TROLL

TROLL

A.F. JANSSON

For Hasna

ASGARD

VANAHEIM

ÁLFHEIM

MIDGARD

MUSPELHEIM

NIFLHEIM

SVARTALFHEIM

JÖTUNNHEIM

HELHEIM

YGGDRASIL

Dornsborg

Beli's cave

Gurmr & Grundr

Gjallarholm

Fjellborg

Hidden runes shalt thou seek,
and interpret secret signs.
Many symbols of might and power,
sung and carved by the high ones.

- ODIN, HAVAMAL

CHAPTER 1

"**I** SAID, PICK THAT SHIT UP!"

Ash looked down on the pile of horse dung on the cobblestones. The horse had been sick. The look that the stable master gave him let him know that he was only moments away from a thrashing. He had felt Roghald's calloused hands across his ears enough times to know better than to test the brute when he was irritable.

"Right away, Roghald", he sighed and dragged himself towards the stables, to find a bucket and shovel.

"And jump to it, before I'll give you something to jump about!"

Ash increased his pace somewhat.

"Stupid Roghald, stupid horses, stupid fortress," he muttered as he waited for his eyes to adjust to the gloom of the stable after the bright sunlight.

All in all, Ash's existence was a miserable one. He worked from sunrise to sunset as a stable hand in the fortress of Hornsborg, for very little pay. Life was hard in the north and he was lucky to have food and shelter, safe behind Hornsborg's walls. At least that's what people kept telling him.

Truth be told, he wasn't sure that it was so dangerous out there anymore. The elders would talk of trolls and giants roaming the land when they were young. Cunning and deceitful, they would lure people to their death and even attack settlements and towns if there were enough of them. But few trolls had been seen for many years. People said there had been a big war in their home world, Jotunheim, where a lot of their magic was lost and they couldn't travel here with ease anymore. The trolls that had remained here on Midgard, the world of the humans, were hunted down by the legendary Jomsvikings and killed. Most of them, anyway. News would reach Hornsborg from time to time about the discovery of a troll and the ensuing battle as they were tracked down and killed, but those tales were few and far in between these days. Nonetheless, people remained cautious of the forests. After all, there was more to fear than trolls in the deep forests of the north. Their world was a lot older than the humankind that populated it, and there remained great swaths of forest and wilderness that had yet to be explored.

Ash sighed as he picked up a bucket and a shovel. The one thought that sustained him through the endless monotony of work in the stables, and the only thing keeping him in Hornsborg for the last few years, was next year's Viking trials.

All children of the Jarldom were allowed to attend the trials on their sixteenth summer. People travelled from near and far to drop off their hopeful sons and daughters, and to watch the largest spectacle of the year outside of the solstice celebrations. The young people would compete against each other in wrestling, archery and feats of strength and speed. Those who did well in the trials would be selected to train as warriors and serve the Jarl as Vikings. The Vikings enjoyed a high status in their society, raiding in the East during the summer and reclining with their feet up by the warm fire in the Jarl's hall during the winter, talking to the other warriors. Mostly about raiding in the East.

Ash was fifteen summers old. That meant that by this time next year, he could already be on his way to becoming a one. The Vikings didn't have to pick up steaming horse manure in the summer or fetch endless buckets of icy water in the winter. If Ash could make the selection and be allowed to train as a warrior, the only time he would have to talk to Roghald would be when he ordered him to fetch a horse. He liked to muse that maybe he would even be in the Jarl's *hird* one day.

Life in the hird, as one of the Jarl's bodyguards and elite fighters, was full of adventure and peril, but well rewarded in silver and honour. Those warriors and shieldmaidens enjoyed the highest status in their society and were given mead to drink every night. Yes, as a hirdsman he might die fighting, but if he did, he would go to Valhalla and feast at Odin's table where all the great warriors ended up. And even if he didn't, at least no one but the Jarl could order him around, especially not Roghald. And he wouldn't have to pick up so much animal excrement.

The blow caught him across his left ear and sent him spinning to the ground as his bucket and shovel clattered to the ground. His vision blurred for a second and he looked up at Roghald's flushed face and flaring nostrils as the large, black bearded man bent down so close that Ash could smell the stale beer on his breath.

"Daydreaming again?" the large man snarled. "The Jomsvikings, led by Jarl Olaf himself, are only moments away from riding through the gates and into a great, steaming pile of horse shit and the one idiot whose job it is to do something about it, is standing around dreaming about milk maidens! You better run to it, boy, or by Odin, I will dig your grave tonight!"

Ash stumbled to his feet, picked up the bucket and a shovel, and scurried outside, leaving Roghald in the gloom of the stables still throwing curses after him.

The man had always had it in for Ash. Already a petty man, Roghald's attitude towards Ash had been bordering on hostile, ever since Ash had moved into the stables. He had tried everything to win the man over, for the only reason to make his own existence more bearable, but whatever he tried, the stable master had never warmed up to him. If Ash worked hard in the stables to impress him, Roghald would give him more work to do. If he tried being friendly with him, his reward would only be a haughty stare. In the end, Ash had just settled for trying to stay out of the man's way, looking after the animals and accepting the occasional beating.

He made his way to the cobblestoned courtyard and the offensive pile of dung. Whilst filling his bucket, Ash spared a glance toward the timber palisade surrounding the central courtyard of Jarl Erik's fortress. The already impressive defences built from large, vertical pine logs with battlements, archers towers on every corner and a sturdy gate house, had been spruced up to prepare for the famed visitors soon to arrive.

Ash doubted that some fresh banners and ribbons would do much to impress a battle-hardened Jarl like Olaf or any member of the most feared fighting force in all the lands. Some say that Thor, the Thundergod, himself had founded the Jomsvikings and even lent some of his power to them.

Either way, it was almost impossible to join their ranks, unless you had been blessed by the gods, since all the warriors under Jarl Olaf's banner were Ulfhednar or Berserkers to begin with. This meant that they shared their spirits with wolves or bears, granting them extraordinary powers in battle. Ash wasn't sure what he would have preferred, the speed and cunning of a wolf, or the strength and rage of a bear. He imagined himself having either, standing against a throng of enemies on a blood-soaked battlefield. He could hear the clang of steel against shields and the thunder of hooves all around him, as he faced an army of trolls, giants and dark elves, horns blasting him and the Jomsvikings to battle.

The second blow of the day was much more forceful than the first. A horse shouldered him in the back, sending him sprawling onto the cobblestones, knocking the wind out of him. His daydream of great battles was torn away, with only the thunder of hooves remaining as the first Jomsviking rode in through the gatehouse and straight into Ash. The big, bearded warrior had not even spared Ash a glance as he knocked him out of the way. Ash lay in the dust and shot a murderous look at the man's back. He got to his feet just in time to watch as more Jomsvikings rode through the gates in pairs. He couldn't help but stare at the tough men and women in their battle-worn leathers and chain mail. And then came the Jarl.

Jarl Olaf was shorter than Ash would have imagined him to be but was built like a tree trunk. He was also older, with a smattering of grey through his otherwise dark beard that reached to his chest, but he radiated vigour, strength and power. He was dressed in a plain black linen tunic over a chain mail shirt and leggings, with a few gold trimmings being the only allowance to his station of a nobleman and a Jarl.

All of Hornsborg had come out to watch him and his warriors ride into the now dust filled and crowded courtyard. Close to a hundred men and shieldmaidens, dressed in furs over heavy chain mail, shields on their backs and swords and axes on their hips, scanned the courtyard with cold eyes as they entered. And although their helmets hung off their saddles and the men's beards were free and unbraided as a sign of coming in peace, it was clear to all that there was nothing peaceful about them. These were men and women bred for war, Ash knew, and death and fire followed in their footsteps. A strange sense of foreboding gripped him as he saw Jarl Erik enter the courtyard and raise his arm in greeting to Jarl Olaf. The leader of the Jomsvikings smiled and raised his, although the smile never quite reached his eyes.

ASH WAS KEPT busy for the rest of the day, leading away horses and making sure they were fed, watered and brushed down. By the time his work had finished, the sun had already set, and he filled the last horse's trough by the light of a lonely lantern on a hook next to him. The mare in the stall, a playful and bright thing, nipped at his collar, almost pulling him into the cold water.

"Hey!" He scolded the horse. "I thought after all I have done for you this afternoon, we would be friends?"

The horse bobbed its head in a way that made Ash feel like it was laughing at him.

He reached into his pocket for an apple he had been saving for later and offered it to the animal. The mare sniffed at it for a second before crunching into it as Ash held it in the flat palm of his hand.

"There," he stroked her muzzle with his other hand. "I hope this seals our deal of friendship?" The horse closed her eyes as she kept munching, and Ash took that as a yes.

"She doesn't let just anyone touch her, you know."

Ash startled at the voice and dropped what remained of the apple into the trough. The horse turned and gave a disapproving snort to the interruption.

Jarl Olaf had stepped into the small circle of light and Ash looked into a weathered face, crisscrossed by scars and several faded runic tattoos. A worn bearskin lay over his shoulders and he held his thumbs tucked into a broad leather belt. Ash noticed that the Jarl's arms were as thick as Ash's legs. Up close, the man was the very image of a hardened warrior, and Ash couldn't believe that he had even imagined himself as the man's equal in his daydreams.

"I didn't mean to startle you, lad," the Jarl rumbled, reaching out to stroke the mare.

Despite looking like a brute, the man had kind and honest eyes, which put Ash at ease, but he remained vigilant. "She likes you," Olaf continued. "Most people she will bite, or worse. That's why I came down here, to put her away myself, since most people cannot approach her."

"I get along with animals," Ash mumbled, blushing with the praise.

"Few people do," the Jarl said, busy scratching the horse's neck. "A fine quality in a person. Your mother and father must be proud."

Ash cringed as he always did when the subject of his parents was brought up. He was an orphan, having been found as a toddler in the remains of a house ravaged by the fire that had also killed his parents. The only memory he had of his mother was a sensation of warmth in her presence, but he had no memories of his father at all.

Jarl Erik himself had found him outside a house that had been reduced to rubble and ashes. As no one knew what his actual name was, and since he was covered in a thick layer of ashes, the Jarl named him Ash. His only comfort was that he had not been named Soot.

Having taken pity on him, the Jarl, as the chieftain of the area, took him in and ordered for him to be raised in the servant's quarters. He had been happy there, playing with the other children in Hornsborg, the Jarl's fortress, and was raised by the cooks and the maids in their spare time.

Then, on his tenth summer, he was sent to live in the stables. Here, he would brush down horses and pick up dung until the end of his days under the watchful eyes of Roghald, the stable master.

"I don't have a father. He died when I was a child. Same with my mother."

"Oh?" said the warrior, looking at him sideways. "Well, you've done a good job raising yourself then."

The big man gave the horse a last pat, then raised a warning finger to it. "Behave."

When he turned back to Ash, he reached out and pressed something in his hand.

"Find me in the fortress if she causes any trouble."

Ash nodded, and the warrior slapped him on the shoulder before turning around and walking off into the night. He listened to the Jarl's heavy footsteps getting further away until they disappeared.

He looked down into his hand and saw a shiny silver coin. The mare snorted and Ash looked up at her.

"I'm buying you another apple tomorrow."

CHAPTER 2

HORNSBORG AND THE SURROUNDING TOWN LAY FAR TO the north, near the coast. It was well positioned as a launch site for raiding the eastern lands but was also far enough removed from the main population of the Norse Jarldoms that any real trouble seldom found its way there. Since very few things out of the ordinary ever happened, the town was abuzz with rumours about Jarl Olaf's visit.

Over the years, Jarl Erik had made himself a wealthy man by sending his warriors out every summer. He had increased his power and reputation to a degree that he was now considered a man to watch in the Norse kingdom. The old king down south, in Hammershall, had been in poor health for quite some time, and with no heirs in line, it was assumed that one Jarl or another would have to seize power soon. The local people whispered that Erik had his eyes on the throne.

So, it was to everyone's surprise that Erik didn't call for a raid this summer. No one understood why, when all Jarls of renown were gathering as much wealth and reputation as they could in the bid to be king. Instead, Erik had all his men see to the fortifications of Hornsborg. He had extended the walls in some places, and the beginnings of a moat were taking shape on the western side of the fortress.

Men and women who had spent all winter looking forward to gripping the oars of their longships and swinging their swords and axes were now gripping shovels and swinging pickaxes. Morale was low, but the people still followed Erik, as he had proven his worth to them repeatedly in the years he had been Jarl. And now he had called on Jarl Olaf to come to the north. And Olaf had come.

"There will be a fight for the crown, mark my words." One of Erik's hirdsmen told Roghald in a matter-of-fact way, as he led his pony into an empty stall. "That's the only thing that makes sense. Some Jarl will take the fight to our doorstep, and Erik has gotten wind of it and now he is preparing for an attack."

The two men were talking as the hirdsman returned from an outlying patrol at the borders of Erik's lands. They seemed oblivious of Ash, who was oiling a tack in the next stall. The fact was that he paid far more attention to the words spoken by the men, than the task at hand. He ducked down low, so as not to be seen.

"That explains why Jarl Olaf and the Jomsvikings are here. Erik will hire them as mercenaries for the upcoming battle," the man continued while lifting his saddlebags off the pony's back. "The two of them have been holed up in Erik's quarters for the last two days along with Rani the Seidwoman. They have allowed none other to enter."

Ash gave an involuntary shiver at the mention of the Seidwoman's name. It was said that the old, blind witch could talk to the spirits, and sometimes even the gods. She could read the future in bones and runes and talk to the wild animals, but what frightened Ash the most was that even in a crowd, although she was blind, she sometimes appeared to look straight at him. Before he would be able to look away, she would give him a grin that would turn his blood to ice.

"But Erik hasn't even challenged for the crown yet. There is nothing saying he ever will," Roghald replied.

"Only a matter of time, Roghald," the hirdsman sighed. "Anyway, he has called for a feast in the hall tomorrow night, perhaps to let us know what all this is about." The man lifted his saddlebags onto his shoulder. "Whatever it is, we'll be the ones fighting for it," he muttered. "At least you get to hide out in your snug stables while we spill our blood in the fields."

Ash heard the tension and anger in Roghald's voice as he snapped back.

"There was a time when I could have bested you, Grim Swordbreaker, and all who lift a shield in the hird, don't you forget that! Had things gone otherwise, I would have been Captain and held command over all of you!"

"But they didn't, and all you command now is a feeble lad and a stinky stable." The man laughed as he pushed the reins of his horse into Roghald's trembling hands. "Don't forget to brush her down well and check her hooves." Exulting at his own wit, the warrior walked out of the stables, leaving a fuming Roghald behind.

Silence settled, and only an occasional soft snort was heard from the horse as the minutes dragged by. Ash kept his eyes closed in the next stall, wishing himself invisible. He knew that Roghald was an ornery man, the kind to always kick downwards, and if he knew that Ash had witnessed him being humiliated by the warrior, he would beat him within an inch of his life.

Everyone at Hornsborg knew how Roghald had ended up in the stables. Ash had been told it several times by people in the fortress, but always before the speaker checked over their shoulder to make sure Roghald wasn't within earshot. Although the tale had varied somewhat from person to person, the basic story was that Roghald was once a respected warrior in Erik's father's hird. Great things were expected for his future, but that all changed on one fateful night on a distant shore.

The Jarl and his Vikings had been raiding in the east and were preparing to return home after a successful summer. Four long-ships had set out from Hornsborg and they sailed further to the east than they had ever done before; so far up a river that they arrived in a land never before seen by Norsemen. They found fat cattle and fat men, not prepared for the threat that they presented, and all was theirs for the taking.

Roghald was young, only twenty summers of age, but already on his third year of raiding. Following his father, Einar - the Captain of the Jarl's hird, he lived only for raiding and making his father proud.

A month's successful plundering in new lands saw the long-boats loaded high with goods and sitting low in the water. In high spirits, they turned their ships towards home but were making slow progress, because of the ships being weighed down by all the marauded riches. When they arrived at the end of the river where it spilled into the northern sea, they sacrificed four sheep to appease Njord, the god of the Seas and Winds for a safe journey home. They ate the sheep, and the Jarl awarded them with a cask of stolen wine for all to enjoy.

They settled for the night, having made all preparations for the sail across the sea in the morning. Einar gave himself the first watch over the ships and the sleeping crews, sending all the warriors to sleep. Tired from rowing for an entire day, no one argued that one man might not be enough to watch four ships. However, Einar had his reason in doing so. He had developed quite a taste for the eastern wine. It was stronger than the mead or beer he was accustomed to at home and returned to the cask several times while the crew slept. Before long, he was asleep in a drunken stupor. Had anyone in the crew been awake only a short while after, by the light of the moon, they would have seen dark shadows materialise from the forest and creep across the riverbank. They headed for the water where the ships lay anchored in a row, right in the middle of the river.

It was only when several sleeping throats had already been cut that the alarm was raised, and the men and women scrambled for their weapons. The people of the lands where they spent the summer raiding had eventually mounted an armed force to repel the Norsemen and sent them down the river in pursuit.

Steel was ringing against steel as the soldiers boarded the two ships furthest upriver. Meanwhile, archers on the beach began raining down death on the last two ships. The night filled with screams of pain and rage, and the deck of the longships became slick with blood. The last two ships suffered only a few casualties, as the raiders of Hornsborg were in the habit of sleeping on their shields, and most raised their shields overhead against the slew of arrows pelting the deck. They were pinned down, however, and could not come to the aid of their comrades, watching in horror as they fought for their lives in the light of the full moon.

It was a hopeless fight, and one by one the Norsemen fell as the attackers fought their way from one end of the two ships to the other. Torches were lit on the beach and burning arrows slammed into their shields and ships and soon the flames spread.

"Cut the anchor rope or we will go down in fire!" cried a burly man on the last boat, whose leg had an arrow sticking out of it. People on both of the rear ships raised their axes and cut through the sturdy ropes, setting them adrift. The current was pushing them out to sea as they rushed to extinguish the flames onboard. Less and fewer arrows reached them as they drifted further, until they were well out of range, and the Norsemen could raise their sails. The beautiful sunrise that soon followed heralded a dark day.

Half of the crew they set out with were dead, including the Jarl, and half of their spoil was lost.

Einar, Roghald's father, was found dead, under a canvas tarp next to the cask of wine in the stern of the last ship where he had fallen asleep. Several arrows protruded from his chest and limbs. By his wine-stained lips and beard, the crew soon realized what had happened. Roghald's eyes had burned with shame as his father's body was dumped overboard, denied the funeral pyre that would allow him entrance into the hall of the gods. Some even spat after the body.

His shame was made complete when Erik, next in line to be Jarl after his father, cursed his family's name, took Roghald's sword and shield and relegated him to an oar.

"None of your father's blood will fight again, Roghald Einarsson. None of your father's blood shall reach Valhalla." With those words he turned his back on Roghald, and though Roghald was still a free man, they considered him a little above a serf from that day forward.

Ash was sure that something must have broken in Roghald that day, since he only ever knew the man to be petty, cruel and quick to anger. Most of Ash's life seemed to comprise avoiding the beatings the man was so generous with. He held his breath and sat in silence for what seemed like a lifetime, before peaking over the edge of the stall. The pony was still there, but no sight of Roghald, thank the gods.

Without making a sound, he hung the tack back on its hook and slipped out of the stall, with a grin on his face. Ash felt smug that he had avoided his tormentor. All he needed to do was lie low for the rest of the day and he would have saved himself a lot of trouble.

His grin dropped from his face when Roghald stood up from inspecting the pony's hooves, but not before Roghald saw his smile. They both stood silent for a moment.

"Sneaking around in the shadows, eh, boy?" Roghald's voice came out as a hoarse whisper, and his eyes filled with a rage even Ash hadn't seen before. "And you dare laugh at me?"

Ash stood as frozen to the spot. In desperation, he sought an explanation to offer the man, but in his panic could think of none.

Roghald looked around, his eyes finding Ash's shovel leaning against the stall rail. With a murderous grimace, he snatched the shovel and swung it high, bringing it down towards Ash's head.

Paralysed with fear, Ash could only watch as Roghald struck at him and from the man's mad anger, he knew he would die. Roghald would kill him, and he still couldn't move, like a deer staring at the hunter drawing his bow. But as the shovel flew towards him, something happened inside Ash. As he was about to be struck down, it was as if an icy fire burst in his chest and flashed through the rest of his body. A calm settled over him and he felt like he was floating. The world around him came into crystal clear focus, and he could see even the smallest specks of dust as they hung in the air in front of him. But the strangest thing was that Roghald's lethal blow slowed down, as if he was swinging the shovel through mud.

Ash sidestepped the blow with ease and watched confused as the shovel slowly drifted past his face. It hit the edge of the stall behind him with a loud and drawn out 'chunk'. It was lodged deep into the wood. Roghald's face mirrored his own confusion for a moment, before twisting into anger once again. The stable master let go of the shovel and drew his arm back, his large hand balled into a fist aimed at Ash's face. But before Roghald's fist even begun moving towards his face, Ash's arm shot out of its own accord, in a backhanded blow that connected with the side of the brute's face.

The large man spun and fell backwards. It happened so slow that to Ash it looked like Roghald was sinking in water, not falling through the air. As soon as he landed on the dirty and hay-strewn stable floor, Roghald sat up with a look of utter surprise on his face. A trickle of blood stained the front of his tunic from where his bottom lip had split. They stared at each other for a long, drawn out moment. Then Roghald's eyes narrowed, and he pressed his lips together in anger, causing another trickle of blood to dribble down his chin.

"Why, you little shit... Challenge me, will you?!" Roghald roared, but his voice was deep and so drawn out that Ash had difficulty understanding what he said. He leapt up and threw himself at Ash. Closing the distance, he drew his arm back and swung a punch that would devastate Ash's face. Once again, the fist was coming at Ash at slow speed. The tingling that flowed through Ash like a burning river sent him into action again. He moved around the blow and delivered a lightning punch to the man's nose, flattening it and lifting him off his feet. He watched as Roghald drifted through the air and landed several paces away. Bleeding from his broken nose and lip, the man lay still on the dirty stable floor.

The strange tingling still possessed Ash's body, continuing as he stood over the beaten stable master. Something strange was happening, but he was finding it difficult to think and his ears started ringing. The tingling intensified and became increasingly uncomfortable. In a matter of seconds, it turned to a burning pain and he felt like he was on fire, both inside and out.

He fell to his knees next to the unconscious stable master; the pain consuming him. He looked at his hands, expecting to see them charred and blistered, but no harm had come to them, his skin still intact. However, the burning continued and was still getting worse by the second. His jaw clenched, eyes shut, and flashing images of a burning house filled his mind. He could feel his lungs fill with wood smoke, threatening to choke him, and his ears filled with the sound of crackling fire.

He saw the back of a woman surrounded by flames in a small kitchen as she fought a hulking, dark creature. She was fast, jabbing at the much larger creature with a short spear. She moved in a fluid way and Ash found it difficult to follow all her blurry movements. Still, it wasn't enough. The creature, larger and stronger in the confined space, swept a clawed hand across her throat.

She staggered and fell face down on the scorched floor, a pool of blood spreading around her. The pain flashed through him once again and he would have screamed, if he could only draw a breath. The creature stepped over the woman's body, and walked towards him through flames, as if they were only tall grass. When it reached the hearth where he was curled up, it stooped down and reached out for him with a large, clawed hand that filled his entire vision. Fear and helplessness overcame him, a nightmare come alive.

Just as the creature's claw touched one of his tiny, chubby arms, a gust of cold wind cleared the surrounding smoke and it was re-placed by the icy smell of winter. The monster in front of him hesitated, and a second later something large and grey slammed into it, throwing it to the side. A second grey blur followed behind the first, and Ash's ears filled with snarls and a loud roar that was abruptly cut off, before the vision faded.

He was lying on the stable floor taking slow, deep breaths, the pain all but gone. His mind was reeling from the events of the last few minutes. What had happened to him? He felt confused by the fight with Roghald and shaken by the vision he had seen. Some madness must have been brought on by his pain. Surely that wasn't real? Then he remembered Roghald. Ash lifted his head off the ground and turned around. There he saw the still body of the stable master.

"I've killed him..." Ash whispered, sitting up, his entire body aching.

He crawled over to Roghald. The man looked a mess, but was still breathing, though unconscious. Relief flooded Ash, but a sec-ond later he realized with a sinking heart that Roghald would soon wake up. And would kill him when he did.

Ash's first instinct was to get as far away as he could. If he didn't leave Hornsborg before Roghald woke up his life wouldn't be worth two copper pieces. It was miserable around here, so it was not to be a significant loss to leave Hornsborg behind, after all. His heart sank in his chest when he remembered the Viking trials. They had been his hopes and dreams for years, and the only thing that kept him going in an otherwise miserable existence. If he left now, he would miss out on his chance to become a warrior. But then again, if he stayed here, he wouldn't be able to attend the trials anyway, since he was sure that having been beaten to death in the back of a stable would disqualify you from entering.

Could he approach the Jarl and explain what happened? The Jarl had been kind to him now and again when their paths crossed. He envisioned being laughed at by the Jarl and his warriors in the great hall, when the grievances of a lowly stable boy were brought to them. Besides, even if the Jarl intervened somehow, Roghald's pettiness would always find a way, and Ash was sure to meet with some kind of 'accident' down the track.

No, he had to leave, there was no other option. Maybe he could go to a town further down the coast? It shouldn't be hard to find work, and he had plenty of experience with horses and stables. A spark of hope lit in his chest when he realized that the Viking trials were held in all the Norse lands. Perhaps he could attend them in Gjallarholm or Fjellborg further south? He might have to settle in and be known in their communities. That would take a while, but if he lied about his age from the start, saying he was a year or two younger than he was, he would have time to do that.

The more he thought about it, the more determined he got about leaving Hornsborg behind forever. He scrambled up the ladder to the stable loft, and the little nook where he had slept for the last five years. Ash gathered up his few belongings - a knife, a woollen vest, a blanket and a small purse with the few coins he had scraped together.

"Not much, to be honest," he muttered as he threw it all into an old knapsack someone had left behind in the stables.

Hanging on a nail above his bedding was his most prized possession, a bow and a quiver of arrows. It had been a midsummer solstice gift from the Jarl himself. No doubt that the Jarl's generosity was fuelled by the great many horns of mead he was enjoying, but it was one of Ash's fondest memories all the same. He had practiced whenever he could, hoping to make archery one of his strengths for the trials, but never quite got the hang of it. Ash more often than not missed the target, no matter how much he tried. He did manage to shoot a couple of rabbits over time but suspected that luck had had a lot to do with it.

Ash hung the bow and quiver over his shoulder and climbed back down the ladder. Holding his breath, he snuck past the still unconscious stable master.

Standing in the stable doorway, blinking in the sunlight, he wondered if this was the wisest thing to do. Should he go to the Jarl and explain what had happened, after all? He could even ask the Jarl to be put to work somewhere else in the fortress, maybe in the kitchens or in the fields? Ash sighed when he realized that even if he did work somewhere else, he would be forever looking over his shoulder, and one day Roghald would stand there.

He heard a groan behind him and turned to see Roghald stirring on the floor as he was waking up. That was all the motivation Ash needed to run into the courtyard and out of the gatehouse. The guards outside barely glanced at him as he hurried away from the fortress, their concern being more about who was entering than leaving.

Ash made his way into the little town surrounding the fortress where he only stopped at the market. He spent a few of his coins on apples, a loaf of bread and a small hunk of cheese. His small purse was already much lighter.

A short time after weaving his way through the squat log houses, Ash stood before the road heading south. He watched it stretch through wheat fields and paddocks before disappearing into the forest, some distance away. Although he had never been down this road before, he knew that within half a day it would reach the coast and the ocean, before turning inland again. Four or five days' travel would see him at the gates of Gjallarholm, a trading town much larger than Hornsborg.

He would go there first, before deciding if he should stay or keep moving down the coast. He hesitated for a second, but soon steeled himself, adjusted his knapsack to rest better on his shoulders, and with a determined look on his face, took the first steps away from the only home he had ever known.

CHAPTER 3

HULDA WIPED HER BROW AND CAUGHT HER BREATH FOR
a moment. She and the other servants had been hard at work
for the last few hours. Jarl Erik's hall was loud and warm, and she
could feel the beginnings of a headache settling in. The few windows that were spaced out along the stone walls had been thrown
open but did little to disperse the heat from the crowd as well as the
multitude of candles and torches that lit the feast. Most of the free
men and women of Hornsborg were sitting shoulder to shoulder
at long tables that filled the large hall. People were laughing and
eating, as Hulda and the other servants weaved their way through
the gathering, carrying big trays laden with fresh loaves of bread,
sausages, meats, steaming potatoes and pitchers of ale and mead. A
group of musicians were crowded in a corner, playing pipes, flutes
and lutes, their music competing with the clatter and din of the
guests, and losing. At the end of the hall was a raised dais where
the Jarl's table stood. There sat both the Jarls next to each other
with their second-in-commands and some other prominent warriors, hirdsmen, shieldmaidens and relatives. The Jarls were deep in
conversation, their faces serious and austere. The other members of
the table appeared to reflect the foreboding mood.

Several loud bangs drew everyone's attention when Erik slammed his horn on the table in a call to silence. As the music and the many voices died down, all heads were turned towards the Jarl and Hulda was glad for the reprieve in the festivities. Standing up, the Jarl let his gaze sweep over the people gathered, before he spoke in a firm voice that would carry across the hall.

"People of Hornsborg - firstly, welcome one and all." The hall was overcome with thunder as the people drummed their fists on the tables in appreciation of his hospitality and generosity. Erik held his hands up for silence and the noise settled again.

"I have hosted this feast in honour of our guests, Jarl Olaf and the Jomsvikings, to welcome them as friends to our lands." A few people drummed their fists on their table, but most noted the stern and serious look on their Jarl's face and waited for him to continue with some trepidation.

"-but also, to mark the newly formed alliance between myself and Jarl Olaf. An alliance we both have entered into willingly but have also been forced into out of necessity." Erik paused, and only the crackle of the burning logs in the fireplace could be heard in the great hall.

"A great danger threatens our lands." he continued. "Scattered reports have come in since the end of winter, and Rani the Seid-woman has long foreseen it in the bones. I was reluctant to believe it, but now our friend Jarl Olaf has brought us his own eyewitness account." He took a breath before continuing, "Not five days' ride from Hornsborg; on their way here, the Jomsvikings were accosted and attacked by the *draugr*."

It took a moment for his words to sink in before the hall erupted with dozens of voices calling out in disbelief. Hulda's mouth fell open as she considered what the Jarl had said and the horror that was the *draugr*, the dead walking again. A *draugr* was an evil or greedy person in life who had found no peace in death. A walking corpse, driven by its own anger and hunger with nothing but blind hate for the living. No one had reported seeing a *draugr* for

20

generations, and most people believed it was now just a story used to frighten misbehaving children. Hulda tried to swallow, but her tongue had gone dry.

The protests escalated as people argued and tried to yell over each other. A resounding boom cut through the noise and all turned their heads towards the Jarl's table again. Standing up with a scowl on his face, Jarl Olaf had a commanding presence. His hand resting on a large war hammer lying on the thick oak table where he had struck it. His stare dared anyone to raise their voice again.

"It is as your Jarl says." he said in a raspy voice. "I have seen inland farmhouses and outposts that have fallen to the creatures, their dead inhabitants scattered about, or what little was left of them, in any case." His gaze swept over the room. "None escaped their attacks; my trackers have confirmed it. Every man, woman and child - dead to a terrible fate." The people stared at Olaf, their mouths open and faces pale.

"They tread lightly and they travel fast, having no need to rest, driven only by their hunger. Their numbers were near a hundred at the last outpost. We followed their trail, but they split into smaller groups and we lost them in the mountains." His eyes became distant as he continued, "We returned to the coast, to travel here to give warning to Jarl Erik, not realising that one such group had circled around and were now following us. Late in the night they came. The guards heard not a sound, as the draugr encircled the sleeping camp, but they later reported a stench of rot on the wind just before the attack. Only once they shambled into the light of the fires, and could be seen, was the alarm raised. But Jomsvikings sleep lightly, upon their shields with their axes and spears in their hands, and in a moment all were standing, facing the foe who now let out bone-chilling moans of hunger." He paused and wet his throat with a long draught of mead before continuing.

"Death has changed them. They are broad over the shoulders, their large mouths agape, showing rows of jagged teeth. Their eyes are white, but are not unseeing, the hunger for the living clear in them. They attack with a ferocity I have seldom seen, and pain affects them but a little. Only the most mortal blows to the head or to the heart will kill them. We cut them down to the last, but not before losing two of our warriors. There was thirty of us and only twelve of them. And mind you, we are the Jomsvikings, and none can fight like we do. Had there been any other group, I doubt they would have survived the attack."

The hall remained silent as he sat down, taking another long drink from his horn.

Hulda looked down to see that she was gripping her apron so hard that her knuckles were white. She let it go and saw that her hands were trembling when Jarl Erik stood to break the silence once again.

"Rani has seen this evil in the bones. It is raised in the deep forests of the west by an old magic, long thought gone from the land. She says it smells of giants and trolls." A communal gasp was heard in the hall.

"Earlier today, we sent word to the King and all the Jarls down the coast, advising them to fortify themselves until we can estimate how large the threat is. All townspeople are to bring only the essentials and move in behind the walls of Hornsborg. Bring what foods you have and leave no one behind. No one is to travel, and no one is to go into the forest."

CHAPTER 4

ASH FELT MISERABLE, WRAPPED IN HIS DAMP BLANKET, under the lowest branches of a spruce tree as the rain poured down on the surrounding forest. His temporary lodging had, by the smell of it, been inhabited by a badger and Ash hoped that it wouldn't return. Through a gap in the branches, he could see the road from where he was huddled up and stared at the large water puddles filling. He thought with longing of the old barn he had found and spent the previous night in, wishing he had taken more time to appreciate how comfortable and dry it had been.

Ash had been traveling that road for two days now, making his way down the coast. He estimated that he had at least two or three days left until he reached Gjallarholm, where it sprawled on the edge of the North Sea. Perhaps four days, if it continued to rain. He was considering his diminishing supply of apples, cheese and bread and realized that he would have to go hungry for the last day or so. He might be able to shoot a rabbit or squirrel if it stopped raining. At least he would have plenty of water to drink, he thought with irony.

Had he made the right decision to leave? A part of him, at least the part that missed his warm spot in the stable loft, regretted leaving. Roghald might have settled for just giving him a beating, and he had had plenty of them before. The thought brought back the memory of Roghald swinging the shovel at his head, and he knew that the stable master would not rest until Ash was dead. He wondered where he had found the courage to fight back against his tormentor. And what had happened to him when time slowed down and the visions had flashed before his eyes? He remembered the pain burning through his body with a sense of unease and uncertainty. What if it happened again? What if it killed him?

The thunder of hooves drew his attention back to the road. Two riders flashed by and were gone in an instant. They had come from Hornsborg, he concluded. The riders had pushed their horses as if the trolls were chasing them, and in the rain, at that. At least someone was more miserable than him, he noted with a chuckle. Although, they probably had a warm fire and a dry bed waiting for them, wherever they were going.

He tried to make himself a little more comfortable and had just started drifting off to sleep when a slow drip started on his head. As the grey dusk faded to darkness, he sighed. He knew he was in for a rough night.

A MOSAIC OF light filtered in through the branches as the sun reached his hiding place. It had stopped raining sometime in the early morning. At one point during the night, just after the rain stopped, he thought he heard something moving around in the forest. Fearing the return of the badger, he had held his knife in a firm grip whilst staying dead quiet. When nothing came to evict him from his sleeping nest, he relaxed again and had drifted off to sleep.

His eyes felt like they were full of sand and his body was hurting in so many places it was just one enormous ache. He was damp and cold, so he needed to get moving to warm up. He tried a few stretches he had seen Jarl Erik's hird do before battle practice, but they did little to ease his aching muscles.

24

A quick breakfast of soggy bread and cheese was the best he could do before scrambling back out onto the road. He had had to unstring his bow the night before to keep the moisture from ruining the string. He only had one string, and if it snapped, his bow would be nothing but a bent stick. Now he fumbled with cold fingers to restring it, but after several failed attempts, he strung the bow and it was ready to be used again.

The warm morning sun on his face lifted his spirits as he made his way south, taking care to avoid the larger puddles in his path. He kept his bow and arrow at hand, hoping a rabbit would jump out on the road in front of him. Preferably a fat one that would stand still for some time while he adjusted his aim.

It wasn't until the sun stood at its highest point that his clothes had dried out and the spring returned to his step. It was a beautiful summer day and as he walked along, Ash felt a sense of freedom he had never known before. He whistled a joyful tune as he imagined all the mounds of horse dung that Roghald was now left to pick up on his own, back at the stables.

As he made his way around a bend in the road, something caught his attention up ahead. Closing the distance, he saw it was a horse lying in the middle of the road, on its side with its legs towards Ash. He stood watching it for a while, but it didn't move. It must be dead, he thought. He remembered the riders last night, riding at high speeds, pushing their mounts so hard that one might have stumbled and broken its leg. They'd elected to kill it rather than leaving it to suffer. He frowned at the thought. Poor animal. That was no way to treat any living thing, let alone a horse that had probably been in Ash's care.

As he moved closer, he could make out a darker area on the ground where the blood would have pooled before being washed away by the rain. This confirmed his suspicion that the horse was dead.

But why in the middle of the road, he wondered. Wouldn't it have been better to lead the poor animal to the side and into the forest, so travellers wouldn't have to make their way around a rotting carcass? That's when he realized that the saddle was still on the horse. Saddles were expensive and would never have been left behind. Unless they had no choice, he thought. He stopped and scanned the forest on both sides of the road for any movement. When nothing presented itself, he crept closer still. Ash came close enough that he could see a man lying on the other side of the horse, his legs trapped under the animal.

To his horror, he realized that half of the man's face was missing, and the other half was frozen in a grimace of terror. Ash's eyes widened for a second, before he doubled over and lost his breakfast. He retched until there was nothing left, pressing his eyes shut, trying hard to push away the image.

As his stomach settled, he sat back on the ground; the horse shielding his view of the rider. He could see part of a boot protruding under the horse's belly, and he could not stop staring at it while his mind raced. Who could have done this? It must have been some wild animal, he thought. Maybe it was a bear.

Ash realized he was very exposed where he sat in the middle of the road, next to what was possible to be a bear's next planned meal. He jumped to his feet and gathered up his belongings. He had to get as far away from here as possible, before whatever it was, returned.

Ash hurried past the gruesome scene, and when he was level with it he turned his head in the other direction, to avoid looking at it. That's when he saw the second rider. Laying just a few strides into the forest, along the edge of the road, the man was face down into the dirt, his tunic red with blood. Ash started running.

CHAPTER 5

ROGHALD MUTTERED UNDER HIS BREATH AS HE FILLED the manure bucket. He imagined all the things he would do to Ash if he ever laid eyes on him again. Not only had the lout somehow bested him, knocking him senseless, but also Roghald now had to do all the menial chores around the place.

He suspected Ash was lying low in town somewhere, lazing about and having a laugh at the turn of events, but the gods help him when Roghald found him.

"Where's the lad?"

Roghald startled at the gruff voice. Turning around, he saw a shadow outlined in the stable doorway. Roghald squinted to make out who it was.

"What?" he croaked.

"I said, where's the lad?" The hirdsman took a step into the stable, coming into Roghald's view. The man's long, blonde beard stood in stark contrast to his blackened chain mail shirt. He looked around the stable, taking everything in before his eyes settled back on Roghald.

"The Jarl has called for him. Where is he?"

Roghald was stumped. Why would the Jarl call for Ash, of all people? Maybe he had been seen stealing or causing trouble in town and was to be punished, he thought. A warm feeling spread through his chest. Maybe even a public flogging was in order, he hoped.

"Haven't seen him for a few days. He's probably up to no good somewhere." he told the warrior.

The hirdsman paused for a moment, then replied, "You better come with me, then," before turning around and walking out of the stable.

Roghald smiled, the flash of pain in his split lip not enough to stop it. This should be good, he thought, rubbing his hands together. He rested the shovel against the wall and hurried after the warrior.

ROGHALD STEPPED INTO Jarl Erik's hall behind the hirdsman. Few people were in here at this time of day, so only a few torches were lit along the back wall, casting the place in gloom. He could see Erik, Olaf and two shieldmaidens sitting at one of the smaller tables, picking at a tray of cold meats.

As they approached the Jarls, Roghald stumbled when he saw the Seidwoman sitting on a low bench in the corner, a little away from the others. That old hag always gave him the shivers. She was wearing her usual, once-white, tattered robes, the hood pulled down to cover the gaping holes where her eyes once were. Her face was dusted white as always and her lips blackened by soot. She was leaning on a gnarled stick and turned her head when they walked towards the Jarl's table, as if listening to their footsteps.

The people at the table looked up as they approached; a perplexed look on Erik's face as he saw Roghald. The hirdsman bent down and spoke a few quiet words to him.

"What happened to you?" the Jarl asked, scrutinizing Roghald's swollen face and flattened nose.

"Kicked by a horse," the stable master mumbled.

One of the shieldmaidens said something under her breath, and the other, sitting next to her, snorted and raised a hand to hide her smile. Even the corners of Jarl Erik's mouth pulled up, but he coughed once and composed himself before addressing Roghald again.

"Where's the lad?" Erik demanded.

"I haven't seen him for a few days, Jarl Erik. Not since after I caught him stealing from one of the patrol's saddlebags. I gave him the beating he deserved and he ran off, and I haven't seen him since. He is a lazy good-for-nothing, and if he has caused any trouble, it has nothing to do with me."

Erik looked like he was about to answer when a sharp rattle reached them from the corner. All eyes turned to Rani the Seid-woman as she ran a hand over a collection of small white bones on the floor in front of her. She straightened up on her sitting bench before she spoke; her blackened lips a grimace of disgust.

"You speak with a cloven tongue, like that of a snake, Roghald Einarson." Her voice was only a whisper, but it carried through the entire hall. "Nothing but lies have fallen from your broken lips since you entered here." With those words, she gathered up the bones and placed them in a pouch that hung around her neck. All eyes turned to Roghald, and he couldn't help but notice how the hirdsman moved to stand behind him.

The Jarl had steel in his voice and in his eyes when he said, "Tell me again, Roghald. Where is the lad, and what happened to your face?"

CHAPTER 6

ASH RAN UNTIL HE COULDN'T DRAW BREATH ANYMORE. He tried to ignore the terrible pain in his side for quite some time, but after a while, he had to slow down to a brisk walk. He drew big gulps of air as he stumbled along, his hands on his hips. He turned to look behind him several times, but the road was always empty. It had now been hours since he had come across the dead riders, but the fear in his belly had not lessened. It was with dread that he had watched the sun descend lower and lower towards the horizon. Ash now found himself in the darkening shade of the surrounding trees as dusk set in.

He needed to find somewhere to spend the night. Somewhere safe. The forest loomed dark on either side of the road, as uninviting as could be. Not far away, a large, rocky hill reached up above the treetops. Yes! He'd camp up high and build a large fire! Wild animals feared fire, he knew, and would keep well away from him until he could move again at first light. He hoped he had put enough distance between himself and the horror sight he'd left behind on the road, but a fire would offer extra assurance.

He pushed into the forest and toward the hill. The ground elevated and large, moss-covered rocks protruded here and there as the trees started thinning out. He made his way up the slope, using his hands to scramble up as the ground steepened.

He crested the rock-studded hill in the last rays of the dying sun. A cool breeze reached him, and he pulled the laces of his tunic tighter as he surveyed his surroundings. His heart sank as he saw very little in the way of firewood. He would have to drag some up to the top if he wanted to make a fire. Darkness was settling around him and the night-time insects had already begun their symphony, joined by the occasional frog croak. He knew he would have to work fast because night was already upon him.

He made his way down the hill again in search of firewood, when something glinted in the corner of his eye and he stopped. Ash turned his head but couldn't see anything except the dark forest. He took a few steps back and stared at the dark silhouette of the forest canopy and surrounding hills. And then he saw it again – a light! Almost at the top of another craggy hill, further off into the sea of trees that now spread out before him, if he turned his head just right, there was a faint flickering light. A fire, he thought, or maybe even a lit window. He considered the possibility that this might be a bandit camp or someone equally unwelcoming. Then he remembered the grimace of horror on the dead rider's face and decided he was willing to take his chances.

He set off down the hill and into the forest, heading as straight as he could towards the peak where he'd seen the light.

The sun was gone, but it was a clear night. The stars and the already risen moon offered enough light to navigate the forest by, if he didn't move too fast. Then a branch cracked somewhere behind him.

Ash stopped to listen, but fear had set his heart racing, and at first all he could hear was his pulse throbbing in his ears. He stood in silence for a while, listening for the slightest sound that didn't belong. Ash had just taken a deep breath and reassured himself that it had been a figment of his imagination when he realized that there were no insect sounds anymore. The forest had gone deadly quiet. Then he heard another crack, this time much closer.

Ash set off like a rabbit through the forest. He scrambled as he made his way through thickets and spruce trees. His clothes tore several times, and he collected dozens of scratches on his face and hands while he raced towards the hill. Ash heard several large snapping branches and occasional heavy thuds behind him, and each time, it fuelled his flight and he pushed himself to go even faster. When he reached a clearing at the bottom of the hill, he cursed when, in the pale light of the moon, he saw how steep it was.

Whatever was behind him was now crashing through the deep brush, getting closer by the second. Deep, drawn out sounds reached him, like wails or moans. The hair on his neck stood on end at the eerie sounds. Convinced that a certain death awaited him and was only a few steps behind, he darted up the hill, first on two legs, then on all fours. Soon he was climbing, seeking handholds and perches for his feet in desperation as his ascent slowed down to a snail-like climb. There were many protruding stones and the occasional tree root to grasp, and he scrabbled up them as fast as he could. His pack was heavy and weighing him down, making the climb much harder. He cursed at not having dropped it at the bottom. Ash was running out of breath from the effort and had to force himself to stop, or he would risk passing out and fall to his death.

He took a moment to glance down. He had made it perhaps twenty feet up the hill. Holding himself still, he eyed the clearing as he waited for his breathing to slow. He could still hear the moans, very close by now, but scanning the dark shadows of the tree line revealed nothing at first.

A brief movement just at the edge of the trees caught his eye. Ash stared, trying to penetrate the gloom, before he glimpsed it again a dozen paces to the left. Not moving a muscle, he wished himself invisible as he held on to the rock wall. After what felt like an eternity, the eerie moaning lessened and seemed to drift off into the dark woods.

When the noise had died away, Ash waited a little while longer before he resumed his climb, trying to not make a sound. As he progressed up the crag, he often looked down, but saw nothing at the base of the rock wall or at the edge of the forest.

He almost lost his grip once when an owl hooted nearby and startled him. While he cursed the owl and its ancestors all the way back to the creation of the world, he realized that its presence maybe meant that whatever had chased him was gone. As he climbed higher, the chirping and buzzing sounds of the night returned, offering reassurance that the immediate danger was over.

His arms were tiring, and his fingers had gone numb from gripping and scraping on rocks, so it was with great relief when he looked up and saw only the star-studded sky above him instead of the dark silhouette of the rock wall. He raised his head over the edge and looked around. It was a wide, uneven plateau, surrounding a wide stone monolith in the centre. The monolith stood as high as three men and was twice as wide again. It had a few stunted spruce trees growing in some crevices, but mostly it was barren rock.

Seeing nothing threatening, he pulled himself up and allowed himself to collapse on the level ground, one leg still hanging over the edge. Lying on his back, he stared up at the night sky, taking deep breaths until sensation returned to his arms and shoulders. After giving a quick glance over the edge, to ensure that whatever was out there hadn't changed its mind about climbing, he crept forwards in search of the light he had seen. He made his way to the central stone, deciding to stay close to it and work his way around the plateau. He had to be quiet, as there was no guarantee that whoever's light he had seen would welcome strangers sneaking up on them in the night.

Pressing his back against the stone, he felt it move. He pulled away and stared at the dark rock. Nothing happened. With caution, he placed his hand on it and he felt it again. Every few seconds, there was a soft vibration, like the beating of a heart, only slower. It was almost soothing; a steady rhythm pulsating through the stone, and Ash couldn't help to linger for a moment. Something about the vibrations resonated with him, and he felt an urge to be part of it. He removed his hand and started moving along the rock. It wasn't long before a soft light spilled onto the ground in front of him. He craned his neck around a protrusion and saw that light was escaping from a crack in the monolith's side.

Ash forced himself forwards and soon he stood next to an opening, about as tall as him, but twice as wide as his shoulders. The gap continued a few steps in, before it made a sharp turn to the right and then down, from where a warm light flickered and reflected out into the night. Hot air pushed out of the crevice and rolled over his skin. A rhythmic, metallic clang resounded from inside the passageway; the same rhythm as the vibration he had felt on the rock.

He stood there pondering his options for a moment. There was potentially something dangerous inside. On the other hand, there was definitely something dangerous in the forest behind him. He decided to go in.

Trying to be as stealthy as possible, he sidled into the passage and followed it down. After only a few steps, the ground levelled out and a large cave opened up in front of him. It was awash with light and an almost stifling heat. The air was dry and smelled of tin and sour sweat. The cave was dominated by a massive forge. Whatever was used for fuel was burning with an intense ferocity, filling the cave with heat and an almost blinding white light. The forge seemed to be built into the very rock, its round opening surrounded by a band of green, glowing runes, unlike any Ash had ever seen.

Next to the forge, in front of a large anvil, stood the ugliest creature imaginable. It was short, with stocky legs, a broad and round torso that seemed to be all ribcage, and enormous hands attached to sinewy arms. It had an unruly tuft of grey hair on top of its head and its back and arms were covered in bristly, grey locks. Its skin, where visible, appeared to be a muted green, and the creature had a large, bulbous nose over a wide mouth with almost no chin at all. Its eyes were hidden under bushy white eyebrows. It wore only a stained loincloth and was glistening with sweat as it worked in front of the forge.

Ash couldn't take his eyes off the creature as it hammered something glowing on the anvil in a steady rhythm. The hammer seemed far too large for the creature, but it swung it with such ease in its right hand, that Ash couldn't help but marvel at the creature's strength. In its left hand, it was holding whatever it was working on, on the anvil, with a pair of long pliers. The creature paused, set the hammer down on the anvil and hobbled over to a large, water-filled stone basin where it dunked the glowing item, pliers and all, into the water.

Ash heard a loud hissing as the water boiled and churned. Steam filled the cave, obscuring Ash's view as the creature disappeared in the cloud. The steam soon dissipated, and Ash saw the creature holding something small up to its eye, scrutinising it, turning it this way and that, in front of its enormous nose.

"You might as well step in here so old Beli can get a look at you." The creature had spoken in a raspy, nasal voice, while not taking its eyes off the item.

"Humans have a stink about them, and Beli is finding it difficult to concentrate, so we might as well talk so Beli can decide what to do with you."

Ash was more than a little uncertain, but he shuffled forward a few steps, still ready to dart out of the cave if the creature turned out to be dangerous. He stopped a few steps into the cavern and the thing finally turned to look at him. It had small, angry, deep-set eyes, and it took all of Ash's self-control to not run away when they locked on him.

"This cave is warded." it said, while taking stock of Ash. "None should be able to see it, let alone approach. Perhaps old Beli is getting forgetful and just didn't power the wards, but he thinks not…" He glared at Ash. "What is the human doing here?" Ash stared at the creature, his mouth opening and closing as he tried to find words to explain his situation.

"Well?!" the creature snapped, half growling the word.

Ash startled and blurted out everything that had happened since this morning, about finding the dead horses and men and how something had chased him through the forest. He described how he had climbed up the rock to escape his pursuer and had stumbled upon the cave opening as he was looking for somewhere to hide. He left out the part about seeing the light of Beli's cave across the forest. Something gave him the sense that he'd better keep that part of the story to himself, since that had roused the most suspicion in the creature.

As he finished his explanation, Beli looked him up and down again before breaking into a broad smile, showing a mouth full of sharp teeth.

"Well, do not worry, little human. Old Beli will keep you warm and safe in his cave. It was great luck that you found it, great luck indeed." He hobbled over to Ash, reached up and grabbed him by the shoulders and steered him towards the unbearable warmth of the forge. Ash didn't pay attention to the fact that Beli pinched his shoulders, as if to feel the meat in them, when he led him to a small table and chairs off to one side.

"Sit, sit and rest, little human, and Beli will see about some supper. Some nice warm stew, he thinks." He gave a perplexed Ash a light shove towards the chair and then darted across the room where he opened a large chest and rummaged in it. With his head and shoulders in the coffer, Ash missed the malicious grin on Beli's face when he placed his hand on a long, sharp knife at the bottom of the chest.

"Yes, some nice stew…"

CHAPTER 7

ROGHALD LACED UP HIS KNAPSACK. IN IT, HE HAD placed all the worldly possessions that he could carry. The humiliation still burned in his chest from the Jarl calling him a liar and drawing the story of Ash's disappearance out of him. He recalled the laughter of the shieldmaidens as he told of how Ash had bested him and knocked him senseless. No doubt the tale had spread throughout Hornsborg by now, and he was the laughing-stock of all. The mere thought of Ash conjured a burning anger in him.

The Jarl had banished him, saying there was no longer a place for him in Hornsborg. Roghald was to collect his belongings and leave in the morning with a delegation of hirdsmen heading to Gjallarholm, a large town to the south of Hornsborg. The hirds-men were on their way there to liaise with the southern Jarls.

At least Jarl Erik wasn't just throwing him out into the for-est, considering the current threat from the draugr. Roghald had a feeling that this small mercy from the Jarl was only to protect his own good name and had little to do with any concern for the stable master's wellbeing.

No doubt he would suffer some ridicule during the ride to Gjal-larholm, he thought with building anger. The Norse warrior culture was brutal, and any kind of weakness was pounced on, so he would expect only gloating and mockery from the warriors he was to travel with.

He told himself he was glad to leave Hornsborg. The fortress was getting crowded with the evacuation of the townspeople. Several families had been moved into the stables and were already getting on Roghald's nerves anyway.

He had heard earlier, while still in Jarl Erik's hall, that Ash had been seen leaving town and walking south. He was sure the boy was headed for Gjallarholm, and Roghald would look for him there if he hadn't already gotten himself eaten by the draugr. The thought of Ash meeting a violent end at the hands of the undead cheered him up a little.

He bent down and pulled a long wooden case from under his bed. Kneeling on the floor, he opened it and looked down on the sword it contained. Roghald lifted his father's sword out of the box with reverence. It was a thing of beauty that had been discretely given to him by one of his father's friends after that fateful summer of raiding in the east. It was a traditional Norse style weapon with a narrow cross guard and a larger pommel that allowed for better balance. He slid it out of the slim wooden scabbard and for the thousandth time admired the runes carved in the fuller along the length of the blade. '*TOR HIELPE*', he read. A call to Thor, the Thundergod, to lend strength to the bearer. Well, he would need all the strength he could get for the next few weeks, as he sought a new life for himself.

He had been practicing in secret all these years and still knew how to wield the weapon, like it was an extension of his arm. Hard work had kept his strength up, and he knew he could even squeeze the life out of a man if he had to.

Once he was out from under the Jarl's feet, he could call himself by a different name and maybe even seek a new Jarl across the narrow sea to the south. For certain this draugr business would be short lived and the raids would start again next summer. He thought about holding a sword and shield again, plundering the coastlines of lands far away, but the excitement these thoughts would always bring did not come. There was nothing left in his heart but resentment and hate. Hate for the Jarl who shamed him and his father. Hate for the hirdsmen and people of Hornsborg who always looked down their noses at him. But most of all, hate for Ash. That stupid boy with his head in the clouds, always talking about attending the Viking trials so he could become a great warrior.

Although he never said it out loud, he knew that Ash thought he was better than him, and that he could follow the warrior's path that had been denied Roghald. It was as if an ember burned in his stomach when he thought of the lout. This was all Ash's fault. Roghald had worked hard for decades to prove his worth to the Jarl. He had been certain that the Jarl would at some point realise his mistake and would allow Roghald to go raiding again. Then, in the heat of battle, on some foreign shore, Roghald would slip his sword between the Jarl's ribs and his father would be avenged. With the Jarl dead with no sons or daughters, it would be the strongest in the hird who would seize power over the Jarldom. There was no doubt in Roghald's mind that that would have been him. But Ash, along with Eric and Rani, had ruined all that. Roghald would seek his revenge on them all, but more than anything, he longed to look into Ash's eyes as he ran his father's sword through his guts. The boy was out there somewhere and if he was alive, Roghald would find him. And when he was done with Ash, he would turn his attention to Jarl Erik. He would dedicate his life to revenging himself and his father.

He slid the sword back into its scabbard and placed it with his other belongings at the foot of the bed. His helmet was already in the pack. He would have to see about a shield in the near future. Roghald laid down on his bed, now prepared to leave in the morning. As he closed his eyes and sleep came to him, he dreamt of death and fire and vengeance.

The courtyard was bustling with activity as Roghald tightened the last strap on his saddlebags. The pony was restless, sensing the excitement all around it, trying to pull its head around to look at everything that was going on. Roghald gave it a whack on the neck. He would have none of that from the beast.

The pony settled somewhat and stood still for him to finish checking his gear.

Two groups were setting out this morning. First was Roghald's group, which consisted of about a dozen men and women from Jarl Erik's hird. They would make haste along the coast towards Gjallarholm, where they would deliver a message for the local Jarl and leave Roghald to his fate and banishment. No doubt the message would contain a line or two about Roghald, so he doubted he would be welcome to remain in the town. He was hoping he would have enough time to look around for Ash before he pressed further south. The lout would likely go south as well, should he not stay in Gjallarholm.

After Roghald's group, a second larger team of Jomsvikings lead by Jarl Olaf himself were setting out, and the gods only knew where they were headed. He was surprised to see Rani the Seidwoman being led out by a servant and onto a horse. Why would they drag that old bat across the countryside?

No sooner had this thought flashed through his mind, when Rani's head swivelled towards him and he could see a scowl under her hood. He snapped his gaze away and onto the task at hand. The trolls take that old hag! He had heard that in the far southern lands they burned witches at the stake. People seemed to be more sensible in that part of the world.

The lead hirdsman for Roghald's group, an older, silver bearded warrior named Arne, gave them the signal to mount and Roghald pulled himself onto his pony. A few moments later they set off,

Roghald riding last. As he rode through the gatehouse, he looked back at the courtyard and the hive of activity. Three dozen Jomsvikings were mounted and waited in formation as Jarl Olaf and Erik clasped hands and were talking, their heads close to each other. Roghald would have loved to listen in on their conversation.

He straightened up in the saddle as they rode through the town surrounding Hornsborg. The town was quiet and eery after the evacuation, and no one in the party spoke as they rode through. Soon they left the last few dwellings behind and picked up the pace as they started on the road south through the Great Forest.

It had rained a few days ago, but the road had dried out by now and Roghald, riding last, was riding in a constant cloud of dust thrown up by the horses in front to him. With a few muttered curses, he tied his spare shirt across his face to keep the worst of it out of his nostrils.

THEY KEPT UP a rapid pace throughout the day, only making brief stops to rest the horses every few hours. Roghald would always sit a little away from the rest of the group when they rested. They had all made it clear that he was not welcome amongst them, and he had no interest in suffering their jeers anyway. The hirdsmen and women all spoke in hushed tones because of the draugr threat, so at least they couldn't call out insults at him or laugh at jokes at his expense. This meant Roghald was spared the constant mockery he knew he would have experienced otherwise. Everyone was on high alert for any sign of impending attack, and all eyes were scanning the tree line as they rode on.

It was in the middle of the day, when they came around a bend in the road, that a shieldmaiden at the head of the group called out a warning. A hiss went through the air as swords and axes were pulled from scabbards and bindings. They slowed to a trot and everyone could see the horse lying across the road. As they drew closer, the smell of death reached their nostrils and the horses became skittish, requiring a firm hand to even move them forward.

When they reached the bloated and fly-covered carcass, they saw the rider lying trapped beneath it. He was purple and swollen, but a grimace of terror was still fixed on his half-torn face. The stench was overpowering, and Roghald was glad for the shirt covering his nose and mouth. One warrior pointed out another body to the side of the road, just inside the forest edge. Arne, the hirdsman in charge, slid off his horse and walked up to the fallen rider, his eyes never leaving the forest as he approached. He bent down and inspected the dead body.

"It is Thorvald, so that one over there must be Jorn." he said pointing to the other body with his sword. "We sent them as messengers to Gjallarholm three days ago." Angry scowls flashed over the Hornsborg warriors as they recognised their kinsmen and friends. Arne looked thoughtful for a moment before saying, "We ride. Now." The other warriors looked uncomfortable.

"We need to bury or burn them, Arne." one said, tension in his voice.

Arne shook his head, his lips tight.

"No. There is no time. The enemy is upon us and we must be swift. We need to get word to Gjallarholm and more lives than ours depend on it," he said as he swung himself back into the saddle. Looking down at the corpses he said, "I hope they will forgive us."

He shielded his eyes and looked at the sun. "We will make it to Gjallarholm by nightfall if we push the horses," he said as he set off, followed by the rest of the group. *If* we make it, Roghald couldn't help thinking, as he took a last look at the dead rider and spurred his horse onwards.

CHAPTER 8

ASH WATCHED THE UGLY CREATURE SCURRY OFF TO THE other end of the cave to open a large chest. What was it and what was this strange place? He took a good look around the cave. The stone was too regular to be a natural cave, though he couldn't see any marks from tools on the smooth surfaces of the floor and walls. The heat from the forge was making him lightheaded, and he removed his tunic, but kept his undershirt on.

His eyes returned to Beli, who by now was rummaging deep in the chest. There were said to be many magical creatures in Midgard, but it was difficult to know what was true and not just a tale or superstition. He had heard many stories around the fire at night while growing up in Hornsborg. Stories of trolls, giants and the gods in Asgard, but also of fairies, elves and other supernatural beings. The land was old, yet not all of it had been explored, and it still harboured many secrets and remnants of long forgotten magic.

Ash was pretty certain that Beli was a troll. The creature seemed odd and harmless enough, but Ash couldn't help feeling suspicious about him. Something didn't feel right. He knew from the stories that not all trolls were bad, some were just indifferent to humanity, happy to live their life undisturbed, but others were violent and cruel. He was happy to have found a sanctuary from whatever roamed the forest though, and he'd been promised a meal, which was definitely an improvement in his situation. Only now did he realise that he hadn't eaten all day. His stomach rumbled with hunger, and he decided to trust Beli, at least enough to share a meal. Ash wondered what the creature considered food. He reminded himself that he still had a bit of cheese and a few apples in his knapsack, should the meal turn out to be something horrendous.

Ash looked around the smithy again and his eyes landed on the giant forge. It was made of stone and was burning with ferocity. The strange runes were glowing and flickering around the opening, mesmerising Ash. Surely, this was magic at play, he thought. In front of the forge stood the anvil and on it rested the smithing hammer Beli had been working with, next to something small and shiny. After a quick glance to ensure that the creature was still busy at the bottom of the chest, Ash walked over for a closer inspection.

Beli appeared to have been working on a small sparrow made of pure gold. The little bird was so detailed and lifelike, it looked like it would take flight any second. He struggled to imagine Beli working on this intricate little thing with such great hammer blows as Ash had witnessed when he entered.

But that was not what caught Ash's attention. The golden bird might as well have been a horseshoe in his eyes, compared to the smithing hammer lying next to it. Made of a dark stone, strange and intricate silver runes had been engraved on the head and shaft. It was the most beautiful thing he had ever seen.

He felt an urge to hold it and glanced around to ensure that Beli was still rummaging in his chest. The troll was still distracted, so he reached out and closed his hand around the handle.

A sense of completeness filled him, like an itch he didn't even know he'd had was being soothed. The hammer was light as a feather and felt like a part of him that had been missing his entire life. It radiated power and purpose and felt alive in his hand. He ran his other hand over the smooth stone of the hammerhead.

Ash couldn't help but laugh as little tendrils of light leapt from the runes to his fingers as he touched them.

A clatter nudged him back to reality. Beli was standing by the chest, a long knife laying by his feet. He stood as if frozen. His large bushy eyebrows were raised all the way to the tuft of hair on his head, his mouth agape and his beady little eyes fixed on Ash.

His eyes moved back and forth between the boy and the hammer.

"But... What...? How...?" he croaked, still not seeming to believe what he was seeing. Ash felt embarrassed and put the hammer back down on the anvil with a sheepish expression.

"I'm sorry," he started. "It is such a beautiful thing and I couldn't resist..."

He was cut short as the creature closed the distance between them in a flash. Before he realized what had happened, Beli's large, rough hands were holding his wrists in a vice like grip. He turned Ash's hands around with ease, even though Ash resisted, and stared at his palms. Then, the troll swung his head up, far too close to Ash's face for comfort, and his eyes burrowed into his. For a few long seconds, the creature just stared at him and Ash felt an uncomfortable tickle in the back of his head. He somehow felt violated, like Beli could see his innermost secrets. As suddenly as he had seized Ash, Beli let go and took a few steps back, looking perplexed.

"I'm really sorry. I shouldn't have touched your hammer and I won't do it again." Ash explained. A small smile appeared on Beli's face and grew larger as he seemed to have come to some conclusion.

"Beli forgives the boy." he said, spreading his arms in a magnanimous gesture. "No harm done, but do not touch again." he said as he raised a warning finger. Ash assured him he would not, although a part of him was longing for the hammer and his eyes kept returning to it.

"Sit, little human. Beli promised supper!" the creature declared.

This time Beli waited until Ash was indeed seated before he spun around and hurried off to the end of the cave again. As he passed it, he swept up the knife where it was dropped and put it back in the chest. Next to the coffer was a solid timber cupboard. Opening it, Beli retrieved a few bundles wrapped in cloth and a large ceramic jar and returned to the table where Ash was waiting.

He sat down, opened the bundles and spread the contents onto the table. A large loaf of dark bread of a type that Ash had never seen before, a piece of moist honeycomb wrapped in waxed cloth and a stone jar filled to the brim with pickled mushrooms. Beli tore off a hunk of the bread, picked up the honeycomb and smeared it on one side of the bread. Then he fished out a few mushrooms from the jar and placed them on the honeyed side. The troll shoved the whole thing in his large mouth, then chewed and smacked his lips a few times before swallowing.

Ash followed his example. He was starving and surprised by how delicious this simple meal was. The bread was dark and rich, unlike the white bread he was used to, the mushrooms were earthy and flavoursome, and the honey added a delightful sweet touch.

Consumed by his ravenous appetite, Ash did not pay much attention to Beli, who never took his eyes off him. The creature studied him as they ate several pieces each. When they were done, Beli cleared the remaining food away before retrieving a long, curved pipe from the same cupboard. The creature sat back down after lighting his pipe with a stick poked into the forge for a second. With a happy sigh, the troll blew out a blue cloud of smoke. When it reached Ash, the smoke burned his throat, and he coughed a few times, making the troll chuckle.

With a full belly, the exhaustion of the day finally caught up with Ash. His eyelids were getting heavy and his head bobbed a couple of times. Beli smiled and pointed to the corner of the room with his pipe. Ash turned to see a pile of discarded sacks amongst old crates and chests. Giving Beli a greatful smile, he got up, spread his blanket over the sacks and set his knapsack up as a pillow. He took off his boots and as he laid down on his improvised bed, Beli turned to him.

"What is the boy's name?".

"Ash." he mumbled half asleep. "Ash from Hornsborg." His eyes already closed; he couldn't see the grin on Beli's face as he replied.

"Sleep well, Ash from Hornsborg."

Ash tossed and turned in his sleep. He dreamt of a dark landscape under a pale sun. Ash was hiding, knowing something was hunting him. He was cautious as he moved from shadow to shadow across the dark land. If he stayed on the move, he knew he had a chance of escaping whatever was stalking him. A light appeared on the horizon. Ash should have welcomed it in this dark place, but seeing it turned his blood to ice as a dark sense of foreboding came over him.

He pressed himself into a small crevice in the rock to hide. The light was fast approaching and soon he could see there was a dark and towering shape behind it. The ground trembled with every step as the giant took long, purposeful steps towards Ash. In front, it swept a lantern from side to side, casting a searching light across the landscape. In its other hand, it dragged a large stone club; the tip carving a broad furrow in the ground as the giant lumbered forwards.

The light fell on Ash's hiding place and the giant stopped. Its face was a mask of anger and its two eyes burned with hate when they locked on the crevice where he was hiding. Towering high, as tall as a hundred men, the giant raised the club over its head. With a resounding grunt, the creature swung the club. Petrified with fear, Ash could only watch as it fell towards him.

"Wake up, Ash from Hornsborg!" Ash jolted awake and blinking, looked around confused. When he found himself in Beli's smithy he was relieved, and the dream already faded from his memory.

"The sun is long risen and the stench of you is unbearable and

Beli needs to get back to his work." Beli was standing next to him with his arms crossed. Behind him, Ash could see a large pot with a ladle and two bowls sitting on the table. Following his gaze, Beli smiled and said, "Eat, Ash from Hornsborg. Eat and gain the strength to travel far, far from Beli's home."

Ash got up and rubbed the last of the sleep from his eyes. His back was stiff from sleeping on the pile of sacks. He walked over to the table and sat down, his nightmare now forgotten. Beli ladled a large helping of some kind of porridge into his bowl and broke off a piece of the same bread from last night for his visitor, before helping himself.

"Nothing comes from nothing, Ash from Hornsborg, and you are now indebted to Beli," his host began. Ash paused with the spoon halfway to his mouth. "You have been fed and kept safe by Beli, and this comes at a price." He could see the look of concern on Ash's face and laughed, spraying bits of porridge across the table.

"Don't be alarmed, boy! Old Beli only asks for a small errand to be done for him. Beli has already fallen behind in his work, thanks to Ash from Hornsborg, and has little time for anything else." Ash relaxed somewhat and continued eating. "Beli needs a message delivered to his brothers, not three days' walk from here." At this, he left the table and retrieved an item from a bench near the forge. He placed a thin stone rod, as long as Ash's forearm and about two fingers thick on the table in front of Ash. On it were carved strange runes, similar to the ones around the forge. They were spindly and intricate, and it amazed Ash that the troll had been able to carve such fine inscriptions into the narrow stone.

"Beli, being very generous, will also gift Ash some food and better clothes to make the journey easier." Ash looked down at what he was wearing, torn and dirty from his flight through the forest. This also reminded him of what led to his arrival at Beli's smithy. He remembered the grotesque scene of the riders and horses, and that something had been chasing him only last night.

As if knowing what Ash was thinking, Beli smiled and holding out his large hand said, "This will allow you to travel safely through the forest, Ash from Hornsborg." In his hand rested a smooth, white stone with another of the strange runes carved on the surface and a hole with a leather strap through it. "Hang this about your neck and no harm will come to you from what haunts this forest."

The look of scepticism must have been obvious on Ash's face, because Beli laughed again.

"There are things in this land that are much older than your kind, little human, and old Beli knows them all. You would be wise to accept my help. You may even keep this stone when you have completed the errand and safely travel wherever you are headed to." Ash hesitated for a second before he accepted the pendant. When he hung it around his neck, it felt a lot heavier than it looked. Ash nodded an agreement to Beli. After all, he had nowhere he had to be and as long as he was getting further away from Hornsborg and Roghald, he was content.

When Ash had finished his meal, Beli took him to a chest next to where he slept. Upon opening it, Ash saw it was full of clothes of all sizes, some old, some newer. Ash was about to ask where all the clothes had come from, as nothing would appear to fit the creature's strange shape, but decided against it, not wanting to seem ungrateful. He found new leggings, a shirt and a tunic with no stains on it and discarded his old clothes. The new clothes smelled musty from having been in the chest for a long time, but they were of better quality than his old ones and fitted him well enough.

"Beli has put food in your pack already." Ash saw that his knapsack was larger than it had been when he arrived. He opened the flap on his pack and slipped in the rune-covered stone cylinder before swinging it onto his back along with his bow and quiver. When he was ready, Beli patted him on the shoulder and led the way out of the cave. Ash followed him, but not before casting a last, longing look at the smithing hammer, still lying on the anvil. What a beautiful thing it was.

The cool morning air was soothing on his face after the constant heat of the forge, and it was a great relief to stand out in the breeze. It was a cloudless morning, the sun already well above the horizon, with only a few small clouds chasing across the blue sky. The creature took him to the edge of the plateau and pointed its long, muscular arm out over the forest.

"There, Ash of Hornsborg. There lives Gurmr and Grundr, Beli's brothers." Ash followed his arm and saw that he pointed to one of the many peaks visible in the distance, surrounded by forest. The peak the troll pointed to was split in two, and was like a small mountain, reaching high into the sky. It was different from the other hills and would be easy to spot from any direction. It seemed to be really far away, Ash thought. And in the wrong direction to where he had been traveling. This peak would take him inland instead of along the coast, and there were very few towns and settlements that deep in the forest.

Once again seeming to sense what he was thinking, the creature scowled at him and in a raspy voice said, "Do not betray Beli's trust, little human. Beli will know and will find you." Beli's eyes flicked to the runestone around Ash's neck. It was only the briefest of glances, but Ash saw it.

"Don't worry, Beli. I will do as agreed." At this, a giant smile broke the creature's face in two and he slapped Ash on the shoulder again. This time, however, it was like being hit by a log and he had to take two steps sideways to steady himself, or he would have toppled over. He felt the threat hidden in the harder than necessary slap.

"Good boy, Ash from Hornsborg! Gurmr and Grundr are just as kind and generous as Beli and will reward Ash with delicious foods and gifts, no doubt."

Beli led him around the side of the plateau and pointed out vague steps in the rock leading down.

"Beli would wish Ash from Hornsborg a safe journey," a smiling Beli said, before giving him a light shove in the back, sending him on his way. He stopped halfway down the steps. Ash took several minutes to scan the forest below and seeing nothing move, walked to the bottom. The forest seemed much less threatening than the night before, with rays of sunshine breaking through the canopy of the trees. He now walked along accompanied by birdsong and the odd lazy bumblebee buzzing past. Ash turned back once, when entering a small meadow, and looked back towards Beli's hill. He saw the creature standing on the plateau, looking in his direction. A chill went through Ash when he felt Beli's eyes on him, so he turned around and continued on his way. Whatever Beli was, he gave Ash a sense of unease and he was keen to put as much distance between himself and the ugly creature as possible.

CHAPTER 9

ROGHALD WAS LEADING HIS HORSE THROUGH THE BACK streets of Gjallarholm. He'd given the Hornsborg hirdsmen the slip, disappearing in the early morning. Much better this way, or he might not have been able to keep the horse since, in reality, it belonged to the Jarl. Small payment for decades of service, he reasoned.

They had made it to the town just as the sun set last night. The group of riders had taken a collective sigh of relief as they reached a crest and saw the town spread out before them. It was several times larger than Hornsborg, looking like it could accommodate several thousand inhabitants. The harbour, stretching its many wooden and stone jetties out into a protected inlet of the North Sea, was crowded with ships and fishing boats.

Dominating the sight, at the edge of the harbour, sat the fortress that was the centre of Jarl Astrid's power. A large stone and wood construction behind a tall, crenelated wall, it looked out over the town and the high seas. Jarl Astrid's banner of two crossed spears on a red background flew from every corner of the fortress.

The town itself was surrounded by tall stone walls between four well-spaced towers. Roghald could see guards patrolling the walls, but the gate stood wide open. The road they were on lead straight through the gate and into the Northern end of town. Gjallar-holm was a bustling hub that had grown through its trade with the northern Jarldoms for centuries and hosted one of the largest marketplaces in the Norse lands.

They had pushed on and soon were riding through the gates under the watchful eyes of the guards in the towers and on the wall. A guard captain in a red tunic and chain mail shirt hailed them at the gate. Arne exchanged a quick word with him, and they were ushered through in the direction of the fortress.

After following a broad street and being led through another gate, they soon entered a large courtyard and rode into the stables belonging to the fortress. Their horses were tired, having been pushed hard all day. Roghald's trained eye had told him that some of the horses would be lame by the morning, and so he had told Arne. He was ordered to remain in the stable and care for the horses overnight, while the rest of their group met with the Jarl and delivered their message. Roghald had stayed in the stables and had ministered to his horse with cool compresses until late in the night, making sure it would carry him again the next day. But his affection extended only to his horse. He knew the other animals would be fine after a few days' rest, but they wouldn't be riding anywhere for a while.

EARLY NEXT MORNING, Roghald made his way down to the marketplace in town. Like in all large trading towns, he knew there was always a need for hired swords. In troubled times, there would be people who needed a strong arm and were happy to pay good silver for it without asking many questions.

This would work well for Roghald. He would find employment as a caravan guard and move further down the coast. As far as he knew, the draugr threat was isolated to the northern parts of the land. When he was far enough away from the threat, he would join a lawless or mercenary band, lie low for a while and make some silver. All the while, he would plot his revenge on Ash and Jarl

Erik. Roghald fumed as soon as the lad entered his mind, but he pushed the thoughts aside. He needed to keep his wits about him and focus on his escape, before anyone from Hornsborg discovered that he was making off with the horse.

Roghald had returned to the northern gate at first light. Pretending to be a concerned uncle, he asked the guard captain if anyone fitting Ash's description had entered in the last few days. The burly man assured him that only two wagons had arrived, and they had seen no lonesome lad.

Roghald entertained the idea that Ash might have been killed along the way and had mixed feelings about the thought. On the one hand, he enjoyed imagining the lad torn to pieces by the undead, but on the other, he would be disappointed for having his sworn revenge snatched from him. However, Ash might also have skirted right past the town and continued south or could even have been hiding in one of the wagons.

Roghald finally reached the marketplace. It was a large open area, where traders had set up tents for living and for displaying goods. Besides everyday items such as bread, cloth and simple tools, precious goods from far away kingdoms could be found here, such as spices, gems, ornate fabrics and silverware. Since the Norse raided and traded far away from their own borders, many exotic things were available in their local marketplaces.

By the bustle of the marketplace, Roghald gathered that the local Jarl hadn't informed the people of the draugr threat yet, or this place would be empty. The merchants would clear out quick enough once the word got out about the attack Roghald's group had witnessed only half a day's ride from the gates. Most would make a fast escape down the coast, and Roghald would move with them.

He arrived at a section where the tents were sturdier and of better quality. The more exotic and expensive items could be found for sale here, and he saw grim, armed men and women keeping guard, eyeing all who approached with suspicion. He knew he was in the right part of the marketplace.

Roghald ignored the vendors calling their wares to him and found what he was looking for next to a mead tent.

A group of merchant guards sat at a table enjoying mugs of mead and ale in the sunshine. Roghald weighed them up, seeing scars and warrior tattoos on their hands and faces, accompanied by dents and scratches on the shields and helmets resting next to them. These were seasoned warriors, hard men and women, not in the service of any Jarl for one reason or another. He liked them already. He squared his shoulders and strode up to the group.

"Who's in charge here?" he demanded.

JARL ASTRID READ through Jarl Erik's message for the third time. She knew he was a pragmatic, honourable man without a tendency to exaggerate or embellish, but she still had difficulty accepting what she'd just read. She entertained for a moment, the thought that this could be some kind of ruse in a bid for the throne, but she could not see the benefit of fabricating such a scheme. Jarl Erik, she knew, for all his virtues, was not a political strategist, but more a 'sword and axe' type of leader. She paused to rub her eyes.

Close to her fortieth summer, she felt more like sixty; the responsibilities of a Jarl weighing her down. She never had to worry about these things when she fought in the ranks as a shieldmaiden, and she longed for the carefree days of raiding and sailing the North Sea. How long had it been since she even saw battle? Seven, maybe eight years? She sighed.

Now it was just endless days of monotonous decisions on trade routes, crop rotations, building armaments, raising or lowering taxes and making sure the people were fed and clothed. And now, this.

She lowered the parchment and looked at the older hirdsman in front of her. He had added his own testimony from his trip here from Hornsborg. He was at an age rarely reached by any hirdsman, and the multitude of scars on his hands and face spoke of countless battles won. Yet, she could still see something in his eyes she would never have expected to see in someone like him. They held a hint of fear.

If this was a ruse, it was an elaborate one.

"And Olaf of the Jomsvikings is on his way to discuss with me in person?"

"Yes, Jarl Astrid." Arne replied. "He has something to take care of first but should arrive shortly."

CHAPTER 10

ASH WAS SITTING BY A FIRE HE HAD MADE IN THE BOT-
tom of a gully. It was a sheltered spot and if he kept the fire
small, he didn't think anyone, or anything, would see it. His feet
were sore from a full day of walking and he was rubbing them to
ease the aches. He had made few stops, wanting to get as far away
from Beli as he could. Ash had been walking straight towards the
split peak, but it seemed no closer now than when he had set out.
He wondered if the ugly creature had told him the truth about
how far it was, since it seemed to be further than a few days' travel.

Leaning back against a fallen tree trunk, Ash ate some mushrooms and an apple, then spent some time just staring into the fire.
He had reached the road early in the afternoon. Standing on it for
a while, he had contemplated whether or not he should abandon
Beli's errand, and just continue to Gjallarholm instead. Looking
back, he saw the monolith on the plateau in the distance, still too
close for comfort, so he sighed and crossed the road, continuing
into the forest.

Having not heard or sensed anything unusual during the day,
he wondered if whatever haunted the forest was gone or if Beli's
strange necklace worked. He lifted the runestone around his neck
and turned it over in his hand, scrutinizing it in the flickering fire-

light. The stone made him uncomfortable. It felt tainted somehow, the exact opposite of how he had felt holding the stone hammer in Beli's smithy. He had an urge to wipe his hands when holding it and allowed it to fall back onto his chest. Sighing, he stared into the fire once again. He sat there unmoving, but thinking, until it had burnt down and darkness settled around him.

IN THE MORNING, when the first light of the day filtered in through the forest canopy, Ash broke his camp and set off again. The only thing left behind in the small gully were the remnant ashes of his fire, an apple core and a runestone pendant hanging from a tree branch.

He felt lighter after removing it, and it only strengthened his decision. He didn't like not honouring his word, even when it was given to someone like Beli, but he felt he had no choice. There was a sense of wrong about the whole situation. The gnawing suspicion he had felt about the troll had only gotten worse the further he had walked, to where he decided it was madness to continue. Without looking back, he set out towards the road to Gjallarholm, but it was via an indirect route, so he could remain far from Beli's hill. He kept a brisk pace throughout the morning and he only stopped to eat and drink when the sun stood high in the sky, before setting out again.

In the late afternoon, he found himself back on the road, but Beli's hill was now long out of sight. Feeling much better with his feet on firm ground and out of the forest, he set off south, whistling a little tune as he walked. It would be dark soon, but he decided to push on a little longer, eager to get to Gjallarholm. A small stone seemed to have found its way into his boot, but he decided to ignore it and carry on. Ash imagined finding a soft hayloft to sleep in when he got to the town. He would spend some of his few remaining coins on a hot meal and maybe even a bath in a washhouse. Gjallarholm was a large, bustling town and he was certain he could find work there, maybe even an apprenticeship if he could impress a tradesperson with some hard work. He imagined a comfortable life for himself in the large town and never seeing Roghald or strange creatures in the forest ever again.

He stepped on the pebble in his boot for the hundredth time and threw his arms up in frustration. His boots had long laces, and it would take a while to extract the offending pebble, but he could take it no longer. Ash dropped his knapsack and bow on the ground and bent down to undo his laces. A double knot had occurred on the top lace and he muttered a curse as he started to tease the knot open.

A foul smell reached his nose. It smelled like a dead cat he had once found behind the stables and wrinkling his nose he looked around for the source. He saw it standing just inside the trees along the road, not ten steps away from him. It was a man, or at least it had been once. He was broad shouldered, much more so than a normal man with long powerful arms that ended in large hands with claw-like nails. His clothes were in tatters and stained with dirt. Dark, dried blood stained its jaw and the front of his chest. His skin was ghostly pale, with black, rotting patches and dark veins spreading across the entire body. The worst of it were the white, dead eyes that were locked on Ash.

A fear that took his breath away spread through his body and knotted his stomach. He could only stare at the creature; his limbs had become like lead. The draugr parted its black lips and revealed a broad mouth, full of jagged and broken teeth. It let out a loud, blood-curdling moan that was answered by others in the forest behind it.

Ash ran. He ran like he'd never run before. He heard more than one creature run out onto the road behind him, but he didn't look back, he just kept running. His heart sank as he could see more creatures spilling out of the forest ahead of him, cutting him off. With terrifying moans, they turned their dead eyes on him. They started running fast, in a shambling, leaping way, and Ash realized that he would never outrun them in the open. He darted into the forest on the opposite side, hoping to get away once amongst the trees, due to his smaller size.

The forest seemed dark after the sunlit glare of the road, but he had no time to let his eyes adjust. He ran between trees, constantly being whipped by low branches. However, soon his eyes had adjusted, and he could duck under the larger branches, but he could hear his pursuers closing in all the same. Their hungry moans filled his world as he ran around trees and scrambled over stones and fallen logs.

The thicket opened up to a broad, shallow stream, but as he splashed across it, he slipped and stumbled and one of the creatures caught up with him. It raked a clawed hand across the back of his neck and Ash was thrown face first into the shallow water. He felt the crushing weight of the creature as it landed on his back, nails digging into his shoulders. Ash cried out, the pain excruciating, as the creature tore at his flesh.

His cry of pain was cut off as, without warning, a burst of icy fire erupted in his chest. The same strange tingling he had experienced when fighting Roghald spread through his body and a great sense of calm came over him. His fear and pain were swept away and time slowed, distorting the moans of the draugr on his back. The world around him once again came into extreme sharp focus. He saw the sunlight reflecting from the smallest of water drops that splashed in front of him as they appeared almost suspended in the air.

Ash reached out and closing his hand around a stone as large as a fist, pushed off the streambed and spun, lashing out with his arm. He connected with the side of the creature's head, caving its skull in. The force of the blow threw the creature clear of Ash and it landed several paces away in a spray of water.

Another two of the monsters were just entering the stream, and Ash could see more movement all around him. He leapt to his feet and punched the closest one in the chest, sending it sprawling backwards. The fire in his body intensified, roaring in his ears, but his mind remained calm. The stone still in his hand, he swung it at the second creature's head. Ash was fast, but it was fast too, ducking away from the blow, only to throw itself at Ash. Snarling, its clawed hands reached for his unprotected throat as the creature launched forwards.

Ash jumped back and prepared to strike again, when he could feel the flame in his chest flicker and die down. He tried to hold on to it, willing it back, but it was like holding on to mist and it dissipated, leaving his chest feeling empty. It was replaced with fear as time sped up to normal and the creature crashed into him at full speed.

Ash fell on his back, the draugr on top of him. Its hands wrapped around his throat, the pressure unbearable as it lowered its open mouth towards him. The creature's hungry moan sent a breath of putrid air into his face. From the corner of his eye, Ash saw another rotting, undead face sink its teeth into his shoulder and he felt warm blood running down his arm and neck. His world became one of pain and helplessness as the creatures tore into him.

A great sorrow filled him when he realized he would die. He closed his eyes and prepared for the end, hoping it would be quick so the pain would go away. In the darkness of his mind, a woman appeared in front of him. She had raven black, flowing hair, and although she had powerful features and posture, her eyes were soft and kind. She smiled at him and it felt warm and familiar as she knelt down to stroke his cheek like she had done countless times before.

"Mother." He croaked, opening his eyes, but the woman's face was gone as fast as it had appeared, replaced by the rotten, gaping mouth of the draugr.

He thought he heard a horn somewhere nearby, then a roar as if by a large animal. His vision darkened as the beast was crushing his windpipe and his lungs felt like they were on fire. In desperation, he ran his free hand over the streambed next to him, seeking another stone, but he found only sand and pebbles.

There was a crashing sound and the draugr was thrown off him. He couldn't feel any of the monsters on him anymore and he took a deep, painful breath, filling his burning lungs. His vision was blurry from tears and lack of air, but he looked up to see a large bear standing above him, roaring. He blinked to clear his eyes, and the bear resolved into the largest man Ash had ever seen. The man had brown, braided hair and beard, with a bearskin over his shoulders and looked familiar somehow. In a flash, Ash remembered where they'd last met - this was the man who had knocked him down with his pony in Hornsborg, when Jarl Olaf had just arrived with the Jomsvikings. Holding an enormous axe, with both the man and weapon splattered in black blood, he stood over Ash, turning in a circle.

Ash was so tired, he just wanted to sleep, but when he heard more moans to his left, he turned his head with a tremendous effort. A dozen of the creatures were entering the stream from the forest, their dead eyes set on the bear-man. Ash heard a shout from the side of the undead monsters before a group of men and women with shields and spears broke out of the forest. They ran fast, in a fluid way, and in no time closed the distance to the pale creatures. Their short spears flashed, glinting in the last rays of the sun, so fast that they became a blur. They overcame their enemies with brutal force and the river ran dark with undead blood.

Another familiar man appeared from the forest. Jarl Olaf strode out, a war hammer resting on his broad shoulder. He had a dark look on his face as his gaze swept over the stream and the dead draugr. Turning to the bear-man standing over Ash, he made a questioning gesture with his hand. The huge warrior looked down on Ash for a moment, before turning back to the Jarl, nodding. Olaf barked an order and turned back into the forest, followed by the warriors.

The large man stooped down and swept Ash into his arms, cradling him to his chest. His face in the man's fur, Ash breathed in the musty smell, letting it drown out the rot that had filled his nostrils. He could no longer hear the moans of the undead, and his last thought before giving in to unconsciousness, was how nice that was.

ASH WAS FLOATING in blissful darkness for what seemed like an endless time. He felt himself drifting through the dark. When a soft light appeared in the distance, he could feel himself pulled towards it. Soon he could make out a doorway, suspended in the dark. It was open and a light came from within. As he got closer, the door became larger and larger, until Ash drifted through it, small as a mouse.

The room inside was as big as the world. Countless strings, disappearing into the shadows, formed a web so large and complex, his head was spinning just looking at it. Three giant women stood in the centre of the room, the web surrounding them. They were older than anyone he had ever seen before, their skin wrinkled and leathery, and their white hair long enough to lie at their feet. Yet, they moved with purpose and vigour. One would spin a thread between her hands, one would fasten a thread to the web, and one would cut threads from the web with a silvery scissor.

Ash knew he was seeing the Norns -Urd, Skuld and Verdandi, who controlled the fate of all who lived. When you were born, they spun a string, giving you your fate and placed you in the web of the world. When your time came to an end, they cut your string from the web and you would be no more. They held power even over the fate of the gods.

He watched them with fascination as they spun, fastened and cut, constantly altering the web of the world, the shape ever changing. But then, one pulled a string toward herself, her scissors at the ready, and Ash felt an uncomfortable tug within. It was his string; he knew it with all of his heart. As she placed the scissors on it, Ash closed his eyes and he felt his heart stop.

"What's this?" A voice as old as time filled the room. He opened his eyes.

The Norns had stopped their activity, and all three were bent over the string, their long noses almost touching it as they stared at it.

"This string should be cut," one said.

"Twisted by the All-father it is." said another.

"Spun with fire and spun with stone." the third whispered.

"But still so, fate comes to all." the first said.

"To cut it now would unravel the web, back to the beginning." the second said, gazing across the room and the complex web that filled it.

"Best left uncut. For now, for now…" the three said in unison. They let the string go and it fell back into the web. Ash felt his heart start again, as if it'd never stopped. The Norns returned to their places and resumed their work. Ash drifted out the doorway, and he watched the room and the doorway disappear into the darkness that once again surrounded him.

CHAPTER 11

ROGHALD ADJUSTED THE HELMET STRAP AS HE RODE alongside the wagon. He had forgotten how uncomfortable these things were to wear for an extended period of time, and not having worn one for years, his neck was becoming stiff from the weight of the iron. He looked over at the man driving the wagon next to him. The man had been whistling the same annoying tune on and off for hours, and Roghald imagined throttling the man to death.

The caravan carried expensive fabrics and spices and was escorted by six armed men and women, including Roghald. He'd had no problem securing the job when talking to Gorm, the captain of the caravan guards, at the mead tent the previous day. The pay wasn't as good as he had hoped, but it was a quick way out of the north and away from the Hornsborg hirdsmen.

As he predicted, word got out about the draugr attack and the marketplace had packed up under the shouting of the merchants. Asmund, the merchant who owned this caravan, was a weasel of a man, and seemed like he was about to wet his pants when he was told of the undead threat. He had insisted on leaving immediately, and not to wait for the morning to leave in a group like most other caravans.

They had travelled south through the night, but their progress was slow with the four oxen-pulled wagons setting the pace. Still, Roghald was happy to be on his way. When the first morning light coloured the horizon, the first riders from Gjallarholm had overtaken them. Fast messengers heading south, as the news broke about the draugr and the pending closure of the city gates, no doubt.

Whenever he heard the approaching thunder of hooves behind them, he was glad for the helmet. Its guard covered the top of his face, nose and cheekbones, making him harder to recognise if they were riders who knew him from Hornsborg. Roghald had made some further inquiries in Gjallarholm, and no one fitting Ash's description had been seen in town. He must have passed through and carried on south, Roghald thought. He took a moment to imagine throttling Ash to death, and that lifted his spirits. Gorm rode up to him, his chain mail jingling in rhythm with the trot of his pony.

"Egil," the captain addressed him. Roghald had given a false name when seeking employment, something he was sure most of his new brothers and sisters in arms had done too when they joined the ranks of the caravan guards.

"There is a spot by the river up ahead where we will halt to eat and water the animals. Stick with the rearmost wagon when we do and keep a sharp eye out."

"Will do," Roghald replied. Gorm nodded and rode on to another of the guards to relay his message. Roghald scanned the forest for the thousandth time. Nothing. His eyes drifted to the lead wagon, where Asmund sat dozing, wrapped in a blanket. The little weasel had fretted all night as they travelled along, jumping at every shadow. He smiled when he remembered the caravan startling a pheasant from its sleep. It made a great flapping ruckus in the tree branches as it flew off, with Asmund squealing and throwing himself off the wagon and onto the ground.

Everyone had laughed when the caravan master climbed back into his wagon with a red face, swearing at them for their insolence and reminding everyone who held the purse strings. Roghald had exchanged amused glances with a few of the guards as they tried to hide their smiles. He enjoyed the camaraderie in the group, having been outside the warrior culture for so long. He could tell by their different dialects that they came from all over the Norse lands. They were far from their homes for undisclosed reasons, exiled or outcast, and he couldn't help but feel a certain kinship with them, that fate had dealt them similar hands. He reminded himself that this was just a means to an end, and he mustn't forget his priorities. His revenge against Ash and Jarl Erik was all that mattered.

The caravan reached an open spot where a river bend came close to the road. The wagons pulled in in a row, and the drivers alighted and went to fill their buckets with water for the oxen to drink. Roghald rode back to the rear wagon as ordered and stepped off his horse to stretch his legs. He led the shaggy mare the short distance to the river and let her drink a little, before returning to the wagon. As he was about to tie her off, she became skittish, wanting to pull away, and Roghald snapped her reins and pulled her back into control. Perhaps she could smell the caravan master's fear, he thought with mirth.

He tied her off to the back of the wagon and was about to reach into his saddlebags for something to eat, when he heard a yell from the front of the caravan. Asmund must have seen his own shadow, he thought with a chuckle, but then a great commotion ensued. He stepped around from the back of the wagon to a sight of horror.

Spilling out of the forest ahead were dozens of beings that could only be something out of a nightmare. Pale and hunched, their clothes in tatters, they threw themselves at the people in the lead caravan who were racing to unsheathe their weapons, as hungry moans filled the clearing. At first, Roghald could only stare in disbelief at what he saw, but then the first creature reached one of the guards and laid into him with teeth and claws. Before the spray of blood from the guard's neck reached the ground, Roghald got moving. He pulled his sword, cursing that he hadn't purchased a shield when in Gjallarholm, and moved to join the other defenders. Their only chance was to stay together as a unit.

The frantic neighing of his horse made him spin around. The mare was pulling at the reins, trying to get away from a handful of creatures that ran out of the woods behind the caravan. Roghald noted that they ignored the horse and came straight for him. Maybe not completely mindless creatures after all, he thought.

A terrible stench reached him a second before the first draugr did. With a snarl, the creature leapt at Roghald, who sidestepped and swung his sword in a downward arc. The sword bit into the back of the creature, cutting a deep gash, and made it crash to the ground. Not even pausing, the monster scrambled back up and launched at him again. Roghald cursed again as he remembered Jarl Olaf's words about how only strikes to the head and heart would kill these monsters. Two more draugr were closing in on him, and he knew that he would have no hope of living through this fight alone. He had to join the other defenders; it was his only chance.

He turned to run towards the front of the caravan where the guards had gathered to fight off the initial attack. He only made it two steps before he realized that there was no one left standing. All had fallen or fled. Bodies littered the ground and in places the creatures were heaped in piles, a lone arm or leg sticking out from under their writhing mass. He heard a few screams from down the road and the forest and knew that those who ran away did not make it far. Roghald was thrown to the ground when a draugr crashed into him from behind, and as his head hit the side of the wagon with force, the world turned black.

CHAPTER 12

THE OLD SEIDWOMAN SAT BY THE FIRE IN A CHAMBER inside the Gjallarholm fortress. She was turning a grey stone rod over and over in her hands, running her fingers along the intricate runes carved into it.

"Jotnar," she whispered to herself, a thoughtful look on her white-dusted face. A thousand years had passed, but the trolls had not forgotten. Her mind drifted to the creation of their world and what had made most trolls hate humankind.

In the beginning, the great world tree, *Yggdrasil*, stood at the centre of the cosmos, its mighty branches and roots connecting the eight worlds which made up the universe. The twin boughs at the tree's crown held *Asgard* and *Vanaheim*, the homes of the gods; the Aesir and Vanir.

On a branch, not far below, sat Alfheim, the land of the Light Elves. At the very base of the world tree, lay the two oldest worlds; *Muspelheim*, the world of fire and brimstone and *Niflheim*, the land of ice and frozen mist. The roots of Yggdrasil stretched deep into the underworld, and wrapped around *Jotunheim*, a place of stone and tall mountains, *Svartalfheim*, the home of the *Svartalfr*, or dark elves, and the *dvergr*, the dwarfs. Even further down, at its deepest root, sprawled *Hel*, the kingdom of the dead.

In Jotunheim had lived *Ymir*, a cruel and vile giant, whose appetite knew no bounds. As he fed and fed, he grew larger and larger and was soon threatening to outgrow the limits of his world. When he laid down to rest, the sweat from his body flowed over the rocks and mountains and gave birth to trolls and giants, who sprang from the stone itself.

From Asgard, the ruler of the gods, *Odin* the Allfather, and his two brothers, *Vili* and *Ve*, watched the growth of Ymir and the spawning of trolls and giants with concern. They knew that soon Ymir would outgrow Jotunheim, and would move to the other worlds, to feed off them. Hordes of giants and trolls would follow in his wake.

The balance of the worlds thus threatened, the three gods armed themselves and set out to kill Ymir. A terrible battle ensued, and they fought for centuries, until Odin delivered the fatal blow, cracking Ymir's head in half. So much blood flowed from his body that it drowned most of the giants and trolls on Jotunheim. Only a few survived - those who held on to the mountains, and those who were washed away to other worlds and did not drown.

Some remained in Jotunheim, where they hid underground until the flow of blood stopped, and they became the Jotnar, the trolls of Jotunheim. Some were washed away to Niflheim, where the frozen mists changed them, turning them into ice trolls and giants. And some were swept to Muspelheim, where they became fire trolls and giants.

Odin and his brothers took the body of the slain Ymir and shaped it into a ninth world. They placed it at the heart of the world tree and called it *Midgard*. From the giant's cracked skull, they made the sky and from his bones and teeth they made the mountains and stones. His blood filled the hollows to make the lakes and the seas.

Midgard became the most beautiful of the worlds, and Odin and his brothers would often walk through it. One day, after a storm had raged across the world, they came upon two trees that had fallen. Not wanting the trees to perish, the gods shaped them into the first man and woman. Having breathed life into their new creations, they named them Aske and Embla, and left Midgard to them.

Aske and Embla had many children, who spread to all corners of their new world. Odin took a great interest in them and would often wander around Midgard in disguise, to watch over the humans. When kingdoms and empires rose and fell amongst his children, he would collect their best warriors, after they died in battle, and take them to his great hall, Valhalla.

But he was not the only one whose eyes were on the new land. From the other worlds, the trolls watched with hate and anger. They had not forgotten what the gods did to their father *Ymir*, and while the humans went about their lives, they plotted their revenge.

Rani turned the rod over in her hands, reading the runes again with the tip of her fingers. The boy was sleeping behind her, his breaths deep and regular. She was blind, having sacrificed her eyes in exchange for True Sight; the ability to see into the spirit realm. The gods drove a hard bargain, but she had never regretted the arrangement. She could see what others couldn't and knew more than most about the workings of gods, trolls and giants.

Rani had sat there for hours, at times reaching out a hand to feel the boy's skin. She didn't have to, since she could always sense him when he was near, ever since he was a little boy, but it was reassuring all the same. She picked up a small bowl sitting on the floor beside her feet and tipped out the many small bones it contained, letting them rattle out on the floor in front of her. Rani ran her hand over them, reading them with the touch of her fingers, but she already knew what they would say. This was the tenth time she had cast them in the last couple of hours and, once again, they fell in the same pattern.

"He's too young…" she whispered. Having gathered up the bones and dropped them back in the bowl, she sat in silence for some time, before sighing and reaching into a bag next to her. She withdrew an old, slim piece of deer antler, as long as her hand. It was polished smooth by years of handling, but she could still feel the faint runes carved into the surface.

Rani stood from the chair, only to sit down next to the boy on his bed. She sat there listening to his soft breathing for a moment before pulling down the blanket, exposing his chest, careful not to touch his bandaged shoulder wound. Rani sat in silence next to him for a while, her hand resting over his heart, feeling his slow and steady pulse. Then she began to sing softly, a tune that followed his heartbeat. It was a song as old as the world, in a language long forgotten. It was a song of deep forests and icy winds, of snow crunching under paws and red blood spilled in the hunt. She sang of running over ice and mountains with howls echoing from peak to peak.

The boy stirred, his head turning like an animal listening. As she sang, she touched the bone to his chest. It sizzled and the smell of burned flesh filled the small chamber as she ran it down his front from his collarbone, down to his navel. She added line after line as she sang until the intricate rune covered his entire torso. When she drew the last line, the rune glowed in a blue light and the boy's back arched when a spasm shook his entire body. The old woman let the song fade out as he settled back into bed.

"This is your birthright, Ash of the Ulfhednar." Rani whispered, stroking his cheek. She sat next to him long after he had drifted back into a deep sleep. She couldn't see, but she knew the rune she had burned into his chest would be gone, faded into his skin. Gone were also the wounds he sustained in the draugr attack, with only faint scars remaining, and she removed the bandages from his shoulder with gentle hands.

She heard a flapping of wings from the window and a large raven cawed at her from the sill. He needn't have bothered. The bird was shining like a beacon to her True Sight, because it was not of this world.

It cawed again and she turned towards it.

"Tell your master that his cub now has its teeth." There was another flapping of wings and the raven was gone. She turned back to the boy and pulled his covers back up, before returning to her chair next to him. She continued her vigil over him, her face a mask of worry.

THE HIRDSMEN PULLED in their horses, a bloodbath spread out on the road before them. They dismounted with their weapons drawn, but all was still. The warm sunlight and birdsong felt like a mockery amongst the carnage. Reports had returned to Gjallarholm about one of the earlier caravans to leave the town being attacked on their way south. As other caravans reached the site, some had turned back, and some had pushed on, hoping to slip past the attackers.

When word reached Jarl Astrid, she sent a host of armed men and women to investigate and to engage the draugr, should they have remained in the area. Jarl Erik's hirdsmen, who had just arrived from Hornsborg and were eager to seek vengeance for their slain brothers, joined them. Dead bodies, horses and oxen littered the ground around the four wagons. The wagons had been rummaged through, no doubt by the passing caravans, but were mostly left untouched since no one had wanted to linger long enough to unload them. A younger hirdsman bent down next to the rearmost wagon and picked up a sword. It was smeared in black blood, but the beauty and quality of the sword was still obvious.

"Hey, Arne! Look at this!" He called to the captain who walked over to where the young man stood, trying to read the runes carved in the fuller through the blood.

"*TOR HIELPE.*" he read. The older man glanced at the sword.

"That sword belonged to Einar Halvarson a long time ago. The last time I saw it, it was strapped to his son, Roghald Einarson's waist." He looked around the clearing and the dead bodies there.

"I guess we can count Roghald among the dead, although I can't see him anywhere. But he would never have parted from his father's sword if there was still breath in his body, of that much I am sure."

"Some of the bodies have been eaten on." the young warrior observed, wiping the foul blood off the sword with a cloth. "Maybe they ate Roghald?"

The older hirdsman laughed.

"That would have been a bitter morsel to eat, I imagine. Probably kept them up all night, squatting in the bushes." Both men laughed.

"I'm keeping the sword." the younger ventured. "It's a far sight better than mine, and Roghald won't be needing it." He turned the blade, letting it catch and reflect the sunlight. "Besides, I found it, so it's good luck." Arne gave the young warrior a pensive look.

"That sword didn't bring Einar any luck, nor his son, as you can see here today."

"Nevertheless, I'm keeping it." He said, swinging it a few times to test the weight. A large raven sat in a birch tree next to the road, watching him, but the warrior was too busy admiring his new sword to notice it.

CHAPTER 13

Ash could hear people talking. He had been asleep for what felt like eons, and the sleep was accompanied by very strange dreams. In one dream, had run over frozen grounds with a pack of wolves. He had been fast and strong and part of the pack, following a scent of blood on the wind. He had felt free and revelled in the sensation of the hunt, when a feeling of being watched came over him. He turned his head to see that on top of a hill stood a tall man in robes and a slouch hat. Two other wolves sat by the man's feet, and Ash felt a strange kinship to them. The wolves were watching him with curiosity. Two black birds swooped in and landed on the man's shoulders and whispered in his ear. The man nodded once and turned to leave, and Ash returned to the hunt with his pack.

He was pretty sure he was awake now but didn't dare open his eyes. The memories of the last few days came back to him, so he decided to find out what was going on before he let anyone know he was awake. He heard a man and two women talking, one of them sounded old.

"... has been several attacks in the last few days. So far only on people traveling on the roads, even large groups, but no attempts have been made on any fortified positions. We are spreading the warriors rather thin, though, and I fear what will happen if a larger assault befalls us." The woman who had spoken was articulate and calm, but her voice held a hint of steel.

"We are wasting our time sitting like rabbits in a field waiting for the eagle to pounce." This was a harsh voice, firm and used to command. It seemed familiar to Ash, but he was not able to place it. "We need to find the source and destroy it, or we all shall perish. What say the bones Rani?"

Rani the Seidwoman? Ash dreaded the fact that he was in the same room as her.

"The bones reveal nothing, Olaf. They have powerful wards, protecting them from my scrying. Odin himself couldn't find them even if he wanted." The man let out a "Bah!", punctuated by the sound of a fist hitting the arm of a chair. Ignoring him, the old woman continued, "I am hoping that the lad can shed some light when he is up. He has had dealings with trolls, and not to his best interest, might I add. If they have something to do with this, the situation is even more serious than we originally thought." Some-one spat three times as if to ward off evil, and the man cursed under his breath.

"Well, when do you think he will wake up? He has been asleep for days." he demanded.

"Oh, he has been awake for a short while, listening to our con-versation." the old woman said. The room fell quiet. Ash could feel people watching him. He opened his eyes. On his left, Rani the Seidwoman sat on a chair, a small smile on her blackened lips. In front of her sat a tall woman in a simple, yet well spun green dress and beside her, a stocky, bearded man in chain mail. Ash hadn't seen the woman before, but the man he recognized as Jarl Olaf of the Jomsvikings. He wanted to pull the covers over his head and escape the scrutiny of them all.

"Erh… Good morning," he ventured.

"How are you feeling, lad?" Olaf grunted.

"I'm fine, thank you, Jarl Olaf." Ash replied in a small voice.

"Do you need anything?" the woman offered. She had two long, blonde braids in an intricate pattern, framing her face. A strong jawline and high cheekbones displayed a mature beauty that had only been enhanced by the years, despite several long since healed scars. She looked on Ash with kind eyes.

"Erh… No, I'm fine, thank you."

"What's this we hear about you dealing with the Jotnar, boy?" Olaf grunted.

"The what?" Ash looked perplexed, rubbing the last of his sleep from his eyes.

"The trolls, lad! Ugly things, live underground, just as easily eat you as look at you."

"I… I don't…" Ash stuttered.

"I think that's enough, Olaf Shieldbreaker." Rani cut in. "The boy has been through a lot and has just woken up. The last thing he needs is to be berated by you." Her voice was firm, and although Olaf looked imposing and held a strong posture, there was a slight nervous flicker of his eyes in her direction.

"It is better if I speak with him alone," she continued. "Go see to your warriors. Your rusting chain mail is stinking up my chamber, anyway." Both the visitors stood up to leave. Ash felt a pang of panic at the prospect of being left alone with the Seidwoman. Olaf mumbled something about being dismissed like a child, but the woman gave Ash a reassuring smile before turning around. They shut the door behind them and for a moment there was only the crackle of the fire.

"I am sure you have a question or two," Rani said, breaking the silence.

Ash fidgeted with his blanket. He had a lot of questions, but he didn't know where to start. He also didn't know if he could trust the old woman. Ash had been afraid of her his entire life, and now he found himself trapped in a small room with her. Torn between his desire to know what had happened and a fear of speaking to the Seidwoman, he summoned a touch of courage.

"Who was the woman?" Ash asked in a small voice.

"That was Jarl Astrid of Gjallarholm, in whose fortress you are now a guest." Her voice was calm and settling, putting him a bit more at ease. For a moment he wondered if she was casting a spell on him, and he put his thumb and forefinger together in a circle under the blanket in the sign to ward off evil, just in case. A bemused smile crept onto Rani's face and he stopped.

"You are right to be fearful of me; most people are. I have worked hard to establish my reputation. It keeps people from bothering me about love potions and sick goats, but I need you to put that aside and remember that I am your Jarl's Seidwoman. If Eric has trust in me, then so should you." She turned her head towards him and Ash could glimpse her empty eye sockets under her cowl. Her white dusted face and black lips hardened into a grimace.

"Besides," she hissed. "I can curse you to tell me everything I want to hear."

Ash couldn't help but flinch and he stared wide eyed at the Seidwoman.

"R-really?" he stuttered, again filled with fear.

"No, not really," she said, her face still stern.

He stared at Rani, mouth opening and closing without saying a word in utter confusion. Then the Seidwoman burst out laughing.

"I rarely miss my eyes, but I wish I had them now," she cackled. "I bet you look like a fish on dry land."

Feeling foolish, Ash added a polite, yet nervous, laughter to hers.

"Really, boy. I am on your side, and so are the Jarls. It is very important that you answer my questions truthfully, understood?"

The old woman's attempt at humour had eased him a bit, crude as it was. Besides, he trusted Jarl Eric and decided to extend that to include his Seidwoman.

"I will."

"Good. Do you remember what brought you here?" she asked. Ash swallowed.

"I was attacked in the forest." He shivered as the incident flashed back in his mind. "These monsters were chasing me. They... They were about to kill me, when a big man, who looked like a bear, fought them off." He raised his arm up to touch his shoulder, surprised to find no wound, and only a pink scar.

"You were very lucky. We were searching for you for days, before we came across your belongings in the middle of the road. One of the hirdsmen recognised the bow you were gifted by the Jarl once, and the scouts saw fresh tracks leading into the forest. We heard their moaning in the distance, and Olaf sent his warriors in after you. The man who saved you was Torsten Grimmson, a Jomsviking Berserker." Ash sat as if stunned for a while, processing what she had said. Then he looked up at Rani.

"How did the hirdsman know that it was my bow?"

"Well, because it was his bow first, before the Jarl got drunk, and gave it away to you," Rani chuckled.

Ash stared at her in disbelief. "Really?" She nodded, still smiling. He sat in silence for another moment.

"Why were you looking for me?"

Rani's face became grave once again. "I think you better tell me what you have been up to since you left Hornsborg first. And leave nothing out, no matter how small it seems."

OVER THE NEXT hour, Ash laid out the days following his running away from Hornsborg; the fight with Roghald, the dead riders, his flight through the forest and how he stumbled upon Beli's cave. He told her in detail what had occurred there and about his agreement with the troll and how he had subsequently broken that agreement and travelled towards Gjallarholm. When he came to his ambush by the monsters in the forest, his stomach hurt as he relived the fear of that moment. Rani often interjected with questions, focussing on minor details and asking for absolute clarity on some things.

Ash spoke and felt a weight lift from his shoulders as he could tell someone about what he'd been through. But when attempting to convey the vision of his mother before he was rescued by the Jomsvikings, a lump settled in his throat, making his voice hoarse. They sat in silence for a long while after he had finished talking. When Rani spoke, it was in a soft voice, full of sorrow, and it seemed that her years weighed heavier upon her.

"I knew your mother." she started. "She was my sister's daughter and her name was Gunnr. We lived in a village in the west, beyond the Great Forest. She was beautiful, full of life, and always had a smile for anyone she spoke to." Ash gasped and sat up straight, but Rani didn't notice, lost in the mists of time as she continued. "She was also a fierce fighter, a shieldmaiden and an Ulfhed."

Ash's mouth fell open. "She... She was a Jomsviking?"

A sad smile touched Rani's black lips. "She was far too good for that lot. They have their uses, but they are a bunch of drunken brawlers." Ash felt confused. All Ulfhednar joined the Jomsvikings, didn't they?

"She shared the same ability and powers as all Ulfhednar, her soul part wolf and all the gifts that come with that, but not all of Odin's warriors are equal. Sometimes an Ulfhed is born that is faster, stronger and smarter than the others. These are the true Ulfhednar; the Wolves of Odin." Wide-eyed, Ash didn't even dare to breathe, hanging on every word she said.

"The Wolves follow only the bidding of the Allfather himself. She would be sent all over Midgard as he saw fit, acting as his hands where he would not, or could not, go. She even travelled across the world tree Yggdrasil, to Svartalfheim, the lands of the dark elves and dwarves, and Vanaheim, home of the Vanir, the second tribe of gods..." She hesitated for a moment, as if she wasn't sure she should continue.

"… but mostly she would be sent to Jotunheim, home of the Jotnar. This is also where she met your father." If Rani had eyes, she would have been able to see the shock and confusion on Ash's face. How could she have met her father in the land of the trolls and giants?

"Was… Was he also a Wolf of Odin? Is that why they met there?" Ash ventured hopefully.

"She told me your father was very handsome." The old woman smoothed out her robes in her lap. "He was quick of wit and had a laugh like the ringing of bells. She said he was kind and considerate and when she was with him, she felt nothing but joy. You see, most men looked at her as something to fear or control, but your father saw her for the person she really was, despite her abilities and loved her truly. And she loved him…"

She took a deep breath before continuing. "…even though he was a troll."

Ash's mouth fell open and his eyes locked on Ranis' face, hoping to see any sign of this being a joke, but none showed itself.

"I'm a troll?" he whimpered in a high-pitched voice.

"Half a troll."

Ash sat in disbelief for a few minutes before feeling his face and scrutinizing his hands. "But I look normal." he started. "Maybe there has been some mistake?"

Rani laughed. "Not all trolls are as big as houses with mushrooms growing out of their ears. Some are, but not all. Your father was handsome and by your mother's description, he looked like most men, if a bit taller than average." She paused and lifted a clay cup to Ash. "Be a good lad and pour me a cup of tea. All this talking is hard on an old throat."

Ash pulled his covers off and got up, unsteady at first, but soon found his balance. He took the cup proffered by Rani and walked up to a pot sitting by the fire. An aroma of forest herbs and berries enticed his nostrils, making his stomach rumble, as he filled Rani's cup. When had he last eaten? Days ago, it felt like.

Rani must have sensed his hunger, because when he handed her the cup she smiled and said, "There is some food on the table. I had it brought for you while you were still asleep. I have never met a lad your age that wasn't in a constant state of hunger."

Ash walked up to the table where he found a plate covered with a linen cloth. Removing the cloth revealed a block of cheese, a hunk of roasted venison, and a thick piece of bread. Ash was salivating at the sight. Next to it was a large jug with fresh milk. They sat in silence as he ate and Rani drank her tea. Ash was sure she had offered him the food as a diversion for her to gather her thoughts and to stem the dozens of questions that had sprung into his mind. He finished his food, mopping up the last of the venison juice with the bread. His hunger now satiated, he returned to the bed and sat down in front of Rani.

Something had been in the back of his mind, but he had been distracted by what the Seidwoman had said about his mother, but now it came to the forefront of his attention.

"You are my aunt?"

Rani smiled.

"I am. I have changed more of your soiled diapers than I care to remember."

Ash sat in silence as conflicting emotions chased around his mind. He had grown up thinking himself alone in the world, and there had been family within arm's reach the whole time. He felt betrayed and mournful.

"Why didn't you tell me?" he whispered around the thick lump that had formed in his throat.

Rani's face turned into one of sorrow and in a brief moment, she looked not like the frightening Seidwoman, but an old woman, stooped with the burdens of a lifetime.

"You will soon understand, when I tell you what happened to your mother."

Rani spoke in a soft voice, as if drawing on old, painful memories.

"Your mother made several journeys to Jotunheim over the years, often away for a month, maybe two, but her last journey was different. She didn't come back like she used to. The months passed, turning into a year, then two. The bones told me very little. Aside from knowing she was still alive; the bones did not reveal in what circumstances. My sister had died a few years previous, so your mother was my only living relative. I was consumed by worry and grief." She looked old and frail as she spoke.

"It was in the middle of a cold, long winter when I heard a knock on my door, so weak I almost missed it. When I opened the door, I saw her lying on my doorstep; I still had my eyes then. I carried her in and laid her in front of the fire. Taking off her cold, wet clothes, I saw her body in a state. She was burned in many places and had several deep cuts on her arms, back and chest. I also saw that she was with child, only a month or so from giving birth. I cared for her and dressed her wounds, but I didn't expect her to live through the night." The old woman took a sip of her now cold tea.

"But Gunnr was always strong and Ulfhednar are hardier than most, so she lived, although it must have been very close. When your mother regained her strength, she told me what had happened." Rani scowled as she went on. "She had met your father, Jordr, in Jotunheim and they had fallen in love. They had lived in his mountain and had been very happy, but unfortunately, only for a short time. Jordr's mother, Gundaganr, was an old troll witch and shaman who was not happy with their union. She hated Gunnr and raged at her son, of which she had hundreds, by the way, for being in love with an Ulfhed. She cursed and raved, but Jordr would not send your mother away, so strong was his love for her. When your mother fell pregnant, they knew they couldn't stay in Jotunheim, for fear of what Gundaganr could do to their child, to you." At these words, she turned her head towards Ash.

"They kept it a secret while they planned their move to Midgard. But Gundaganr had powerful magic, and no such secret could be kept from her. She saw this as an opportunity to rid herself of your mother once and for all. She took what she knew to a *jotunn* chieftain, one of the ruling elites of the Jotnar, and he too was enraged at what he heard. Not only was there the shame of a troll in union with a human, and an Ulfhed at that, but Jordr was also a renowned Stonesmith, and could not be lost to Midgard. The jotunn, Burrugandr, was wiser than most trolls, and I think he knew that a child of their union could be very special. A child like that would have the potential to be powerful. A half-troll and half-Ulfhed had never been seen before, but if the child inherited powers from both sides, it could be a force unlike any other in the nine worlds."

Rani paused and let her words sink in. Ash's palms had started sweating, and he wiped them on his blanket. He knew she was talking about him, and a fear gripped him at his very core. He wished he could just go back to the stable and look after his horses, but instead he felt himself propelled into something he couldn't even hope to control.

Rani cleared her throat and continued.

"Burrugandr would have known that growing up in Midgard, the child would come to side with the Aesir, the gods of human-kind, and turn against the troll and giant kind. But if Burrugandr could take this child and raise it in his own mountain and secure its loyalties, he would be powerful enough to challenge even the Troll King of Jotunheim."

"So, the jotunn ordered his trolls and giants to storm Jordr's mountain, to Gundaganr's great delight."

Ash couldn't believe what he was hearing. Trolls and giants and other worlds, and he was not only a part, but the cause of such a wild exploit. However, as Rani spoke, he knew in his heart that it was true. It felt like long-lost pieces of a whole fell into place, as the old woman wove her tale.

"Your parents made a formidable force together. They slayed trolls and giants as they came for them, your father swinging his smithing hammer in crushing blows and your mother's spear, fast as lightning, always finding its mark. But there were just too many of them, and they were eventually overcome. Your father fell to the blows of a raging *thursr*, a powerful battle troll, and the last your mother saw of him was his lifeless body being cast into the depths of the mountain."

Ash felt tears running down his cheek, mourning a father he had never known, but had longed for in his heart on so many lonely nights.

"Your mother's heart broke at the sight of his death, and unable and unwilling to live anymore, she threw herself without caution at the enemy, seeking a fast death. But Burrungandr had other plans. He had ordered her capture, and for her to be brought to his mountain. You see, he wanted the child, you, to be raised amongst his kind, to be tied to Jotunheim. You were to be another weapon in his arsenal.

"Your mother was sealed in a cave with food and light, in the heart of his mountain, to await the arrival of you. No doubt, she would be discarded once she had given birth." She paused for a minute, allowing Ash to gather himself a little, but he was sitting on the edge of his bed, pleading for her to continue.

"She was trapped there for several months. As her belly grew, so did her love for you, and she found a reason to live again, but try as she might, she could not find a way out of the cave. When she had all but abandoned the faintest of hopes of an escape, a hole appeared in the wall. It was as if the stone had turned soft and parted to make an opening. At first, her heart filled with joy, as this was the work of a Stonesmith, and she thought Jordr had somehow survived and had returned for her. However, she was soon disappointed when a small, stocky man with a short white beard stepped through the opening and upon seeing her, waved her over before disappearing back through the hole.

"She followed through what was a long tunnel, but there was no sign of the man. She ran through the dark and the tunnel opened up to a cold, windy landscape at the bottom of the mountain. The only trace of anyone having been there was a softly glowing rune-stone at her feet. It was a portal stone. Your mother was well familiar with them, having used them to travel between the worlds that lay on the branches and roots of the world tree. She snatched it up and set off. She needed to find a 'soft spot' where one root that wrapped around Jotunheim was close enough that she could open a portal back to Midgard.

"But Burrungandr was no fool. He had expected her to attempt an escape and had his forces at the ready. As soon as she had set foot on the windblown ground outside his mountain, his magical wards told him, and he set his trolls on her. They threw spears and magic at her, and they attacked with clubs and stones. Gunnr fought them as they came, taking their weapons and turning them against the trolls. She was wounded and tired, but her love for you kept her going, moving along the valleys, fighting them off with all her strength. She was about to abandon her hope when the rune-stone began humming, sensing the world tree beneath her feet.

"She cast the stone on the ground and fell into the portal that opened, landing in deep snow, back on Midgard. It was good luck that she recognised where she was and only had to walk a short way to my door, where she collapsed."

Ash had so many emotions about what he was being told, that his head was spinning.

"Why don't you pour me another cup of tea and one for yourself, lad?"

Grateful for the reprieve, Ash stood up and busied himself with the pot and cups. Handing Rani a cup and clutching his own, he sat down on the bed again, as the old woman spoke.

"We decided it was best to move away. Too many people knew who your mother was and plenty of other Jotnar live in Midgard; well hidden, but they are here, nonetheless. Someone like Burrungandr would not give up easily, and while you were young, you could still be corrupted. So, we moved northeast, to the outskirts of a village on the edges of Jarl Erik's domain. You were born and we settled into a quiet life. Your mother had hung up her spear and shield, finding happiness in the simple life. She never named you, a last act of love to your father, as trolls do not name their young until they come of age. She called you 'little heart' or 'tuft' because of your unruly hair. We believed we were safe in our new home; but trolls have a way of finding things out. Their magic is powerful, and their shamans can scry across the worlds. While we were preparing to celebrate your second birthday, they came for you. As a Seidwoman, I would often spend long periods in the forest, unravelling its mysteries and talking to the spirits, and so I was away the night the trolls came for you. I was asleep by a creek when a raven landed on my chest and cawed three times before flying away. I knew something terrible had happened. I raced back to the village, only to find the house in smouldering ashes."

Her voice was thick with sorrow as she went on. "Your mother's body lay where the kitchen had been, in a pool of her own blood, deep cuts in her throat. I knew that no human alive could have overpowered her, and that Burrugandr had finally found us."

Ash was sobbing into his sleeve. There was just so much to take in and he felt a heart-wrenching pain, knowing that his mother had died defending him. As if she could read his mind, Rani spoke in a soft voice, "She loved you very much. You were the light of her world, and she would have died for you a thousand times." She reached out and placed an old hand on his knee.

Ash raised his head and wiped his nose. "I saw her. In the forest when those, those… things came after me."

"Well, of course. She was a shieldmaiden and a Wolf of Odin. Once she died, she went on to serve the gods as a Valkyrie, collecting the fallen on the battlefield for Odin's Valhalla. You were dying and she would let no one else collect your soul, I am sure of it." She smiled a sad smile. "You will see your mother again, when your time comes. Be mindful of your gods, fight bravely, and one day she will carry your soul to Odin's hall."

Then she cackled and raised a bony finger. "But don't rush to the appointment!" He wiped his tears on his sleeve and he took some comfort in the fact that he would see her again, although it would be a very long time. Hopefully.

The Seidwoman's voice took a serious tone once more as she continued, "As I stood there over your mother's body, I cast my eyes around looking for you, but you were nowhere to be seen. My heart broke for the second time that day, and I feared that you had been carried off to Jotunheim. I was startled as two large ravens, black as night, swept in from the darkness and landed in a nearby tree. In the glow of the embers an old man strode into what was left of the house, with two immense wolves by his side. He wore a large-brimmed hat, was dressed in aged, grey clothing and had a long grey beard reaching down to his waist. I wanted to run, but his one eye held me stronger than any chain could. His other eye was missing; the socket seemed to contain the entire night's sky, stars glittering as if far, far away. He walked up to me and then I knew him. I had seen him in the leaves of trees, moving in the wind on a summer's day and in the flowing streams in the forest. I had seen him in the falling snow, in the cold of winter and in the life and death of all things.

"Odin, the Allfather, the Wanderer, stood before me, and in his arms, covered in soot, you slept peacefully. The father of the gods held you out to me, but I didn't take you. Instead, I begged him to hide you, to hide who you were so the Jotnar wouldn't find you. And hide you he did, in plain sight. He bared your chest and with a piece of coal from the fire, he drew a rune on you. As soon as it was finished, the rune disappeared, and with it, it took the gifts from your mother and your father. It buried the part of your soul that is wolf and the troll magic in your blood, so the trolls couldn't use their magic to find you again."

She drained the last of her tea.

"I heard horses and voices approach behind me and turned around to see armed men with Jarl Erik in the point, ride up to the house. Apparently, they had seen the light of the fire from their camp further away and came to investigate. When I turned back, the old man and his wolves were gone. I knew Jarl Erik to be a good, kind man, and in private I explained everything to him. He agreed to hide you in a lowly position in Hornsborg until you came of age and I could explain everything to you. I had hoped to have a few years yet, but alas, that was not to be. I became the Jarl's Seidwoman so I could be close to you, but I was afraid of being too close, as the Jotnar likely knew of me. You were hidden from their eyes, unless they looked closely. Part of the reason I gave my eyes for the Second Sight, was so I could keep an eye on you from afar while you were safely hidden away."

A pang of guilt hit Ash when he heard that she had sacrificed her eyes, to keep him safe.

"We waited for you to take the Viking trials. There was no doubt that you would pass and once you had trained as a warrior with Erik, we were to send you to the Jomsvikings to train as an Ulfhed and bring your powers out from within. But blood will out, as they say." she sighed. "It sounds like the gifts are strong in you, Ash of the Ulfhednar and Jotnar, and when you were in trouble, they both resurfaced, even with Odin's spell on you. The Ulfhed and the troll magic raged within you, fighting to control one body. It could have killed you, you know, and nearly did, by the sound of things. The rune that bound you worked like a bottleneck, creating immense pressure as the powers within you rushed to get out. The fire could have burned you to death from within. While you were sleeping, I removed the binding the Allfather placed on you, so now you must learn how to control your abilities a lot sooner than expected."

"But how will I do that? I know nothing of these things!" Ash blurted out, distraught.

"Jarl Olaf has arranged for your training to begin tomorrow." she replied with a mirthless smile.

CHAPTER 14

ROGHALD'S HEAD WAS POUNDING. THERE WAS AN UN-comfortable sensation of movement, making him nauseous and sending jolts of pain through his body. He tried to open his eyes, but it was as if they were glued shut. A terrible smell filled his nostrils, making the nausea so much worse. The memories came flooding back to him, all at once. They had been attacked by the draugr at the river. He forced his eyelids open and a small sliver of light pierced his left eye. A wave of nausea hit him, and he let his stomach settle before attempting to open his eyes again.

His next attempt was more successful, letting in a flood of day-light. Roghald's vision was a blur, but he blinked a few times and soon he could see the ground speeding past in front of him. His nose was caked in dried blood and his arms hung limp in front of him, slapping against dirty, torn linens. He was flopped over someone's shoulder, he realized. They were moving at great speed and Roghald was a large man, so it was someone very strong. The stench of the thing and the strength could only mean one thing; he was carried off by the draugr. No doubt they thought him dead and were carrying him off to a larder for eating later. His guts twisted in horror as he visualised being eaten alive by the monsters. He wished he had died during the attack, so he wouldn't have to endure what was coming. Another wave of nausea overcame Roghald, and as he pressed his eyes together to will it away, unconsciousness claimed him again.

Asʜ ᴡᴀs sɪᴛᴛɪɴɢ in the hall in Gjallarholm, eating a breakfast of porridge and honey cakes. The hall was full of the people who lived in the fortress, enjoying their morning meal. He was hurrying, however, because he didn't want to be late for his first training session. Jarl Olaf had come to see him again last night, instructing him to present himself at the training grounds first thing in the morning. He finished his meal in great haste and hurried off to follow the directions the Jarl had given him last night.

He took a few wrong turns, but before long he arrived at a wooden door which opened up to a smaller courtyard. There were several battered dummies made of wood and hay lined up along one wall, and plenty of wooden and metal weaponry stored in racks. As he opened the door, he interrupted a conversation.

"... don't understand why I have to babysit like this, Olaf!" a tall woman, her arms crossed, stood in a defiant stance in front of Jarl Olaf. She was young, not far beyond twenty summers, but held herself with great confidence. The sides of her head were shaven and her top hair lay in long and matted, auburn braids that were tied back with a leather thong. She had tattoos on the side of her head and arms, crude depictions of wolves and runes that identified her as an Ulfhednar shieldmaiden. The scars on her arms and hands showed that she had fought in the ranks for a while, despite her young age. They both turned towards him and fell silent as he entered.

"Ah, there's the lad! Right on time!" Olaf grinned, finding the situation humorous. The sturdy Jarl laid a heavy hand on Ash's shoulder, turning him towards the woman.

"This is Yrsa, lad. She has the great pleasure of being responsible for your training from here on." Ash looked at the woman, whose arms were still crossed, and whose eyes were appraising him from head to foot. She didn't seem impressed, a slight frown on her face. She wore a sleeveless, green cotton tunic and trousers, showing her athletic build, lean and muscular, the very image of a shieldmaiden.

"Erh, hello?" he squeaked, cringing at the lack of control of his voice. Yrsa snorted and turned her head to Olaf, and if looks could kill, there wouldn't have been much left of the Jarl. Olaf let out a hearty laugh, slapped Ash on the shoulder and walked out the door through which Ash had just entered.

"Have fun, you two!" he called as he shut the door behind him. They stood in silence while a frowning Yrsa looked him up and down, before appearing to come to a decision.

"Well, let's get on with it," she spat, before turning around and walking to the rack which held the wooden training weapons. Ash followed her, fearing he was in for a long morning. She grabbed a short stave from the rack and held it up for Ash to inspect.

"This is a spear, the preferred weapon for most Ulfhednar, because it suits our battle style of fighting as a pack."

"It hasn't got a pointy bit." Ash remarked, believing that was an essential criterion for a spear.

"You are not ready for 'pointy bits' just yet, little cub." she said, her voice like ice. She gripped the stave about halfway down the shaft in a one-handed grip. "The short spear is more versatile than people think. It is light enough that you can move swiftly and not be encumbered by it, like with a heavy sword. It can be used with one hand, or two when more force is needed, and is easily combined with a small shield or even a seax," she said, patting the traditional Norse, long-bladed knife that hung at her belt.

"This can be particularly useful in a melee, when the enemy has difficulty keeping an eye on both your hands." She made two quick jabs with the tip of the stave over Ash's left shoulder. As a reflex, he sidestepped right and felt a sharp prick in his ribs. Looking below his right arm he saw that Yrsa somehow had drawn her seax and poked his side with it, without him even noticing what she was doing. She gave him a cruel little smile. "You're dead, little cub."

She sheathed her blade and returned his attention to the stave. "So, the spear, when used with the speed and tactics of the Ulfhednar, makes it a formidable weapon. This will be our focus as far as weaponry goes, for now."

She threw the stave to Ash, who thankfully caught it, before helping herself to one of her own. She walked him over to one of the dummies along the wall and stood herself in front of it.

"Place your leading leg forward, in your case the left, and bend your knees slightly, to allow yourself to change direction and position as needed."

She showed him as she talked him through the position.

"Use your left arm to balance yourself and grab the spear just behind the middle in an overhand grip, like so, and when ready, lean forward and strike."

Holding the spear at her waist, she shot her arm forward and thrust the tip into the chest of the dummy with a solid 'thunk', before returning to her original stance. "Got it? Good. Now you do it. Over and over and over."

ASH'S BODY HURT in places he wasn't even aware he had, as he dragged himself up the stairs to the room he had been allocated. He had felt embarrassed, having a room to himself in the fortress, something the visiting hirdsmen didn't even get. However, Rani had insisted he remained close to her, and Ash didn't think even Jarl Astrid was prepared to go against the Seidwoman's wishes. But right now, he was glad to have a quiet place to curl up after the long day of training Yrsa had put him through.

She had kept a rapid pace through the day, making him thrust at the dummies in every way imaginable. Early on, various Jomsvikings had come past to watch for a short while, often heartily mocking Yrsa and her student. They shouted unnecessary encouragements and lamented Ash's fate for having such an ill-tempered teacher. This all stopped when Yrsa threw an axe at a Berserker, which only just missed his head as it lodged in the doorframe with a splintering of timber. The man yelped and withdrew, and neither he nor any other tormentors returned.

It didn't help Ash, though, that after every such visit, Yrsa's face would darken with anger and she would double the intensity of whatever exercise Ash was doing. She had finished the day by making him run three laps around the fortress, to "improve your poor condition." The whole time he was running, she sat on a wagon at the gate, drinking a horn of ale, commenting on his form every time he passed.

Ash got to his room, and tears welled in his eyes when he saw that some kind soul had left a bowl of stew, a loaf of bread and a pitcher of milk on a small table next to his bed. He had bypassed the hall and dinner downstairs, as he wasn't even sure that he would make it to his bed before falling asleep. After he wolfed down the meal and drank the whole pitcher of milk, Ash wriggled his sore limbs out of his clothes. He was asleep as soon as his head hit the pillow.

ASH'S WEEK PROCEEDED in a similar fashion, with the only addition of Yrsa beating him with a stick from the third day onwards. She called it 'sparring', but Ash saw it for what it was; a beating. She hounded him from sunrise to sunset, always watching and criticizing his every move. Nothing he ever did was good enough and he would often have to repeat, over and over, heavy and menial tasks for the sake of 'conditioning'.

He endured the endless drills, exercises and runs with a determination he didn't know he had. But on the afternoon of the sixth day, he lost his willpower along with his temper. Yrsa had had him moving heavy sandbags from one end of the courtyard to the other. When he had finished and sat panting on the pile, she looked at them critically before saying, "No. I think they would look better over there," showing toward a point twenty paces to the left. "Snap to it," she barked before she went and sat down in the shade.

Ash fumed and grumbled but did as she said and moved the bags again. When he was about halfway done, he felt a painful sting on the back of his thigh. He cried out and spun around to see Yrsa standing there, twirling a stave in her hand.

"Tsk, tsk, tsk. You have to keep your wits about you, if you want to be a Jomsviking." she sneered. Something burst in Ash's mind and his chest filled with hot, white rage. He lunged forward and snatched the stave from her hand, and roaring with anger, he turned around and threw it as hard as he could into the air. They both watched it spin end over end until it disappeared behind the wall of the training grounds. Breathing heavily, Ash turned back to the shield maiden, expecting a few good whacks from her, but she just stood there, her face a mask of stone.

"Congratulations, little cub. You have just advanced from 'completely useless' to 'useless but mouldable.'"

Ash caught his breath for a second before replying. "You're not upset?"

Yrsa snorted. "We are trying to raise a wolf here, not a sheep. You were making me sick with your blind obedience." She turned and walked away, heading towards the door to the fortress.

Before walking through it, she called to him, "Take tomorrow off. The next day we start in earnest!" Then she disappeared into the gloom of the fortress. Ash grabbed another stave and gave a wooden dummy a few whacks for good measure before he left the courtyard. He decided to spend the entire next day sleeping.

CHAPTER 15

ROGHALD HIT THE GROUND HARD. HE HAD BEEN AWAKE for a short while, as the draugr carried him along, but he hadn't dared to move. He risked opening his eye a sliver and saw they had stopped in a clearing. Several draugr were spread out before him, standing unmoving, in eery stillness. Turning his head slow, so as not to draw attention to himself, he got a good look of the area.

There were other people from the caravan lying on the ground at the feet of the draugr. He recognized a warrior and a shield-maiden from the caravan guards, and Asmund, the merchant. They were all injured, with dried blood on their faces and tunics, and Roghald could see that the shieldmaiden had a severely broken arm, which was bent at an unnatural angle.

The guards were more or less conscious, pain and fear written on their faces as their eyes darted between themselves and their captors. Asmund lay prone on the grass, his eyes closed. As if by a hidden signal, all the draugr moved at once and Roghald felt two pairs of powerful hands grabbing hold of his arms in crushing grips. He heard the shieldmaiden scream as her broken arm was grabbed and held taught. Roghald felt himself being pulled up on his knees and turned around. He tried to resist but failed. In their vice like grips, he was no more likely to pull loose than if he was clasped in irons.

Looking up, he saw that he was facing a granite rock face. It stretched up higher than he could raise his head to see in his uncomfortable position, but what caught his attention was the cavern in front of him. It was a natural opening in the stone, as tall as three men and just as wide. There was nothing remarkable about it, but it filled him with an inexplicable sense of dread, all the same.

"What is happening?! Where... Where am I?!" a shrill voice called out.

Roghald turned to see Asmund squirming and throwing himself around in panic, but to no avail in the firm grasp of the two draugr holding him. "No! Please! I..." Asmund fell quiet. He had turned white as a ghost, his mouth open and a look of incredulous fear on his face.

Roghald followed the merchant's gaze back towards the cavern. He could see a large creature standing in the opening. It was tall and lanky, reaching almost to the top of the cave. Roghald realized that he wouldn't even have reached the creature's waist. It had mottled skin, as grey as the granite that surrounded it, with too long, spindly arms and legs for its body. Its clothing was a patchwork of furs, skins and dirty woollen fabrics, and several grimy golden rings wrapped around its wrists and above its elbows. Around its waist hung a belt adorned with human skulls, and from its shoulders a necklace of various bones. What horrified Roghald the most was that the creature had two heads, side by side.

Two monstrous and ugly faces now looked down upon the captives with morbid grins. The left one had a bald head, with an immense nose, set under two beady and cruel eyes. The other had long matted hair that fell down the sides of its head in long clumps, framing a broad face with enormous eyes under thick eyebrows. It had a smaller nose than the first head, but had a massive mouth and jaw, displaying two large bottom tusks when it grinned. Although he had never seen one before, Roghald knew he was looking at a troll. Asmund, having been stunned for a moment, once again began shrieking and screaming in panic.

Both heads on the monstrosity swivelled to regard the merchant, and their grins grew even wider. Asmund screamed even louder at this unwanted attention.

In two giant strides, the troll reached the merchant and bent down before him. From its belt, it removed a large flask of some stiff leathery material and on pulling the cork, tendrils of black smoke spilled out and floated to the ground. It almost gently placed a giant hand behind the merchant's head. With an enormous thumb and forefinger on each of Asmund's cheeks, it pressed down so the merchant's mouth opened while bending his head backwards.

The troll brought the flask up to Asmund's lips and began pouring. A thick, dark liquid spilled out over the unfortunate man's face and into his mouth, and the dark tendrils of smoke seemed to find their way into his eyes, nose and ears. He was coughing and spluttering, too busy gasping for air to scream anymore. When he went limp, the giant removed the flask and took a step back, watching the little man, who now hung unconscious in the grips of the two draugr. A spasm shook his body and at a wave of the troll's hand, the draugr let him go and the merchant dropped to the ground. Another spasm had him arching his back and his heels drummed on the grass covered ground.

The most gut-wrenching, drawn out sound Roghald had ever heard escaped through Asmund's clenched teeth and the black liquid spurted through his nose. The jerkin he was wearing tore as his arms grew longer and shoulders grew wider. Thick, dark veins appeared on his face and arms, and his skin faded to a ghostly white. He roared when his mouth flew open and stretched and tore as his jaw widened. Then, with one final jerk, he fell still and lay in the grass. There was no breath left in Asmund's body. His eyelids opened and dead white eyes looked up on the blue summer sky. He stood up with slow movements and remained there, unmoving, oblivious to anything around him.

Roghald looked on in horror, realising that he had not only witnessed the birth of a draugr, but that his own turn was coming. This was how his days would end; as a senseless monster, doing the bidding of trolls. His life and soul would be lost, his planned revenge too. Anger pushed away his fear as he thought of Ash and how he had forever escaped him. He would never know Roghald's wrath and he would live safe and happy in a southern town somewhere, while Roghald would serve an eternity as a ghoul, forever deprived of his rightful vengeance. The anger at the injustice filled his chest, and he prepared to curse Ash with his dying breath.

The troll, both heads beaming, turned and walked towards the shieldmaiden. Tears of pain and fear ran down her cheeks as she sobbed and shook her head, when the bald, rightmost head swivelled around and sniffed the air with its massive nose.

"Wait!" it hissed in a hoarse, deep voice. It stopped, then sniffed again a few more times. "Can you not smell it, brother? Such sweet, sweet hate." It turned around and lumbered over to Roghald. Bending down, the large nosed head pushed into his face and sniffed deep. The troll smelled of earth and leaves, not at all the foul stench Roghald had expected.

"Yes, yes…" it said between sniffs, before the head opened its mouth and extracted a large, black tongue which licked him from his neck to his forehead, leaving a slimy film behind. "Such delicious, tasty, hate," it moaned with yearning as its eyes rolled back in its head. Another nose assaulted him, sniffing and snorting against his cheek.

"Yes, but it also stinks of Asgard and the one-eyed's pets." the second head rumbled. Roghald was picked up by his shoulders, lifted like a child into the air and held at arm's length in front of the two heads.

The first head scrutinized him.

"But it's not him, its someone he's been near…" the large nosed one said with a thoughtful look, before pulling him close and smelling him again. "And he smells of troll, but not quite… hmm."

It adjusted its grip on Roghald, pulling him close to its chest with one arm. It wrapped its other hand around his head, covering it.

At first nothing happened, but soon Roghald felt warmth radiating from the large hand and a strange tickle inside his head. The massive hand obscured his vision, but then he saw a burst of light, accompanied by images flashing before his eyes. He realized that he was reliving his life, but in reverse, as if time was counting backwards, but at great speed. He saw the attack by the river, followed by him travelling with the caravan, walking through Gjallarholm marketplace and beyond. When his memory had arrived at the banishment from Hornsborg, and into Erik's hall, the vision slowed. As it went further back to his confrontation with Ash, it ground to a halt, only to start again, but now moving his memory forward in time.

Reliving himself getting bested by Ash caused the hate for the lout to flare up anew and his stomach burned with it. He heard a barking laugh from the troll and the hand was removed from his head; the vision disappearing with it.

"The halfbreed. It has been with the halfbreed!"

The second head spun to face its brother. "Are you sure? If you are wrong, our heads will be on a stake."

The first head, having never taken its eyes of Roghald, smiled even wider as it nodded.

"And it hates him. All its delicious hate is for the half-breed. We have found a suitable vessel. Burrugandr will be pleased." Both heads burst out in laughter. They handed him back to the draugr, who on some silent command began dragging him towards the cave opening. The giant was still laughing as it picked up the flask where it had dropped it and then continued towards the restrained shieldmaiden. The last thing Roghald saw as they pulled him into the darkness of the cave, was the giant grabbing the back of the shieldmaiden's head and lifting the flask up to her terrified face.

CHAPTER 16

ASH SAT DOWN ON A BENCH NEXT TO YRSA IN THE training courtyard. The first light of the day spilled over the walls as she greeted him with a nod. Her attitude towards him had improved since last week, although she made it clear she would rather be employed elsewhere.

"So," she started. "What makes us Ulfhednar different is that we have a power called Shifting, which allows us to move with a speed and clarity of mind that would be impossible for other people. This was a gift bestowed upon a select few by Odin himself at the dawn of Midgard. As you know, the Father of the gods has two wolf companions, Freki and Geri. It is said that when Odin had created humankind, he took a part of the wolves' spirits and infused them into the souls of warriors of his choosing; creating the first Ulfhednar. This gift is most often hereditary, usually inherited from a parent with the same gift, although once in a while it shows up in a person outside the bloodline. This, I have been informed, is not the case with you."

She turned to Ash and looked him in the eyes, "Olaf has told me you are the son of Gunnr Ulfsdaughter, the last Wolf of Odin." She seemed to look for a reaction in him, but Ash kept his face neutral, only nodding. "Your mother was a legendary shieldmaiden. I never met her, as I was too young, but Olaf did once, and he recounts the tales of her feats with awe."

Ash wondered if this had anything to do with her change in attitude towards him. He felt somewhat awkward with her scrutiny and blushed a little. Yrsa smiled at his embarrassment, but continued, turning her head to look out over the courtyard. "It is the same for the Berserkers, but their souls are part bear. Their gift comes from Thor, the Thundergod, and is manifest in the rage and strength that fills them when in battle, just like Thor. They, because of their particular gifts, prefer to fight as solitary units on the battlefield, whilst we will always fight as a pack if we can."

She stood up and waved for him to follow. She went to a rack, selected a stave and walked up to one of the dummies along the wall. "Observe." Ash took a step back, but didn't take his eyes off her. She did a series of thrusts and jabs on the dummy, the blows ringing out a fast tattoo against the wood. Ash was impressed. He pitied anyone that would have to face her in battle. She moved with a relentless speed and grace.

"And now, the same movements, but while I am Shifted." She seemed to ready herself for a second, and then her body became a blur. A quick rattle rang out, and she stood still once again. Ash looked at the dummy, some dust settling around it, the wood chipped and scuffed much more than before. He must have had an incredulous look on his face, because Yrsa laughed.

"With the great speed comes some extra force, making the blows harder than they otherwise would be, although we couldn't even begin to compare ourselves with the strength of the Berserkers." She walked over to the rack and returned the stave. "I have seen Torsten Grimsson, the giant of a man who swatted those draugr off your back in the forest, demolish a small house with only three blows of that enormous axe he drags around."

Ash remembered the man who had saved him very well. He had kept an eye out for him around Gjallarholm, wanting to thank him, but hadn't seen him since the incident.

"You need to learn how to channel your ability to Shift, so you can control when it starts and stops. If you stay Shifted for too long, you will burn out and collapse. It wouldn't serve you well to fall unconscious in the middle of a fight because you stretched yourself too far." She pointed for Ash to sit down on the bench again. She sat down next to him and picked up a small stone from the ground in front of her.

"Close your eyes and relax. It is easier the first few times if you have no distractions." He closed his eyes and took a deep, calming breath.

"Now, focus on a point deep in your chest. Feel around until you can sense a dense cluster, that isn't quite a part of you."

Ash concentrated as hard as he could, all his focus on his chest. At first, he couldn't feel anything, but as he imagined floating around inside of himself, there was a part that seemed different. It was like a knot on an otherwise smooth rope. He focussed on it and drifted closer.

"Can you feel it?" Yrsa asked. Ash nodded, too afraid to speak in case he lost it. "Now imagine yourself pouring into it and allow your awareness to permeate it."

He imagined himself drifting into the lump, filling it like water soaking into fabric. "Are you there?" She whispered and once again Ash nodded.

"Then tear it open." Ash hesitated a moment, then concentrated and tore it asunder like a loaf of bread. Warmth burst from the strange lump and the tingling sensation he had experienced a few times before filled his entire body. He opened his eyes to a smiling Yrsa, who flung the stone from her hand. Ash watched it sail a dozen steps away across the courtyard, like it was floating through water. Yrsa stood up, her movements unnatural and slow as she took a few steps, before she sped up to normal.

"Now we are at the same speed." she said, her voice deep and metallic. "Sound is different like this, and you will have difficulty understanding someone who isn't Shifted like you."

He nodded, too amazed to reply.

"Stand up and walk around."

Ash stood up and took a few steps, but the tingling feeling dissipated from his body as soon as he stood up and the sharp focus disappeared from the world. He felt back to normal and felt a bit foolish.

"I lost it," he said.

Yrsa, who must have stopped shifting too, only smiled.

"You need to reserve a little concentration for keeping the cluster open, or it will shut itself again and you will stop shifting. Try it again."

Ash closed his eyes and concentrated on the mass in his chest again. Now that he knew where it was and how to let his awareness fill it, he shifted faster and revelled in the sensation of the tingling spreading through his body. He opened his eyes and looked around, making sure a little of his awareness remained with the cluster, holding it open.

Yrsa, who must have started shifting again, spoke in that strange, metallic voice, "That's better. Now, jump as far as you can."

Ash took a few steps forwards. It felt almost like normal, besides the drawn out crunches he could hear as his feet left and met the ground and a slight resistance in the surrounding air when he moved. He took a few quick steps and jumped as far as he could. He leaped almost twice the distance he otherwise would and landed with a scattering of gravel.

"You will get better at it the more you practice." Yrsa informed him in her strange voice. "Now stop Shifting and sit back down."

Ash let his mind leave the cluster in his chest and he felt it pull back together as the tingling feeling left his body.

When they sat back down on the bench, Ash was grinning from ear to ear.

"Don't get cocky," she scolded him. "You still have a long way to go, little cub." He tried to wipe the smile from his face but failed.

"Not bad for a start." Yrsa smiled and elbowed him in the ribs.

Ash was tired and drained from the experience and thought a lie down would be nice, but Yrsa had other plans.

"Now, you need to take a refreshing run around the fortress. Four laps will do it, I think. Then we start weapon drills. We will alternate between Shifted and non-Shifted sparring for the rest of the afternoon. We need to increase your tolerance to Shifting and, as always, we need to improve your conditioning." She said all this far too cheerfully for Ash's liking, and he couldn't hide the disappointment from his face, which seemed to make her smile even wider.

CHAPTER 17

ROGHALD'S ENTIRE BODY WAS THROBBING. HE WAS BE-
yond pain now, his body and mind felt numb. He couldn't tell
how long the strange singing had been going on, but it might as
well have been an eternity. The two-headed troll sat cross legged
on the ground in front of him, rocking backwards and forward as
it sang a deep, rhythmic, wordless song in an eerie harmony with
itself. It was beating a slow rhythm on a shallow, broad drum in
its lap with what seemed to be a human thigh bone. Red staves
and runes painted on its surface appeared to move and dance with
every beat, and the painful throbbing in Roghald's body matched
the beat.

Gurmr and Grundr, he thought in a detached way. He had
learned their names from listening to them talking. Had had been
dragged into the cave by the draugr and held down, while the giant
took care of his companions outside. Their screams and howls had
echoed into the cave as they were transformed. Roghald couldn't
help wondering what gruesome fate awaited him inside the cave.
They had taken him through pitch darkness on a twisting path.

Rounding a corner, a dim cavern, large enough to fit the entire fortress of Hornsborg, opened up before him. It was lit by a

pale glow, appearing to originate in large patches of mushrooms growing on the walls and ceiling of the cave. His eyes were drawn to the very centre where he saw an earthen mound from which grew the strangest tree Roghald had ever seen. It had the shape of an old oak, its thick, black trunk glistening in the soft glow from the walls. The branches were twisted, reaching in all directions, and although it bore only a small amount of purple-tinted leaves, the branches were laden with bulbous, black fruit, weighing them down. It was a sickening sight; a perversion of nature and Roghald was filled a sense of repulsion looking at it.

The draugr had held him to the ground, their dead eyes never leaving him until Gurmr and Grundr stepped into the cave. As soon as the giant laid its enormous hands on him, the draugr had let him go and shuffled out of the cave. He was once again effortlessly lifted by the troll and placed under one of its arms, as it set off across the cavern floor. They stopped along the wall, in front of a pile of clothes, weapons, armour and various personal items. No doubt, Roghald thought, things that had been stripped from their previous victims when they were turned to draugr.

Gurmr and Grundr bent down and picked up two seaxes from the pile before turning around and walking towards the centre of the cave and the strange tree. As the troll drew close, Roghald could see that the bark of the tree was smooth and covered in black scales, like that of a snake or a lizard. The glistening fruits hanging in great clusters from the branches were the size of apples. A thick, dark sap coated them and would occasionally drip, causing small tendrils of smoke to erupt where a drop splashed on the earthen mound with a hiss.

The troll pulled Roghald out from under his arm and pushed his back against the tree. Roghald could swear he felt it move behind him as he was held against it. The grip around his chest was released and the giant instead grabbed his left arm with one hand, holding it in a crushing grasp. With sinister grins on both of its faces, it used its other hand to push one of the seaxes through Roghald's forearm and into the tree.

His screams seemed to only entertain the troll who chuckled as it let go of his arm only to grab his other and repeat with the other long knife.

Gurmr and Grundr stood back and looked down on Roghald where he was nailed to the tree, his arms spread wide. The troll turned around and disappeared from Roghald's view for a while, only to return with the drum. It sat down and began its deep, horrible song. That had been days ago, and not once had the troll stopped singing. At times, it would stop drumming, only to lean towards Roghald and cut him with a clawed finger. He now had cuts on his arms, legs, torso and face. Every time the troll cut him and a trickle of blood reached the trunk of the tree, a small tendril of smoke would rise from the bark and find its way along the trickle and seep into the wound.

Roghald was waiting for death or unconsciousness, hoping for it, but it never came, although he felt his body trying to shut down from weariness and blood loss. He had been kept awake for days, every moment filled with agony. When the troll struck the drum, Roghald's body would throb with the beat, his mind and body jolted awake and kept from the blissful darkness just outside of his reach. Just beyond his hearing, he thought he could hear a mad laughter in the distance, but every time he tried to focus on it, it slipped away.

As he watched, thick, grey tendrils of vapour extended from the tree, rising like snakes around him.

The troll's singing and drumming intensified, changing in pitch for the first time since it had begun. The tendrils turned down towards his body, and when they touched him, they burned like fire. He screamed, but in doing so, one ringlet found its way into his mouth, prying his jaws open and flowing down his throat. It was like swallowing fire. In seconds, all the tendrils had made their way in between his teeth and his body was burning from the inside.

A pressure filled his head as if something was entering his mind, threatening to burst his skull.

Reality exploded in a thousand stars that fell like rain all around him. When the stars receded, a world under a dark sun appeared. It was a world of stone and mountains with sparse purple vegetation. An icy wind swept across the land, making eerie howling sounds as it found cracks and crevices in the rock.

Before him, on a throne of intricately carved stone, sat an enormous giant, taller than ten men. As grey as the stone surrounding it, its skin stretched over a massive, fat body, horribly scarred by intricate runes and symbols, long ago carved into its flesh. A mane of pale hair flowed down its shoulders over arms laden with thick, golden armbands. The facial features were exaggerated compared to a human's, a large protruding nose, with a broad mouth and jaw. But Roghald could not have described it as ugly; It had a strange beauty to it, almost divine. As the giant turned an ancient, intelligent gaze on Roghald, he felt like the thing could see into his soul. He was in awe of it. This was true power, he realized, and the means for his revenge. With a single thought, the giant made him a promise of fire and blood and vengeance. It would give him his revenge in exchange for his servitude, for his loyalty and his soul. He was being offered the opportunity to leave behind the humankind that had trodden on him forever and transcend the boundaries of his existence. He laid himself flat on the cold ground, prostrating himself in servitude, and gave himself to his new master. Deep inside him he felt a word spoken, and with it every bone in his body trembled in ecstasy.

"BURRUGANDR!" Fire erupted all around Roghald.

THE VISION FADED and after a moment of confusion, Roghald opened his eyes to see the two-headed troll grinning down at him. The seaxes had been pulled out of his arms and he was free again. He rubbed his arms where the long knives had been pushed through, but only thin scars remained. As he surveyed the rest of his body, Roghald found that every cut made during the ritual had healed, leaving only the faintest of marks. He looked up on his captor and now knew them for what they were: brothers.

"Welcome, thursr Roghald," the large nosed face said. "You are blessed to now share your body with a battle troll from Jotunheim."

Roghald knew that something had changed within him. There was a new presence in the back of his head, and he felt stronger than he ever had before. He thought he could hear an echo of a guttural laugh off in the distance.

"A half-breed to catch a half-breed," the other head laughed, and Roghald couldn't help but smile. He saw his path with renewed clarity. He would capture or kill Ash and serve his master by conquering the world of man, in the name of Jotunheim.

CHAPTER 18

ASH RAN ALONG A STONE CORRIDOR INSIDE THE GJAL-larholm fortress. He had nodded off while resting on his bed, exhausted as he was from training, and now he was late. He'd been in the fortress for several weeks, but he had either been too busy training or too exhausted to do any real exploring of the place. As a result, he didn't know how to get to Jarl Astrid's private rooms and had to stop and ask for directions from a pair of red cloaked guards along the way.

In the end, when he had found where he needed to be, he took a moment to catch his breath before reaching up to knock on the thick wooden door. He heard a muffled "Enter!" and pushed the heavy door open.

"Ah, Ash. How good of you to join us." A smiling Jarl Astrid said in good humour. A room full of people had their heads turned towards him, but Ash only recognised a few - Jarl Olaf, sprawling on a bench with a horn of mead in his hand, Yrsa, shooting an angry look his way, letting Ash know that the subject of tardiness would be discussed later and Rani, sitting off to the side as was her habit. There were also several men and women he had not met before. Most of them were wearing blue capes, signifying they were all members of Astrid's hird and personal guards.

The room was large, sparsely decorated and dominated by a sizeable table in the centre, covered in maps and small coloured markers. Jarl Astrid's war room, it seemed to Ash. He had no idea why he had been called to attend.

"My apologies." Ash stammered. He glanced at Yrsa again, but her face had not softened. He knew he would pay for being late with pain, blood and sweat tomorrow.

"Well, now that we are all here, let's get started," Jarl Astrid said, clapping her hands together. "Torsten, how are things on the roads?"

Ash recognized the man who had saved him in the forest, sitting on a chair close to Jarl Olaf. He was a large man with long hair and beard, braided for battle and held together by an assortment of silver rings. He had a network of scars criss-crossing his face and hands and a large blue tattoo covering most of his forehead. Ash had heard of the Berserker runic tattoos that were said to make the bearers invincible in battle. Looking at the number of scars on the man, tokens of all the injuries he had survived, Ash would say that the tattoo probably worked. Torsten saw that Ash was studying him and winked at him before turning to Astrid and Olaf.

"There has been no further advancement south past Fjellborg." Ash knew the name of the town a few days' ride south along the coast. "Most attacks happen within three days south from here and as far north as Hornsborg." The large man was thoughtful for a moment, stroking his beard braid. "Also, I don't think they are just random attacks by mindless monsters, or we would've had them at the gates here a long time ago. They are calculated, attacking only smaller patrols, isolated groups or the occasional merchant caravan taking their chances and running south. They are always long gone when we find an attack site and they have never attacked a larger patrol, such as ours. It seems that they also split their numbers up after an attack, making it harder to track them through the forest. Oh, and they carry off some of the dead at every attack, because there are people missing from whatever group we come across."

Jarl Olaf slammed his hand on the bench he was sitting on, spilling mead on the floor. "Curse them! Why are they playing this cat-and-mouse game?"

"They are building their numbers," Rani's soft voice silenced the room. "The missing people from the attacks have no doubt been added to their ranks."

"But how?" Jarl Olaf cut in. "How is that possible?"

"Trolls," Rani said matter-of-factly, holding up the carved cylinder Ash had been charged to deliver to Beli's brothers. Most people in the room had sceptical looks on their faces.

"They are behind this. The fact that the bones could not tell me who is behind the draugr made me suspect them in the first place. There are very few creatures in the nine worlds that have magic and wards strong enough to hide them from my scrying, and trolls are one of them." She placed the stone cylinder on the table for all to see the spindly runes carved on it. "Finding out that there are trolls nearby has confirmed my suspicions. There are many dark sides to troll magic; no doubt they would be able to turn men and women to ghouls."

"But why?" Jarl Astrid asked. "I thought that what few trolls were left on Midgard did their very best to remain hidden?"

"I think this is orchestrated from Jotunheim or Muspelheim, not by some fledgling trolls still living in our world. If they could conquer all of Midgard and turn whoever survived to draugr, the armies of Asgard would be pretty thin when Ragnarok, the last battle between the gods and the giants, happens. Maybe they think they can change the prophecy of the outcome of Ragnarok?"

Ash, like everyone in the Norse lands, knew the prophecy of Ragnarok very well. It foretold the end of the world, when the hordes of trolls and giants from Jotunheim and Muspelheim will lay waste to all of Midgard, before turning their armies on Asgard, the home of the gods. The god Heimdall will blow his mighty horn, calling all the other gods to battle as the invaders cross the rainbow bridge to Asgard. All the warriors who'd been slain in battle since the dawn of the world and brought to Valhalla, would prepare themselves alongside the gods, to meet the oncoming hordes on a great field. There, the final battle will take place, shaking the entire world tree *Yggdrasil* to its roots.

When these two great armies clash, most of the gods will fall. Odin will be swallowed whole by the giant wolf *Fenrir*. Thor, the Thundergod, will slay *Jormungandr*, the great serpent, but not before being poisoned by it, and will walk only nine steps before falling to his own death. Soon Tyr and Frey will also be slain. But although many Aesir will fall, so will many of the Muspel and Jotnar armies, and the battle will be even. Then, in a desperate act, the awful *Surtr*, the fire giant of Muspelheim, will raise his flaming sword and with one mighty blow, will burn the entire world. All of its inhabitants, including the gods and the armies of the trolls and giants, will perish in the flames.

All would be still, and no life would be seen to stir in any of the worlds. But then a new world will rise from the ashes, a world born anew, with sprouting fields of wildflowers. Two small children, Lif and Lifthrasir, will climb out from the roots of Yggdrasil, where they had been hiding and humanity will once again populate Midgard. Two of the Aesir gods, Baldur and Hoder, will rise from the kingdom of the dead and walk the earth again. A new dawn will begin for the world of man, and all will live in peace for a thousand years.

"If the trolls can prevent a large army from presenting on the field of battle to face the armies of the giants, they may defeat the gods. Then, Surtr will not need to burn the world and all in it. The new world will not be born; instead the old world will remain, but now ruled by trolls and giants. What few humans would survive would be nothing but slaves and a living larder for the new rulers." There was silence in the room as Rani's words sunk in.

"We must stop them at all cost," hissed Jarl Astrid.

"Then we must find the source of their power," Rani said. "The power to corrupt a man's soul and turn him to a draugr is beyond anything found on Midgard. The power must come from Jotun-heim or Muspelheim. There must be a source, a channel from their realm, where this power flows into our world from theirs. It will be well hidden, and no doubt warded, therefore only visible to trolls and giants, but we must find it and destroy it."

"But how? If it is so well hidden from human eyes?" Jarl Olaf barked.

Rani raised her hand and pointed a finger across the room, straight at Ash, and all heads turned to follow it.

"Luckily, we have a troll of our own," she said with a sad smile.

FOR ALMOST AN hour, Rani recounted Ash's tale to everyone in the room. There were a lot of incredulous looks back and forth between Ash and Rani as she spoke. Yrsa's eyes never left Ash as Rani told his tale and conflicting emotions crossed her face. Ash felt very uncomfortable under all this scrutiny and wished he could sink into the chair where he was sitting and disappear. Rani finished the story by describing Ash's encounter with Beli and holding up the stone rod with the intricate runes on it.

"It is written in troll, of course, and spells out: *Great Gurmr and Grundr. Remember loyal Beli in this gift.*" Everyone in the room looked perplexed as silence once again hung in the air. Rani sighed.

"You really are only good for brawling, aren't you? *Ash* was the gift. When he picked up Beli's hammer, something only a troll should be able to do, Beli saw past Odin's spell, realising that Ash was of troll blood. There is no doubt that by now Burrungandr has put out word about the lad to all of his people on Midgard, and likely promised a reward for his capture."

"If that is the case, why didn't he capture Ash himself? He had him in his bloody cave!" Olaf burst in.

Rani smiled. "Being half troll and half Ulfhed, he was potentially far more dangerous than Beli had first thought. I am certain that this Beli, by his description, is a lowly *vaettr* and would not dare attempt the capture. These Gurmr and Grundr, whom he was sending Ash to, are likely to be a thursr, or even worse, a lesser jotunn and much more adept at capturing a dangerous foe."

"Erh," Ash said, raising his hand and all eyes turned to him. "What's a vaettr?"

Torsten, the warrior who had saved him, cleared his throat.

"Trolls have a very strict hierarchy," he began. "At the bottom of the ladder are the vaettr; often small, dumb and, unless they are under firm leadership, cowardly. Next are the thursrs, the battle trolls. They are strong, fast and powerful and just smart enough to fight well and to think on their feet. The Jomsvikings have fought a few, and even taking down just one thursr comes at a terrible cost. Then, there are the jotunns." He straightened up in his seat, his face serious. "They are the leaders of the trolls, their ruling elite, and controls everything in their world. We sometimes call them giants, because they can grow to enormous sizes, but at the end of the day, they are trolls. They are smart, cunning and ruthless and take up all the positions of power, such as chieftains and shamans. What power they have amassed, they guard ferociously. They scheme and battle amongst themselves and often fight wars against other troll clans back on their own worlds. The fact that there might be one here in Midgard is a big problem."

Ash's face was white when he cut in with a touch of panic in his voice. "So, all these trolls know that I am in the area and are searching for me?"

Rani looked sad once again when she replied. "Maybe. But it is far more likely that Beli is still the only one aware of you. Troll hierarchy is brutal and is governed by fear. If, whoever these Gurmr and Grundr are, were to find out that Beli had you and lost you, he would probably meet a swift and terrible death. So, at the moment, we can almost be certain that your secret is safe with him. You must remember though, that since the hiding spell placed on you has been removed, even the briefest of glances will reveal you as a troll to them."

"But how will all this help us?" Jarl Astrid ventured.

"The point is that the troll's wards hide their caves and locations from all but trolls. This is how Ash found Beli's cave in the first place. A normal human should not be able to find it, let alone cross over the ward. But the boy can. He can lead us to the trolls and the source of all this."

Once again, all eyes turned to Ash who was now as wide eyed as an owl and he swallowed a lump that seemed to have formed in his throat.

"Is that really the best approach? What of the southern Jarls?" Olaf said, changing the subject. "Have they heeded our call to arms? Perhaps we can lead an army against the trolls and draugr instead?"

Jarl Astrid sighed and shook her head. "They are all very politely declining any requests for assistance," she started, unable to hide the bitterness in her voice. "It seems they believe this to be a ruse for the king's throne and have no intention of playing anything into our hands. They are all aware that neither myself nor Jarl Erik have sent our Vikings raiding this season, and as they are expecting us to attack to seize the kingdom, they have not sent theirs either."

"I guess that's something," Jarl Olaf grumbled. "At least they are fortified and ready if the draugr move south."

"Yes, but that would mean that we have been overrun and have swelled the ranks of the undead ourselves." Astrid said, rubbing her eyes.

A FEW DAYS later Ash was riding in the middle of a column of Ulfhednar and Berserkers. They were on their way north, towards Beli's cave. The council had decided that it was the safest place to start, as the lowly troll would be the least threat. If he could be captured, information may be gained about Gurmr and Grundr and what to expect from them. There was always the risk that Beli may get away and raise the alarm, so care had to be taken to ensure his capture. A plan had been hatched and agreed upon, though protested by Yrsa of all people; Ash would lead the warriors to the cave and while they surrounded the hill, he would sneak in to either draw Beli out or destroy the ward that kept them from entering.

"He is only a boy! You are sending him to his death!" Yrsa had railed against Jarl Olaf, pacing the training courtyard.

"Come now," the Jarl had interjected. "He is a clever lad, and pretty quick on his legs too. Besides, he has been training with you for weeks. Surely that counts for something?"

"Bah, he barely knows which end of the spear to stick in the enemy," she said, crossing her arms. Ash was mortified hearing this. He felt he had made significant progress lately, even earning a rare compliment from Yrsa from time to time, but he said nothing.

"He is not much younger than you were the first time you set your foot on a battlefield, Yrsa."

"Yes, and I nearly died, and I had been training for *years* beforehand. He wouldn't last two minutes in a full battle!"

"Well, take comfort in the fact that even the youngest warriors get a seat at Odin's table if they fight bravely." Then his eyes turned to steel as they bored into her. "He is an Ulfhed, gifted by Odin. There is no room for weakness in our ranks, and that's the end of it." Yrsa met Olaf's eyes for a moment before looking away.

"As you say, Jarl Olaf," she said through clenched teeth and walked away. The Jarl's eyes followed her as she left, and Ash saw his shoulders sag a little when she exited the courtyard. He turned his head towards Ash, as if only now remembering that he was there and smiled at him.

"Daughters!" he sighed. "It is harder being a father than it is being a Jarl, mark my words, lad."

"I wouldn't know, Jarl Olaf." Ash replied. Olaf laughed and reached out, placing a fatherly hand on his shoulder.

"You'll be fine, lad. We're all behind you. No doubt you will make us proud."

"I will do my best, Jarl Olaf." Ash tried to come across as brave, but his voice betrayed him.

Now THEY WERE riding north at a good pace, forty Ulfhednar at the front and twenty Berserkers in the rear, with Ash tucked away in the middle. At times, he would turn in his saddle to look back at the Berserkers. They fascinated him, with their large axes and war hammers, draped in bearskins and very little else. Some had painted their faces with black or red paint for the anticipated battles, and Ash could not imagine a fiercer force in this world.

Occasionally when he looked back, Torsten would meet his gaze, grin and wave at Ash. Sometimes he would make a fierce grimace instead of smiling, shaking his heavy axe at him, before breaking out in laughter. After the meeting in Jarl Astrid's rooms, Ash had approached Torsten to thank the Berserker for saving him in the forest. The large man had given him a broad smile and told Ash to think nothing of it, with a slap on the back. Torsten had turned out to be as jovial and good-natured as he was vicious looking, and Ash found himself liking the man more and more.

They made camp overnight and a third of the force were kept awake in rotations, guarding for any sign of a draugr attack. Torsten had sought out Ash and Yrsa's fire in the centre of the camp and sat down with a grunt.

"Getting old, Torsten?" Yrsa teased. Torsten shot her a mock murderous look.

"You forget, young whelp, that an old bear is still a damn bear, and would do best to watch your tongue." Yrsa rolled her eyes and Torsten winked at Ash, who grinned.

"Seeing how you and that moth-eaten old bearskin of yours have decided to stink out our fire, I will take this opportunity to go have a word with Olaf," she said, standing up.

"My apologies," Torsten said, bowing his head. "I forget how sensitive dog noses are."

Yrsa laughed and made a rude gesture to Torsten as she turned

119

around and walked away, weaving between the campfires to get to Jarl Olaf's.

Torsten turned to Ash, smiling.

"We have always bickered, ever since she was a little pup hanging off her father's pant legs."

"Where is her mother?" Ash asked.

"Long since dead," Torsten replied. "She was a decent Ulfhed shieldmaiden and fought in our ranks. Yrsa inherited her abilities from her mother, although I always thought that was some kind of mistake, since her temper would have made her an excellent Berserker, had she gotten her father's abilities instead." Torsten pulled out a skin of mead and took a long swig of it, before offering it to Ash, who declined.

"Her mother was killed not long after Yrsa was born, in a battle with another Jarl and his forces. Although death is our constant companion, and she is surely serving as a Valkyrie to the gods now, Olaf took it hard. He sought out and killed every single person of the Jarl's family and relatives, burned their goods and fortresses and hung them from a tree as a sacrifice to Odin. The Jarl himself, Olaf gave the Blood Eagle."

Ash swallowed at the mention of the Blood Eagle. It was a punishment reserved for the worst of criminals and traitors. The offender would have his arms tied to two stakes, then two deep cuts would be made with an axe down the back, separating the ribs from the spine. The ribs would then be bent outward and the lungs pulled out and draped over the exposed ribcage. All this while the person was still alive, so that his or her last breaths would make the lungs flutter like wings.

Ash looked over at Jarl Olaf, who now was talking to Yrsa. He saw the two of them in a new light. The respect he already had for Jarl Olaf had increased, for the actions he had taken to avenge his lover's death. He couldn't help but see Yrsa with a new sense of kinship as well. He too had lost a mother he was too young to remember. He knew what it was like to grow up, desperately searching for a memory to cling on to. He had always felt alone in this strange grief, but now he had someone who would understand, who would know how it felt. He was certain that he had found the real reason for Yrsa's attitude change towards him.

"Anyway," Torsten cut in on his thoughts. "Yrsa can be a right pain in the backside, but she means well, lad, and you'd do well to learn from her." He took another swig of his mead and looked at Ash, while shaking his head with a grin. "You poor bastard." Then he broke out into a deep belly laugh when Ash frowned. It was a big contagious laugh and Ash soon found himself laughing along with the bear-man. He was rough, yet Ash couldn't help liking him.

"Well, aren't you two getting along splendidly?" There was disapproval in Yrsa's voice as she materialised between them. "I'm not sure I want you corrupting the young pup with your influence, Torsten. Before you know it, he'll stop bathing and my life will be overcome by the stench of two mangy bears." Torsten wiped a tear from the corner of his eye, before putting the stopper in his mead skin and wiping his moustaches with his sleeve.

"Well, I know when I have overstayed my welcome. You're on your own, lad." He stood with a grunt and an exaggerated bow towards Yrsa as he left. Ash looked up at Yrsa who was watching Torsten leave with a warm smile. When she realized that Ash was watching her, her face melted into a stern look.

"You choose your company poorly, boy. That man is nothing but a bundle of bad habits. Now go to bed." Ash nodded and spread out his sleeping roll and crawled in under the blanket. He laid on his back listening to the sounds of the nighttime forest and let his mind wander. Although it had been weeks, the attack on him by the draugr was fresh in his mind and he couldn't help returning to that horrible moment, time and time again. He had felt so helpless when the claws of the undead sunk into him, and he remembered the pain and fear only too well. But when he had Shifted, for a short while, that fear had gone away. Ash had been able to think with a clear mind, devoid of fear, and had fought back. He realized that the Ulfhed path was the path to conquering his fears. He muttered a silent vow to the gods, that he would double his efforts at training and commit wholly to the Ulfhednar, so he would never have to succumb to fear again. A raven cawed twice somewhere in the treetops behind him. Strange to hear a raven at night, he thought. He turned on his side only to discover Yrsa lying awake looking at him.

"Try to get some sleep." She said in a soft voice. "We have a long day ahead of us tomorrow." Ash nodded and closed his eyes. Eventually he drifted off into a restless sleep, and when someone shook his shoulder at first light, he felt like he'd had no sleep at all. He was handed a bowl of porridge and a hunk of bread for breakfast, and these helped to chase the chill and sleep from his body.

They broke camp fast and efficient and were soon on the road again.

Scouts and trackers rode forwards and would return at regular intervals, but with nothing to report as there were no sightings of the draugr, or anyone else for that matter. Jarl Olaf explained that they hadn't expected an attack, since they were a larger force and the monsters had been avoiding such confrontations. But the trackers did see tracks and signs of their movements. There had been heavy rains a week ago, and no new tracks had been made along the road since then.

"I wonder what they are up to?" the Jarl had muttered as he stared into the forest, as if trying to see through it. They rode on for a few hours until Ash started to recognise a few landmarks and it wasn't long until he could see Beli's hill in the distance. He pointed this out to Olaf, who nodded and called a scout to him. He gave a few orders, and the scout rode forwards to inform the other trackers. Before long, the rider returned to Olaf with a report.

"There is a suitable area about three leagues ahead, Jarl Olaf, in reasonable proximity to the hill. Still no sign of the enemy."

"Good." Olaf replied. "Have them prepare the area for camp."

The rider nodded and turned his horse around before riding ahead of the column again, disappearing around a bend in the road.

As they travelled on, Ash found it difficult to take his eyes off Beli's hill, which was steadily getting closer. He had an urge to duck down low, to hide himself from view behind the trees that lined the road. After about an hour, they reached a large, clear parcel of land where Ash could see several horses tethered, eating grass in the open area. There was a small stream nearby, and the ground was level and free of rocks. It seemed that this had been a commonly used camp area for riders and caravans traveling up and down the coast, but Ash doubted it had had much use since the draugr attacks had begun. The sun had only just reached its highest point of the day, when Olaf ordered for camp to be set up, while also being prepared to depart on short notice.

"We don't want to linger for too long," he told Ash and Yrsa as they were tethering their horses. "The longer we are out here, the more we risk discovery, by either the draugr or your friend on top of that hill." He waved at Torsten to join them. When the large man lumbered over, Olaf continued.

"I need half of the Berserkers to come with us to the hill. The other half is to remain here, guarding the horses. Same goes for the Ulfhednar, Yrsa." The shield maiden and the big man nodded at his words. The Jarl looked around the camp.

"I don't like splitting the force when in hostile lands, but we can't take the horses with us through the forest. We will have to make haste and use the horns if there is any sign of trouble." He turned towards Ash. "Get ready, lad. We leave as soon as camp is set." Ash nodded and turned back to his horse to retrieve his equipment.

Jarl Astrid had given him a spear and a seax from the Gjallarholm armoury. It was a traditional, longer spear, so Yrsa had cut it down to make it the short kind favoured by the Ulfhednar. He had also been given a padded leather chest and back piece, since any chain mail kept in Gjallarholm was too large for him. He had tried one on and hadn't liked the weight of it anyway, feeling like it was pulling him down towards the ground. Ash couldn't imagine wearing it all the time, like most of the Jomsvikings did, let alone having to fight in one. He had been training wearing his leathers for a week and felt that he could move comfortably in his new armour by now.

Yrsa had shown him how to pull his hair back and braid it like the warriors did, to prevent it blowing into his face during a fight. She had looked at the soft down on his upper lip and chin and laughed that he needn't worry about braiding them just yet. Ash had flushed at this, making her laugh even harder.

Holding his spear in his right hand and resting the other on the seax in his belt, he felt like quite the warrior in his armour and stood a little bit taller than he usually did.

He turned his head towards Beli's hill and his heart skipped a beat. He was about to find out if his bravery would hold or not. Looking up, he could see some rain clouds moving in from the north across an otherwise clear sky. Go on, make it worse, he thought.

CHAPTER 19

ROGHALD PULLED HIS HOOD AS FAR FORWARD AS HE could, trying to keep the rain out. He was glad for the foul weather. It gave him a good excuse to keep the hood up as he passed through the gates of Hornsborg. If he was to be recognised now, his plan might be for nothing, and he wouldn't have the opportunity to look for Ash inside the walls. He doubted the kid would be here, but his masters had insisted he start at the beginning and follow the trail from there.

He had snuck into the town under the cover of darkness and had waited for daybreak in an abandoned house. The people of Hornsborg were dismantling parts of the town below the fortress to salvage materials that Roghald could see had been used to extend and fortify the walls. It had been a simple matter for him to sweep up some boards, set them on his shoulder and fall in behind a work crew carrying timber through the gates. Dozens of guards were manning the gates, but they were watching the road and tree line, barely sparing a glance to the people entering.

He smiled as he entered the familiar courtyard and deposited his planks in a growing pile in the centre. Many hands were busy inside the fortress, not only fortifying the walls but also building shacks along the inside of them. Obviously, the housing situation hadn't improved since he'd left, and a dank smell hung over the place. It wasn't just the stench of sewage, muck and sweat of too many people and animals crowded together, but also the smell of fear permeating everything.

Well, they were right to be fearful, he mused, but they needn't fear for much longer.

He walked over to the stables where he'd spent the last twenty years of his life. He stepped into the building and frowned when he saw the mess. There was no one here, except sleeping rolls and stacks of people's belongings which were spread everywhere, and not in a tidy manner either, he noticed in disgust.

They live worse than animals, he thought as he picked his way across the floor between bedding, unwashed food bowls and piles of clothing. They deserve everything they are about to get.

He walked up to the stalls and noticed that a few horses still remained, to his astonishment. He was surprised they hadn't killed and eaten them yet, to make room for the human filth cowering behind the walls. They had been well cared for too, he noticed with approval, running his hand down the flank of a gelding he knew well. The horse snorted and bobbed its head when it recognised him.

"Excuse me. No one is supposed to be in here in the daytime," a small voice chimed behind him. Roghald stroked the gelding one last time before turning around. He looked down on a young boy, maybe twelve years old, who looked vaguely familiar, straining to hold a bucket, water dripping off his clothing.

Roghald pulled his hood back.

"Don't worry lad, I'm only greeting an old friend."

"Roghald? You're back?" the boy looked surprised.

"Only stopping in for a quick errand, lad." He reached into his pocket and pulled out a silver coin that he flicked to the boy who caught it with his free hand.

"Take that for your troubles, and not a word to anyone that you have seen me, alright?" he smiled and winked.

"Whatever you say, Roghald." the boy said, his voice thick with suspicion. "I'm just going to water the horses."

He pocketed the coin he had been given. With a cautious eye on Roghald, he walked around him, giving him a wide berth, before emptying his bucket in a trough for the gelding to drink. Roghald smiled at the boy's cautiousness and clear distrust before walking towards the ladder leading up to the loft.

"I'm just popping up here for a minute," he told the boy who only nodded, but Roghald saw his eyes flicker to the stable doors.

As soon as he had climbed up to the low-ceilinged loft, where extra hay and grain were sometimes kept, he heard running footsteps from below. He laughed at the poor deal he had gotten, attempting to buy the boy's loyalty. He made his way to the corner where Ash used to sleep. Not much was left there, besides an old blanket and a few little trinkets. A good layer of dust also covered everything, confirming his belief that Ash hadn't returned. Thinking of the boy stirred his hateful feelings anew.

It had shocked him to learn from his new master that Ash was a half-blood and his father was a troll. That explained how he had beat Roghald in a fight. Typical of the lout to cheat and use his powers to defeat him. Well, now two can play at that game, he thought with a cruel smile. He had learned a thing or two after spending the last couple of weeks being instructed by Gurmr and Grundr. He had several scars to show for it, since the troll was a tough taskmaster, but it had been effective learning.

Roghald now had powers of his own, having had the soul of a dead battle troll, a thursr, merge with his. He could feel its presence always, sometimes pushing in on his thoughts, sometimes mumbling to him, sometimes laughing. Roghald was never able to make out any words, so he assumed it was just mad blabbering. But Roghald remained in control of himself, and that was the most important part. Like a hound, his new master had set him on Ash's trail. Gurmr and Grundr had ordered him to bring the boy back alive when he found him, but Roghald had other plans. He would make the little clod suffer for as long as he could before snapping his neck. Ash was to die at his hands and there was no force in all the worlds that would stop Roghald when the time came. He could feel the dead troll get excited and laugh like a madman when Roghald's hate permeated their shared consciousness. He was starting to like his new companion.

"Roghald Einarson!" A harsh voice called up from the stables below. "You are in breach of your banishment! Come down and face the Jarl's justice!"

Roghald's grin threatened to split his head in two.

"Is that you, Arne Skaldison?" he called down in a cheerful voice. "Are you guarding the stables these days?"

"Come down, Roghald, and you better be unarmed, or the lads here will fill you with arrows."

Roghald climbed down the rickety ladder. There were six warriors greeting him when he got down; three carried bows with arrows nocked, two had spears and Arne, the captain, stood with his arms crossed and a serious look on his face.

"Good to see you, old friend," Roghald smiled at the older hirdsman.

"You were counted as dead, Roghald, and most were glad for it," Arne scowled at him. "You are mad to have returned here. I doubt the Jarl will be merciful this time around."

Roghald looked around at the warriors surrounding him, who all looked at him with contempt. He smiled at them.

"I'm sure I can explain everything to the Jarl." he said.

"Oh, you'll have your say, Roghald, don't you worry. Now, hold your hands out." Arne held out a length of rope and indicated to Roghald's hands. He held his hands out and Arne tied them together at the wrist. One of the other warriors patted Roghald down, confirming that he was unarmed.

Roghald saw movement from the corner of his eye and turned his head towards it. It was the stableboy he had given the silver to, watching from a dark corner. The boy pulled himself a little further back into the shadows, but his eyes never left Roghald. Roghald smiled and winked at the boy as he was taken away.

THEY MARCHED HIM across the courtyard, full of people, and into the fortress through familiar corridors, and he was brought into Jarl Erik's hall. Jarl Erik was sitting at his usual table. He seemed irritated, no doubt from the news of Roghald's return to Hornsborg. The former stable master was shoved over the threshold and had to take a few stumbling steps to regain his balance. Erik shook his head, meeting Roghald's eyes with a dark look.

"I see my mercy was wasted on you. What could possibly possess you to return here?"

"You would be amazed, Jarl Erik, if you believed it." Roghald laughed. Erik looked perplexed for a second, but soon recovered and assumed his stern look once again.

"Before I declare my sentence over you, would you care to enlighten me as to why you came back?" Erik pressed.

"Oh, I have come to look for Ash the half-troll, Jarl Erik." Roghald said in a cheerful voice. Erik's face paled and his eyes bored into Roghald's as he stood up from the table.

"How could you possibly know about that?" he said in a strangled voice.

"… and when I find him, I will tear him limb from limb. Since he doesn't appear to be here, I will have to settle for killing you and everyone who resides behind your walls, Jarl Erik."

Erik stood speechless, staring at Roghald, bewildered. One of the hirdsmen who had brought him in struck Roghald with the shaft of his spear across the back of his legs, driving him onto his knees. Erik shook his head in contempt, looking down at the madman kneeling before him.

"By the laws of banishment, your life is now forfeit, Roghald Einarson. You will be taken from here to the gallows where you will hang by the neck, as you deserve. Do you have any final words?"

Roghald, whose head was bowed with his chin against his chest, was calm, almost serene as he replied. "I don't think you have enough men here for that, Jarl Erik."

Erik smiled a sad smile for his old stable master. "How so, Roghald?"

When Roghald lifted his head and looked at him, Erik couldn't help but gasp and take a step backwards. Roghald's eyes were as black as the darkest night, and a cruel smile revealed two rows of sharp teeth. With a deep, inhuman voice Roghald said, "Because the trolls are upon you, Erik."

All in the room took a step back when Roghald tore his bonds as if they were made of cobwebs. He began to grow, his clothes tearing as his back and shoulders widened to that of a bull. His arms grew long and soon were thicker than a man's waist, and from his fingertips, long claws sprouted. His head enlarged and his jaw widened and teeth like knives crowded his maw under a long nose. Roghald's forehead bulged and two points pushed through the skin as curved horns grew out, curling backwards over his head, while short, bone-coloured spikes sprouted on his shoulders and upper arms. His skin turned a shade of green, with darker patches and thick, moss-coloured fur on his back, shoulders and the back of his arms. With his head and shoulders reached the ceiling, he had to stoop over to accommodate his enormous size.

A terrible roar filled the hall. The hirdsmen, shaking themselves from the initial shock, launched what arrows and spears they had at the monstrosity that had appeared in their midst. The arrows failed to penetrate its thick skin and fell harmlessly to the floor. Only one spear struck true and lodged itself in Roghald's thigh. He roared and ripped the spear out, only to thrust it through the chest of the nearest hirdsman.

Jarl Erik was shouting orders, attempting to rally his men, but panic had now struck and the room fell into chaos as the slaughter began. Roghald grabbed a warrior and snapped her neck with ease, a mighty blow of his fist crushed another's ribcage. He felt ecstatic, their pain and death filling him with an unimaginable pleasure, and the maniacal laughter of the troll inside him spilled out of his own mouth as he brought violent death to all in the hall.

A sharp pain burst in his leg and he looked down to see an axe embedded in his thigh. The axe head had runes etched along the edges, and they were glowing softly. It had cut into his thigh bone where it seemed to be firmly lodged. The pain was excruciating, but it took more than that to stop a thursr, the pain only fuelling his rage. His eyes met Jarl Erik's who was pulling at the axe handle, trying to dislodge it for another blow. Roghald's arm shot out and seized the Jarl by his throat, lifting him off the floor with ease. He smashed him into a pillar, then shook the man like a rag doll until he fell limp. When he noticed two hirdsmen advancing on him from behind, he threw the Jarl into them, sending them all sprawling across the hall.

With a snarl, he ripped the axe from his thigh and threw it across the room. He could already feel his flesh knitting itself back together thanks to the innate magic of battle trolls. He turned to face the few remaining warriors in the hall. It took only a few more moments before they were all lying dead at Roghald's feet.

He walked up to the broken body of Jarl Erik. Somehow the man was still alive, even after the thrashing Roghald had given him.

The Jarl's eyes were locked on Roghald, filled with hate. He tried to speak, but his chest was crushed, and he could only gurgle as foamy blood trickled from his lips. Roghald laughed. Clearly, the pathetic Jarl was trying to curse Roghald with his dying breath, only to no avail. Laughing, Roghald lifted his leg up high before bringing his clawed foot down on his head with force, thus ending the rule of Jarl Erik Erikson.

Roghald had to be quick. He could already hear the alarm being raised inside the fortress. He ran, not toward the door, but to one of the large windows that would at times be opened to air out the hall. At this time, it was boarded shut. Even so, the timber splintered when his large body slammed through it. Though it was a second-story window, he barely noticed the drop onto the cobblestones, his body radiating with power and strength.

The courtyard was still full of people and many screamed in horror as his monstrous shape exploded from the window and landed amongst them. He scrambled to his feet as people all around him shouted and scattered away in fear and confusion. But he paid them no attention, and as soon as he found his footing he began to run straight for the gates, swatting anyone within reach out of his way. Half a dozen men and women were busy closing them by hand when he got there.

Roghald leapt on the people from behind, his claws tearing their backs and throwing them to the side, as if they were made of straw. He slammed his shoulder into the heavy gates and pushed them open. As they swung out, he put his head in the opening and roared, loud and long, carrying far beyond the town and over the forest. A chorus of hungry moans rose from the tree line.

A cry was heard from the top of the fortified wall.

"The draugr! The draugr! They are coming!" Roghald pushed the gates wide open and lifted his head to see hundreds of draugr spill out of the forest and rush towards the town and fortress. More cries of alarm were raised.

"Kill it! We must shut the gates, or we are all dead!" A few of the warriors threw themselves at the pulling mechanism, trying to force the gate shut.

The first spear lodged in Roghald's back, then a second. Soon spears fell like rain on him, the pain almost unbearable, but he stayed firm and held the gate. He turned around and roared at the people throwing their spears, while reaching his arms out to the sides, holding the gates open. Some flinched back or were so frightened that their throw missed their mark, but plenty found their target. He dodged a few, but it was getting harder and harder as one after another slammed into him. Roghald had dozens of spears protruding from his back and front, black blood seeping from his wounds, pooling on the ground beneath him. His vision swam, and he felt slow and heavy.

"He is fading! Attack now and drive him out! There is still time!" one warrior yelled. Roghald could see a fylking battle formation; a wall of round shields and gleaming steel, advancing towards him. He had difficulty focusing on the warriors that came towards him, their swords and axes raised. Roghald readied himself for the rain of blows that would come at any moment, determined to hold the gates open.

When the fylking was only two paces away from him, and the Vikings raised their weapons to strike, the first draugr shot past underneath his out-stretched arm and slammed into their shields. Then a second, and soon after a third, before the entire horde pushed past him, spilling into the courtyard. In seconds they had overwhelmed the fylking and shouts of surprise turned to screams of pain and horror as the draugr attacked anyone in sight.

Roghald gave a triumphant roar where he stood. He let his arms fall by his side as more draugr ran past him, in an endless flow, into the courtyard. He removed spear after spear from his body, watching as the wounds closed and healed before his eyes, leaving only pale scars behind. All spears now removed, he looked out over the gruesome scene spread out before him, as his draugr pushed further into the fortress, unstoppable as the tide. Time to get to work, he thought. And the troll in his head laughed and laughed.

CHAPTER 20

ASH PAUSED AT THE BASE OF THE STEPS TO BELI'S CAVE. His heart was beating fast, threatening to burst from his chest. He craned his neck to look up to the top, half expecting to find Beli standing there glaring at him, but the ledge was empty. He turned around to ensure that Yrsa and Torsten still waited for him just inside the tree line. A sense of unease had filled the Jomsvikings, growing stronger the closer they got to the hill, only their iron wills allowing them to push forward, until eventually the air had become a solid barrier for them. Ash knew that was the ward working, conjured to turn away anyone not of troll blood. Even the things that had chased him that night, most likely draugr, he remembered with a shiver, hadn't been able to follow him beyond the tree line. Yrsa's eyes met his, and she gave a quick nod of encouragement. Reassured that his friends were close, he turned to face the steps once again. Ash balled his hands into fists to stop them shaking.

"You can't be brave unless you are afraid," Torsten had told him as they crept through the forest. "The gods know that too, that's why they value bravery above all. Only a complete idiot is never afraid." The thought had made Ash feel a bit better. He felt that he must then be the bravest person in this forest, because no one could be more frightened than him right now. Taking a deep breath, Ash steeled himself, before placing his foot on the first step and began his slow ascent up the steep hill. He took slow, careful steps, often stopping to listen at the slightest of sounds, eyes locked on the hilltop, but when nothing appeared, he kept moving.

When his hand touched the top step, he raised his head over it, ready to turn and run in the event of an ambush, but it was all still and quiet. The approaching clouds had hidden the late afternoon sun and a few light raindrops fell on his face as he crept towards the large rock in the middle of the plateau. He moved in a semicircle to ensure that the cave opening would be on the opposite side of his approach, so he wouldn't be spotted in case Beli popped his head out.

Moving up to the rock, he reached his hand out and placed it on the grey stone. There it was, the rhythmic pulsation that meant that Beli was beating on his anvil.

WHILE THEY RODE to Beli's cave, the Jomsvikings had made a plan for Ash to lure Beli out into the forest, for the warriors to capture. Ash, who knew Beli, knew that the troll was far too cunning to be lured out of the safety of its cave, but his protests had fallen on deaf ears. So, he had made his own plan, one that was more of a risk to himself, however. Ash knew that the only way to beat the troll was at its own game. At first, Ash had felt bad for going against Yrsa's instructions, but she had told him to be a wolf, not a sheep, so a wolf he would be.

Unfortunately, for Ash's plan to work, he had to remove all his weapons and armour. He took off his belt holding his seax and wriggled out of his leather armour. He placed it all in a pile next to the rock where he also leaned his spear. Even though they had only belonged to him for a short while, he felt a little naked without the weapons.

He ran his hands along the ground before rubbing the dirt in his hair and on his face. Then he dropped to the ground and rolled around, while being as quiet as he could. Standing up, he examined himself and feeling that he looked sufficiently dishevelled, he took a deep breath and walked around the rock towards the opening.

The cave opening soon appeared and the familiar heat radiated out of it in stark contrast to the cool air outside. He could hear the regular clangs of the hammer on the anvil and they became louder as he slipped inside the passage. He stepped into the cave and found it the same as during his visit several weeks ago. Beli stood before his anvil, just like the first time Ash had found him. The troll halted, his hammer held above his head with a look of surprise on his face. His expression was just turning to one of anger when Ash cut in:

"Beli! Thank the gods I found you again!" He aimed to portray an air of relief when seeing the ugly troll, when all of his instinct told him to run. Although lying always made Ash uncomfortable, he had, as a means of self-preservation, often had to lie to Roghald and had gotten quite good at it. The prospect of a beating was an excellent motivator, after all. Beli's face shifted from anger to confusion.

"The message you gave me to hand to your brothers must have fallen from my bag as I travelled through the forest. I retraced my steps as best I could and I have been searching for weeks, but could not find it." If the creature had seemed confused for a while, he now looked doubtful as he glared at Ash.

"I gave up hope and came back to ask for the message again from you. This time, if you give it again, I will not lose it, I swear!" Ash extended both his hands in a pleading gesture, but Beli still looked suspicious. The troll stared at him for a long moment and Ash was just prepared to turn and run, ready to abandon his plan. He hoped Beli would at least follow him, and maybe he would make it to his friends before the troll could catch him. But like before, he didn't think Beli would fall for such a trap and he feared they would fail. But then the troll's features softened somewhat.

"Ash of Hornsborg is a stupid, stupid boy," Beli spat. "Beli worked hard carving a beautiful message for his brother." He put down the hammer on the anvil and turned to walk towards his workbench next to the hearth. Ash's eyes were drawn to the forge, spewing out the heat that was stifling the cave, but more precisely to the glowing runes around the opening. Rani had said that the wards protecting the cave would be magical runes. It had to be them.

"Beli will carve another message and will hang it from a string around Ash's neck, so he does not lose it, stupid as he is." When he had almost gotten to the workbench, he stopped and turned to face Ash, his face full of suspicion again.

"What of the boy's knapsack? And the clothes Beli kindly gifted to you? Did Ash of Hornsborg lose them as well?"

Ash wanted to smack himself on the forehead. He hadn't thought about that. They had given him new clothes in Gjallarholm, as the ones he wore when he left here had been torn in the draugr attack. The knapsack he had left behind in the fortress.

"Well, I…" he began, but the troll squinted at him and said in a stern voice:

"Show Beli the stone he gave you. It is not around the boy's neck, so how did he walk through the forest all this time?"

Ash met the troll's stare, his mind racing to come up with an explanation. The troll was still only a few paces away from the anvil. Not far enough. Ash's eyes flicked to the anvil and back. It was only the briefest of glances, but Beli had seen it and his eyes widened in understanding. As soon as the troll moved, Ash sprang into action. The weeks of training with Yrsa had paid off, and he could Shift at a heartbeat's notice. The air thickened around him, and the troll's movement slowed down. He could see the heat coming from the forge as a shimmer in the air as the world came into crystal focus.

He darted across the cave, towards the anvil, but the troll was much closer. A drawn-out snarl bellowed from the creature, as he threw himself to cut off Ash from his most prized possession. Ash took the last few steps as long leaps, and reaching out, he closed his hand around the shaft of the large smithing hammer, snatching it up while the troll's hand was only inches away.

Using the momentum of his lunge he spun around swinging the hammer in a wide arc as the troll, clawed hands out, was closing on him, but now had a look of fear on its face. Beli flinched away from the blow, but Ash had never intended to hit the troll. He drove the hammer home with as much force as he could muster. It slammed into the rune at the top of the forge's opening with a dull thud, followed by a boom and a flash of green light.

A big crack spread across the smooth stone from where he had hit it and the rune there flickered, but it was still whole. Then the troll was upon him. His sinewy hands closed around Ash's throat and squeezed. His vision darkened and losing his concentration, he could no longer stay Shifted. The world sped up and the pain and discomfort became so much worse.

The troll was shaking him, choking the life out of him, and Ash knew he only had one chance before he blacked out and died at the hands of this monster. Still holding the hammer, as light in his hand as the first time he had picked it up, he drove it as hard as he could into the creature's face. The grip around his throat loosened and blood rushed back into his head, clearing his vision somewhat. He hit Beli again and again until the troll let go and it staggered backwards, blood running from its big nose and mouth.

Free once again, before the troll could recover, he gripped the hammer in two hands and swung it at the runes. This time the hearth crumbled with a crack and a blinding light exploded from the rune. It shattered with a loud boom that shook the entire cave and threw Ash across the floor. He scraped his elbows and face against the rough surface, before he came to a sprawling stop. Ash sat up, rubbing his eyes, trying to get his vision back after the blinding light, when a wave of intense heat rolled over him and he heard Beli yelling.

"What has he done?!" His vision clearing, he saw Beli running for the exit. Ash felt the skin on his back burning from the heat, and he turned to see molten rock and black smoke spilling out of the now ruined forge. The air was so hot it was hard to breathe and, covering his nose and mouth with his sleeve, he jogged to follow the troll. He stopped at the end of the cave and looked back to the hammer where he had dropped it in the explosion. The lava was only a step away from it and closing in. For a split second he considered making a dash for it, but the air was now so hot and full of sulphur that he choked on it. Coughing and gagging, he ran for the fresh air outside.

Ash threw himself out of the opening and into a cool rain, and it felt like he had plunged himself into a frozen river. He still felt burning hot, but the rain soothed his reddened skin and he spared a moment to let the soothing droplets wash over his face.

A rumble from beneath his feet brought him back and reminded him of the urgency at hand. Looking around, the troll was nowhere to be seen, but soon he heard clanging and a roar of anger that turned into a yelp of pain. Another, much more powerful rumble, made Ash decide that the best move for the foreseeable future would be to get off the hill. He ran around the rock and snatched up his belongings before heading for the steps. When he reached the ledge, an anxious Yrsa came running up, visibly relaxing when she saw him approaching.

"You idiot!" she spat. "We will talk about this later." She attempted to look stern, but she couldn't quite hide the relieved look in her eyes. As another rumble shook the ground, Ash turned to see black smoke and molten rock spilling out of the opening.

"Let's go!" Yrsa snapped and turned to run down the steps with Ash close behind her. They made their way down as fast as they could. Ash slipped several times on the wet stone as tremors made him lose his footing, scraping his hands and elbows. At the bottom they found the rest of the Ulfhednar waiting for them.

The troll was hanging between two large Berserkers, like a hunted deer, tied up and suspended from the ground by a rough-cut pole carried across their shoulders. Beli was bleeding from a cut on his head but was conscious and stared at Ash with murder in his eyes. Ash avoided looking at the troll and busied himself putting on his leather jerkin and belt.

Another quake shook the hill, this one so violent that a large crack appeared in the crag next to them. Olaf ordered everyone to make haste back to camp. With no reason to remain concealed anymore, they made better speed heading back and soon they broke clear of the forest and were back in the camp area. The sun had set by now and Ash turned around to see the hill aglow with molten rock as a large black plume of smoke climbed to the skies. He felt a pang of remorse when he remembered Beli's smithing hammer. The tool had connected with him and he had wanted to keep it, but it was now lost forever in a pool of molten stone.

Many of the Jomsviking gathered around to look at the troll who was dropped on the hard ground with a thump. He kept silent but defiant, glaring at the captors surrounding him. Olaf stepped forward and placed his large war hammer on the creature's chest, crossed his arms and rested them on the bottom of the shaft, creating an uncomfortable pressure for Beli.

"So, you miserable son of Ymer," Olaf began, referring to the father of all trolls and giants. "Care to tell us what has brought this plague unto our lands, and maybe I will grant you a quick, clean death?" Beli squirmed under the weight but remained silent. Olaf shrugged his shoulders and turned to his warriors.

"Well, we can't expect that a lowly vaettr would know anything about it, anyway. He is too stupid for his masters to confide in him about their plans."

Beli exploded in a burst of curses and swear words that put even the burliest of Berserkers to shame, but Olaf continued.

"Someone as slow as him would've only been good for emptying the piss pots in Jotunheim, and probably couldn't even manage that, and was therefore exiled to Midgard." The laughter of the men and women surrounding him sent Beli into a rage. He thrashed and tore at his bonds, but to no avail. "And why shouldn't they? Obviously, he is simple, even by troll standards, and why would you keep the village idiot around to get in the way and upset things? No, this one knows nothing, as he is less than a dog to them."

"The stupid humans will all die at the hands of the Jotnar!" Beli roared. "A jotunn sits in their lands and his power is great! More and more humans are turned every day by the great Gurmr and Grundr's hand, and soon they will be overrun!" The surrounding laughter died, and he continued with glee, "For generations a vine has grown all the way from Jotunheim while they slept, the stupid humans. The old magic has grown in their midst! Can't they see its too late? It's too late!" He chuckled at Olaf standing over him and continued with a taunting voice. "The sons of Muspel and Jotnar will trample their lands and crops. Their kind is not long for this world. The age of the troll is here," he said with a wicked smile. Olaf looked grim as he stared down on his captive.

"Well, at least I can take comfort in the fact that you will never know." With those words he lifted his war hammer and brought it down with full force on the troll's head with a loud thud, splitting his head like a melon. Ash had just turned away a second before the blow had struck, but the sound was forever etched in his memory.

Torsten placed a heavy hand on Ash's shoulder and turned the boy around to face him and looked him in the eyes. "You are not to feel any guilt for your part in this, lad." The man had a sombre look on his face. "When we were waiting for you at the bottom of the hill, we found his refuse pile and it was full of human bones. Some were from children. He was a wicked thing that would prey on travellers on this road for his larder. His death is well-deserved and as a Jarl, Olaf has a duty to see to it, but anyone here would have gladly done the same."

Ash nodded and realized that the Berserker was right. He remembered the clothes he had rifled through when he first met Beli and felt sick at the thought. Only chance had saved him from the same fate. He turned to look at the troll and gasped at what he saw. Where his body had been only a pile of rocks remained. They were vaguely in the shape of the troll, but all signs of its life were gone, and only withered granite lay in its place.

"When the trolls and giants were created, they sprung from the very rock of Jotunheim and so when they die, they return to their true form." Torsten explained. "Some hills and mountains are said to have been trolls and giants once, slain by Thor and his mighty hammer."

Ash had heard the tales as a child, like everyone growing up in the Norse lands, but he hadn't believed them to be literally true. He would never look at a mountain the same way again. Or enter a cave, for that matter, in case he made his way into a giant's ear. Or worse.

Olaf and Yrsa came to join them. Torsten turned to the Jarl, "What do you make of what he said?" Olaf looked pensive for a moment before replying, "I think we better ride north to Hornsborg. We need to discuss what we've learned with Erik, sooner rather than later and we need more warriors. If it is as the troll said, and there is an actual jotunn here, we have little time and we must strike at their heart before they grow much stronger. If Rani is right, our jotunn sits where Ash was being sent by the vaettr. We at least know where to aim our forces, and we might have a chance at thwarting their plans." The warriors agreed with their Jarl, who turned to the rest of the camp.

"Listen up! Stretch the canvases between the trees so we can get out of the rain for the night, but don't get too comfortable. We ride for Hornsborg at first light!"

CHAPTER 21

R ANI SAT BY THE FIRE, ROCKING BACK AND FORTH, MUM-
bling to herself. Her Second Sight often allowed her to see
things that were happening far away and sometimes even things
yet to be, although they were often clouded and difficult to interpret. Now, however, she could see the turn of events with unusual
clarity, and they filled her with dread.

There was a rustle of feathers close to her and a raven's caw
broke the silence in the room. Rani could sense someone sitting on
the bench next to her, where no one had been a moment ago. She
had heard no one enter or walk across the room, and after years of
physical blindness, her hearing was as acute as that of a fox. Nor
had she felt anyone sitting down next to her. One second there was
no one in the room, and the next it was as if someone had been
sitting there all along. It could only be one being.

"Allfather," she greeted him, bowing her head.

"Seidwoman," he returned, a touch of amusement in his voice.

"The tides are bad in the north and about to get worse. Jotunheim is building its forces with great speed and has found a
new champion," she told him. For several heartbeats, the room
remained silent.

"Hornsborg has fallen," the old man said in a grave voice. "Jarl Erik sits at my table in Valhalla."

"And the boy?" she asked, the concern in her voice betraying her.

"He still lives, but for how long, even I cannot foretell."

"He wasn't... *isn't* ready for this," she corrected herself.

"None are," the old man replied. "The fate of Midgard hangs in the balance. None are yet prepared for what might come."

"Can you help him?" she asked, but already knew his answer.

"I cannot. The laws of the universe would claim a high price if I did. I'm afraid that when I stepped in and aided the boy when his mother died, I unleashed this very curse on the land. In aiding him, I gave the ice and fire giants the right to aid their people. They gave Jotunheim the secret to turning men to draugr. Every action reaps a reaction, and I cannot afford to give them any more advances." They sat in silence for a moment.

"I can act indirectly though." Rani could hear some mischief in his voice. "I have called upon Eikinri of the dvergir to see to the boy," he said. The Seidwoman raised her head in surprise.

"Surely not!" Rani's voice was high pitched in disbelief. The air became at once cold and a smell of snow was brought on an icy breeze that swirled in the room, pulling at her robes. She knew she had overstepped the mark, angering the god in questioning him. She had forgotten how irritable the old sod could be.

"Forgive me, Allfather. My concern for the boy got the better of me," Rani said while bowing her head. After a moment, the warmth returned to the room and the smell of winter left to be replaced by the smell of burning pine logs in the fireplace.

"Can he be trusted?" she asked.

"No," Odin replied. "But he owes me a great deal, and I will free him of his debt in this final repayment. It has been a source of shame for him to be indebted to an Aesir, so I'm almost certain he can be relied upon in this matter," he said with some enjoyment. Rani's lips tightened in disapproval, but she dared not question the god further. All she could do was hope that Ash was ready for what he was about to face. And she was not thinking of the draugr.

CHAPTER 22

ASH DREW HIS CLOAK CLOSER AROUND HIMSELF AND pulled the hood forwards as far as he could. The rain had stopped, though a stiff wind whistled under a cloud covered sky. It was a stark contrast from the warm days of the last few weeks, but the northern weather was always unreliable.

They had been riding since the break of dawn and had made good headway toward Hornsborg. Ash had mixed feelings about returning to his home. One part of him missed the familiar environment, and the few kind people that lived there, but he couldn't stop worrying about the reason he left.

Roghald the stable master. No one could hold a grudge like Roghald, and he would without doubt beat Ash within an inch of his life, given the opportunity. Although, a lot had changed in the months since Ash left. He had learnt how to fight and he now had control of his abilities, so he could no doubt hold his own against the stable master. But just in case, he would make sure he kept close to Yrsa for the time they were there. If anyone had a worse temper than Roghald, it was her.

He rode on, lost in his thoughts, when they passed yet another abandoned house next to the road. He found the empty, silent homesteads and farms a disconcerting sight, and his worry grew with each one. Sometimes the doors or windows were unlatched, swinging in the wind, as if the owners had left in a hurry. Or they hadn't had a chance to leave at all. Endless horror scenarios played out in his mind, and they filled him with sorrow for the people who had lived there. Trying to distract himself, he practiced Shifting. He went in and out of that heightened, Ulfhed state, finding it easier to do each time. When Ash tired, he knew he had reached the limits of his ability and had to stop.

He drove his pony forwards and drew level with Yrsa, who greeted him with a nod. He looked at the forceful woman and thought of the bond they had formed in the last few weeks. She was rough and strict, in particular when it came to his training, but he had glimpsed a warm, caring core underneath all the steel and chain mail. He realized that he trusted her, even if she made his life miserable most of the time. Having grown up as an orphan, he didn't know what it was like to have a family, but Yrsa felt like something he'd imagined of it. She was like a big sister, perhaps. An older, mean, bossy, domineering sister, sure, but someone who he felt cared about him all the same.

A little overcome by the emotion, he smiled his warmest smile at her, and she proved his point by glaring at him and asking, "What are you smirking at, pup?"

Ash rolled his eyes and slumped his shoulders. "Nothing." They rode on in silence for a few minutes before Yrsa spoke.

"When we get to Hornsborg and gather what warriors Erik can spare, we will leave as soon as possible," she paused for a second. "You will, however, be staying behind."

Ash snapped his head up. "What?"

"I have spoken to Jarl Olaf about it, and he agrees that it will be too dangerous for you to continue on with us. A jotunn is something completely different from a vaettr and he would not use your... abilities in the same way against such a foe."

Ash was mortified. He had been brave, and it was thanks to him and his quick thinking that Beli had been captured with no one getting hurt. He had embraced his fate and had felt himself part of the Ulfhednar, yet now he was to be left behind in the fortress like a child. With Roghald. He looked over to the Jarl, who rode at the head of the column, and was just about to spur his horse to ride up to him when Yrsa cut in.

"Don't bother. His mind is made up. You will only irritate him if you push the matter, and he will only dig his heels in further. Trust me, I know." Ash's face was like a storm cloud and he rode in silence, ruminating. Yrsa glanced at him out of the corner of her eye.

"A warrior is always wise to surrender to the inevitable. Don't rush to your grave, young Ulfhed, you will find it soon enough in our line of work," she chuckled with a bitter edge. Ash nodded but was not appeased. He was determined to leave with the Jomsvikings, and he would find a way.

He heard a shout up ahead as one of the scouts came riding back at high speed. The scout pulled up next to Olaf and spoke hurriedly. Olaf's face darkened and he raised his hammer as a call to arms. A ruckus broke out as sixty warriors strapped their shields to their arms and drew their weapons. At another sign from Olaf they rearranged their formation, riding four abreast in rows.

"Stay to my left." Yrsa instructed Ash as she took the rightmost position in their row. Ash pulled his horse in next to the shield maiden just as the unit moved out in a slow canter. His heart was racing. What was this about? By his estimation, they were very close to Hornsborg now and should be under the protection of the Jarl.

They rode on for a short while, before the forest on the sides of the road opened up into a large, cleared area. Ash looked out over the familiar town of Hornsborg and the fortress he had called home for most of his life. At first, he felt relief at seeing the grey stone building, but soon an uneasy feeling struck him. It was dead quiet, and he could see no movement in the surrounding town. He scanned the walls of the fortress where guards were always patrolling, but these too were empty.

The remaining scouts waited for them at the first of the many small timber and stone houses that made up the town. They seemed tense, and all wore serious expressions. Ash noticed that their horses were skittish and anxious, sensing the concern of their riders.

When the main body of the warriors reached them, the lead scout spoke with the Jarl. Ash strained his ears to hear them, but he was far back in the column and any words he might have heard were drowned out by the sounds of creaking armour and the snorts from the now restless horses they all sat on. Jarl Olaf's eyes never left the fortress as the scout spoke. He soon nodded and turned to face the warriors.

"Listen up." His usually loud voice was a little muted and Ash had to lean in to hear him. "Hornsborg appears to have fallen. It happened no sooner than yesterday, according to the scouts." The tension amongst the Jomsvikings became palpable and more than a few of them turned their heads to eye the tree line of the forest surrounding them with suspicion. "There appear to be no enemies in the town or inside the walls, nor any sign of survivors, but they might just be holed up inside the fortress and not aware of our presence yet."

"The survivors or the enemy?" a shieldmaiden asked.

"Either," Olaf replied. "We need to investigate for both survivors to rescue or enemies to bring vengeance to, so we will enter the fortress." The rustle of tightening straps and helmets secured filled the silence for a moment as sixty heavily armed warriors prepared themselves for what was to come.

"We will secure the courtyard first, then we will re-assess and take it from there. Apparently, the main gates have been torn clean off, so we will have a pathway of retreat should we need it. I want Scouts to the walls immediately to watch the town and the forest." He tightened the strap on his shield arm and drew his war hammer from the saddle.

"And steel yourselves. A bloodbath lies beyond the gates."

Ash's mouth was dry, and he fumbled with his spear, almost dropping it. He had no shield, but he was glad for it since his hands were so sweaty, he thought he would have dropped the spear if he had to rely on only one hand.

"Stay with me, no matter what," Yrsa ordered him. The steel cheek and nose guard on her helmet did little to mask the concern he saw in her eyes. They set off in a slow canter, the Berserkers fanning out in front as they made their way through the abandoned town. They would have preferred to dismount and proceed to the fortress on foot, as both Berserkers and Ulfhednar fought better off a horseback than on it, but Olaf had insisted they remain as they were, in case they met an overwhelming force and had to retreat. Ash thought they moved far too slow and kept looking over his shoulder as they moved past house after house. Something felt wrong. He had to fight the urge to turn his horse around and ride for Gjallarholm as fast as he could.

They soon approached the main entrance and Ash could see the thick gates lying discarded outside the walls. If someone had stormed the gate, shouldn't they be broken inwards? The hairs on his neck stood on end and he leant over to mention this to Yrsa, but as soon as he opened his mouth she raised her hand, signalling for him to be quiet.

They rode through the gates and into the once familiar courtyard. There were bodies scattered throughout the open space, and flies had gathered to feast. The large window shutters that he knew were from Jarl Erik's hall were shattered, one of them hanging limp on a single hinge, creaking mournfully in the wind. Ash saw there were almost as many draugr amongst the dead as there had been defenders, and the terrible smell of rot filled his nostrils. At least they had sold themselves dearly, he thought as he tried to swallow a big lump in his throat. He had known many of these people, and for their lives to have ended in such a horrific way struck grief in his heart. He looked away, so he wouldn't sob in front of the other warriors.

"At least the crows haven't gotten to them yet," a shieldmaiden said in a low voice to Yrsa, who nodded. That was strange, Ash thought. The crows around here were pretty quick to get their next meal, and any dead animal or discarded waste never got to lay alone for long. The shieldmaiden that had spoken to Yrsa bent down and stabbed her spear in a fallen draugr a few times. When it didn't move or stir, she straightened up and resumed inspecting the courtyard.

They all dismounted, and the Berserkers formed a defensive semicircle facing the fortress while the Ulfhednar separated into three small battle units, spaced behind them. Ash's eyes were drawn to the stables where he had spent much of his life. He peered into the darkness of the stable, and a sudden movement in the gloom made him flinch and draw a sharp breath. He opened his mouth to call out a warning to the warriors behind him, when the movement materialised to a bird hopping towards him on the ground. It was a raven, and a large one at that. Ash let his breath out and relaxed a little.

The strange bird stood watching him, its head cocked to one side. Ash felt a strange compulsion to get closer to the bird and took a step towards it. It turned around and took a few hops back toward the stables before stopping and turning its head sideways to watch him again. Ash took another step towards the bird and it hopped off into the stable, disappearing into the darkness. Ash looked behind him. The Jomsvikings were still in their battle formation whilst Olaf and Torsten were head to head, talking in low voices. He turned back to the stable and followed the bird in.

It took his eyes a moment to adjust to the low light, but soon the same carnage he had seen in the courtyard greeted him inside the stable too. Bodies lay strewn across the floor, with the only difference being that he could see no draugr amongst the slain. A rustle of wings turned his attention to the far wall where the raven sat atop a body. It cawed at him before flapping its wings, flying up to the rafters and disappearing into the darkness.

Ash walked towards the figure, taking great care to not look into the stalls as he passed them. The large shapes that laid still in the corners of his eyes, no doubt belonging to the horses he had loved and cared for over many years. He doubted his heart could stand seeing them slaughtered and kept his eyes fixed on the far wall.

He reached the body, vaguely recognising it as a young hirdsman he had seen around the fortress. Across his chest, where the raven had sat, rested a sword, the hilt still in the dead man's hand. It was a beautiful sword, and what parts of it that weren't covered in black blood shone, as if it was made only yesterday. Down the centre of the blade runes had been carved into the steel, and although he couldn't read them, Ash found the beautiful symbols somehow comforting but didn't know why. A sword like this shouldn't be left to rust. Maybe the young hirdsman had family elsewhere who would like it returned? He would take it and give it to Torsten, he would know what to do with it. With care, he pried the sword loose from the dead man's hand and was holding the sword up for closer inspection when he heard a shout from outside, startling him.

"Ho there, in the fortress!"

He scurried outside to find Olaf gripping his large war hammer, eyeing every window in the building, peering as if he could breech the gloom inside.

"I am Jarl Olaf of the Jomsvikings!" he called out in a resounding voice. "Friend or foe, come out to meet your salvation or your doom!" His words echoed around the courtyard, but nothing stirred. He waited a minute and was just opening his mouth to call again when a shout came from the wall.

"The forest! They are coming from the forest!" One of the scouts who had been watching the town from the wall was calling out as he laid an arrow on the string of his bow.

"How many?" Olaf called up to him.

"At least a hundred," the scout said, the colour draining from his face. "And they are coming fast!"

"Goblin shit!" Olaf cursed. "We are cornered in here. Defensive formation at the gate! If we use it as a choke, we have a good chance against their numbers!"

The Berserkers ran to the gate and lined up shoulder to shoulder. It took four of the large warriors to fill the opening and just as many again stood behind them, ready to rotate in as their brethren tired or fell. The Ulfhednar formed up behind them, ready to lend a spear where needed.

A tall woman at the front began a deep growling chant that was taken up by the rest of the Berserkers in the courtyard. They stomped their feet and slammed their swords and axes on their shields in a steady rhythm as the chant grew in intensity. The hairs on Ash's arms and neck stood up as something he had only heard stories about took place all around him. He was hearing a Berserker battle song for the first time. He stood in awe as the song echoed around the courtyard and the rhythm seemed to resound in his very bones. Ash could have sworn that a soft red glow escaped their eyes as they worked themselves into a state of rage and power. To him, they seemed to grow taller, and at times he couldn't tell if men and women in skins surrounded him or enormous bears.

Olaf let out a bellowing roar and was joined by the other Berserkers. It was a wordless, primal challenge to anything that would stand against them. A heartbeat later, heavy thuds were heard as bodies slammed against the shield wall and the roaring Berserkers began their lethal dance, axes and swords becoming a blur, black blood spraying into the air. They were ferocious and Ash couldn't see how any foe could possibly stand against them.

Their line held and Ash felt a glimmer of hope, but he still couldn't shake the terrible feeling that something was wrong. He turned and ran his eyes over all the windows but could see nothing. He forced himself to look at the many corpses in the courtyard. There were a lot of dead draugr littering the courtyard. Maybe that's why there weren't any crows? There was the strange raven, but there should've been hundreds of birds. Not even the ever-hungry crows would scavenge them, he imagined. Plenty of humans, though, that should have attracted the birds. Unless…

He looked closer at a fallen draugr that laid a few paces from him. Did it just move? Ash stared at it, holding his breath so he could remain still, looking for the slightest movement. He was just about to give up when the creature opened its eyelids and locked its dead, milky eyes on him. Ash stumbled backwards, tripping over the body of a hirdsman, stepped on his own cloak and could not right himself and fell hard on his back. He had let go of his spear to brace himself and watched it tumble away, out of his reach.

"Trap! It's a trap! Behind you!" Ash yelled as loud as he could, a second before all the draugr in the courtyards stood up, as if on an invisible signal, and launched themselves towards the Jomsvikings. Ash's yell had given them only a second's warning, but that was enough for the fast Ulfhednar to launch against the monsters and push them back. This came at the price of terrible losses, and Ash saw several Ulfhednar dragged into the mass of draugr.

The draugr that had awoken close to Ash still had its milky eyes on him and came at him with terrible speed, its horrible jaw wide open, a moan of hunger escaping it. Ash Shifted and rolled backwards and landing on his feet, he swapped the sword, now his only weapon, into his right hand and sprung up to face his attacker. Its movements were slowed, but the draugr still moved much faster than a normal human would. What little training Ash had received from Yrsa kicked in. He dodged down under the creature's arms and thrust the sword in the chest of his attacker like he would a spear. It slid into the draugr with ease, all the way to the handle. He must have driven the sword into its heart, because the ghoul fell to the ground, unmoving. He pulled the sword from the body, before looking around for any other attackers near him, but seeing none, he turned to find Yrsa.

He saw her duck and weave, fighting the draugr in the courtyard, her spear flashing with incredible speed and bodies piling up at her feet. Ash moved to stand behind the line of Ulfhednar, ready to fight if he had to. Looking at the horrid, undead faces of the draugr pushing closer, his legs felt numb, and he had to grasp the sword tightly so it didn't slip out of his sweaty hand. Their hungry moans echoed around the courtyard, and he had to fight the temptation to drop his weapon to cover his ears from the unsettling sound.

The ground in the courtyard had turned slick with blood as the battle raged. To his horror, he saw more draugr spilling out of the main fortress, adding to the already overwhelming force facing them in the courtyard. Many Berserkers had run to the aid of the Ulfhednar as they were buckling under the sheer numbers of attackers. However, that had left them thin at the gates and before long the defensive line there broke and more of the monsters entered the melee from outside the walls. He saw the scouts on the walls being cut off from the rest of the warriors and it wasn't long before a wave of draugr swept over them and they were torn to pieces.

"Fall back! Fall back!" Olaf's voice roared. The Jomsvikings began moving backwards, closing their formation. They now stood with the stables on their left and the fortress on their right, creating another choking point, allowing them to fight on one front again. There were, however, at the end of the two buildings behind them, only the protective palisade connecting the two and they were trapped, with no way out.

The Jomsvikings fought well, cutting down the enemy like saplings, but there seemed to be an endless supply of the draugr. Soon the warriors tired and died by the dozens as the horde threw themselves at them in overwhelming numbers.

From the back, Ash saw that just six Berserkers held the front line, with not even a dozen Ulfhednar behind them, jabbing their spears with lightning-quick thrusts between the larger warriors.

Ash searched among the Berserkers for Torsten, and his heart dropped when he couldn't see his friend.

He looked around and with relief saw the large man standing next to Olaf, in a discussion with the Jarl. Wounded in several places, Torsten stood panting and leaning on his great axe, but he was alive. Ash saw the men look around and Olaf pointed behind them and Torsten nodded. The large man ran off and kicked open a smaller wooden door set in the fortress's wall. He peeked inside, then turned to Olaf and waved.

"Fall back into the fortress!" Olaf called to the remaining fighters. Yrsa grabbed Ash by the shoulder and began pushing him towards the small door. It caught him by surprise and he once again stepped on his cloak, the clasp tearing as it fell to the ground. As he bent to pick it up, Yrsa snapped, "Leave it!" before pushing him towards the door again.

A terrible roar blasted out from inside the fortress, and a second later a large shape launched from the broken window of the Jarl's hall. With a crash, it landed amongst the horde of draugr and a black eyed, muscular, drab-green creature stood up, almost twice as tall as the undead surrounding it. Curled horns grew from its forehead and vicious looking, short spikes protruded from its shoulders and upper arms. The thing snarled, revealing two rows of long, sharp teeth as it hunched forward and spread out two enormous arms. It felt like Ash's heart stopped when he felt the creature's eyes land on him, pure hate radiating out from the monster.

"It's a thursr! Quick, fall back! Fall back!" Olaf's voice rang out over the sounds of battle. This was the first time Ash had ever heard a touch of fear in the Jarl's voice. The large battle troll began throwing draugr out of his way as he pushed towards the combatants. To Ash, it seemed like the troll was focussed on him and the fear made his legs weak. The Jomsvikings disappeared one by one through the door.

Ash stood wide eyed, staring at the enormous troll ploughing through the draugr towards them. He had imagined big trolls before, but seeing one in reality, heading straight for him was the most frightening thing he had ever seen. A firm hand grabbed the nape of his tunic and pulled him backwards.

"Nothing but death out here, lad," Torsten's voice cut through the moans and wails of the undead as he pulled Ash through the doorway.

When only the last two Berserkers remained outside, they refused to follow the other Jomsvikings, and still fighting one yelled, "Me and Bjarke will hold them while you barricade the door! Tonight we feast in Valhalla!" Then, as tired and battle-weary as they both seemed, they looked at each other and laughed, attacking the horde of draugr with renewed strength, pushing them back a step.

"Save me a seat!" Torsten called to them. "We might not be far behind!"

They were still laughing when Torsten slammed the thick wooden door shut and the remaining warriors pushed a heavy table in front of the door, followed by an assortment of other furniture. They found themselves in the fortress's kitchen. Three large fireplaces with spits ran along one wall, but the fires had gone cold. Large, well-worn tables filled most of the floor space, still laden with breads, vegetables and meat, which now had drawn flies, having been left unattended for a while.

There were several doors leading out of the kitchen, into the fortress, so there were plenty of ways for the draugr to reach them. There remained only three Berserkers, including Torsten and Olaf, and four Ulfhednar, including Yrsa and Ash. They could hear the sounds of battle on the other side of the door, but soon they grew quiet. A solid thud rattled the hinges, pushing the furniture half an inch.

"It won't take the thursr long to get through," Olaf sighed. "We are trapped and will join Bjorn and Bjarke in Valhalla shortly. The best we can do is to take as many of them with us as possible, preferably the troll."

"There is a way out." All eyes turned to Ash, who felt awkward with the attention, but pushed on. "I used to play here as a child. We can go through the storerooms into the cellar. From there, there is a passage through the rock that leads to a small exit by the river. They sometimes take the big pots there for scrubbing. We can get out that way!"

Olaf smiled and slapped Ash on the shoulder. "Lead the way, lad, and be quick about it!"

Ash crossed the kitchen and opened a door into a large store-room that held shelves laden with various dry goods. He paused for a second, seeing several bodies in a corner, lying in a pool of blood. Another wave of sorrow came over him when he rec-ognised Hulda, one of the serving girls among the bodies. She had always been kind to him, often giving him a smile and a friendly word as they passed each other. Now her usually radiant face wore a grimace of fear and her always neat and clean apron was stained black by her own blood. Ash blinked away the tears that filled his eyes and he could feel a physical pain in his heart. He tore his eyes away from the sight and rushed through the room. With the warriors in tow, he reached another door at the end of the shelving and ripped it open. He was looking at a broad set of stone stairs leading down into the dark. His heart sank as he realized that it was pitch black in the cellar and it would be impossible to navigate it.

As if reading his mind, Yrsa reached into her pouch and pulled out a smooth stone, the size of her palm and spoke, "*Lyse.*" No sooner had she said the word than a rune appeared on the stone and shone bright as daylight, lighting up the darkened stairs. "A gift from Rani," she smiled.

A crash rang out from the kitchen behind them, and the troll's roar filled the room. That was all the encouragement Ash needed and he ran down the stairs as fast as he could, Yrsa and the others only a step behind him. The light from Yrsa's stone spilled over his shoulders, illuminating the staircase, allowing Ash to move down the steps as fast as his legs would carry him. They came down into a large cold-cellar, full of barrels, crates and sacks that Ash weaved around as fast as he could. Slams and cracks from up the stairs told him that the enemies had turned the barricading furniture to splinters and were now in the kitchen.

When he reached the door at the end of the cellar, he ripped it open and was greeted with cold, damp air. He looked out over the natural cave set in the stone that Hornsborg rested on. He had explored here as a child, when he still lived in the servant's quarters and knew that although there were several tunnels to their sides, they were all dead ends. The only exit from here was through a fortified door in a thick stonewall that had been built to seal off the naturally occurring cave opening that led to the river outside the fortress.

He ran down the passage on hard dirt, compacted by generations of pot scrubbers, towards the door and freedom. Yrsa's light was throwing shadows around them as they ran, and Ash couldn't help letting out a triumphant whoop when it fell on the man-made stone wall and the door that would lead them out of the fortress.

Reaching the door, he tore off the wooden spar that secured the door from the inside and put his shoulder to it. It didn't move. He tried again, but to no avail.

"It's stuck!" he yelled; the panic obvious in his voice. The moans and thuds could be heard from the cellar as the draugr made their way towards them.

"Step aside," Torsten swept him out of the way with a thick arm before throwing his shoulder with full force into the door. A sliver of daylight appeared as the door opened a finger's width, but that was as far as it got. Torsten put his face to the crack, peering out, and swore.

"It has been blocked off. Stones and logs piled high against it." He slammed his shoulder against the door a few more times, but it would not give any further. Ash could hear the burbling of the river just beyond the door and had never longed for anything more in his life. They heard a moan as the first draugr entered the doorway

159

behind them, followed by others, dozens spilling out, their wails echoing around the cave.

"So, we fight," Olaf said, hefting his war hammer in two hands. The few remaining Jomsvikings lined up in formation, preparing to meet death as they had lived their lives. Their faces were serious and showed no fear; some even seemed calm, verging on serene. Yrsa pulled Ash backwards so they stood with their backs against the rock. Torsten went to stand in the line, but Yrsa put a hand on his arm, stopping him.

"Let's stay with the boy," she said. "We'll help him make his mother proud." Torsten looked her in the eyes for a second then shrugged, taking a step back, placing his hand on Ash's shoulder. Yrsa positioned herself on his other side and gave him an encouraging smile before turning towards the enemy.

"You have all done me proud, each and every one," Olaf said in a loud voice, eyes never leaving the enemy as they lumbered towards them. "I will personally fill your horns at Odin's table tonight."

A shieldmaiden laughed, "If there is any left for us when you're done with it, Olaf." They were all still laughing when the horde crashed into them and their weapons became a blur, draugr after draugr falling before them. Ash's stomach was a painful knot of fear, but he knew if he fought bravely, he would soon meet his mother as she and the other Valkyries would come to collect their souls from the battlefield. He just hoped it wouldn't hurt too much.

He Shifted for the last time and the battle in front of him slowed down. The flow of draugr stopped as the large troll squeezed himself through the door, its raging roars sounding deep and strange because of his slowed perception of time. He couldn't help thinking that the troll looked familiar somehow. Not that it mattered anymore.

Ash saw the remaining warriors fall, one by one, in front of him. Olaf swung his hammer like a whirlwind, swatting away a dozen of the undead, limbs and heads crushed, splattering him with dark blood. He was a terrible force to behold, his strength and power beyond any human Ash had ever seen. The undead threw themselves at him, and Olaf crushed them like they were insects, his hammer always finding its mark, moving in a blur. But there were just too many. Olaf over-reached and in smashing a draugr to the side of him, he opened himself to another on the other side. The ghoul jumped on him, latching on in a deadly embrace as it tried to sink its teeth into his shoulder through his chain mail. Olaf staggered and several others threw themselves at him and he was pushed to the ground, his hammer falling from his hand with a clatter on the stone floor. Soon, the jarl was overwhelmed and disappeared under their writhing mass.

Yrsa cried out as her father fell. Ash looked at her and saw tears running down her cheeks, her face a grimace of pain, but she stayed next to him, her spear ready in her hands. The troll was through the doorway and was pushing forwards with giant strides, knocking the draugr out of the way as it went with the sheer force of its momentum. Its eyes were locked on Ash and it had a triumphant grin on its bestial face as it drew back a clawed hand to strike.

CHAPTER 23

R OGHALD WATCHED THE RIDERS APPROACH HORNSBORG with excitement. He had known that it wouldn't be long before Gjallarholm or one of the other southern Jarls would send warriors to the fortress, but sheer luck had brought some the very next day. Having worked through the night, he had made all the preparations for a warm welcome.

Although the draugr were mindless and difficult to steer, his control of them over a short distance was improving and he was confident the trap he had set would be successful. The hard part had been the draugr waiting in the forest. They were too far away for him to control with his mind, so he had placed one hidden outside the fortress wall, within his range. He would send the draugr on an indirect route to rouse the others as soon as a target entered the gate. The draugr didn't need to eat for long periods of time. If they didn't, they would just emaciate over time until their bones could not be held together anymore and they would fall apart, but that would take months. Nor did they ever need to sleep, so his trap could be waiting to spring for a long time.

The best part was that he didn't need to roam the countryside in the rain, whittling down the humans one patrol at a time. This way he could sit as comfortable as a spider in its web, waiting for the humans to come to him. He was sure his masters would be pleased. He just needed to make sure that enough people survived for him to deliver to his masters in order to fill the ranks of the draugr, but also so he could question them about the boy. There were often more than a few wounded, unable to fight, that would suit that purpose well.

With Jarl Erik dead, and he savoured the thought, half his revenge was claimed already. When he found Ash, his master's promise to him would be fulfilled and his revenge would be complete. At first, his pact with the trolls had only been to meet his own ends, but a sense of loyalty had grown for Jotunheim. Humankind had always let him down and had turned against him, through no fault of his own, but with the trolls, he felt a part of something greater than himself. He finally had the recognition as a warrior that had always been denied him, and it felt like he belonged. He was determined to serve his masters well, even after his sworn vengeance on Ash was achieved.

Roghald watched the humans ride through the gate, and after dismounting they spread out across the courtyard. He sent a mental command to the hidden draugr, who set off towards the forest to fetch the rest.

Jomsvikings, he noted, Berserkers and Ulfhednar. And Jarl Olaf himself! He assessed how many draugr he had and reassured himself that there were enough, even against such a formidable force. Besides, the whole point of the trap was to surprise attack their flank and overcome them with sheer numbers. And if they should for some reason defeat the horde, he would just slip away and start anew.

Waiting for the message to reach the draugr in the forest, he watched the group. All were typical warriors and shieldmaidens, except one. Male or female, he couldn't tell, because they wore a hooded cloak, but they were a bit shorter and ganglier than the others and didn't move with the same confidence as the seasoned warriors. He had a strange feeling when he looked at them, as if they were familiar in some way, but couldn't put his finger on it. He watched the person disappear into the stables for a minute, but soon forgot about it as Jarl Olaf began shouting in the courtyard.

"You will have your answer soon enough, Jarl Olaf," he whispered to himself. Soon one of the guards that had been sent to the wall shouted, and the Jomsvikings changed their formation to defend the gate. Looking out over the town, he could see his draugr running and shambling at high speed towards the fortress. Excellent.

The draugr reached the gate and threw themselves at the Berserkers holding the frontline and were cut down by the dozens before even a single defender fell. Roghald waited a little longer, making sure that everyone's attention was on the battle, before sending his next mental command to the very much alive, if you could call it that, draugr lying around the courtyard. Draugr didn't breathe and could therefore appear dead until roused. Even if they had kicked one, it would not have flinched.

He snapped away from his train of thought when he heard a shout and looked up to see the gangly one lying on the ground, calling out a warning to the others, who were now turning to face the new threat. Roghald swore to himself as the surprise element of his trap had been ruined, but soon he saw that the draugr were overwhelming the Jomsvikings all the same.

They were down to just a handful of defenders and were pushed in between the fortress and the stable, and it would be just a matter of time now. Roghald was just about to congratulate himself, when he saw one of the Berserkers kick in the side door to the kitchens and wave to the others. Roghald sighed. He hoped this wouldn't be a drawn-out affair that would see him combing through the whole fortress again, searching for hidden humans. He reminded himself to barricade that door before next time.

Roghald was watching the warriors retreat towards the door when the gangly one tripped and its cloak fell off. His breath caught in his throat as he realized he was looking at Ash. The boy looked somewhat different, and he could tell, clear as day, that the boy was troll like himself, but there was no doubt that it was him.

The rage filled Roghald like a volcano about to erupt and he could not have stopped himself even if he had wanted to. His body began growing and changing as the laughter of the troll within filled his mind. The pain of the horns and spikes growing from his body was intense, but it was swept away by the fury that filled him and escaped in a great roar. Roghald threw himself out the window once more and into the courtyard, crushing several draugr as he landed with a heavy thud. Ash would meet his end by Roghald's claws.

He waded through his undead and was infuriated to see the door to the kitchens slam shut before he got there. Two men had stayed behind, holding the door. They had shields and axes and were laughing as they cut down his draugr as soon as they got within reach. Roghald picked up an undead next to him and, raising it over his head with two arms, threw it as hard as he could. It slammed into the man on the left, pushing him into the door before he fell, the draugr on top of him. His comrade turned to help him, but in doing so exposed his back and several of the monsters threw themselves on him, tearing and biting as they went down.

It took Roghald only a few seconds to clear the draugr and throw the now dead or dying warriors to the side so he could kick at the kitchen entry. On the second strike, the door and frame splintered, and he could push into the room through a hastily assembled barricade. He looked around the kitchen and found it empty. There were several doorways leading out of the kitchens, but he saw the one leading to the store and cellars ajar. He smiled. He knew the building as well as anyone who had lived here, and one of the first things he had done when he had seized the fortress was to barricade the small entryway leading out to the river. They were trapped.

Roghald sent some draugr ahead, in case they had set an ambush. He followed them through the storeroom, coming to the stairs leading down to the cellars. It was a narrow stone passage and he had to squeeze through, only just being able to work his bulk down the steps. He entered the cellar to see a light shining through the open passage at the other end. Draugr were now running past him, pushing to get to the humans.

He hurried up to the door and stuck his head through. A light was shining from the end of the cave, right by the blocked door, where his draugr were fighting what was left of the Jomsvikings. The doorway was a small one, but he forced himself through. He could see Ash at the back of the group and his rage ignited anew.

Once through the door, Roghald ran towards Ash. The boy's face was a mask of fear when he saw his death approaching, and the sweet taste of vengeance filled Roghald. The troll in his mind was laughing a maniacal cackle, and Roghald could feel its excitement in their shared mind. He was only a few steps away, his arm pulled back so he could tear Ash's head off with one blow, when the very rock behind Ash shimmered and moved. Then it parted, like it was made of clay, revealing an opening. The boy, having pressed himself against the wall, fell backwards into the rift. A shieldmaiden and a warrior who had been standing next to the boy, turned at the movement and, weapons raised, launched after him through the opening.

Roghald threw himself past the last combatants but could only watch as the stone closed itself a heartbeat before he got there, the light disappearing with the shieldmaiden.

"No!" He slammed his fists on the rock but was rewarded by nothing but dull thuds against the solid stone.

"NO!"

ASH WAS WATCHING the troll closing in on them. It was slow, as he was Shifted, but relentless. Ash pressed himself against the rock behind him. He prepared himself to go down fighting, but the sheer size of the thursr removed all hope from his heart. He saw the troll who seemed to have had its eyes locked on Ash, look over Ash's shoulder and its face changed from triumphant to surprised. Then Ash fell backwards.

Where there had been nothing but stone a moment before, there was now open air. Ash fell hard, knocking the air from his lungs.

Confused, he looked up to see stone walls all around him, like he was lying in a tunnel. Seconds later, a firm hand closed around the nape of his tunic and with a jerk, he was dragged further and further into the darkness, only able to watch as the walls rushed by. He bumped along the ground and losing his concentration; he stopped Shifting and time sped up to normal again.

Soon he was shrouded in darkness and lost all sense of direction. The grip on his collar released and he hit the back of his head on the hard ground. A weak light appeared from an opening in front of him. The light grew brighter and soon Yrsa and Torsten jumped out of the tunnel he had come through, their weapons drawn. Behind them the tunnel closed, immovable granite once more.

The light from Yrsa's stone revealed that they were in a massive cavern. It felt cold and damp. Any sound they made would turn into a strange echo, and the air was as still as the grave. His friends stood where they had entered, seeming uncertain about how to proceed. He could tell by Yrsa's movements and rapid breathing that she was still Shifted and Torsten had an angry, restless air about him, looking like he was about to launch into an attack. They both had their weapons trailed on something behind him.

Ash turned around and saw what had pulled him into the cave; a short, sturdy man, who would only reach to Ash's shoulder, but twice as broad. The man wore a sleeveless vest and worn leather pants. He had golden bracelets wrapped around thick arms crossed over a round belly and a stern expression aimed at his friends. Wide set, piercing blue eyes over a broad nose and a thick, short white beard, bored into them. The head was broad, with thick, fleshy ears that stood straight out, and golden earrings glittered in Yrsa's light.

"No need for that. The wolf and the bear can put their teeth away," The voice was deep, and spoke slow. It was paced as if it didn't speak often and had to think about every word. Ash heard a rustle and turned to see Torsten fastening his axe on his belt. Yrsa turned to the Berserker, her eyes wide and questioning, but the burly man only shook his head.

"It's a *dvergir*. If he wanted it so, we would be dead by now."

She looked surprised but lowered her spear. A dvergir? A dwarf? They were the legendary smiths and crafters, who had created Thor's hammer, *Mjolnir*, and Odin's spear, *Gungnir*, amongst other fantastical items. They were also said to be shrewd and highly untrustworthy. According to legend, anytime anyone had dealings with them it more often ended poorly than not. Ash turned around and stared at the dwarf in disbelief.

"I am Eikinri. I came for the trolling, not a bear and not a wolf, this was not agreed."

Trolling? That must be him. But who would send a dwarf for him? Ash remembered being told about the jotunn that hunted his parents and a chill went through his body.

"Are you sent by Burrugandr?" Ash asked with caution. The dwarf grimaced and spat at his feet, angered. He crunched his jaw in hesitation for a moment before answering.

"No. Odin of the Aesir sends me. A debt has to be paid," he grumbled. "But the agreement was for the trolling, no other. I will return the bear and the wolf from whence they came."

"No, please!" Ash pleaded. "They will be killed. There is no hope where we came from." The dwarf didn't reply, he just crossed his arms again and jutted out his lower jaw in a clear denial of his request. Ash felt anger blossoming in the pit of his stomach. He had lost most things precious to him, the death of the two Jarls, Jomsvikings and everyone he had known in Hornsborg still fresh in his mind. Not to mention the lives of all the innocent men,

women and children who had been slain since this had all started. Midgard lay open for the trolls to ravage and conquer, and he
knew in his heart that he had to do all he could to stop it. If the key
to defeating them was in his troll blood, then so be it. But he could
not do it alone. He needed Torsten and Yrsa to face what was to
come. Their support and guidance felt like a beacon of light in a
dark world, and he knew he would be lost without them. Besides,
he had grown very fond of them both and could not stand the
thought of losing them.

He pulled himself up to his full height, which wasn't very impressive to begin with, but he crossed his arms, mirroring the dwarf
and said in a firm voice, "No." The stocky dwarf raised his eyebrows
for a second, but soon resumed his stern face and growled, a deep
sound that vibrated through the air in the cavern. Ash didn't care
anymore. He was sick of being afraid, sick of having no say in his
own fate, always being thrown from one end to the other.

"No." he repeated. "If you return them, you will have to return
me as well, and the debt you owe will remain unpaid."

He met Eikinri's glare head on and a lifetime seemed to pass
before the dwarf snarled, "So be it!" and stomped off down the
cavern. Ash turned to his friends who looked at him like he had
grown a horn in the middle of his forehead.

"What?" he said, but they both raised their hands, showing that
they had nothing to say. Yrsa looked over his shoulder as the dwarf
disappeared around a block of stone.

"We should probably follow him. We are underground with no
idea about how to get out," she said. Torsten and Ash looked in
the direction the dwarf had taken, and with no sight of him, they
hurried along the same path. Before long, they caught up with the
morose dwarf and heeled him as he led them through a maze of
caverns and passages, naturally occurring in the rock. Ash was glad
for Yrsa's luminous stone since their rescuer appeared to have no
problems finding his way in the dark. The thought of navigating
through the unknown with no light was an unpleasant one.

A.F. JANSSON

The first time they came to a dead end at a rock wall, Ash was astounded to see the short man sink his arm into the solid stone all the way to the elbow, as if it was made of warm butter. The dwarf then mumbled under his breath and the stone parted from his arm until a tunnel large enough to fit him opened up, and he walked through. Unfortunately for Torsten, who was twice the height of the dwarf, that meant that he had to crawl on his hands and knees to fit through. His muttered swearing reverberated through the tunnel. Ash, himself having to stoop, followed close behind the dwarf, eyeing the newly opened tunnel with suspicion, fearing it would start closing around them.

They travelled like this for hours, always moving down, deeper and deeper into the underground. They walked through narrow tunnels and enormous caverns and skirted on thin ledges along bottomless crevasses through an ever-changing landscape never seen before by human eyes. They would come across patches of fluorescent mushrooms, sometimes covering the surrounding walls. At these times, Yrsa would cover her stone and they could admire the strange beauty of the underworld. Sometimes things would scurry away into the dark as they drew near, and Ash couldn't help imagining the untold horrors that hid just outside their radius of light. He also tried not to think about the tonnes and tonnes of rock above their heads, and he imagined its weight pressing down on them. The feeling got worse the deeper they got, but he pushed it to the back of his mind, focusing on the ground before him and placing one foot in front of the other.

He had attempted to talk to Eikinri to distract himself several times, but the dwarf ignored him and continued his relentless march into the underworld. The only time he spoke was when they entered an enormous cavern that had a wide lake of still, black water in the middle of it. The path around it was wide enough for ten horses to ride abreast, but Eikinri warned them to stay close to the wall as they passed without elaborating further. They followed behind the dwarf, skirting the wall. Once Ash spotted a large ripple in the water near the bank keeping pace with them, he continued with his back pressed against the wall until they were clear of the underground lake.

After long hours, they stopped at another wall, but looking at it, Ash saw that it differed from the world of grey granite they had been travelling through. It was white and smooth, with no cracks or marks blemishing its surface. Eikinri stopped in front of it and pushed his hand into the white stone, having much more difficulty than before. Beads of sweat broke out on his broad nose and forehead as he muttered under his breath. It was slow, but the stone gave way and expanded into a tunnel. The dwarf was breathless when he finished, wiping his brow, but quickly stepped into the tunnel, turning to Ash and his friends to bark, "Make haste!"

He set off at a much faster pace. Ash and Yrsa had to jog to keep up and Ash turned to see the tunnel already sealing, only a dozen steps behind them. Torsten was crawling like a madman, the rattle of his weapons and armour filling the tunnel while the Berserker swore with every breath. They followed the tunnel for only a short distance, before they stumbled into a softly lit room, furnished with a long bench along one wall and a small table with two chairs. All the furniture was made of grey stone, but delicately carved with intricate patterns. The walls were of the same white rock that they had passed through. Bands of runes, the size of Ash's hand, framed the floor, ceiling and walls. It was these runes that provided the glowing light. There was an arched doorway at one end, large enough to accommodate the dwarf; it too had a band of runes around it, and through it they could see another room furnished in the same fashion. The tunnel closed behind them almost as soon as they had entered, the wall assuming the same smooth surface as the others. The air in the room was dry and held a hint of sulphur.

"Where are we?" Yrsa whispered, looking around the room. The dwarf gave her an irritated look.

"My home. In Yggdrasil."

"Everything is on Yggdrasil," Torsten said lying on his back on the floor where he had collapsed after his high-speed crawl. "It is the tree at the centre of the universe and all the worlds rest on its branches."

"No, human. Inside Yggdrasil, beneath Midgard, is where I have made my home." All their jaws fell open as what Eikinri said sunk in. They were inside a branch of the tree at the centre of the universe, a whole world resting above their heads. They couldn't help but look up and stare at the ceiling.

"I have tired myself and need to rest." the dwarf sagged his shoulders. "I suggest you do the same. You may rest in this room." He turned to walk out the arched doorway.

"Wait," Yrsa called after him. "What is going on? Why was Ash brought here?" Eikinri gave her a haughty stare before turning to Ash.

"Rest, then we will speak," he replied. Backing out of the room, he reached up above the arched doorway and mumbled a few words. The glow in the runes surrounding the opening faded and went out, and the walls closed in and sealed the gap. They were locked in the small room that now only had four blank walls and no way in or out. Torsten walked up to the wall and ran his hands over it, before knocking on the solid surface at various spots.

"Curses!" He muttered. "We are trapped in the underground, in the very world tree itself, at the mercy of an irritable dwarf that can walk through stone. I wonder who is better off, our brothers and sisters feasting in Valhalla, or us?" He sat down on the stone bench with a heavy thud, placing his head in his hands. It had been a long day for everyone. Ash sat down next to his friend, having to reach up to put his hand on the Berserker's shoulder.

"I'm sure we'll be fine," he said to Torsten. "We will rest and talk to Eikinri later."

"At least we are safe for the moment," Yrsa chimed in, pushing off the wall she had been leaning against. "Let me see to your wounds, Torsten."

The big man gave her a tired smile and allowed her to tend to him with a salve and bandages from her pack. When she was done, Torsten caught her eye.

"I'm sorry about Olaf." Yrsa met his gaze. Her eyes watered and she pressed her lips together, but she took a deep breath and nodded once at the Berserker.

"Thanks. The old badger is probably busy drinking Valhalla dry as we speak. I will see him soon enough."

Torsten slapped her on the shoulder and gave her a mischievous grin. "He's probably just enjoying the peace and quiet until you get there."

Yrsa gave him a brief smile before punching his arm. Torsten laughed at this, but the second she turned away to pack up her remaining bandages, the Berserker rubbed his arm with a grimace, and stretched it as if trying to get the sensation back.

The bench was long enough that they could all stretch out and Ash took off his leather armour and tunic and rolling it into a ball, he fashioned a pillow for himself. The room was warm and he was comfortable in his undershirt. Lying down, he made himself as comfortable as one could expect on a stone bench and drifted off to sleep to the sound of his friends' hushed conversation.

Ash opened his eyes to find himself standing on a ridge, high above the surrounding lands. Before him, rolling hills and lush forests surrounded yellow wheat fields gently swaying in the wind. He saw little towns dotting the landscape. Within them he could make out children at play as adults laughed and worked together. He felt the warm sun on his shoulders and a sense of peace and harmony filled him.

Ash realized someone was standing next to him and looked up to see a tall man with a long grey beard, leaning on a spear. He was gazing out over the landscape but turned to look down on Ash. He saw that the man was old, his face a map of fine wrinkles and he was missing an eye. The socket where his eye should have been was a gaping hollow, and in it he could see stars glinting and swirling, like the sky on a clear and frosty night.

The old man smiled at him, but soon his face became serious and he raised his arm and pointed to the horizon. Ash followed his arm and he could see a large shape in the distance. It was the enormous creature that had haunted Ash's dreams before, searching for him with its lantern. The giant lifted one foot, as large as a city, and stomped once onto the ground. An entire forest crumbled beneath the giant. The force of the stomp caused a blast of wind to roll across the landscape, spreading further and further out.

When it reached Ash, it tore at his clothes and he had to lean forward so as not to lose his balance. The wind died down, but it had carried a stench of decay, unlike anything Ash had experienced before. It smelled of putrid death and the stench lingered. Ash watched as a blight spread out from the giant, like dark veins snaking their way across the land. Everything these dark rivers touched withered and died - trees lost their leaves and distorted into black spindly things, grass turned to dust, and fields to stinking marshes. In the towns that had been so full of life, lay nothing but bleached bones around crumbling buildings.

When the veins of sickness reached the ground Ash was standing on, he had to take a few steps sideways to avoid them. His heart filled with nothing but hopelessness and despair. He turned back to the old man.

"You have to stop this. Why aren't you doing anything?" Ash demanded. He could see that the decay had affected the old man too. His cheeks were hollow, and his skin was cracked and blistered, blood filling his one good eye.

"That is the wrong question," the old man croaked.

Ash stared at the man who started to fall apart, little pieces breaking off his face and drifting away on the wind.

"What can we do?" Ash pleaded with him, his voice breaking. "Where is this coming from?"

"Ah!" the old man said, smiling and raising a disintegrating finger in front of Ash. "That is a much better question."

In seconds, the old man was nothing but dust, drifting on the wind and Ash found himself alone again. He turned to look at the giant on the horizon. His eyes met Ash's and he could feel the hate radiating from the creature.

Ash could only watch as he raised his enormous club, high into the air, before bringing it down on the ground in front of him in an explosion of dust and debris and as the cloud reached him, the entire world turned black.

CHAPTER 24

ROGHALD PUSHED HIS WAY PAST THE DRAUGR IN THE courtyard. He transformed back from thursr to his usual self. It was always with a sense of longing that he resumed his human shape. The powers and anger of the troll were intoxicating, but he found it difficult to think when the soul he shared a body with was always laughing or babbling gibberish. No doubt the creature was mad. Maybe because it was trapped in Roghald's head, but maybe it had always been mad? He had tried to communicate with it, but it had never responded in any sensible way. At times, he could still hear the troll, even after he resumed his human form, and he felt a niggle of concern about it.

As he waited for the last mad sobs to die away, he tried to concentrate on the problem at hand. The anger still seethed in him, but he brought it under control. How had Ash escaped him? What had snatched Roghald's revenge from right under his claws? It hadn't been a troll, or he would've known when he looked at it, but it wasn't human either. He had so many questions he could not answer. As fortune would have it, he had someone to ask.

He stopped by a body being held down on the cobblestones by two draugr. Bite marks covered his face and hands and his right leg was pointing at a painful angle, but he was breathing through gritted teeth and he stared at Roghald with murder in his eyes. Roghald smiled at the man.

"Welcome to slavery, Jarl Olaf."

"WAKE UP, TROLLING." A firm hand shook Ash's shoulder. He looked up to see Eikinri the dwarf standing above him, a sour look on his face. Ash's eyelids felt like they had been glued together, and his body ached from a restless night on a stone bench, but he sat up, stretching his sore limbs. He looked further down the bench, at his friends, still asleep, stretched out and snoring. That was strange. They were both light sleepers and would have woken up when the dwarf had spoken.

Eikinri saw the questioning look on his face and muttered, "I have seen to it that they shall sleep a little longer. We have matters to discuss." He turned on the spot and marched out through the now reappeared doorway. Ash stood up and followed him out. He came into a room, very much like the one they had slept in, only this was better furnished, with another arched doorway at the opposite end. All the furniture was made of stone, except the bed, which had an actual mattress and several furs spread out on top of it.

Eikinri nodded to the bench whilst seating himself at the table. He gave Ash a long appraising stare and didn't seem to think much of what he saw.

"You are here because I have a debt to Odin of the Aesir. I am reluctant to share my home with anyone, let alone a troll-blood, and while you are here you will abide by my will, is that clear?"

Ash was still confused, but he nodded.

"Your friends will remain asleep while you are here. You are not to plead for them to be awoken until we are done. To them, no time will seem to have passed since we left the room, until I once again open it. No harm will come to them, upon my word."

Ash turned to look behind him, only to see that the doorway had once again disappeared, leaving his friends on the other side. He turned back to the dwarf and nodded again.

"While you are here, you will under no circumstances use any tools or items unless specifically instructed by me. Is that understood?"

Once again Ash was forced to agree.

"Good," Eikinri slapped his hand on the table. "Any questions?"

"Erh…" Ash started. "Why exactly am I here?"

The dwarf mumbled something into his beard that Ash couldn't make out.

"Sorry?" Ash asked, leaning forward.

"I said, you are to be my apprentice!" he growled, standing up and walked out of the one remaining doorway.

Ash watched the dwarf leave, eyebrows raised. Apprentice? Apprentice doing what? He got up and hurried after the dwarf. As he got through the doorway, he stopped and his mouth fell open. It was a much larger chamber than the rooms he had seen so far. He couldn't have hit the other end with a stone's throw if he tried.

The space was cluttered with workbenches along all the walls, broken up only by various forges and other strange constructs. Ash counted dozens of anvils spread around the room and saw piles of different rock and ore laying all about the place. In the centre of the large workshop was a wide, stone bricked well, full to the brim with clear water.

Looking around the walls, he could see that every workbench was in a state of disarray; tools and strange metallic shapes and rods were cluttering most of the working space. It seemed as if the dwarf preferred to build a new workbench whenever he started a new project, rather than clearing up the previous one. The sight mesmerised Ash, and a part of him felt great excitement as he tried to take everything in at once. The dwarf came and stood next to him.

"I have a system and I know where everything is, so touch nothing if I don't give you reason to," Eikinri said, raising a warning finger.

"What is it you do, exactly?" Ash asked.

"I am a Stonesmith," he said, looking out over the tools and benches. "Like your father was, I am told. And let me add that that was the *only* reason I agreed to have a troll-blood in my workshop, debt or no debt."

"You mean you are going to teach me to move through stone like you do?" Ash said, raising his eyebrows.

"That's only a part of it and hardly the most important part." Eikinri snorted.

Ash's fingers were itching to get started. To learn the trade would bring him closer to the father he had never known. Last night's strange dream still fresh in his mind, he was ready to learn any new skill that he could use against the trolls and giants threatening Midgard.

Then a thought struck him. "Eikinri. How long does an apprenticeship take to complete?"

The dwarf looked at him. "Well, not long, really."

Ash breathed a sigh of relief.

"Since you are part troll, you are probably a bit dimmer than would be expected of an apprentice, so I would say around ten or twelve years until you reach Journeyman status and are free to set out into the world."

Ash's mouth fell open. Ten or twelve years? He didn't have that much time to spare. Midgard would be long fallen by then.

Eikinri must have seen his crestfallen face, because he said, "Here we are outside of the time in Midgard. What is a year here is less than a day in the world above us. Not even two weeks will have passed in the time you complete your apprenticeship."

Relief flooded him as what the dwarf said sunk in.

"If!" Eikinri added, raising a finger. "-you complete your apprenticeship. It is hard and heavy work, ill-suited for the human constitution, and fraught with danger, not only to the body but also the mind."

Ash swallowed nervously but reminded himself that the lives of many were at stake and that he had committed to doing everything he could. He looked Eikinri in the eyes, squaring his shoulders. "I'm ready."

The dwarf met his gaze and snorted. "We'll see."

ASH WAS DISAPPOINTED that his first duty as an apprentice Stonesmith was to sort through a gigantic pile of rocks. It didn't seem fair that every time someone set out to teach him something, he ended up moving heavy things around. This was the biggest pile yet, reaching halfway to what could only be called a distant ceiling. Yrsa would have been very pleased indeed, had she seen it. Eikinri had explained that it was his junk pile, where he had thrown any leftover rock over the years, and probably centuries, if the dwarf was to be believed.

Any time Ash came across a new type of stone, he had to call Eikinri over to name it for him. Ash then had to commit the stone to memory. Eikinri would explain the properties of the ore or mineral and told him to "sense" the stone, to hold it and feel the structure of it, inside and out. After a while, Ash began to understand what the dwarf meant. The stones felt different if he concentrated on them, and as the weeks and months went by, he could even tell if there were contaminants of other minerals present. Soon, Eikinri had him making a scrap pile of stones of poorer quality that were of no use to him and dozens of tidy piles of quality ore.

Ash marvelled at the world of stone and minerals that opened up in his hands. Prior to coming here, he had only known one or two types of stone, and even then he was mostly guessing. Now he could tell the difference between epidosite, boronalite and appinite, with just a glance or a touch. Holding a piece, he could feel the composition, minerals and grain sizes of the rock and could detect any fault lines or weak points. It was as if his mind could see into the stone and he could visualise the small crystalline building blocks that it was made up of. Eikinri had called it Stonesight, explaining that it was the very foundation of Stonesmithing.

He had laboured in that fashion for several months, sinking the pile to about half its original size. He felt stronger from moving so much stone all day long, and he had noticed that his shirt was getting a little tight around his arms and shoulders. However, he was feeling stiff, especially in his back. He decided to take up some drills that Yrsa had taught him, in order to maintain what little agility he had gained from his training in Gjallarholm. Eikinri gave him an hour or two of free time at the end of his working day. Ash would often spend it resting before the shared evening meal, but now, he decided, he would be more productive, and do his drills. This did mean that he would be exhausted at the end of each day, but he hoped he would get used to it.

Ash now lived in a corner that Eikinri had cleared for him and also kept what little belongings he had there. The dwarf had even come up with a sleeping roll for him, which was a significant improvement from the original stone bench.

Passing by the dwarf's room on his way to his corner, he glanced at the wall behind which his friends still slept. Eikinri had placed runestones on them, putting them in an enchanted sleep, and there they were, unaffected by time while Ash had been slaving away for months. He missed them a lot, even their constant banter.

By his bedroll, he picked up the sword he had found in Hornsborg. He had cleaned it up, and it was indeed a beautiful weapon, the steel reflecting the light from the forges. He still intended to find and return it to the rightful owner once he was back in Midgard. Since he had lost his spear, this would now have to do for his practice drills. He walked to an empty area on the workshop floor and, after a quick stretch, he fell into one of the basic drills Yrsa had taught him. His movements were stiff and clumsy at first, but soon they became more fluid and he switched from one form to the other, faster and faster. Ash began to sweat, but pushed himself harder, losing himself in the movements as he stopped thinking and just flowed through the drills. He came to a stop and gasping for air, sat down on a pile of rocks to catch his breath and wipe the sweat from his eyes. Once his breathing settled, he noticed Eikinri was sitting down, smoking his pipe, watching him.

"Not bad," the dwarf offered, and Ash felt a glow in his chest. He had never received a word of praise from Eikinri before. "If you are trying to swat flies off a cow's arse, that is. Maybe you are more suited to farming than fighting?"

Ash tried not to let his wounded pride show when he replied. "Those drills are meant for a spear, not a sword," he said, wiping his eyes and brow with his sleeve so he didn't have to look at the dwarf.

"A spear?" Eikinri scoffed. "Fighting with a spear might be well and good when everyone is nicely lined up against each other on a field, but what of close quarter fighting, in a building or underground? Your spear would be useless. Better to use that shiny sword of yours the way it was intended."

"I am an Ulfhed, and we fight with spears," Ash replied, sounding more sullen than he intended.

"Why?" Eikinri asked, seeming genuinely perplexed.

"Well," he said, a bit of irritability sneaking into his voice. "Because that's what works when we fight in a group. It is very effective."

He barely saw the dwarf move. Like a blur Eikinri shot up from where he was sitting, to standing inches from Ash, holding the edge of a long knife against his neck.

"A lot of good your spear would do you now," the dwarf grumbled, before putting his knife away. "Your group won't always be around for you. You can't rely on others in order to walk away from a fight in one piece. That sword will serve you better than any spear will." The dwarf's eyes landed on the sword and he stared at it for a second before his eyes widened.

"Now where did you get that, lad?" He whispered, his eyes never leaving the blade.

Ash, feeling embarrassed about what had just happened, mumbled sheepishly, "I found it. I intend to find the rightful owner and return it when I can."

Eikinri took the sword from Ash's unresisting hand and ran a calloused finger over the runes on the fuller.

"*TOR HIELPE*" he read out loud, before turning to Ash again. "What do you know about it?" he asked.

"Erh… Nothing, really. I only found it the day you rescued us."

The dwarf handed it back to him. "Feel it like you would the stone you have been sorting. In essence, it is just minerals that have been reforged."

Ash took the sword and after a quick look at Eikinri to make sure he wasn't being mocked somehow, he took a deep breath and let his mind flow into the weapon. In his mind's eye he could see the iron throughout the sword. But it was bent around other minerals, like cobalt and nickel, and all were clustered around each other so tight that it was difficult to tell them apart at first. This must be how steel is forged, he reasoned, and reported his findings to Eikinri.

"Good," the dwarf said. "Now look deeper."

Ash focused on a single forged cluster and delved deeper into it. To his mind the minerals appeared as large as houses and he could feel a sweat breaking out on his forehead from the concentration.

"What do you see?" Eikinri rumbled.

Ash was just about to reply that he could see nothing unusual, when a glimmer caught his attention. He focused on it until he realized that the cluster had little flashes of lightning racing across its surface. This was something he had not seen in any of the stones he had been inspecting. He withdrew his mind from the sword and told Eikinri what he had seen.

"There is hope for you yet," the dwarf replied. "The runes carved on the blade are a call to Thor, the Thundergod, for aid. This is common enough on weapons, but what you saw is a touch of his power imbued into the sword. This is rune magic."

Ash looked wide-eyed at the sword. "What does it do?" he asked.

"I don't know," Eikinri let out a laugh. "But seeing how old Thunder-Thor is also called the Trollslayer, I'd be careful to not cut my finger on it, if I were you!"

Ash froze for a second, staring at the sword. He turned around and, with caution, carried the sword back to his bedroll to put it away where he wouldn't risk accidentally cutting himself. He was half troll, after all. The dwarf's laughter followed him all the way.

THE NEXT DAY, Ash laboured in silence, sorting the never-ending pile of rock. He thought about the evening before and decided to ask Eikinri for something that resembled a spear so he could continue his drills. He was also determined to ignore the dwarf's taunts and stick with his usual training schedule, since that was all he knew. He would ask Torsten to show him how to use a sword or an axe later. Then he remembered that that might be a decade from now.

Eikinri had worked in various places, all around the workshop, as was his habit, and he was always engulfed in his projects, paying little attention to Ash. He had learned early on that interrupting the dwarf when he was busy was a sure-fire way of rousing his anger, resulting in more work for Ash. So, he would wait until the end of the working day to speak to the dwarf about things not directly related to his work.

When he heard his master's raspy voice calling an end to the working day, he finished with the stone he was working on, and turned to find the dwarf to speak with him. Eikinri was standing right behind him, arms folded over his belly, and Ash took a startled step backward.

"I have decided to protect my investment," Eikinri said, but before Ash could open his mouth to ask, the dwarf turned around and walked away. "Come with me," he grunted.

Ash followed him with curiosity as they walked across the workshop, and through another archway in the wall that had not been there this morning, or ever, as far as Ash could remember. On entry, he was faced with a large room, covered from floor to ceiling with weapons of all sorts. He gawked at swords, maces, axes, all kinds of shields and strange, edged weapons he had never seen before, but their cruel and pointy designs left little doubt as to their intent. They were all hanging in neat order on hooks, and the floor space was open and clear of any furniture. The purpose of this room was obvious, and Ash's stomach knotted with excitement.

"I didn't realise you had this room," he said to the dwarf as he perused the various implements of death surrounding him.

"I have many rooms that are none of your business," Eikinri grumbled. "It just so happens that this one has now become a part of your apprenticeship." The dwarf wiped a minute speck of dust from a well-worn, double-bladed axe suspended in front of him. "There is no point in me spending all this time teaching you, only for you to drop dead as soon as the first person who takes offence to your ugly mug sticks a blade in you."

Ash ignored the insult and grinned at the dwarf, the prospect of training with all these new weapons exciting him.

"Oh, I'll wipe that thing off your face in a minute," the dwarf spat, and Ash's smile fell from his face.

"Sorry, master," Ash offered.

Somewhat placated, the dwarf walked along the wall and took down two swords. They were a little shorter and broader than the swords Ash had seen most warriors carry around.

"These are dwarven swords," Eikinri explained. "They differ from the ones used in Midgard, but the weight and balance are similar. They will do for now."

"Erh..." Ash started. "We usually use wooden practice weapons in training," he said.

The dwarf rewarded him with a grim smile. "That doesn't encourage you to not get hit, does it?"

He accepted one of the swords and was somewhat relieved to see it was blunt, but he knew with every bone in his body that this was going to hurt either way.

"Let's start with your stance."

CHAPTER 25

ROGHALD HALTED THE SHAMBLING GROUP OF DRAUGR around him with a thought command. They had been making their way through the forest for almost a week. The undead surrounding him were inexhaustible, but he still needed to rest and sleep from time to time. He could have transformed to his thursr shape and made better pace, but the laughing voice in his head was getting harder to shake each time he changed back, so he didn't want to transform more than necessary. Even now if he stood quiet and listened hard, he thought he could hear the insane laughter in the distance. A seed of concern had grown in his chest.

He had left a good portion of the draugr in Hornsborg. He knew humans would continue to travel there, with nothing but violent death awaiting them inside the gates of the fortress. Looking around him, more than a hundred draugr stood dead quiet among the trees, awaiting his next command. A dozen of them were carrying survivors from the ambush of the Jomsvikings. Some had died on the way, which was only to be expected, but a surprising number still had breath in their bodies, ready to receive the elixir of the jotunn shaman that would damn them to the ranks of the draugr.

He walked up to the undead nearest to him and its unconscious parcel slung over its shoulder. He grabbed a fistful of Jarl Olaf's hair and lifted his head up for inspection. Dried blood was caked on his face and his eyes were swollen shut. He was still alive, though only just. The man had resisted all the way, not once giving him any information about Ash or the humans' plans. Roghald had been very persuasive, but Olaf's only reply to his questions were defiant stares with hate and loathing in his eyes. But Roghald wasn't worried, as Gurmr and Grundr were now only a short distance away, and his masters had means to get into a man's head. Olaf might think he had defeated Roghald in a small way by not disclosing what he knew, but it would all be for nothing in a moment. His master would find out everything the Jarl knew. Roghald would then take great delight in watching Olaf's transformation to a ghoul, knowing that the man would be forever robbed of his seat in Valhalla.

Satisfied that the Jarl was still alive, he ordered the draugr forward, and it wasn't long before they broke into the clearing in front of the jotunn's cave.

Roghald waited until all the draugr had come out of the forest, before he pulled a curved horn from a satchel on his hip, put it to his lips and blew a long, mournful tone. Soon the large, two-headed shape of his master filled the cave opening, with wicked grins on both its faces.

"The thursr returns." Gurmr remarked, scratching his big nose.

"With gifts for his betters," Grundr cackled, looking at the draugr carrying wounded warriors as he removed the round flask from his hip. "He does not disappoint!"

"Even better than that," Roghald boasted, sweeping his arm over the clearing. "These are pets of Asgard, Ulfhednar and Berserkers, all of them!" He waited for another bout of praise, but none came. He looked to his master to see only disappointed looks on both faces.

"I told you he is as dumb as a rock," Grundr muttered, replacing the flask in his belt.

Gurmr ignored his brother, but was stern in his voice when he spoke, "They cannot be transformed. The bile of the Aesir fills them and the elixir will not take. We are pleased to see them defeated, yes, but they are of no use to us."

Roghald felt deflated. He had been sent to gather more people to fill their ranks and had failed. He should have realized that they could not turn, given that they were gifted by the gods. There was still hope of pleasing the giant, though. He pointed to Olaf where he lay over the draugr's shoulder.

"This one is the leader of the Jomsvikings, and he also knows the half-breed. He knows all the humans' plans."

At the mention of Ash, even Grundr perked up. "Maybe he is not completely useless after all," he said to his brother.

"Bring him inside," Gurmr told Roghald. As an afterthought he added, "Kill the rest," before turning and walking back inside the cave. Roghald smiled and followed, ordering Olaf's draugr to do the same. The sound of the rest of the draugr, tearing through flesh and chain mail as they feasted, followed him into the dark passage.

It was night before Roghald emerged from the cave. He stood and let the breeze flow over his face as it swept away the cold and damp of the cave. He felt discontented that Olaf had not been turned undead. Still, they had got what they needed from him and at least when he died; it had been in pain.

Looking down, he spun a wooden spike in his hands. It was as long as his forearm, with a sharp point at the end. His master had made it for him by breaking a thorn off the tree of Jotunheim, before carefully carving runes around it. When it was done, the giant had grabbed Roghald's arm slicing it with the thorn and then allowed the blood to soak into the carvings. The runes now glowed a dull red in the night, and the thorn felt like a part of him, the light pulsating with the beat of his own heart. It was a formidable weapon, and he knew that a small part of his soul had gone into making it. The Jotun had explained that he needed to use it with caution, as its power was limited and would run out, should he waste it.

The draugr stood unmoving where he had left them, with remnants of the captured Jomsvikings at their feet. He was tired, and probably should sleep before setting off, but the dead Jomsvikings reminded him of his failure to fill the ranks, and also his failure to capture Ash. His master was most displeased with him on finding out from Olaf that Ash had been within his grasp and had somehow escaped. His back still burned from the lashes he had received as punishment, and he felt a trickle of blood running down the back of his leg. But the wounds were already closing, and pain didn't bother him much anymore. Even so, Gurmr and Grundr had been merciful, giving him a chance to amend his failures with a new task. Roghald was determined not to fail them again. Mostly because he doubted they would extend him mercy a second time.

Upon reading Olaf's mind, his master gathered that with the Jarl's death, there was really only one person who threatened to halt the draugr from sweeping across the lands. She was the only one who commanded authority enough with the Seidwomen scattered across the Jarldoms to force all the chieftains to listen. The internal squabbling of the southern Jarls for the king's throne prevented the humans from mounting a unified defence, and his master would sweep across the Norse lands, one Jarldom at a time, and finally, the whole of Midgard. By the time the humans realized the extent of the threat, it would be too late. Midgard would fall and it would usher in a new era. The age of the troll was at hand, and Roghald was the vanguard.

Only one death and the world would be theirs for the taking. He adjusted the straps of his knapsack and set off alone through the trees. He had a witch to kill.

CHAPTER 26

JARL ASTRID DISMISSED THE MESSENGER AND HAD DIFFI-
culty hiding the disappointment from her face. Yet another polite refusal of sending troops to support the northern Jarldoms.
The message had been dressed in fanciful words of praise of the
capabilities of her hird and the Jomsvikings, but also doubt as to
the legitimacy of the threat. Even the town Fjellborg, only a few
days' ride south, had been 'unable' to spare any warriors at this
time, choosing to barricade themselves behind their walls.

They were alone. Their one hope was Rani. As a Seidwoman
with Second Sight, she was respected, even among her own kind.
Since most Jarls had a Seidwoman of their own and often heeded
their advice, Jarl Astrid knew that they were the key to unifying
the Norse lands. When Olaf returned with Ash and the Jomsvikings, they would have to escort her south in a last attempt to gain
troops and support. But Olaf was delayed, and she couldn't ignore
a niggling worry about him.

She sighed and pushed herself up from the bench, leaving the
hall and her hird behind. Astrid entered the narrow spiral stairway leading to the western tower and Rani's rooms. Although the
Seidwoman frightened her a bit, she was happy to have her in
the fortress, her uncanny predictions and wise counsel always be-

ing advantageous, especially in these dark times. She was less impressed with how Rani had commandeered the western tower for her own use, though she had resigned to the fact.

Making her way up the stone spiral, she stood before the Seidwoman's door. She raised her fist to knock, but before she had a chance to rap on the wood, she could hear Rani's voice whisper in her ear, "Surely you need not knock in your own fortress, Jarl Astrid?"

She spun around to look at the empty stairwell behind her. Uncanny.

Pushing the door open, she entered Rani's quarters. The room was dim, lit only by a bed of glowing embers in the fireplace. Astrid's eyes stung from a thin mist in the room, at the same time as being drawn to a bowl of smouldering herbs near her feet.

"Light a candle, if you need it, Jarl Astrid," the Seidwoman spoke from where she sat on a bench next to the fireplace.

"Thank you, Rani, but I won't stay long." She looked at the old woman and saw a scattering of bones on the floor in front of her. "I have come to ask for tidings of Olaf," the Jarl continued. "When can we expect his return to Gjallarholm?"

"You cannot expect him at all, Jarl Astrid." Rani's voice was only a whisper. "The Norns, who wove his fate, have already cut his thread, and he sits at Odin's table in Valhalla."

Astrid staggered, reeling from the news.

"Are you absolutely certain?" she blurted out. The Seidwoman looked insulted and chose to not answer this question. "Forgive me," she added. "It has come as a shock." The Jarl looked thoughtful for a second. "What of the boy?"

"He is safe. For now," she said, but didn't elaborate any further.

"We will have to arrange to escort you south, without the aid of the Jomsvikings. I will have warriors ready in the morning."

The old woman shook her head. "There is no time to travel to every Jarldom to speak with their Seidwomen," Rani said. "In one moon from now, there is a gathering in the sacred grove. Most of the seers will be there, and I will speak with them then. I will require an escort only to where it is safe from the draugr. The grove's location is secret and cannot be revealed to the uninitiated."

"A month?" Astrid sighed. "That means we can expect aid in six weeks. At the earliest! There is a great chance that the draugr numbers have swelled enough by then, that we will not be able to resist them."

Rani shook her head. "No, but the southerners might. If they manage to unite, Midgard still has hope."

"But we in the north do not?"

Rani sat in silence for several heartbeats. "There is always hope, Jarl Astrid. Only the Norns know the fate of humanity."

Astrid bowed her head and put her hand on the door to leave, but the Seidwoman raised a hand and she halted in her step. Before Rani even spoke, a shiver ran down Astrid's spine. Sorrow was written on the old woman's face and even a touch of fear.

"Astrid, something terrible comes this way," she whispered. She looked even older than usual. Old and tired.

"I will double the guard and keep all the warriors ready. Whatever comes, we will ride it out behind our walls, fear not."

Rani nodded and lowered her hand. Astrid bid her farewell and shut the door behind her. "I don't think your walls will be enough, Jarl Astrid," she whispered to the empty room.

CHAPTER 27

ASH HELD UP A PERFECTLY ROUND BALL OF GRANITE for inspection and beamed. It had taken years of practice and hard work, but he finally did it!

When he at first had started his apprenticeship and had spent months and months sorting Eikinri's pile of rocks, the dwarf had finally begun teaching him Stonesmithing.

The dwarf had declared that Ash had developed his Stonesight enough that they could move on.

The next step was merging himself with the stone, filling it with his mind, and then reshaping it according to his will. Eikinri had showed him how to use his inherent Stonesmithing powers to shape it, then taught him chants and songs to force the stone to remain that shape. The songs were ancient, reaching back to when Odin and his brothers had created Midgard. What had been a plain lump of granite was now a shiny, stable orb, and Ash revelled in the beautiful marbling, turning his creation round and round in his hands.

Years of daily practice and he had finally managed it without cracking the rock or leaving it misshapen.

He had also become proficient in most other things the dwarf had schooled him in so far. Even though he was not yet able to make tunnels like Eikinri, he could travel through stone, making it flow around him almost without effort. It did have its limitations, since Ash could only go as far as he could hold his breath while submerged in the stone. This exercise had almost been the death of him at first.

ABOUT TWO YEARS into his apprenticeship, he had been practicing, moving through the massive pile of Eikinri's junk stone. Ash had been pushing through the stone, but not able to make his breath last for the full length of the massive pile, only dipping in and out of the pile at the edges. He needed more time to make it all the way through to the other side of the mound. That's when an idea struck him. Ash concentrated and stepped into the pile, letting the stone flow around him, pushing towards the middle of the mound. Then he Shifted. If time slowed down and he moved faster, he reasoned, he could make it through the entire pile before he ran out of breath.

It had felt like a sledgehammer hit him in the stomach. Something went terribly wrong. Time was spluttering, speeding up and slowing down, and he felt dozens of sharp pricks as the jagged rocks around him cut into him. He tried to stop shifting but wasn't able to. He could still feel time changing around him, and the sharp stone edges pushed and stabbed at his skin, harder and harder. Ash panicked as the pressure from tonnes and tonnes of stone started pressing down on him. He tried to open his mouth to scream, but the rocks were solidifying around him, clamping his mouth shut. The entire time it felt like a battle raged inside him, and he lost all control. His lungs burned from the lack of air, and bursts of light flashed before his eyes.

The next moment, all the pressure from the rocks disappeared and for a blissful split second, he was suspended in the air, before crashing to the ground. He lifted his head to see the outline of Eikinri walking towards him at the end of a tunnel, before he lost consciousness.

When he woke, he was lying on his bedroll; the dwarf sitting on a stool next to him. Eikinri, seeing that he was awake, gave him a long look and Ash cringed under his master's stare.

"Well, that was very foolish," the dwarf had grumbled, shaking his head. "I should have left you there. It is true that a fool seldom reaches old age."

"I was just trying to get through the whole pile," Ash replied sheepishly. "I figured I could move faster that way."

Eikinri sat silent for a few long seconds. "The two sides of you are conflicting. They are the opposite sides of the balance in the universe, Jotnar and Aesir. Their hate for each other runs so deep that they will always fight, even if that battle is within you, and even if it will kill you."

"I... I didn't know," Ash mumbled.

"Well, your wolf friends should have taught you!" Eikinri's face was red and his fists were clenched. "This is the way with the Aesirs, lad. Always full of secrets and riddles. Don't forget that one of Odin's many names is 'The Deceiver'." The dwarf took a deep breath and his features softened somewhat. "Just keep your wits about you when dealing with the gods, lad. Remember that they only work towards their own ends. If their goals align with yours for a while, that is all fine and well, but as soon as that changes, you will see another side of them."

Ash could only nod at Eikinri's words.

"Now, the two very different sides of your soul will always be at odds with each other. Think of them as two beasts, always fighting for dominance. When you use one of your abilities, whether that is your troll-given Stonesmithing, or your Ulfhednar powers, you feed one of them, making it strong enough to rise to the surface. The other beast, who is starved at that time, will shirk away, lest it gets killed by the stronger one, allowing you to use your powers without problems. However, if you try to use both powers at once, you feed both, making them both strong. They will then turn on each other in a fight that could kill either one, or even you. This is the conflict within that will always be a part of you, and you have to live with that. You will either be troll or an Ulfhed, you can never be both at the same time." Eikinri stood up. "Rest for the day, lad. We'll get back to work tomorrow."

And with that the dwarf had left, leaving Ash with a lot to think about.

Ever since, when Ash had continued his Stonesmithing, he had left his Ulfhednar side dormant. He would only practice Shifting when he went to bed at night, to keep the skill, but otherwise he left it well alone. The memory of that terrible pressure from the stone as it crushed down on him served as a reminder of what could have gone wrong.

Now, Ash took stock of the time he had spent with the dwarf as he ran his hands over the orb, looking for the slightest imperfection. By now, almost five years had gone by since he had started his apprenticeship. He knew he had grown a fair bit taller since then, because he now had to duck to get through the doorways in the dwarf's home. All the hard work Ash had invested in moving and working with stone had built his strength, while the night-time weapons training with his master had left him agile and light on his feet.

He remembered the only time he had tried to use his Ulfhed powers and had Shifted to get an advantage against his master and had deeply regretted it. The stocky dwarf had disarmed him without much effort and had bruised him from his ears to his feet with the flat of his sword, letting Ash know what he thought of 'cheaters'. As harsh and grumpy as the dwarf was, a friendship had grown between the two as the years went by, and Ash savoured all the wisdom flowing up from his short friend.

He was yet to learn how to make tunnels in stone, like Eikinri had done when he'd rescued them from Hornsborg, and also when he had pulled Ash from under the rock pile. To Ash's disappointment, Eikinri had told him that this was an advanced skill that would come later and that, using rune magic, he would even be able to make permanent tunnels and hollows in stone. He was determined to learn every skill he could use against the enemies of Midgard. He also felt that in a small way, his apprenticeship had brought him closer to his father, who had also been a Stonesmith.

The dwarf had also taught him blacksmithing in the traditional sense. Although he could reshape rock, he could not change its properties, like merging minerals to make steel. For that, they needed fire. Really hot fire. Eikinri's forges were enchanted and heated to incredible temperatures, allowing the dwarf to forge steel and even elven silver, the hardest and lightest metal in all the worlds. A chain mail or a weapon made from elven silver would be close to unbreakable but would cost a kingdom. Blacksmithing would also pave the path to enchanting, creating magical objects, but this, Eikinri had explained, was a master craft, and could only be undertaken by a skilled Stonesmith. Ash was a decade away from even beginning to understand the process.

Blacksmithing soon became Ash's favourite aspect of his apprenticeship. Eikinri had given him a hammer to use, similar to the one used by Beli, and Ash had felt the same connection and purpose to it. He would lose himself in the process of shaping the metals, his Stonesight allowing him to see the forging of the minute minerals and work them to perfection. Often Eikinri would need to tap him on the shoulder and drag him away from the anvil at the end of the working day.

His master had taught him to read runes as well, when they sat together at night. Not only the *Futhark* rune alphabet, used by the Norse but also *Esh*, the dwarven runes and *Kerach*, used by the trolls and giants.

"Runes," the dwarf had explained, "is the key to enchanting. A Stonesmith can weave the inherent magic in stone or channel spells through it, but to make the effect permanent, runes are needed to bind it to the stone. Although you fuel the runes with your own powers, the runes themselves hold magic of their own, if you know how to release it."

New worlds had opened up before him, and he drank in everything the dwarf offered.

Although Eikinri would never admit it, Ash had a feeling that his master was pleased with his progress. He was keen to show his master the ball of granite, but knew better than to interrupt the dwarf when he was working. Instead, he busied himself with tidying the workshop for a few hours until the end of the working day.

Later on, when they met up in the weapons room in the evening, he presented the ball to the dwarf. Eikinri looked at it with a critical eye, before handing it back to Ash.

"Not the worst thing I have ever seen," the dwarf admitted, but seeing Ash's grin added, "Don't get cocky, you have a long way to go yet."

Ash wiped the smile from his face but was still pleased with himself.

"Just swords tonight, I think." Eikinri said, rubbing his chin as he studied the weapons hanging around the room. The sword had become Ash's favourite weapon since training with his master. He still enjoyed using the spear and axe, but he liked the versatility of the sword, being able to thrust, cut and defend from most situations he found himself in. His master was a formidable warrior, and Ash had never bested him. Although, in the last year, he felt that the dwarf needed to apply extra effort to defeat his student, sometimes even breaking a sweat.

After a few warm-up stretches and exercises, their swords clashed together in a clang of metal. Ash ducked and weaved, staying light on his feet, always searching for an opening in the dwarf's defence. He was familiar with most of his master's favourite attacks and could evade and counter many of them. Whenever he tried to attack, however, his sword was always redirected or just hit plain air as the dwarf moved out of the way with ease.

After an hour he was sweating and breathing heavily, he started to tire. This was when Eikinri would step up his attacks, pushing Ash harder and harder until his arm felt like dough. Before long, he was pushed into a corner and a swift blow sent his sword flying across the room. Eikinri's tapped his sword against Ash's ribs.

"You're dead," the dwarf declared before handing his sword to Ash. "Fix them, then come to dinner," he said. Those words had become a mantra, signifying the end of their weapons training every night.

Ash looked down on the sword in his hand and noted the nicks all along the blade. With care, Ash pinched the edge between his thumb and forefinger, and his fingertips glowed red. Whispering a spell, he pushed his fingers up the blade, erasing the damage from the blunted steel edge. He took great care with this task, because he knew the dwarf was very particular about the weapons being kept in pristine condition. Once he was happy with it, he hung the sword back in its place on the wall and bending over to pick up the sword he had used; he repeated the process.

The rumble in his stomach reminded him how hungry he was, and remembering that Eikinri had been simmering one of his delicious stews for most of the day, he hurried into the room where they took their meals.

He almost tripped over when he ducked under the arch and into the room, only to find Eikinri with company. An old man with a long grey beard occupied Ash's usual seat, and judging by the looks on their faces, he had caught them in an argument. They both stopped speaking and turned to face him as he entered, making Ash feel a bit sheepish. He froze for a second when he saw the old man's face. The long white beard and slouch hat combined with his one eye scrutinising Ash like a man would a prized horse left no doubt who it was. Ash knew him from his dreams and from the words of others as much as he knew it in his very bones.

"Odin," he greeted the god.

The old man smiled at him, "Ash Jordrson. I trust that you have been well, and that Eikinri has taught you everything he knows?"

"That's the point, Odin!" the dwarf cut in. "There hasn't been enough time. The lad is talented, I grant you that much, still he's only halfway through his apprenticeship. What happens if you pull a half-forged sword from the anvil and start banging about with it? It breaks, that's what happens!"

Ash had never seen Eikinri so flushed with anger, yet the dwarf was collected, his hands flat on the table in front of him.

"Though I wish that I could leave him with you for as long as needed, master Stonesmith, our time has run short. The Jotnar have moved sooner than expected, and with the way things are in Midgard, we cannot spare even an hour. Consider your debt to me paid, however."

There was finality in the old god's voice that wouldn't be argued with, and as upset as Eikinri was, even he couldn't oppose the father of the gods.

"What has happened in Midgard?" Ash asked, unable to hide the concern from his voice.

"You need to be in Gjallarholm." Odin's eye locked on his. "Jotunheim have gained an unexpected advantage with the deaths of both Jarl Olaf and Jarl Erik, and the fact that only a few Jomsvikings remain. The north lies open for them to attack. I fear that Rani, who is our last hope to unify the southern Jarls, will be the trolls' next target. Midgard is running out of time to stop them. Left unchecked, their numbers will soon be in the thousands, and humanity will have no chance."

"Why can't you tell the Jarls, Allfather? Surely they will heed to you more than anyone else?"

"I cannot interfere directly or Ragnarok might be upon us much earlier than it is fated to. There are certain… rules that even I have to abide by. Any rule I break allows the enemy freedom to do the same. Considering that the forces we face lack a certain control, things could escalate quickly beyond our ability to prevent it. I fear that since I interfered once to prevent your death at the hands of the fire-thursr, the very source of what infects Midgard was allowed to grow. Many things are yet to happen before the final battle, and all the worlds could be destroyed forever if I act directly to change the course of things. The frost and fire giants know this and are profiting from my hands being tied, as they have the advantage at the moment." He took a swig from the mug in front of him. "I can, however, speak with Rani as she is gifted with Second Sight, and can see into the spirit realm, but no other. The only reason I speak with you now is because here we are outside the worlds and hence the usual rules do not apply," he finished with a wry smile.

"Unfortunately, I suspect that what opposes us in Midgard is a jotunn Shaman with similar magic and privileges as our Seidwoman, although its wards are powerful and I cannot know for sure. What I do know is, that whatever it is, it will come for Rani, and she will need your help."

"Me?" Ash asked in a high-pitched voice. "What can I do to stop a jotunn Shaman?"

"You are one of my Wolves, are you not?" Odin said, his voice like iron.

Ash nodded.

"Then you will stop it or die trying."

Ash sat in silence as he thought about what the Allfather had just said. The god was right. This was what he had been training for all these years. He was a Wolf of Odin, and he would go where the god sent him. A sense of purpose filled him, and he felt a sense of freedom when he accepted his fate, committing to it in his heart. The old man must have sensed his thoughts, because he smiled as he sat back in his chair.

"I must do right by my master, and I will need to ask his leave." Ash said, turning to the dwarf.

Eikinri looked from Ash to Odin and back again, before slumping his shoulders and sighing.

"By the Norns, I have gotten used to having you around, lad. When all this business is sorted, you are welcome to return and finish your apprenticeship with me."

Ash had to swallow down a lump that had appeared in his throat when spoke to the dwarf.

"Then I am ready," he told the god. "Let me fetch my things."

With that, he stood and made his way to his corner. Before he walked out of the arched doorway and into the smithy, Odin spoke again, "Remember Ash, that the gods help those who help themselves."

A bit perplexed, Ash nodded and walked out. He collected his meagre belongings and put on his tunic and cape. He strapped his seax to his belt and hung the runic sword in its scabbard below it. A quick look around confirmed that he had left nothing behind before he went back to join the dwarf and the god.

He found Eikinri alone, however, with no sight of the Allfather. In reply to Ash's questioning look, he shrugged, showing that he didn't know or care where the god had gone. He noticed that his master looked awkward and was spinning a round shield in his hands. He thrust the shield into Ash's hands.

"This is to keep you safe. I don't want a word said about it, just take it," the dwarf muttered, busying himself with the runes that would open the wall to where his friends had been asleep this whole time. Ash examined the shield and saw it was made of brown, marbled stone, yet it weighed as light as a feather, with beautiful runes carved on the face along the rim. It was smaller than the round shields Norsemen would use, but dwarves didn't need large shields, he reasoned. It fit on his arm as if it was made for him, and Ash's heart filled with gratitude towards the dwarf.

A doorway opened into the other room and Ash was excited to see his friends' sleeping forms on the bench where he had left them, years ago. As the runes lit up in the room, Eikinri went in and removed glowing stones from Yrsa and Torsten's chests, and they began to stir. Before long, they were sitting on the bench stretching and yawning. They didn't seem any worse off than if they had had a good night's sleep, but when their eyes fell on Ash, both their mouths fell open. Torsten rubbed his eyes and leaned forward to stare at Ash with his eyebrows raised.

Then it struck Ash that while it had only been one night to them, he had aged five years, give or take. He shot them a winning smile.

"I guess I have some explaining to do."

EIKINRI WAS LEADING them through the underground once again. Ash spent the first few hours answering the multitude of questions his friends bombarded him with, but after a while they seemed satisfied, although amazed. When they had walked through the smooth rock that was Yggdrasil's branch and stepped out among the rough underground granite, a strange sensation came over Ash. It was as if a pressure that he hadn't even been aware of lifted from him, and he knew that they were back in the normal flow of time.

They walked in silence, taking in the underground landscape revealed by Yrsa's glowing rock. Several times, on Torsten's request, Ash had to stick his hand into the stone walls. Each time the Berserker would shake his head and mutter, "Incredible!"

Sometime later, they entered a broad, but low-ceilinged cavern when the dwarf called for a halt. Sitting down on a small ledge, he opened up a pack he had been carrying on his back and started laying out wrapped parcels in front of him. Ash could smell one of the strong cheeses he had come to favour since living with the dwarf and his mouth watered. Besides the cheese, there was bread, dried meat and a jar of pickled onion and they all dug in, enjoying the reprieve.

"Do we have far to go? I'm getting sick of stumbling around underground," Yrsa asked, her mouth full of food, crumbs spattering as she spoke. Eikinri gave her a look that said everything about what he thought of her manners.

"We will rest here and try to sleep for a few hours. When we set out we still have a few days left, unless you want me to drop you back in the hornet's nest where I picked you up?" Eikinri said.

"No," Yrsa replied, pretending to ponder the question. "Far away from there will be fine, I think."

Eikinri gave her a glare, suspecting he was being made fun of. Ash and Torsten laughed at her joke. It was nice to be with the two of them again, Ash thought.

Soon, they spread out their blankets. Eikinri took first watch. He explained that although it was mostly safe in the underground caverns, now and then something would find its way down here that could surprise a careless traveller.

"Or even worse," he added. "Something will find its way up into them."

Ash had some difficulty falling asleep, imagining things hidden from the world that could prey on them in the dark. He was also apprehensive about returning to the world after so many years in Eikinri's smithy and his mind raced, giving him little peace. In time, he drifted off and slept until it was his turn to keep watch.

WHEN THEY SET off again, the only one who seemed well rested was the dwarf who had spent a lot more time in the underworld. As they travelled on over the next few days, Ash relaxed and began feeling more at ease. He marvelled at and admired the ever-changing subterranean landscape and saw beauty in strata and rock formations. He spotted veins of rare minerals all over the place, and once even saw a thick seam of gold glittering in the wall on the other side of a deep, seemingly endless chasm. Ash would often pause and put his hand on an interesting rock face, letting his mind enter it and explore its depth and mineral makeup. A whole new world had opened up to him since he began his Stonesmith apprenticeship. When Eikinri signalled the end of their underground journey, Ash felt a stab of disappointment, but reminded himself that there were more important things at stake.

"On the other side of this rock," the dwarf said, placing his hand on a granite face, "lies the road to what you call Gjallarholm. You will emerge only a few hours north of the place. This is the closest I can get you, as there is only loam and mud between here and the town. I will open a tunnel for you, but this is as far as I am willing to go."

Eikinri bid them all farewell, and when he got to Ash, he reached out to clasp his forearm in a firm grip. Ash struggled to get a hold on the dwarf's thick forearm in return. His master looked him in the eyes and spoke, "Be safe, lad, and come back to finish what you have started."

Ash looked down into the usually grumpy face and smiled. "I promise to come back," he replied, his voice breaking a little. His master returned his smile with a rare one of his own and with a final slap on his shoulder, released Ash before turning to the granite behind him. He sunk his hand into the stone and as he muttered what Ash now knew was a spell, the wall drew away from his arm and a tunnel formed. The group had seen this a dozen times since their journey started, but this time the difference was that daylight spilled in from the other end, flooding them with bright light.

"Go, now." The dwarf said, and they stumbled forwards, shielding their eyes from the bright daylight. They stepped out onto green grass and warm sunlight, which made their cool skin tingle. Their hands were on their weapons as they scouted the surrounding forest. Nothing leapt at them, and birdsong in the trees reassured them that nothing sinister was waiting beyond. Ash took his first deep breath of fresh air in years. The smell of the trees was intoxicating, and the rustle of their leaves in the breeze was the most beautiful sound he had ever heard. He turned around in time to see the stone tunnel close behind them.

"There," Yrsa said, pointing with her spear. "There's the road."

Torsten looked up at the sun. "It's late afternoon. If we want to get to Gjallarholm before dark, but we'd better make haste."

They made their way out to the road and stepped out from the cover of the trees. All was still around them, so they set out at a brisk pace south, but remained vigilant, watching the road ahead as well as behind them. A tense couple of hours later, as the sun was setting in the west, they crested a hill and looked down on the fortress of Gjallarholm. The fortress and town lay nestled in its bay, the ocean lapping at its jetties, rocking the many boats moored there. The sight seemed normal, but a keen observer would notice that all was still in the unprotected town surrounding the fortress, and no one could be seen working the fields surrounding it. Many guards were patrolling the thick stone walls of the largest fortress of the north.

They didn't allow themselves to stop and take in the view, instead they hurried along, eager to get behind the protective walls. But they hadn't taken many steps along the road before the forest erupted in cracks and rustles around them.

CHAPTER 28

"I AM TOLD YOU ARE SAILING TO GJALLARHOLM. GOT room for one more?"

The old sailor looked up from the rope he was splicing, giving Roghald a long appraising look.

"Depends," he said, turning his attention back to his work. "Any good with an oar?"

Roghald grinned at him. "I raided in the east in my youth. It's been a while, but I'm sure I remember which part goes in the water."

The old seafarer let out a raspy laugh and pointed over his back with his thumb. "So long as you're not carrying any goods, since she's pretty full, you can come along. We're a few hands short, what with all the extra shipping to Gjallarholm, so you are welcome to join the crew. Can't say it will be a leisurely trip, though. There is a steady northerly, so we'll be rowing most of the way, and there will only be three of us. You've been warned."

"It is about the destination for me, not the journey," Roghald replied, throwing his knapsack over the low railing and onto a bench where the oarsmen would be seated, and jumped aboard.

It was a small boat with a short mast and only four pairs of oars. Looking at the amount of goods stowed in the bow and stern, it wouldn't have fit more than three people, anyway. The boat was painted dark grey; the old sailor had no doubt made a few smuggling runs before the draugr attack had opened up a profitable shipping market to Gjallarholm for anyone with a boat. With the closure of the roads, the sea was now the only way to traffic goods and supplies into town.

Roghald made himself comfortable on the bench, his pack under his head, and stretched out his aching legs. He had been on his feet for over a week, traveling at a fast pace and sleeping only a few hours every night, racing to make it to Fjellborg, south of Gjallarholm. The woods and lands around Gjallarholm were well patrolled, but he was certain the humans would retreat behind their walls at night. Avoiding them by getting to the fortress under the cover of darkness would not have presented a problem; getting inside was a whole different matter. He doubted he would be able to make it inside unseen if he came over land.

The port was a different matter, however. The warriors were looking to the forest, not the sea, so he had skirted Jarl Astrid's fortress, and continued south to Fjellborg. It was a small town and fortress, now overcrowded, as one of the last safe harbours before Gjallarholm. Roghald had inspected the low timber palisade surrounding the fort as he strolled through the gates. Some efforts had been made to heighten and fortify the walls, even so, he estimated it would take his draugr horde a matter of seconds to breach them. Once Gjallarholm fell, the south would be like a ripe plum ready for picking, he mused.

He dozed off for a moment but was awoken by a thud and the rocking of the little boat.

He lifted his hood and peeked up at a glum-looking man with an unkempt black beard settling in on the bench next to his. The man glanced at Roghald, who gave him a curt nod which the man ignored, and instead turned to his pack. Obviously not a talker, which suiter Roghald just fine. The man pulled out an apple from his pack and began gnawing at it. Roghald became horribly fascinated by the process, since the man seemingly only had three teeth in his mouth, and none of them lined up. It was an animated display of pure determination and the man's beard was soon glistening and dripping with juices as he ferociously attacked the apple with loud smacking noises and grunts.

"We're off, lads." The old sailor's declaration pulled Roghald from his observation, and he was disappointed to see his fellow rower throw the half-gnawed apple overboard and wipe his mouth on an already greasy sleeve. The sailor released the lines securing the boat to the jetty and with an experienced hand, pushed off and jumped onboard in one smooth movement. They mounted the oars and with steady strokes made their way out of the harbour.

It was a pleasant summer's day with very little headwind, and Roghald found himself enjoying being on a boat again, watching little islands slowly pass by as they made their way through the bay. He took a deep breath of the salty sea air and felt more invigorated than he had in a long time. As they came out of the inlet and into the open sea, the swell picked up a little, though not enough to make the rowing difficult or laborious, and they turned the bow north towards Gjallarholm. They rowed along the coast throughout the afternoon and before nightfall they reached a small archipelago comprising several small, rocky islands. Roghald could see a few huts and cabins on one of the larger islands.

"Fishing outpost," the old sailor explained. "Only a few people live here year-round. They shouldn't give us any problems if we don't go ashore. I'd rather anchor up here overnight than close to the mainland shore, what with all the troubles and all."

Happy to be done with rowing for the day, Roghald stretched out on his bench, his feet resting on the railing, and settled in for the night and a long overdue sleep.

ROGHALD WOKE UP to the troll in his head, blabbering incoherently. He opened his eyes to find it was still dark. The troll usually kept quiet at night and seemed to sleep when Roghald did. Now, for some reason, it seemed quite agitated and irritated. He raised his head over the side and scanned the surrounding darkness. I had delighted Roghald to discover that after his transformation to a battle troll, he had near perfect night vision. This ability had remained with him even when he was in human form and now proved very useful. Looking out over the nearest island, he saw four men huddled together on the beach. They were looking out over the sea, talking, their heads close together. Even though the moon wasn't up, and only a few stars shone down on the archipelago, Roghald knew that they could see the silhouette of their boat, anchored a little way out from the island.

He had a feeling that the men had malicious intent, and his suspicions were confirmed when they undressed and walked into the water toward Roghald and his companions. He saw the glimmer of knives as they bit down on them to free their hands for swimming. Roghald watched them push out into the water with slow movements so as not to splash. Judging by the distance and the fact that the men were going to great efforts to not make a sound, it would take them a little while to reach the boat.

Roghald smiled to himself and checked to make sure his crewmates were sound asleep before he removed his clothes. Swinging his legs over the railing, he silently lowered himself into the cold water. He didn't care the slightest about his companions, but if they had their throats slit, he would find it very difficult to sail the boat to Gjallarholm on his own.

He submerged himself and swam down a few strokes before he opened himself up to the troll within. The pain of the transformation was still excruciating, especially when the spikes and horns grew through his skin and muscles, but now that he knew what to expect, it wasn't as bad as the first few times. The voice in his head laughed madly as Roghald homed in on the four swimming bodies approaching the boat that was bobbing above his head. He swam underwater and with only two powerful strokes; he had passed the first pair of his would-be murderers. Roghald stayed submerged in the water until the second pair were right above him. Then he simply reached up and grabbed a leg in each enormous hand and yanked down, making them disappear from the surface with nothing but a slight 'plop'.

The swimmers were completely blind in the dark waters, but Roghald enjoyed watching the fear on their faces as they clawed and pulled at his hands in desperation. Their knives fell from their mouths and disappeared into the depths as their muted screams sent a stream of bubbles to the surface. As soon as they fell limp and stopped struggling, he gave them a last push downward and swam back towards the first pair. They had reached the boat and were treading water next to it. He could tell they were facing the shore, waiting for their friends, so they could launch their attack on the sleeping sailors together. Roghald was more than happy to reunite them, and soon their heads disappeared underneath the surface too. In a couple of swift movements, he snapped their necks and sent them to their watery graves.

Surfacing next to the boat, he listened for a while, but no sounds came from the boat, the two sleeping sailors unaware that Roghald had saved their lives. Changing back to his human form, to the great lamentation and wailing from his inner troll, he lifted himself up and into the boat. He patted the worst of the water off himself with a cloth from his pack before sitting himself on his bench. A gentle breeze dried the last of the water from his skin and hair as he looked up at the stars. When he dressed himself again and laid down on the bench to sleep a few more hours, he didn't take notice when a ripple passed by the hull of the boat, gently rocking it.

THEY WOKE AT first light to a welcome change of wind. A steady south-easterly had set in in the late hours of the night, and they were quick to set off so they could profit from it. Soon the sail was out and filled, pushing them north at a steady pace. The favourable winds lifted the spirits of the old sailor, who sang a few shanties as he trimmed the sail. The dour shipmate remained glum and ignored any attempts at conversation, but that again suited Roghald fine. He stretched out on his bench and dozed throughout the day.

When the sun started to set over the sea in the east, colouring the sky a fiery red, the old sailor spoke up. "The wind is holding, and it will be a bright and clear night, especially once the moon rises. As I am reluctant to anchor near the coast, we shall carry on through the night and reach Gjallarholm a day early. We will take turns doing the night watch, but any man who falls asleep, I will cast overboard, even if that means extra rowing for the remaining two of us."

Roghald was assigned the last watch, so he settled in to sleep while the old sailor navigated them north with a steady hand. The gloomy sailor roused him for his watch with a tap on the shoulder. Sitting himself on the stern board, Roghald took the rudder in his hand, blinking the sleep from his eyes. Like most Norse ships and boats, the rudder sat outside the hull, giving the ship a slight pull towards starboard, but the shallow-keel design made it easily manoeuvrable over the water. Roghald found that he was enjoying himself, guiding the boat onward under a starlit sky, and for the first time in a long time, simple joy found its way into his heart.

The moon and stars reflected on the water, and he could see the dark contour of the coastline at some distance on the port side. He was feeling quite relaxed when a strange sensation of being watched overcame him. It was a strong, undeniable feeling and Roghald could once again hear the mad troll in his mind blabbering away, adding to his uneasiness. The difference was that this time, the troll sounded... anxious.

There were no lights or silhouettes of any other boats around them, and they would have been close to impossible to spot this far out from land. Roghald could not make sense of his unease. He turned to look behind him but could see nothing, except the moonlight glimmering on the water, stirred up by the wake they left behind.

Then he saw it. Within the very wake there was an additional ripple that shouldn't be there. Something was swimming, not ten paces out from their boat, and it was following them. Whatever it was, it must be big enough to leave a large ripple while not even breaking the surface. Could it be a whale, or perhaps a big fish? He had heard of large predatory fish in the warmer southern waters that would take a man for a meal, given the opportunity, but they had never been seen here in the north.

He kept an eye on the ripple as he sailed through the last hours of the night until dawn coloured the horizon a fiery red. As soon as there was enough light, he could make out an elongated shape beneath the ripple. Whatever it was, submerged itself towards the depths of the ocean and did not rise to the surface again. As his shipmates awoke to the light of dawn, he handed over the rudder to the old sailor who, besides trimming the sail slightly, kept her on the same course as they had been on throughout the night.

THEIR GOOD WEATHER fortune held until a few hours after mid-day, when the wind fell out and a swell from the north forced them to break out the oars again.

It was hard rowing against the swell and although they were making progress, by the time the sun began to set, they were all tiring.

"If the wind had held, we would have been in Gjallarholm in a few hours. The way it is now, we cannot row through the night. We will have to anchor until the morning and either the wind will have swung back, or at least we will be rested for the last push against the swell and into port." The old sailor shielded his eyes against the sun setting over the coastline in the west. "There is a sheltered cove near to here. We can anchor in there for the night."

They turned the bow towards land and put their backs into the last leg for the day. Before long, they were gliding into a sheltered bay that Roghald had had difficulty spotting in the cliffs until they were right in front of it. He glanced over at the old sailor expertly steering them into the narrow passage. He was a smuggler, alright.

Once in the bay, the water calmed and was almost as still as a pond. They dropped anchor in the middle of it, as far from the shore as possible. The forest pushed all the way to the water's rocky edge, hiding the little cove from land as well.

The shipmates pulled out what meagre foods they had; bread, cheese and some dried meat, and settled in for their meal. Once they had eaten, the old sailor spoke.

"I want a watch through the night again. We are too close to the land for my comfort and if any trouble finds us, I want a warning as early as possible, so we can set out to sea with haste."

They agreed to use the same rotation as the previous night, so Roghald laid back on his bench to have a sleep, but he wasn't yet aware that he would not find any that night. As soon as the sun had set, the uncomfortable sensation of being watched returned. He sat up to see that a thin mist had settled in the small bay, obscuring most of the water. Scanning around, he soon saw the ripple he had been looking for. Whatever it was; it was circling the boat.

He turned to the old sailor, who was on first watch, to ask him what he made of it, but he was asleep, leaning on the rudder handle. So much for keeping a firm watch, he thought. He stretched his leg out and gave the old man a kick to rouse him, but the sailor slumped forward into the bottom of the boat and remained asleep.

Roghald grabbed his shoulder and shook him, but he did not stir, although he kept snoring. He kicked the surly one as well, for good measure, and he too remained sound asleep. He gave the man a second kick, but mostly because he didn't like him.

Something was amiss. He looked out over the water, but the fog had thickened and now lay like a blanket, so he could not see the surface of the water at all. He heard a light splash and saw two large hands grip one side of the boat. They were soon followed by a tangle of seaweed, from under which two green eyes as large as hen's eggs peered out and locked on him. Roghald backed into the stern as the boat tipped to the side, threatening to capsize, while an immense upper body pulled itself out of the ocean. A cascade of water fell from it, splashing onto the deck as it leaned in.

It was an ugly creature of a dirty, dark green colour. The hair was a mess of seaweed and mussels. Barnacles grew over its shoulders and arms, and at the waistline were green scales which glistened in the moonlight and disappeared under the water. It had the face of an old woman, although the head was twice the size of a human's. Roghald had heard tales of sea hags, and he was fairly certain he was looking at one now. He recognised her as being of troll blood. She opened her mouth, baring two rows of sharp, broad teeth, and a small crab scuttled out of her mouth, disappearing into her tangle of seaweed hair.

"I could smell the stink of a mountain thursr mucking my waters, but I could not believe one would have the nerve." Her voice gurgled and water spilled out of her mouth as she spoke.

"I did not know I was not welcome in your waters, and I am merely traveling through." he replied. It took all of Roghald's self-control to maintain a calm demeanour. The sea hag was terrifying to look at.

"You should know that there is no love lost between our kinds. The sea and land trolls parted way a long time ago. You were foolish to attempt this journey. There will be a price to pay."

"What price would you dare ask of me, thursr Roghald in the service of the jotunn Gurmr and Grundr?" he replied, squaring his shoulders.

Her eyes narrowed and a sneer curled her top lip.

"I am jotunn Havbodr, and I care not for you or your master." She looked at the boat and Roghald's shipmates. "The price I demand of you, thursr Roghald, is your humans and the ship to sink."

Roghald was just about to happily agree, the lives of the men meaningless to him, when her cruel eyes narrowed and she extended a long finger, pointing to Roghald's waist.

"The enchanted wood in your belt. I will also take this as payment for your trespass."

Roghald went cold. He could not part with the thorn. It was soul bonded to him, and he would forever be the slave of the sea hag, should she possess it.

She saw him hesitate, and a wicked grin exposed her sharp teeth once again. "If you do not accept, I will simply drown you and take it from your corpse," she said, certain of her victory.

Roghald thought hard, and an idea came to him, but it would be a close call.

"I will agree to the price you demand, Havbodr, although it will anger my master greatly, and you may yet have to answer for your actions to him," Roghald said, placing his hand on the thorn in his belt. "Since you say that there is no love lost between our kinds, also there would be no trust. I would need some assurance that you will not drown me when I have handed over my most formidable weapon," he said, tapping the thorn. "I will sit in the back of the boat, while you push it to the shore front first. Then I will throw my thorn into the water, giving me time to leave the boat and jump ashore, while you retrieve it. You will be reassured, because if I don't throw it, you will be placed between me and the shore, free to drown me if I do not honour my word."

The sea hag's eyes narrowed with suspicion, but she could not seem to find a fault in what he suggested. As a jotunn, she would defeat Roghald, they both knew that, but it might be costly, since Roghald was a battle troll and also had an enchanted weapon, so it would be in her best interests to claim her prize without a fight, which is what Roghald was betting on.

"Agreed," she hissed. "But cross me, and your slow death will be legendary in all the nine worlds."

With those words she sank back into the misty water and a sudden jolt pushed the boat forwards. Roghald placed himself at the stern, right next to the sleeping old sailor. Making sure that Havbodr was submerged and not watching, he pulled his thorn out and pushed it in between the sailor's ribs. The man died with a sigh, and Roghald could feel the thorn throbbing in his hand and a small tendril of black smoke escaped the man's wound. Roghald watched the man change while he was lying in the bottom of the boat. He could feel how the thorn shrunk a little, shrivelling as some of its power left it.

The throbbing in the thorn ceased just as the boat slid onto the gravelly beach with a crunch and he withdrew the thorn from the man's ribs. Havbodr raised her large body from the water's edge, blocking Roghald's escape.

"Now, little thursr, throw it in the water." She commanded. Looking at her, Roghald could read the deceit in her eyes as clear as day. As he had suspected, she had no intention of letting him pass; she was just waiting for him to be disarmed before she struck.

Roghald turned to the side and drew his arm back as if to throw his thorn. She was staring at it with greedy eyes, so she didn't notice that the old sailor had flicked his dead, white eyes open. Only when he launched himself at her, strong draugr arms extended, did she take her eyes off the thorn. With a shriek of anger, she swatted the draugr away just before it reached her, and he fell in the water with a splash. The moment of distraction had left her open for what Roghald had planned next. No sooner had she snapped her head towards him, her face a mask of rage, than a dark vine whipped into her face, wrapping around her head.

Roghald's thorn had extended into its full form; a long, spiked whip. The hundreds of little thorns leaked burning sap into already painful wounds, and she clawed at her face to tear it off. Roghald, still holding on to the whip, dashed to the bow of the boat as he changed into his thursr form. One powerful leap launched him onto the shore, past the struggling sea hag.

Havbodr was thrashing in the shallow water as the whip stung and burned her flesh, when suddenly it released, and she instinctively dove under the water. Roghald was already amongst the trees when she resurfaced a second later, black, stinging wounds on her face and neck. She looked around for the thursr with bared teeth. Roghald let a laugh ring out from the safety of land.

"I guess you bit off more than you could chew, you overgrown sardine!" Roghald called out as he ran from the shore. Her shrieks of rage were soon followed by the sound of the boat being smashed to pieces.

Roghald let go of his thursr shape when he had put a comfortable distance between himself and the shore. He sat down on a fallen log as he gathered his thought. This latest development was a slight problem, because now he had to approach Gjallarholm from land after all, but he was still feeling quite smug about having outwitted the sea hag. He would continue north through the night. If he needed to sneak past the sentries at the fortress, he was better off doing it under the cover of darkness.

He got up and made good progress through the dark forest, reassured that he was the most dangerous thing in it. Before long, a red glow reflected off the clouds in the northern sky and he knew he was close to Gjallarholm.

Soon he stood at the end of the forest, looking out over unkempt fields. The Gjallarholm fortress sprawled in the background, flooded with light from hundreds of torches and fires.

He moved closer, keeping low as he made his way through the fields, until he reached the town in front of the walls. Though the buildings were long since abandoned, he moved forward at a snail's pace, frequently stopping to listen for any hidden sentries. A sudden movement in an alleyway to his left made him spin around and he raised his thorn in front of him. Roghald scanned the debris and broken crates for several heartbeats until he saw a cat slip around the corner. He let out a breath and chuckled as he continued through the town.

When he came to the last building, he crouched behind an old cart and carefully raised his head to look out over the fortress. Built larger and with much taller walls than Hornsborg, the fortress seemed almost impenetrable where it stood. When it's time came, Roghald thought as he gazed over the stone walls and towers, Gjallarholm would have to fall from deceit and cunning, not brute force. With defence in mind, an empty field had been kept clear between the town buildings and fortress for at least a hundred paces.

Fires burned at regular intervals along the towering walls, lighting up the ground in front of him, making it impossible for an invading force to approach unseen. The gates were firmly shut, and the gatehouse bathed in light from fires and torches above it. Roghald scanned the fortress looking for a weakness, There were four square stone towers protruding from the walls at even distances, and in front of them there was a small strip of darkness, where the light from the fires on the walls could not quite reach. Roghald smiled. He had found his way into the fortress. He just needed a distraction.

CHAPTER 29

Ash, Torsten and Yrsa raised their weapons as soon as they heard the rustling, but within seconds, they found themselves surrounded, a dozen arrows aimed at their heads. After a tense few seconds, they relaxed as the arrows were lowered to reveal scouts and woodsmen from Gjallarholm. They gave their names and were welcomed with relieved smiles when they were identified as friends and not foes.

The captain of the scouts, a short, lean man named Bjarte, offered to escort them to the fortress. As they walked, he explained that there had been no attacks on the roads for several weeks and the scouts patrolling the area had seen no evidence of the draugr roaming nearby. The townspeople had begun to hope that the threat was over.

Ash watched the man's face turn pale when Yrsa told him what had happened in Hornsborg and the trap that had sealed the fate of both Jarl Olaf and the Jomsvikings. When she told him that they expected the draugr horde would turn to Gjallarholm next, he excused himself to turn back for his men, and they walked alone towards the fortress. As night set in around them, they watched a multitude of fires and torches being lit along the walls ahead of them, chasing the darkness away.

They arrived at the first houses and Ash experienced the same eerie feeling walking through the abandoned town surrounding Gjallarholm, as he had at Hornsborg. He looked towards the fortress and the sentries lining the walls reassured him that no draugr lay waiting for them inside.

When they came to the gatehouse, they found it open, but a dozen guards lingered outside, ready to shut it at a moment's notice. Several of the guards recognised them and they were ushered through. The courtyard inside the gates was a hub of activity, even at this time of night. With the townsfolk evacuated from their homes, most of them had opted to stay in the fortress, close to their homes, instead of leaving south. This seemed to have allowed for an improvised marketplace to spring up just inside the walls. Various foods, garments and weaponry were for sale at inflated prices, he noticed, as they weaved their way through the torch-lit marketplace.

Walking up the stone stairs to the fortress proper, they were waved through by a pair of hirdsmen, and were soon stepping through the long corridor, towards Jarl Astrid's hall. Pushing open the doors, they were met by a wall of noise and stale air, as close to a hundred men and women sat eating and drinking in animated conversations.

They saw Jarl Astrid at her table at the end of the hall and headed towards her. As they got closer the Jarl spotted them and a look of relief lit up her face. She stood up to greet them, her eyebrows raising when she laid eyes on Ash, now several hands taller than when she had last seen him, but said nothing about it. She waved her arm at a free bench close to her, indicating for them to sit.

"Eat and rest, we will discuss matters tomorrow."

They sat down gratefully, taking the weight of tired legs, setting their weapons and packs down behind them. Ash's rune covered shield drew many curious looks from the men and women of Astrid's hird, so he threw his cape over it, having no desire to discuss it with anyone. They ate and drank, and some tension fell away as they enjoyed the momentary safety of a hall full of friendly warriors.

Hours passed and Ash had long since eaten his fill. He sat nursing a mug of ale, looking out over the crowd in the hall. It was a strange sensation to be amongst so many people after spending years in Eikinri's workshop with the dwarf as his only company. He found himself missing the Stonesmith and their simple life together. Torsten slapped him on the back, pulling him from his reverie.

"I haven't been described as the cleanliest of Berserkers, but I think what my sore legs and back need most right now is a hot bath. Shall we bring along an ale and go soak for a while?"

To Ash, this sounded like a fantastic idea. The noise of the hall was giving him a headache, and he was more than happy to escape it. He nodded to his big friend, who smiled and filled both their mugs from a frothing jug in front of them.

As they stood, Torsten tapped Yrsa, who was engrossed in a discussion with Jarl Astrid seated next to her, on the shoulder.

"We're off to the bathhouse. Feel free to join us."

Yrsa gave him a disgusted look. "As much joy as the thought of you washing brings me, Torsten, I have better things to do than watch your hairy arse float around in a bathtub."

The big man laughed and winked at Yrsa before grabbing his mug as he walked out of the hall with Ash in tow. Ash had been eager to speak with Rani, but figured it could wait a little while. She would probably prefer it if he didn't stink her rooms out, anyway.

The bath house was located outside, next to the fortress, and they followed a trail of torches that lit the way to a squat timber building against the fortress walls. Ash could see steam escaping from small ventilation holes close to the roof, and a smell of scented oils hung in the air. Torsten pushed the timber door open and a cloud of steam billowed out. Walking inside, Ash's eyes soon adjusted to the gloom, and he saw several large wooden tubs evenly spaced across the floor. A long fire crackled in a hearth on the back wall and large copper pots were suspended over it, heating water.

The bathhouse was almost empty at this time of night; only two women were sitting in a tub, one running a bone comb through the other's hair. Ash knew that men and women bathed together, but he was still not entirely comfortable with the idea of strutting around naked in front of anyone. He moved into a dark corner to remove his clothes, then wrapped a drying cloth around his waist.

Torsten had no such reservations, and Ash turned to see him merrily chatting to the women as he removed his many layers of fur and chain mail. By the tattoos wrapping around their arms and shoulders, he knew they were shieldmaidens and Torsten seemed to know them. Ash had no interest in talking to anyone while he was in the nude, and so he jumped into the tub furthest away from the trio.

The hot, herb scented water enveloped him like a warm blanket, and he sunk into it up to his nose. After soaking for a few minutes, he scrubbed his hair and feet and once satisfied that he was clean; he laid back and relaxed, closing his eyes. He was vaguely aware that the shieldmaidens left, and he heard a splash in the tub next to him, followed by water sloshing onto the floor, no doubt from Torsten's volume added to a too small bathtub.

Ash looked up to see the big man leaning back in the water, smacking his lips happily, having drained his mug of ale. He let the empty wooden mug drop to the floor and began combing his beard out with a similar bone comb to the one the women had used. He looked over at Ash and smiled as he kept combing. "Be good to get the lice out," he rumbled. "I know it's a sign of good health to have them, but there have been a few too many for my liking lately."

Ash ran his hand over his own sparse growth on his chin but didn't think he was at risk of a lice invasion just yet. After a few more minutes of scrubbing and combing, Torsten climbed out of his now murky bath water and emptied a few buckets of cold water from a barrel over his head, snorting and huffing.

"That will do for me. I have run out of ale and I worked up quite a thirst over the last few weeks." he told Ash.

"I will linger for a while, I think," Ash replied.

"Careful that you don't dissolve. Too much water is bad for you," his friend warned him as he was drying himself with a cloth. The Berserker was soon dressed and gave a wave to Ash as he left.

Ash, seeing that he was alone, snuck out of his tub and fetched a couple of buckets of boiling water from one of the copper pots and poured it into his bath.

He sunk into the now steaming water with a happy sigh and felt the knots in his muscles beginning to dissolve as he relaxed. He shut his eyes and with the warmth and the pleasant scent of herbs soothing him; it wasn't long before he nodded off.

He stood in a dark and decayed landscape. Ruined buildings could be seen in the distance, and what remained of the once lush forests were twisted, leafless trunks and stumps. No birds sang, and no animals could be seen in the fields. The air was still and stagnant. Dried bones and rusty armour were scattered across the ground before him; remnants of a battle fought long ago.

He saw sickening, dark veins stretching across the ground, covering the entire landscape. Ash knew he needed to find the source of the decay or the world would be lost to the sickness forever. He moved like a ghost across the silent landscape, following the dark veins. He ran for hours and soon arrived at the rim of what looked like an enormous crater. The dark veins spread out across the land from a hole in the centre of it. Ash slid down the walls of the crater, pebbles and dust racing ahead of him as he tried to keep his balance on the dry, dead surface.

Soon he stood before the hole, so large he would not be able to throw a rock across it. The venations spreading from the hole were much thicker here and appeared to be moving a little at times. Laying his hands on one, he could sense the decay and corruption as clearly as he could see it. It was as if a sickness pulsated through the tendril and he could feel it creep up his arm like a film of grease and he pulled his arm away. Ash wiped his hand on the front of his tunic, but the film remained. He knew he needed to climb down the hole to reach the source, but there were no other purchases except the sickening tendrils. Ash steeled himself and took a firm grip on one as he lowered himself over the edge. He climbed for what felt like hours until he saw a light at the bottom of the hole.

Without Ash realising exactly when, the climbing had changed from moving down the hole to climbing up, so that when he scrambled out of it, he came up, despite having only travelled in what seemed only one direction. He felt nauseated but couldn't tell if it was from touching the sickness or from the disorientation.

Looking around, Ash stood in a cold, mountainous landscape. Endless rocky peaks stretched out to the horizon, surrounded by deep gullies, filled with dense, purple-tinted vegetation. The light was dim, and he looked up to see heavy, low clouds only letting sparse sunlight through. An icy wind sent a shiver through his body, and the air smelled like sulphur and iron. A strange sense of familiarity filled him, but he had never seen this place before, of this he was certain.

The dark veins he had followed did not spread here to cover the entire surface like the previous land he had come from. Here all the veins lay in one direction. Ash could feel a sense of urgency, so he started running alongside the growths, and soon he stood before a dark mountain. Massive gates sealed a huge opening in its side. The gates were made from dark and ancient timber, studded with sharp spikes. Amongst the spikes were intricate carvings of monstrous faces, baring their teeth, threatening all who would dare to enter. The dark veins disappeared underneath the doors. Ash had found the source of the infestation. He took another look at the otherworldly landscape and then knew where he was. He had heard of this place in the Sagas. As children, sitting huddled by the fire, the elders would try to frighten them with tales of this place. He was in Jotunheim; the world of trolls and giants.

He looked beneath the gate, and there was a crack that would be large enough to allow him to squeeze through.

"Ash!"

He stood up. The voice sounded familiar. He spun around but saw nothing but the desolate landscape.

"He is here! Ash, wake up!"

Ash sat up, water splashing over the edge of the tub and onto the floor.

That was Rani's voice. He leapt out of the bath, snatching his shield and pulling the sword from its sheath and ran to the door. He threw it open, almost knocking over a man carrying a stack of cloths on the other side. He pushed past the man, sprinted towards the fortress and Shifted. When he did, the surrounding people slowed down as he sped up.

From the courtyard, he glanced up at the tower where Rani had been residing to see a bright blue light flashing in the window, and he doubled his effort. Please, Odin, don't let him be too late.

CHAPTER 30

ROGHALD WAS MOVING LIKE A GHOST THROUGH THE
forest. He could see the glow from Gjallarholm far in the
distance as he crept from tree to tree. He had picked up the scent
he was looking for a while back and was drawing closer to his prey
by the minute.

Fortune had it that he had gone hunting for one when he was
young and had always remembered the smell of its den. Then, they
had used hounds to track one down, but with Roghald's heightened senses in his thursr shape, he didn't need dogs to track it.
They had also used half a dozen men with long spears to bring it
down, and even then, it was at great risk. Now, Roghald would take
one on with his bare hands, but he had no concerns about what the
outcome would be.

He heard a crack of a branch behind a copse of trees ahead of
him and froze. Roghald listened and soon heard a snuffling sound,
as if the beast was smelling the air. All was still and Roghald knew
that it, like him, was listening intently.

A low, deep growl rumbled amongst the trees ahead of him.
Roghald squinted to see through the thickets and low hanging tree
branches, but to no avail.

Then the forest in front of him exploded as a massive shape shot out from behind the copse and launched at him with a furious roar. The bear was as big as him, and Roghald got a glimpse of vicious teeth and claws as it bore down on him.

But Roghald had been ready. With lightning reflexes, he jumped to the side just as the bear was about to tackle him. He pushed off a tree, jumping back at the animal and wrapped one muscular arm around its neck as he put all his weight on its back. With his other hand, he pushed the thorn deep into the bear's neck and held on.

The bear shook and twisted like mad, but soon its roar of rage turned into a drawn-out yelp of pain as the thorn pumped its sickness into its body. Roghald noticed how the thorn shrunk and shrivelled further in his hand. This better work, he thought. To be honest, he wasn't so sure it would, or if the source tree's magic would work on anything besides humans.

The bear staggered a few times before dropping to the ground under his weight. It sighed deeply once and didn't breathe again.

Roghald pushed itself off its shaggy, brown fur and stood back. Seconds ticked by and nothing happened. Roghald had just started swearing at himself for wasting the thorn's precious magic when the bear shivered. He watched as it opened its eyelid to reveal a milky, dead eye that locked on him.

"Hello, pet."

ROGHALD POKED HIS head up behind a dung heap on the outskirts of town. He was just outside the light radius of the walls, and if he didn't make any sudden movements, he should not be spotted.

He focused and was able to sense the bear that stood idle behind a house close to the gates of the fortress. Roghald was hidden further down the wall, opposite the last of the towers. He looked at the welcoming strip of darkness that ran up the face of the tower. Scanning the walls, he saw the guards evenly spaced out on top of them, most of them looking out at the dark, searching for the draugr horde.

229

Roghald sent a command to the bear, and it started thrashing about, smashing a crate to pieces. Shouts were heard from the gatehouse and the closest guards on the walls ran towards the gate. Jarl Astrid's guards were more disciplined than he had expected, because most of them remained in their positions, however their attention was solely on the area in front of the gate.

Making noises wasn't enough, he decided, and sent another command to the bear. The now mindless beast lumbered out from behind the house and moved around in the street just beyond the light.

A high-pitched shout could be heard from the gatehouse, the fear in it making Roghald snort, before he placed his hand over his mouth, stopping the laughter that threatened to escape.

Several twangs could be heard as the guards fired bows into the night. The excitement was enough for the guards on the walls to break discipline and jog along the crenelations towards the gatehouse. Getting there, they added their bows to the already firing guards and Roghald could hear a smatter of arrows landing around the houses closest to the gate. This was the moment he was waiting for. Roghald dashed out from behind the dung heap and in a dozen long strides, he dove into the strip of darkness in front of the tower.

He held still for a moment, listening for anyone to raise the alarm. Besides the shouting at the gate, the wall above him remained silent. It was time to calm everyone down. He sent a command to the bear who, riddled with arrows, staggered out to the light in front of the gate. He made it drop down on the ground and move no more. There was a moment of silence, followed by laughter from the top of the walls. The laughter was taken up by all the guards as the tension fell off them, followed by a cheer. They all were relieved that it was just an old bear that had come sniffing around the abandoned town.

Roghald sat still in the dark, waiting for all the excitement to die down. He sat there for an hour, reassuring himself that the sentries were sufficiently bored again and the alertness from the bear incident had worn off.

Then he stood, looking up the face of the tower. It was a square tower that protruded somewhat from the walls surrounding the fortress. It would be very effective against a force in a siege, allowing archers to shoot down attackers along the wall, however, for a single enemy to climb unseen at night, it offered nothing but protection. He counted three stories, by the arrow slits on every level.

He ran his hand over the stones in the wall. They were well fitted together, but there was enough of a crack between the stone blocks that something sharp could be inserted and levelled to allow for climbing. Something like a clawed hand, he thought with a grin as he once again assumed his thursr shape, ignoring the mad laughter as it drowned out all other sounds for a moment. The laughter even escaped his own lips for a second before he could stop it, and he felt a pang of concern. It felt like the mad troll in his mind was getting louder each time he changed. He shook his head to clear it before turning his attention back to the wall.

He stuck the inch-long claws of his right hand into the crack and tested the weight. His strength was such that he could lift himself off the ground, even with one hand, and so he hoisted himself a little way up the wall. Slowly, to avoid making a sound, he made his ascent up the wall. Roghald made sure to remain in the centre of the tower where the darkness was thickest and carefully skirted the arrow slits as he passed them, so as not to be seen from within.

It wasn't long until he raised his head above the topmost battlement of the tower. There was a sentry there, dressed in the same uniform red cloak as the guards he'd seen on the walls. The sentry was looking over the edge of the wall and into the courtyard and marketplace on the other side of the tower, having likely grown bored with staring at the dark town and forest on the other side. Roghald was quick to profit on such good fortune and, without a sound, hoisted himself over the crenelation, silently dropping down behind the guard. He reached out and wrapped his large hand around the guard's throat, rendering him voiceless as he pulled him away from the edge and throttled him. The man resisted for a short while but was soon lying dead at Roghald's feet.

Roghald lifted the man's cloak and clothes off of him as well as his spear and helmet. He transformed back to his human shape and dressed in the guard's clothes and threw the cape over his own shoulders. The clothes fitted him well enough, but the helmet was a bit tight, chafing at the back of his head, but it would have to do.

He was suddenly invisible, just a guard amongst many, in a fortress prepared for war. He lifted the man over the outside edge of the battlement; careful to drop him in the shade of the tower from whence he had come. The body landed on the ground with a thud. Roghald stood still for a full minute, listening for any signs that an alarm was being raised, but nothing happened.

There was a timber hatch in the floor of the tower, and Roghald lifted it a crack to peek in. Stone steps led down to the level below, where a lonesome torch lit the way for anyone accessing the tower. The fact that no one was present on the floor to scout out the windows, proved Roghald's suspicion that more importance was placed on the sentries atop the walls, where the light of the fires was assumed to be sufficient for any incoming threats to be seen.

All the other floors were empty and when Roghald reached the bottom floor, equally devoid of guards, he could only see one door. He opened it with caution, and peered out onto a well-lit courtyard, crowded with a variety of market stalls. He slipped out and pushed his way through the bustle of people and soon walked up the stone steps to the fortress, passing two guards who didn't even spare him a glance in his red cloak.

Although he had travelled through Gjallarholm before the draugr took him, he had not been inside the fortress before. However, the layout was familiar, similar to all Norse keeps, with the Jarl's great hall, the heart of his or her power, accessible from the entrance. He followed behind a hirdswoman in a blue cape as he entered through the great doors and into the fortress. Sure enough, to his right, he could see the entrance to the great hall with its doors wide open.

There was clamour and commotion inside as a great many people ate and drank at the Jarl's tables. Roghald looked to the end of the hall where a raised dais marked the Jarl's own table. A handsome woman in her middle age, dressed in a plain but well-tailored green dress, was, without doubt, Jarl Astrid herself. She was head to head with a shieldmaiden involved in a quiet discussion. The shieldmaiden seemed very familiar to Roghald, even though he couldn't quite place her. Someone bumped into him, and he realized he would draw attention to himself, standing in the doorway, gawking like a peasant.

Roghald quickly found a free spot next to some off-duty servants in the corner closest to the doors and sat down. He took his cape off and placed it in his lap under the table. He didn't need anyone wondering why a guard would sit at a servant's table. Helping himself to a platter of hot potatoes and some bread, he smiled and nodded a greeting to the person across from him. It was a rotund, middle-aged man in a servant's garb. The man had a loathsome look to him and as soon as he spoke to Roghald in an arrogant, nasal voice, Roghald had to suppress a sudden urge to punch him in the face.

"Why aren't you sitting with your friends?" the man asked, nodding his head towards the many warriors sitting closer to the Jarl's table.

Roghald pursed his lips before answering. "Had a misunderstanding with the Captain about his sister," he said with a sheepish grin. "I think it might be best to keep a low profile for a while."

The servant let out a barking laugh. "Well, Captain Jorma has never given me a reason to feel kindly towards him, so you are welcome with me."

Roghald gave him an awkward smile and began eating. Between mouthfuls he chatted with the servant, whose name was Birk, steering the conversation where he wanted it.

"So, is there a lot more work to be done with all these extra people now living behind the walls?" he asked between mouthfuls.

"Not really," Birk replied. "I mean, there is for those who work outside, because most of the people who have moved into the fortress are camping out in the courtyard, the stables or down at the docks. Besides the old Seidwoman in the western tower and a few Jomsvikings, there really aren't many extra people inside the fortress, which suits me fine."

Roghald sat up straighter at the mention of Rani. "Can't say I have seen much of the old hag myself," Roghald told the man. "What with being out on patrol most of the time. Does she come down much?"

"She rarely leaves," Birk mumbled, chewing on a piece of bread. "I have to bring her most of her meals, and my poor knees don't fare well on those stairs, let me tell you."

"Surely, they could send food with her guards, and spare your knees?" Roghald asked, feigning annoyance on the man's part.

"That would be a good idea, but she has got no guards, unfortunately. Why would she need them in the heart of the Jarl's fortress?"

It took all of Roghald's willpower not to smile from ear to ear. "Well, you never know," he said.

Roghald endured some further small talk, before excusing himself and leaving the table and stepped out of the hall. Making sure no one was paying him any attention, he swept the red cape over his shoulders once again and put the helmet on his head. During dinner he had watched the movements of the men and women serving and had therefore learned in what direction the kitchen was located, and it took him no time to find it.

Entering through the doorway, he looked out over the large room dedicated to feeding the entire fortress. It was warm and full of enticing aromas. Dozens of servants milled about between tables laden with breads, casks, jugs and fresh meats and vegetables. The kitchen had four broad fireplaces along the back wall, all roasting some kind of meat or another. One even held an entire stag, slowly being rotated on a spit by a sullen-looking kitchen boy.

After a few minutes of watching the bustle closely, a pattern became apparent to Roghald; everything that took place inside the large kitchen revolved around one person. A plump little woman was making the rounds, talking to everyone and tasting everything, as she made her way through all the working spaces. She was resting a large wooden spoon on her shoulder, a symbol of her power and undisputed rule over the kingdom that was the kitchen.

The lad who was turning the spit appeared to have been lost in a daydream, with the rotation of the great beast having slowed down since Roghald entered the kitchens. One great whack to the back of his leg with the wooden spoon woke him up with a yelp and he picked up his speed again.

When the woman approached the door where Roghald was standing, he assumed a bored look and waved her over. She did not look impressed at seeing a guard in her kitchen and after looking Roghald up and down; she marched over to him and crossed her arms.

"What?" she demanded, her rosy cheeks wrinkling as she frowned at him.

"Jarl Astrid sent me. She says the Seidwoman needs a pitcher of water and some bread and I am to take it to her immediately."

Her eyes narrowed. "Why didn't she just send Birk?"

"He had to go see the healer about his knees, or something." Roghald sighed with exasperation. "Either way, I have had a lot of grief from both the Jarl and Captain Jorma today, so let me just be on my way, will you?"

A disgusted look came over the cook. "Serves you right to run a servant's errand, then. Take what you need over there," she said, pointing to some tables with her large spoon.

"And how do I find the tower?" Roghald asked. "I never patrol inside the fortress."

She gave him a long stare before rolling her eyes. "Out the door you came, up the stairs to the end of the corridor, then the door on your left opens up to the stairs leading to the Seidwoman's rooms. Now hurry up and get out of my kitchens!" With those words she turned her back and stomped away, resuming the governance of her small kingdom. She didn't even notice that Roghald had left without collecting any of the items he had requested.

ROGHALD MADE HIS way through the empty corridors. The cook had given clear instructions and soon he was sneaking up the spiral staircase in the central tower. He could feel the excitement building up within him. As he pulled out the thorn from inside his tunic, he could see the soft red light of the runes throb in time with his own accelerated heartbeat.

He came to a rough wooden door at the top of the stairs and placed his ear to it. Nothing. He bent down and looked through the keyhole but could only see the back wall dimly lit by the flickering light from a fire. He placed his hand on the door and pushed ever so gently. It gave way and swung open a crack. So, she hadn't locked it. Big mistake, he thought, smiling to himself.

He put his eye to the crack and could now see one part of the room. All was still, but looking over at the bed, there was a bundle under some furs. He had caught her asleep. This was going to be even easier than he thought. He opened the door wide enough so he could step through it.

The metal hinges creaked a little, but the bundle on the bed didn't move, so he took a few quiet steps towards the bed.

A burning pain exploded in his left side and Roghald fell to his knees. The agony was so great that his entire body seized up. It felt like ice, but it burned like fire, spreading through his entire being. Only able to draw shallow breaths, he slowly forced his head down and saw that a deer antler, about the same size as a dagger, had been stuck in between his ribs. It had small runes on it, which illuminated the room with flashes of bright blue light. An old, frail looking hand held the base of the antler and a voice he only knew too well spoke in his ear from behind him.

"So, Roghald Einarson. The trolls did not find you wanting when it came to betraying your own people." She spoke calmly, but there was steel in her voice.

"Did you not think that I would be able to sense the filth that tarnishes your soul approaching?" She pushed the antler a bit deeper, and the pain intensified. "Though I will gladly grant it to you, death is more than you deserve. Any last words before I send your soul to Helheim?"

Roghald drew a few more ragged breaths. The pain was excruciating, but he had turned, inch by inch, his right hand and pointed the thorn at the Seidwoman.

"Yes," he gasped. "You should have killed me as soon as I entered your room."

Rani's eyes widened for a split second before the vine extended with lightning speed and wrapped around her arm holding the antler. With a snap, it ripped the weapon from her hand and out of Roghald's body. The wound still pained him, but it was nothing compared to his suffering of a moment ago.

With a swipe of his arm, the Seidwoman's frail body was thrown across the room, crashing into a table and chairs. She was moaning and tried to get up, but Roghald whipped the thorn at her again and it coiled around her neck and shoulders, lifting her up and pushing her against the wall. With the thorn bound to his soul, he had full control of it, and it felt like an extension of himself. It was with great pleasure he watched the once feared Seidwoman struggle and suffer under his power.

Still in his human form, his ears filled with the manic laughter of the mad troll and he felt the first tingles of his body changing. No! He was in control! He wrestled the troll away in his mind and the tingling disappeared.

Sensing his distraction, Rani began a deep wordless chant. The room darkened and Roghald could feel a great pressure building in his ears. He grinned at Rani, as the tip of the thorn grew small black sprouts that sought out and entered her mouth and nostrils, ending her chanting. The light soon returned, and the pressure dissipated. He tightened the vine around her neck, suffocating her. He could feel her panic through the thorn as she kicked and tore at the vine, but to no avail. Her death would be something he would treasure for a long time.

CHAPTER 31

ASH WAS STILL SOAKING WET AS HE SPRINTED, ARMED, barefoot and naked, through the doors of the fortress. The guards noticed him coming and though they attempted to step out and block his way; he was Shifted, and they didn't stand a chance.

"Help! The tower!" he called to them, hoping they would understand his sped up words.

He darted inside and leapt up the first set of stairs in a couple of strides before sprinting down the corridor and throwing open the door to the tower staircase. He ran up to Rani's quarters as fast as he could. When he saw that her door was open, he threw himself through the doorway and into a scene of horror.

He saw a big man standing with his back towards him, holding some kind of tree branch. It extended away from him and at the end of it; Rani was hanging several feet off the ground, the branch wrapped around her face, neck and shoulders. She was still moving, but it seemed she wouldn't be for long. Ash let out a cry and raised his sword, but almost dropped it when the man turned his head and Ash recognised the too familiar face.

"Roghald!"

He saw the stable master's face split into a manic grin and

Ash was so shocked that he could not concentrate enough to stay Shifted.

"What-?" was all he had time to say before the vine dropped Rani, who fell in a heap on the floor, then whipped around at him, as quick as a snake strikes. Ash ducked in time but could feel the breeze of it close to his head as it swept by.

"How I have longed for this day!" Roghald's voice sounded unfamiliar. It was deeper, and it sounded almost like when two people speak in unison. "Your death will be as painful as I can make it, and you will finally know that I was always your better!"

Ash could see in his eyes that Roghald was mad, but there was something else unusual about him, yet familiar somehow. He felt a sensation similar to being in Beli's presence. Roghald felt like a troll. Ash could only stare at the man, shocked.

"But first, I will make you suffer for all the pain and shame you have caused me. You will beg me for death before long." The strange vine in his hand contracted and shrunk until it was just a wooden spike and Roghald spread his arms out by his sides. Then his features changed and grew grotesque. Ash took two steps backwards, the colour draining from his face as his old stable master grew taller and wider, spikes growing from his shoulders and horns from his forehead as a monstrosity took form in front of him. Then Ash recognised him. It was the troll from Hornsborg. The very same troll who had killed Jarl Erik and set the trap which killed Jarl Olaf and most of the Jomsvikings.

It only took a second for Ash's shock and fear to turn to rage. The anger burned red hot and grew with every breath he took, as his memories of all the deaths flooded back. He raised his sword and shield and stood to face the beast.

The troll's eyebrows shot up when his eyes fell on the weapon and he recognised it. "You come at me with my own father's sword?" Anger flashed in Roghald's eyes. "I will take it from you and run it into your guts!" The troll moved fast, its giant fist coming straight for Ash, but he Shifted again and raised the shield in time to block it. It was a reflex from training with Eikinri, and before the thursr's powerful blow landed, he wondered for a split second if he had made a mistake. Though the blow struck hard and a white flash filled the room, the shield and Ash held. He looked up at a surprised troll, glancing down at its fist, little tendrils of smoke rising from it.

The surprise only lasted for a second and soon rage filled the troll again, as he threw blow after blow at Ash and his shield. The battle troll moved with incredible speed, even when Ash was Shifted. He had to drop the sword to support the shield with two hands after one particularly hard blow drove it into his face. A trickle of blood ran down his chin from where the rim of the shield had split his bottom lip.

With every strike, light flashed in the room and although the shield held, Ash was pushed further and further back with every powerful blow. Soon he would be in the corner with nowhere else to go, and Roghald could overpower him. He needed to get out of the tower, not only so he could fight better, but so he could get the troll away from Rani, who lay helpless in the corner still. The doorway was a few paces to his right, but he didn't think he could get there without getting clobbered.

Then a simple solution presented itself. Ash waited until his back was against the wall and when the troll drew his arm back for a final blow, he stopped Shifting and simply stepped back and sunk through the stone. He came through the other side of the wall and fell a few feet down until he landed on the spiral staircase. Ash stumbled, and almost fell down the staircase, but regained his balance at the same time as he heard a surprised grunt from the troll. He rushed up the few steps to the doorway and stuck his head inside.

The thursr was running his hand over the wall where Ash had disappeared. When Ash coughed theatrically, his head snapped around, a confused look on his face. Ash smiled and made an obscene gesture he had seen the hirdsmen and shieldmaidens do, enraging the troll who now threw himself at Ash. He pulled his head out of the doorway and started running down the stairs. His immediate instinct was to Shift again, but he would need to preserve his energy for the fight, and he was already feeling a little fatigued from running to the tower Shifted. If he ran out of power now, he would be dead.

Dashing down the stairs, he won some time as the thursr had to squeeze through the doorway, but soon he could hear heavy footfalls on the stairs above him. His heart sank when he heard angry voices from the bottom of the stairs. Sprinting past the guards earlier, followed by loud noises and the commotion from the tower, had set off the alarm.

He should have been glad for the reinforcements, but unfortunately they would block his escape down the stairs and before he would have a chance to explain things, an enraged troll the size of a bull would crash into them, killing everyone. Ash looked around. Every few yards along the stairs, there was a window designed for archers defending the fortress. These windows were covered in shutters for most of the year, but it being summer, they were now open to allow for some ventilation of the stuffy stairway. The windows were just large enough that Ash could slip out of them while the troll certainly couldn't. But where would Ash go, anyway? He was in a tower, and it was a couple of stories drop to the roof of the main fortress, and he had no hope surviving a fall like that.

Then an idea struck him. He removed his shield, dropping it on the stairs before leaping up to the sill of the closest window and stuck his legs out of it. Most of his body was hanging outside of the tower, legs dangling in the open air. Ash clung on to the windowsill as he waited for Roghald. After only a few seconds, the thursr came lumbering down the stairs, and seeing Ash almost completely out of the window, Roghald froze for a second. Ash smiled and waved at him.

"As slow and clumsy as you are ugly," Ash teased. "No wonder they kicked you out of Erik's hird all those years ago."

Roghald exploded in blind rage and threw himself at Ash, who now let go of the windowsill before the troll could catch him. Ash pushed his hands forwards beneath the windowsill and let them sink into the stone on the outside of the tower. When his hands were submerged in the stone, he concentrated and lowered himself by the sheer friction of his hands flowing through the rock. He was coming down fast, but still slow enough to avoid breaking his legs once he landed on the roof.

He was about halfway down when the first boom was heard from the window above. When he landed on the roof, a rain of rocks followed a second boom from above as the troll smashed a hole where the window had been. Ash pulled himself close to the wall to avoid the larger pieces, which were shattering roof tiles as they crashed all around him.

Looking up, he saw the troll swinging down from a hole in the wall, holding on to that thorny vine of his, and getting lower by the second. This was as far as Ash had planned, so all he could do now was run. He had no weapons, so he needed desperately to find some. Quickly. He set off across the roof and soon heard the troll land at the base of the tower with a cracking of roof panes followed by heavy steps running behind him.

Ash had never been up on the roof of the fortress, which seemed to be a haphazard landscape of many smaller wooden and ceramic tiled roofs that had unevenly merged together over the centuries. There had been many additions and extensions to allow the formation of what was now a vast building. An extensive collection of chimneys was scattered across the uneven roof, and Ash weaved around them in an attempt to slow down the troll.

There was a thud next to him as the vine struck a chimney he had just slipped past. The troll was gaining on him. He had wanted to save his Shifting energy until he was armed and could fight back, but he had no choice anymore. The world slowed down, and the air thickened around him as he pulled away from Roghald, running along the ridge of the central rooftop. He scurried down the edge of this roof and onto a smaller perpendicular roof that ran the length of the fortress.

Sprinting about halfway along it, he could see the defensive walls below him and the ground several stories below. It was still too far to jump, and he could see that the roof ended ahead of him with nowhere else to go. If he did not think of something, he was about to be trapped on the edge of the roof. He risked a glance behind him and could see the thursr dropping down from the central roof. He had gained some distance, though not as much as he had hoped.

Then, light-headedness overcame him as the Shifting took its toll. Now at his limits, Ash had no choice but to stop Shifting or he would collapse. Time sped up and he could hear the troll's stomps behind him getting louder. He reached the end of the roof and his heart sank as he saw nothing that he could use to climb down. The roof overhung the wall of the fortress by several feet, and he doubted that he could reach the stone wall underneath in order to repeat his trick of moving through rock.

Below him was nothing other than a big drop to the cobbled stones of the port quay. He was trapped. He considered the option of jumping and attempting to pass the quay so he could land in the waters of the harbour. It would have to be quite the jump, or he would smack onto the stone quay, killing himself.

A terrible pain struck his shoulder and still reeling from the blow, he saw Roghald pulling his arm back for another whip with the vine. He felt warm blood trickling down his arm and knew that the next strike would be the last. Well, that settled it. Ash took three quick steps towards the corner of the roof, and the very last second before he reached it, he Shifted and leapt as far forward as he could. But as soon as he had sprung off the roof, unconsciousness claimed him as the last of his energy drained away.

CHAPTER 32

ASH OPENED HIS EYES. HE WAS LYING ON HIS BACK, looking up at a lush forest canopy. Soft sunlight filtered through the leaves and birdsong filled the air. He could hear burbling water nearby. He sat up and saw that he was next to a small stream, the water playfully splashing over the rocks. It was the most beautiful place he had ever seen. He turned to see Rani sitting on a rock next to him. She had her bag of bones in her lap and she was flicking them one after the other into the stream.

"Am I dead?" he asked her.

"Not quite yet," she replied. "Did I not tell you that when that day comes, your mother would come to collect you?"

He looked around him, confused. "Then why are we here?"

He could see Rani smile in the shadow under her cowl. "Because I am dead. Well, nearly anyway."

"What? No!" he reached out to her.

"Don't be a child, Ash. It is the way of all things. I had hoped I would have more time to guide you through what is to come, but it was not to be," she sighed and flicked another of her bones into the stream.

"Will you go to Valhalla?" Ash asked. "If so, we would meet again."

She shook her head. "I am not a warrior and I will not gain access to the halls of the fallen." She smiled again. "As a Seidwoman, I have other… arrangements. This is where I will spend my time until Ragnarok." She swept her arm around the forest. "As you can see, there are worse places to spend the afterlife."

As beautiful as this place was, Ash couldn't help but feel a lump in his throat at the thought of the Seidwoman's death.

"And stop snivelling," she said, irritation in her voice. "I can't stand it." She turned her head towards him. "You are here because I need to talk to you before I go. You need to kill this thursr that possesses Roghald's body. I have seen its work before." She hesitated for a moment. "You see, it was him who killed your mother all those years ago. Though Odin's two wolves killed its body and saved you, its soul lives on. When I struck it, I felt its true nature; It comes not from Jotunheim, but from Muspelheim, the world of the fire giants. Surtr, who rules Muspelheim, must aid Burrugandr, and that makes the situation far worse than we thought. It was this thursr who tracked your mother back to Midgard. Part of their plan is to change the prophecy of Ragnarok, which would mean completely eradicating the Ulfhednar, and especially the Wolves of Odin. With your mother gone, you are the last one. This thursr lives to hunt you, Ash, and it has been driven mad. Even if you kill Roghald, the soul will return to Muspelheim again and it's only a matter of time until they find a suitable vessel for it and it will hunt you down again. You have to find a way to destroy it completely."

"But how would I do that?" Ash blurted out, his voice breaking a little.

"I don't know." Rani admitted. "But for now, we have to settle for stopping him and stopping the draugr. If you manage to kill or escape Roghald, you have to find and stop his master. The jotunn is spreading the corruption within this land. Stop him and you stop the undead."

"The peak split in two." Ash whispered. "Where Beli meant to send me."

Rani nodded.

"I will do it, Rani," he vowed. "I will do it for you."

She smiled and reached out a hand to stroke his cheek. He noticed her hand was smooth and soft, not wrinkled and frail like he remembered it.

"But I have probably fallen to my death," he sighed. "And if I did make it to the water, I will have drowned anyway, because I have burned out."

"Don't worry about that," she laughed, a warm, youthful sound. "I kept the last of my life's energy just for you." She pulled back the cowl and a young woman looked back at him. She was pretty and had the most beautiful green eyes he had ever seen. In her afterlife, Rani had gained both her youth and her eyes back. She held up her hand in front of him and a golden light rested on her palm.

"Fare well, dear nephew. I will watch over you." she whispered before blowing gently on the light. It rose in wisps and swirls and flowed onto his face. He felt a warmth sink into him.

Ash splashed into the cold, dark water. All around him he could see bubbles and in a moment of disorientation, he couldn't tell what was up or down.

As soon as the bubbles settled, he could see the weak light coming from the surface of the water. A few quick strokes saw him breaking through to the surface, gasping for air.

He heard a large splash somewhere to the right of him, and as the preceding events came back to him, he hurried to get out of the water. Ash had landed uncomfortably close to the stone quay, but at least he had cleared it and made it to the water. He reached out for the stone walkway and began pulling himself up. Though it was slippery, the heavy splashing behind him was an excellent motivator and he scrambled up on the quay with great effort. He stood up and blinking the water out of his eyes, he looked for the fortress. Although his vision was blurry, he saw the flickering of a few torches nearby and started running towards them.

He'd only taken a handful of steps when his eyes cleared enough to allow him to realise his mistake. The torches he had seen had been lit on the end of a wooden jetty that stretched some way into the harbour, not the fortress as he had thought. He had run into another dead end.

Hoping he had enough time to correct his mistake, he turned to run back the other way. Ash stopped short and froze as he saw the troll clambering out of the water on the opposite end of the jetty, cutting him off. Looking up at the roof of the fortress, he could see armed men and women looking down on them from where he had jumped. Ash knew they would never get down here in time, nor did he expect anyone who was wearing chain mail to jump into the ocean.

Roghald smiled at him, with water pooling at his feet, and the wooden spike in hand. Ash felt a shiver down his spine as the spike grew longer, coiling on the ground whilst emitting a soft, pulsating red light.

Although Rani's energy had been enough to bring him back to consciousness, he did not have enough strength to Shift for more than a second or two. Exhaustion hung like a blanket over his shoulders and he tried to clear his mind and find a way out. The thursr laughed as he pulled his arm back and Ash braced himself for the blow that was coming.

WHEN ROGHALD HAD seen Ash jump off the roof, he had feared that the boy had jumped to his death, snatching the revenge away from him. Running up to the ledge, he had been relieved to see that the boy had made it into the water, if only just clearing the stone quay. He took a few steps back for a run up and launched himself into the air with a giant leap. He sailed well past the boy and landed with a big splash. The water was cold and dark, but his strong arms brought him back to the surface in no time.

For some reason, the mad troll in his head stopped its maniacal laughing and was now sobbing. Roghald had had just about enough of sharing his mind with the thing and decided that he would have to find a way to rid himself of the troll whilst keeping his powers. He shook his head, trying to ignore the crying and focus on the boy instead. He saw Ash climb out of the water and stumble down the jetty in the wrong direction. Ha! He would have him trapped!

Roghald swam with powerful strokes towards the quay and climbed up, water gushing off his large frame. He pulled out his thorn and let it grow out into a serrated whip. Enough games. It was time to kill Ash. As much as he wanted to see him suffer, Ash had an uncanny ability to slip between his fingers and now he wouldn't take any more chances.

The boy, having realized that he was cornered without an escape, turned to face him. He could see the defeat in Ash's face. At least the boy knew that his end was here. Roghald couldn't help laughing as he pulled his arm back to strike him down, when the boy's eyes darted up above Roghald's head. If Ash had looked fearful before, now he looked absolutely terrified; his eyes wide and his mouth fell open.

A great sense of foreboding came over Roghald as the troll in his head started wailing. Heavy drops of water started to fall on his head and shoulders. He turned his head slowly to see Havbodr towering above him. She extended out of the water twice as tall as him, her scaly body, shaped like that of an enormous eel, continuing into the dark water. Her grin exposed her rows of sharp teeth and her long, clawed arms were held out to her sides. He had never seen a more hateful look than the one she was now giving him.

He had just opened his mouth to say something in his defence, when she moved as fast as lightning. Throwing herself forward, she wrapped her arms around him, her sharp teeth sinking into his neck. A sudden yank and a splash and they were in the water. Roghald could feel her thick body wrap around him like a snake.

It felt like he was being crushed under a mountain. He was aware that they were moving, first outwards and away from the fortress, but soon they began sinking deeper and deeper. Roghald could feel a terrible pressure all around him, and his last thought was that Ash had escaped him. Then, even the troll in his mind fell silent as he disappeared into the dark of the deep.

ASH HAD DIFFICULTY processing what had just happened. Some monster, another troll maybe, had just saved him, sweeping Roghald out to sea. He wanted to get away from the water as fast as possible, in case either of the trolls came back. As a matter of fact, he was fairly certain that he could never go swimming again. Ever.

Overcome by exhaustion, he stumbled along the jetty. He paused at the place where Roghald had stood and looked down on the wooden spike where it had fallen. He knew it was a dangerous thing and best not left lying around for anyone to find, so he picked it up with two fingers, careful not to hold anywhere near the tip. The runes carved around it were strange to him, and he was cautious not to touch any of them, just in case. They were rapidly flashing in a red light, but they soon flickered and stopped. The spike went dark as he held it.

By the time he made it to the end of the jetty, a crowd of armed warriors reached him, Yrsa two steps ahead of them. Torsten was not far behind her, his axe drawn and panting with laboured breaths. They all stopped and stared at him, and Ash became painfully aware that he was stark naked.

"Cold in the water, eh?" Torsten called, loud enough for all to hear. As all the warriors laughed, Yrsa gave the Berserker a dark look before sweeping her cape around Ash's shoulders, covering him up. Ash's face went red and he pulled the cape tight around him as they walked back towards the fortress.

Yrsa turned to look at him with sorrow in her eyes.

"Rani is dead," her voice was thick with emotion.

"I know," he replied. "She didn't seem too upset about it."

She gave him a strange look but didn't falter in her steps as they entered the fortress.

When they reached the hall, it was now almost empty, save for the servants who were clearing the remnants of the evening meal. A hirdsman greeted them with a message from Jarl Astrid. She wanted to see them in her chambers. They made their way through the long corridors, stopping only briefly in Ash's chambers for him to put on some clothes. He also grabbed a piece of cloth and wrapped the thorn in it, before hurrying out of his room to his friends. Soon they were pushing open the thick oak door leading to the Jarl's war room.

Astrid sat at the table, along with her advisor and the captain of her hird, as well as the captain of her guards. She seemed sombre; her face neutral, not revealing any emotions. She looked up at Ash and his friends as they entered and bade them to sit.

"I am glad you are well, Ash. Erland here has told me what happened."

Ash looked at the captain of the hird who gave him a nod.

Astrid placed her hands on the table and took a deep breath. "Rani, the Seidwoman is dead," she began. "All hope of rallying the southerners died with her. From here on, we are alone." She looked up at them and very little hope could be seen in her eyes, but she kept her chin raised and her shoulders squared.

"We need to strengthen our positions as best we can. I will no longer send scouts outside of the walls. We will buckle down here and hopefully it will come to a siege situation and we can whittle down their numbers against our walls and defences.

As it now seems that the trolls have infested the sea as well, we can no longer rely on it for provisions. I will send my hird and guards to take control of all resources and foods in the fortress, and we will begin rations. With a bit of luck, we can hold out long enough to see this through."

"There is another option." All eyes turned to Torsten.

"What do you suggest, Berserker?" Jarl Astrid asked.

"We attack them," he said. "The trolls have lost a thursr and are at their weakest before they can find another. Now is the time to strike."

"It is madness," said the captain of the guards, rubbing his eyes. "Every single warrior sent will be slain and turned to draugr."

"As they will if they stay here." Ash spoke in a little above a whisper, but all eyes turned to him. "No one is more frightened than me, but I know one thing; we are only delaying the inevitable if we hide behind these walls." His voice grew stronger and he raised his head. "And for what? A few more weeks of miserable existence until the sons of Jotunheim can break down the gates and kill us like rats in a barrel?"

He stood up, placing his knuckles on the table and spoke, his voice now firm with resolve. "I am an Ulfhed, and I will not die that way. I will take the fight to them, even if I have to go alone. We know that I can get around their wards and we know where their lair is, where this undead infestation stems from. If we strike swiftly, they will not have time to prepare for us."

The room was silent, and Ash could see Yrsa and Torsten staring at him, their eyes full of pride. Jarl Astrid started laughing, a rich, resounding laugh.

"The boy is braver than my fiercest warrior!" A radiant smile had chased away her solemn look. "He is also right. We are trapped here and maybe striking now is our only chance, however small. At worst, we take as many draugr with us as possible and earn our place in Valhalla."

Everyone at the table nodded their assent, and the guard captain, now eager to prove his bravery, was the first to vocalise his. Astrid sent for ale and food as they sat down to plan the demise of the trolls in Midgard. They planned, argued and strategized until late into the night, before finally agreeing on a plan. They would start preparations at first light. Ash lingered while the others left the war room and soon found himself alone with the Jarl.

"Was there something else, Ash?" she sat on the edge of the table.

Ash took out the thorn and unwrapped it from the cloth.

"Normally, I would have given this to Rani, but-" He had to stop himself as a lump formed in his throat at the thought of the Seidwoman, and he left the last part unsaid. "I think this is really dangerous and important. It needs to be kept from falling into the wrong hands." He held it out for Astrid's inspection. She looked at it curiously, though she didn't touch it.

"I will keep it safe until we know what to do with it. Maybe we can ask one of the southern Seidwomen to deal with it once this is all over."

Ash looked at her gratefully and wrapped it back up in the cloth before handing it to the Jarl.

"Go to bed, young Ulfhed," she smiled at him. "Long and hard days await us all."

He nodded and left, shutting the oak door behind him. Astrid took the thorn into the next room, where she slept, and walked up to a small chest on a shelf. She opened it and looked down on some valuables and keepsakes that she had collected over the years. She dropped the thorn in a corner of the box.

Since it was wrapped in the cloth, she couldn't see that the runes started pulsating red when she shut the lid.

CHAPTER 33

ASH SWUNG HIMSELF INTO THE SADDLE. HE HAD BEEN given a chestnut mare who seemed well tempered, although he had bought her affection with an apple all the same. He checked that his bags were secure across the flanks of the horse and after adjusting a few straps, he was satisfied. Around him, nearly two hundred hirdsmen, shieldmaidens and warriors were mounting their horses and attempting to line up in something that resembled a formation.

Jarl Astrid had almost emptied the fortress of warriors for this last, desperate push against the draugr. Only a handful of the older fighters would remain, in order to organise the townsfolk in defence of the fortress, should it be needed. There were many tearful farewells as people hugged their children and wives and husbands. No one who was riding out expected to return.

Ash rode to the front to find Torsten, Yrsa and Astrid, who were in the middle of a logistical discussion. Ash had held Astrid in high regard because of her intelligence and confidence as a leader, but now that he saw her dressed for battle, he understood that she was a warrior first and a chieftain second. She was adorned in a worn black steel chain mail shirt and leggings. She seemed as comfortable in these as her linens and silks at the feast. Her hair was braided for war and spilled down over her shoulders. Her eyes were sooted under a black helmet, giving her a fierce look. She wore her shield on her back and a vicious looking axe and a longbow were strapped to her saddle. A well spun, blue cape rested over her shoulders, with gold trimmings around the border marking her rank as a Jarl. She was the most formidable looking warrior Ash had ever seen, and he had no doubt as to how she had risen to power.

"We have approximately six days of riding in order to reach our destination, that is, the camp which we will set up in close proximity to the lair." Astrid spoke loudly for most people around her to hear. "We will only ride along the road for one day. This will allow us to get as close as we can via the grasslands instead of the forest. This way we can keep the horses and we will be harder to ambush. Though it is a further way to travel, I am hoping that they do not expect us to approach from southwest, buying us some time before they can rally their forces to meet us."

The people surrounding her voiced their agreement and, on a signal from Astrid, a hirdsman blew a horn and they set off. Ash was riding between Yrsa and Torsten with what was left of the Jomsvikings. Twenty-eight men and women, including Ash, were all that remained of the most feared fighting force in Midgard. These were the Ulfhednar and Berserkers who had been elsewhere occupied when Jarl Olaf had ridden out on that fateful mission.

Torsten, as the only remaining captain, had assumed command and had placed Yrsa as his second. Already a close-knit unit, the few remaining Jomsvikings had welcomed Ash with open arms and had commended him on his bravery and cunning when leading the thursr away from the tower, no doubt saving many lives. They called him a true Ulfhed, and his back was tender from the many friendly slaps he'd received.

He had been somewhat embarrassed by all the attention, but

the feelings of welcome and belonging that he had felt amongst his new brothers and sisters filled a hole in his heart that he hadn't even known he had. He now had a better idea of what he was fighting for, and he would give everything and anything for them.

"Are you ready for this?" Yrsa asked him, the concern obvious on her face.

He shook his head. "No, but I'm going anyway," he replied. "Not that I think that it matters if I am or not. This will happen either way, might as well try to enjoy it."

Torsten, who had been listening, burst out in a booming laughter, startling the horses closest to him.

"That's my boy!" he laughed and slapped Ash hard on the shoulder. "Death smiles at everyone," he said in a loud voice, "but only a Jomsviking smiles back!" He was rewarded with some laughter and cheers from the other warriors.

And so they rode out, in good humour and banter for a while, which took their minds off what they were about to face.

BIRK STOOD IN the window watching Jarl Astrid ride out with almost all of the warriors. There would be hardly anyone left to defend the fortress, and Birk had been told to report to what remained of the guards, in order to be given a weapon and assigned to guard duty. He couldn't believe that after having served three Jarls faithfully as one of the head servants, with his bad knees and all, they still expected him to man the walls and fight off an army of draugr. This was madness.

He had no doubt that the Jarl and all of her warriors were riding off to face the glorious death they so desired and would leave the rest of them behind to be slaughtered like pigs for a summer solstice celebration. Thanks, but no thanks, he thought bitterly. He had met with his cousin Halvdan, a fisherman, that morning. Even though the port had been closed, his cousin said they could set off in his boat unnoticed in the middle of the night and would be halfway down the coast before anyone even knew they were gone. They would sail as far south as they could and set up a new life for themselves, far away from the troubles of the north.

The only problem was that they had next to no savings between them. Luckily, Birk had a solution to that problem. With Astrid gone, Birk would be the only servant who had any business in her quarters, for cleaning purposes, and without doubt she had some coins or other valuables tucked away. It was very unlikely that she would come back to spend it, anyway. Besides, he had been given very little reward for a lifetime of service at Gjallarholm, so he was entitled to a parting gift.

When the last rider had disappeared over the hill, Birk left the window and walked with a casual stride through the corridors to the Jarl's chambers.

Taking out his key, he unlocked the door and stepped into the war room, careful to lock the door again behind him. He wouldn't want to be seen rummaging through the Jarl's belongings. In times like these, you would get put to the sword for less.

A quick search of the room revealed nothing of value besides a quality dagger, which he tucked away inside his tunic. That would come in handy on his journey. He moved on to the living quarters in the next room, where his expectations were higher. He went straight to the large chest in front of the bed and lifted the lid. Inside, he found some weaponry and bits of armour that might be worth a few coins, but nothing he could carry out of the rooms unseen.

Swearing to himself, he closed the lid and straightened his back when his eyes fell on a small ornamental chest on a shelf. A few quick paces and he stood in front of it, flicking it open. The first thing that caught his eye was a small leather pouch that jingled with promise as he picked it up. His heart raced when he opened it up to see a small fortune in gold and silver coins spill into his hand. With this, he could live in comfort for the rest of his life and even have servants of his own. He put the coins back and laced the pouch up before slipping it inside his tunic next to the dagger.

Looking back into the chest, he saw a lock of hair tied with a ribbon, another dagger and a pair of bone dice. There was something wrapped in cloth in a corner and he picked it up for examination, unwrapping it with care. It was a strange piece of wood. He could feel some warmth coming off it through the cloth as it rested in his hand, and he held it up to the light to examine it closer. It had some strange carvings all around it, and he reached for it with his other hand.

As soon as he came into contact with one of the carved runes, it pulsed in a red light. Startled, he almost dropped it on the floor. It continued to pulsate, and Birk was mesmerised by it. It was clearly magical and would be worth a king's ransom. He couldn't believe the good fortune this day had brought him, and he could not wait to show his cousin. Images of him living like a Jarl flashed before his mind's eye and he grinned from ear to ear.

The glowing red light was beautiful, and he held it up again to inspect it more closely, but suddenly the thing was no longer a stick, and it moved like a snake in his hand. He yelped and attempted to fling it away, but it had coiled around his hand. He shook his hand, but it remained attached to him. As he was flailing his arm about, it slithered up his arm and was soon wrapped around his neck. He tore at it with his hands, but to no avail. He tried to call out for help, but his airway was cut off as the thing started constricting his throat and he couldn't make a sound. As he became lightheaded, Birk fell to his knees, no longer able to stay upright.

He blacked out for a second and when his eyes opened again; he was lying on the floor, the pressure gone from his throat. He was only half conscious, but he became aware that the thing had released his neck, but only so it could slither down his throat. Birk panicked, but then an unspeakable pain exploded in his chest and the world went dark.

ROGHALD OPENED HIS eyes. He was lying on the floor in a room he didn't recognise. A wave of nausea washed over him and turning to his side, he vomited on a carpet he had never seen before. He retched long after he had nothing left to bring up, before collapsing on his back, panting while the room spun around him.

He felt incomplete, like a part of him was gone, but he couldn't put a finger on what part exactly.

He rubbed his eyes to try to stop the vertigo, but even that felt unfamiliar to him. Lifting his hands from his face, he looked at them. They were soft, with short, stubby fingers, not the large, calloused hands he had always known. He felt his face, and that wasn't right either. His cheeks were clean shaven, with only some whiskers on his top lip, with a double chin to boot.

Still too weak to get up, he lay on the floor trying to make sense of it all, when the memories came flooding back. Overcoming Rani, Ash showing up, followed by the chase over the rooftops, before jumping in the water. Then Havbodr appearing behind him, the realisation that she must have somehow sensed him when he fell in the water, before he'd found himself in her crushing grip and being dragged underwater. He shivered as he remembered her biting his neck, the pain overwhelming, before she crushed his lungs, forcing the last of his breath out and drowning him. He remembered dying, so how did he possibly end up here, and why was it he felt so... hollow?

As soon as he gathered enough strength, he pulled himself off the floor. Standing up, the doorways seemed tall for some reason. He looked around and realized that he was in the bedroom of someone well to do. On a small table underneath the window, he spotted a polished metal looking glass next to a set of combs. He staggered over to get a better look at himself.

Lifting up the looking glass, he nearly dropped it as he glimpsed a strange face in it. He took a few breaths and raised it again so he could study the face looking back at him. It seemed familiar, but it wasn't his face. That servant! What was his name? Never mind, but how could this be? He looked out through the window and it only took him a few seconds to realise that he was back in Gjallarholm.

Feeling dizzy again, he sat down on the bed when something uncomfortable poked him in the ribs. Roghald opened up the front of his tunic to pull out a dagger in a sheath that was lying inside his clothing, along with a leather pouch of some sort. He removed the items and was just about to button up the tunic again when a soft red light caught his attention. He opened the tunic again and stared in bewilderment at the place where his heart was. A red light was softly pulsating, just beneath his skin. He put his hand over it and could sense his thorn in the place where his heart should be, and it all made sense.

Havbodr had killed him, but in her eagerness to do so, must have left the thorn behind. It was as much a part of him as his own limbs. A piece of his soul had been infused into it when it was made, and his consciousness, or at least part of it, had always remained inside of the thorn. When he had died, perhaps his soul had drifted towards the sliver of it that was still anchored in this world and the thorn had found a new vessel for it in the servant? Remembering the face in the looking glass, he wished it had made a more striking choice, but any port in a storm, he thought to himself.

He looked inside the pouch he'd found along with the dagger, and seeing the gold and silver, he discarded it on the bed. What need did he have for gold and silver? Looking around the room again, he came to the swift conclusion that this room most likely did not belong to the servant, nor the coins for that matter. He figured he'd best get out of there before his second chance at life found him hung at dawn.

Feeling a bit better, he put the dagger away in the tunic again, before standing up and making his way to the adjacent room, looking for a way out. It was a fairly empty room, mainly occupied by a large table in the centre, maps and charts scattered on it. There was a door at the other end of the room with a key sitting in the lock, most likely the way out. As he walked past the table he glanced down towards the large map in the centre and halted mid-step.

It was a map of the north; he could see Fjellborg, Gjallarholm and even Hornsborg marked out, although Hornsborg had a red cross over it. He smiled at that, remembering his violent revenge on Jarl Eric, as well as the trap he had set there for Jarl Olaf and his warriors. Various red dots, mostly on the roads between the Towns, marked out where the draugr had attacked.

A red circle northwest of Gjallarholm caught his eye. With disbelief, he realized they had marked his master's cave. There were lines drawn from Gjallarholm to the cave. He hurried back to the window in the other room and scrutinised the walls and the guards manning them. Though they were armed, they were not warriors. Fat, skinny, old and young, they were just townsfolk with spears, and no armour, helmets or shields.

Jarl Astrid had emptied the fortress of warriors and it could only mean one thing; they were attacking Gurmr and Grundr. Knowing that half the draugr were in Hornsborg, he feared there might not be enough to defend the cave, depending on how many warriors they had sent. He had to get there as fast as possible to alert his masters.

He walked back towards the door when another wave of nausea washed over him. His head spun, and he had to lean against the wall, or he feared he would fall. Roghald's legs shook and he could feel cold sweat beading on his face. There was an uncomfortable pressure in his chest, and he looked down to see the red light beneath his skin flashing. The flashes were irregular and each time it pulsated; it felt like a worm was twisting inside his ribcage. Roghald closed his eyes, taking deep, slow breaths, and eventually the sensation died down. He opened his eyes and took a minute to gather himself. He felt weaker than he had. The new body seemed to resist him. He needed to get back to Gurmr and Grundr. They alone could help him with this. Perhaps they could even give him a new body all together as he wasn't particularly thrilled about this one. Pushing off the wall, Roghald took some tentative steps towards the door. He seemed to be fine, and the nausea had passed, but he had to put more effort into even this small task, as if he had to force the body to operate. He opened the door a fraction, so he could poke his head out. The corridor was empty on the other side, so he slipped out and shut it silently behind him. Heading towards a staircase he had glimpsed at the other end of the corridor; he'd only taken a few steps when a door opened ahead of him.

A maid stepped out, her arms full of folded linens. He froze in his tracks as she turned to him, a look of surprise on her face.

"Birk!" she gasped. Reminding Roghald of his new name. "Where have you been? Mother Hilda has been furious, swearing over you for the last three days. She said that you were a coward who ran away because all the warriors left and if she ever saw you again, she would see to it that you were skinned alive over an ant-hill."

Impressed, Roghald took a mental note of that punishment so he could use it for Ash when he caught him.

"I've been sick," he mumbled. "When did the warriors leave?"

She looked at him feeble minded. "Why, three days ago. You better go report to Mother Hilda right away."

"I just have to go wash up, then I'll see her." Roghald lied, setting off towards the staircase, leaving the maid to stare after him.

Three days, he thought. They've had a significant head start and on horseback too, no doubt. He hurried down the stairs and soon saw the main doors leading out of the fortress. Once in the courtyard, it was not hard to find the stables. He walked in looking for a horse. He could see none. Most of the stalls had been taken over by cattle and goats in the absence of horses. He found a stableboy who confirmed that the warriors had taken every single able-bodied horse on their mission.

Swearing under his breath, he made his way towards the gate. He would have to make it on foot. He could make better pace in his thursr shape than his current pudgy one, although it would be tiring.

Roghald arrived at the gate to find it open, but his way was blocked by a couple of people in servants' garb, like himself. They had spears and one of them had even managed to dig out an old rusty chain mail shirt from somewhere, although it looked like it would fall to pieces if the man had one good sneeze. The man seemed to be in charge over the makeshift guard patrol and stepped out in front of Roghald with an air of self-importance.

"Halt!" he said in what must have been his most commanding voice. "Going somewhere, Birk?"

Roghald's head started to spin a little again, and the nausea returned. He bit down on the sensation and concentrated on staying in control, pushing it aside.

"Yeah. Out." Roghald snapped. "Now get out of my way."

The man smiled, his voice full of glee as he replied. "Not deserting, are you, Birk? I'd have to cut you down if you did. Put this spear right in your fat belly." The man laughed and when he turned to his cronies, they all laughed too.

"I'm not a warrior, so I can't desert, because I never swore an oath to fight to the death and so on. Now get out of my way."

The guard's face darkened at being opposed and he took a step back, levelling his spear at Roghald. "I'm not telling you again, Birk. Turn around or it's going to get messy."

Roghald smiled. "In that case, I look forward to it." Then he changed.

CHAPTER 34

"Go now!" Astrid called a second before she slammed her axe into the chest of a charging draugr.

"Are you sure?" Yrsa yelled back at her, standing behind the shield wall, stabbing her spear through a small opening and into an undead face.

"Yes, by Odin's beard, now!" the Jarl grunted as a draugr threw itself onto her shield.

Ash picked up his pack and slung it over his shoulder when Yrsa nodded to him as she pulled away from the melee, another warrior taking her place. They ran further up the hill where Torsten was waiting with the horses.

"It is time," he told his friend.

The big man nodded, and after handing Ash and Yrsa the reins to their horses, he swung himself into the saddle. They all turned and looked back down on the raging battle. Jarl Astrid must have seen them, because she raised her fist in the sign of the Hammer, a blessing in the name of Thor, the Thundergod. The three friends raised their fists too, in a solemn moment, as they knew they were unlikely to meet the Jarl again in this world.

"Few warriors outside of the Jomsvikings can compare themselves to her," Torsten rumbled, before turning his horse and setting off. The two Ulfhednar were not far behind and soon the three of them were riding through a narrow gully, away from the sounds of battle. So far, the plan had worked. The force from Gjallarholm had set up camp at a defensible position only a few hours away from where they thought the lair was.

Once they had settled in, they felled trees to build crude walls to funnel a horde of draugr to the bottom of a hill. Here they stood between the two walls in a fifty-warrior wide shield wall, before they sent out a patrol towards the lair. The patrol made a lot of noise, sounding horns and slamming their weapons on their shields, and soon they drew the attention of the undead. At first there were only a few that followed them back to camp, but soon, almost a hundred of the monsters had trickled out of the trees and had thrown themselves at their camp without fear or concern.

Although they'd had losses as the battle raged, the shield wall held, and they were slowly whittling down the draugr. However, there were far more of the undead on the field of battle, and even though the humans had the tactical advantage, Ash knew that they would soon tire, and the draugr would not. After all, they were only buying time for Ash and his friends to circle around and approach the lair from the west, hoping to encounter no resistance.

The plan was for them to scout out the wards that prevented any non-trolls from seeing or entering the lair. Once they had found them, they would destroy them and attack the jotunn before the draugr force could be turned back to defend the troll Shaman. The remaining warriors would follow the returning draugr to the cave for one last battle. Jarl Astrid had wanted them to take at least the remaining Jomsvikings, but Ash had refused, knowing that if the Jarl was to hold back hundreds of draugr, she would need every sword and axe available. Besides, if they wanted to make it to the lair unseen, they were better off keeping their numbers low.

They rode along the gully until they could no longer hear the sounds of fighting, and deeming that they were far enough away, they pushed the horses up the bank and rode north. Ash could see the split peaks where the jotunn's lair was thought to be located beyond the tree line ahead, and his stomach knotted when he realized how close it was. They rode for a few hours and the sun had just reached its zenith when Yrsa signalled for them to leave the horses and continue on foot. They didn't tie them up, since if they didn't make it back, the poor things would at least have a chance to get away from the draugr. Ash figured that if they succeeded in their task, he would gladly walk back to Gjallarholm.

They crept forwards for another hour, and were soon crouching behind a large shrubbery, looking out over a meadow in front of a large cave, at the foot of the mountain.

"So, you can see it?" Ash whispered to his friends. They both nodded.

"And you don't feel uneasy and want to turn around?" he asked them.

"Not more than I should," Torsten rumbled in his interpretation of a whisper.

That was strange, Ash thought. Maybe the trolls hadn't bothered to put up wards given this was so far away from the roads and humans.

"I don't like it," Ash breathed, scanning the cave and meadow for any movement, and seeing none. "And shouldn't there be at least a few draugr guarding it?"

"Pride comes before the fall," Yrsa said. "Maybe they are just too arrogant and sure of themselves by now?"

"Well then, let's go and make sure they fall really far," Torsten grinned as he stood up and hefted his axe, followed by the others.

They kept low and off to the side of the cave's opening, in case something sat in the dark looking out. Ash expected a roar or an attack to come at any moment, yet all was quiet as they made it to the rock wall. With his back up against it, Ash sidled up to the cave and peered into the darkness. Not a sound could be heard, and no movement seen. He signalled to his companions and they crept forward into the dark, weapons drawn.

266

It was dark enough that Torsten stumbled, sending a small rock flying into the pitch black ahead. The sound, in reality, wasn't much of a noise, but to them sounded like the entire mountain had come down. After this, Yrsa pulled out her rune stone, which she wrapped a cloth around, before activating. It only let out the thinnest of light beams where she had folded the cloth back, and now at least they had light enough to see where they should put their feet.

They walked through a large passage that wound and twisted, deeper and deeper into the mountain. The air was stale and still, and there was a vague, unpleasant odour here that Ash couldn't identify. It wasn't long before the cave opened up into an enormous cavern and the friends readied themselves, as they would be easily spotted by anyone or anything there. They stood still for a long, uneventful minute, before Yrsa removed the cloth from her stone and the entire cavern became visible to them as it basked in the enchanted light.

There was no one there. Besides a strange-looking tree growing from a mound in the centre, the whole cold, damp cavern was empty. There were also no other passageways leading onwards. This was the end of the cave.

"Now what?" Torsten asked, relaxing his shoulders and straightening up.

Yrsa, who still had her weapons raised, kept staring all around the cave.

"Last time I checked, trees didn't grow in caves underground. Something's not right."

"Well, let's have a look at it, then." Torsten started walking towards the strange tree, the others following a few steps behind. Ash realized that the smell was coming from the tree. It was a sickening, sweet smell, and he felt uneasy when he looked at it.

"Don't touch it!" he snapped at Torsten, who pulled his hand back, having reached out to one of the bulbous fruits hanging down from a branch. He was just about to tell his friend that there was something very wrong about it when a deep voice echoed around the cavern. It was melodious and sounded like the snippet of a song.

"*OOOO AJ AJ AJ AJ BUFF...*" the song was followed by a chuckle and the air along the cave to the left of them shimmered. They all spun, weapons raised, to see the glow fall like a curtain. In its place stood dozens of draugr. But it wasn't the draugr that made the companions take a step back. Towering over the undead stood a creature unlike anything they had seen before.

Twice as tall as the undead surrounding it, a lanky, grey skinned, two headed troll looked down on them. One of the ugly heads was chuckling, but the other had a dark look on its face. A fire pit had become visible behind them, its heated glow now illuminating the cavern.

"The half-breed has come to seek our doom, Grundr," the cheerful one spoke in a deep, otherworldly voice. "Instead, he will find his own."

Ash could see in the corner of his eye how several draugr had moved to block the only exit.

"You see, little half-breed, your friend Jarl Olaf was most helpful. When he told me that you could see the wards at Beli's dwelling, we made a new ward, that no troll could see," said the same head, twirling his finger around to indicate the cave.

"You have saved us a lot of trouble by coming here, still I cannot grant you and your friends a swift death, because there simply isn't any pleasure in that for me." He grinned, revealing sharp, blackened teeth.

"Olaf was alive?" Yrsa stammered, the colour draining from her face.

"For a short while, yes." The troll gloated. "He eventually met a slow, painful death, very much like the one you are about to receive."

Without a command, all the draugr threw themselves forward at once as the jotunn laughed.

Torsten let out a terrible roar and before the undead reached him, he was frothing at the mouth and had grown taller as the Berserker rage took hold of him. He swung his axe in a wide arc, cleaving the first draugr in half at the waist.

Ash Shifted and from Yrsa's movements, he could see that she had too. Her spear shot forward like a viper and ran through the head of the closest attacker. Then one slammed into Ash's shield and he had his hands full. The runic shield flashed as the draugr hit it and the foul thing was thrown yards away, but two more soon took its place. He could see in his peripheral vision that they were being flanked on all sides and soon would be trapped.

"Together! Together!" Yrsa shouted. "Or we are lost!"

They moved closer and stood with their backs towards each other, forcing the undead to meet them head on. Ash's nose filled with the smell of rot as the undead closed in around them. One swiped a clawed hand at Ash's head, but he ducked and sliced deep into its leg. The creature didn't stop, though it was unsteady as it launched for him and a quick swipe of his sword severed its head from its body.

"Watch out!" Yrsa yelled.

Ash looked up to see the troll striding towards them, an enormous wooden club in its hand. The club was covered in red, glowing runes and radiated power. He had to stop it. He didn't think his friends could stand against such a weapon, so he had to do something. Ash cut down another draugr in front of him before slamming his shield into another, sending it sprawling backwards, and knocking down two others behind him.

"I'm taking him!" He called to his friends.

"Ash, no!" Yrsa yelled, but he was already on his way.

He leapt over the knocked down draugr before they could get up and had a clear run to the troll. He felt a burning pain in his thigh as one of the downed enemies slashed him when he jumped over them, but he pushed on. A quick run up and he launched into the air and swung his sword at the left face. The two heads grinned cruelly as they saw him come and swung the club to swat him out of the air.

The club and the sword met, and a resounding boom followed by a shock wave that threw both him and the troll back, away from each other. Ash landed on his back amongst the draugr and a quick backward roll allowed him to escape the teeth of one as it twisted to bite him. The undead monster had rolled onto his shield, however, and Ash had to let it go, otherwise he would have been pinned to the ground.

Getting back on his feet, Ash looked down on his sword and saw that the runes carved on the fuller were glowing blue. There was a chip in the blade where it had met the club, but it still seemed intact. A quick glance told him that the undead had closed over his shield and he could not get to it.

He saw the troll struggling to its feet, surprise plastered on both faces as they looked down on the club. Ringlets of smoke came off a darkened spot on the weapon where Ash had hit it, and the runes were spluttering and blinking. With a challenging shout, Ash once again threw himself at the draugr, who had now been reduced to half of their original numbers. He was looking for a way to get through them and get to the troll.

The looks of surprise on the troll's faces soon turned to anger as it lumbered forwards towards the battle again. Ash stabbed his sword into the throat of another draugr, making an opening to launch at the jotunn.

Yrsa's shriek made him turn his head. She was overwhelmed by two draugr who had made it past her guard. They tore into her arm and leg, her face a grimace of pain. He saw Torsten spin to see her plight, mad rage in his eyes as he went to help her. In turning his back, Torsten had left himself open and several of the undead threw themselves on him, digging their teeth and claws into him and forcing him to the ground under their weight.

"No!" Ash called, and he turned to help his friends, when the troll's club hit him in a backhanded sweep, sending him flying.

He hit the stonewall hard and landing in a heap, lost control of his Shifting. His entire body hurt, and he looked down to see his left leg bent outwards, broken in several places. He heard a deep chuckle and turned to see the troll coming towards him, triumph written on both faces, swinging its club back and forth in one hand.

Then there was an eruption behind him and draugr were thrown into the air as Torsten rose from where he had fallen, bellowing like a mad bull. Covered in blood, the Berserker was in a state of mad rage. His axe moved in a blur as he ploughed through the undead who could offer no resistance to the ferocity of his attack. The troll turned at the commotion to see the Berserker butchering his draugr at an alarming rate, and after giving Ash a quick glance, made a decision, and turned to face the Berserker instead.

Ash saw in horror how the draugr who had been fighting Yrsa, rose from her unmoving body and lumbered towards Torsten. His friends were dead or dying. He had to do something. He put one hand against the stonewall and leaning on it pushed himself up to stand on his right leg. The pain in his left leg was overwhelming, and his vision darkened when he tried to put some weight on it.

He could only watch helplessly as the troll, towering over the scene, swatted Torsten's axe with his club, sending it flying across the cave. Torsten, in his state of frenzy, threw himself at the troll, striking blow after blow at its torso, even pushing the beast backwards a step under his storm of punches. But even Torsten could not match the strength of a jotunn, and the troll snatched both his arms and pulled them out to the sides, rendering him powerless.

The troll raised the berserker up in front of its faces and pulled hard on his arms. Ash could hear his friend's joints crack from where he stood. The troll's maniacal laughter filled the cavern when Torsten screamed in pain and rage. Ash's eyes flickered to Yrsa's unmoving shape, and he knew he had failed. He had failed his friends, himself and he had failed his people. Odin had put his faith in Ash to save Midgard, but where was Odin now when he needed him?

"The gods help those who help themselves," the Allfather had told him, but where was the help now? His eyes were drawn to the sword in his hand, the runes still aglow from the battle with the troll. *"TOR HIELPE"*, he read.

Then he realized that the gods were there. Eikinri had said that some of the Thundergod's own power dwelled in the sword; he just had to wield it himself, and the god's help would be there. The help of Thor - the troll slayer.

He looked up to the roof of the cavern and then to his hand against the wall. Granite and basalt with veins of mica; an easy composition to work with. Ash let his hand sink into the wall, then his entire arm. He grimaced at the pain in his leg as he hopped closer to the wall. Ash took a deep breath and fell forwards and let himself sink into the stone. He concentrated and made the minerals move around him as if he was walking through stone, but now he forced them to push him up instead.

At first nothing happened, and his heart sank, but then he felt a sensation of movement and he began floating upwards, painfully slow at first, but soon the speed picked up. He was still not moving fast enough, and he pictured his friend being torn from limb to limb, before he could do what he wanted. Yrsa laid dead and Torsten was soon to follow and Ash would be alone in the world again, even if he somehow survived the jotunn. And it would all be because he was too slow.

Ash concentrated and Shifted. He almost lost control of the Stonesmithing as his Ulfhed ability took over and he felt the pressure of the mountain around him threatening to crush him. He tried to push onwards, to move faster through the stone. A taste of iron filled his mouth, and he felt blood trickle from his nose as the two powers struggled for control within him. The troll and Aesir magic struggled against each other and he felt his mind reeling and his head spun as he lost control of both. He attempted to stop Shifting, but it was raging in his body, refusing to relent to the troll magic, and he found himself unable to do anything. Eikinri had described his powers as two beasts fighting for control, even if it would kill both. And him. The two beasts tore into each other's and Ash could only watch, helpless. He felt his heart flutter, then stop.

CHAPTER 35

"Ash."

He opened his eyes and saw his mother's face beaming at him. They were suspended in an endless darkness and she shone like the sun, sitting astride a white horse, armour glittering with a shield strapped across her back. She held a long spear in one hand and the reins of the horse in the other. A cascade of dark hair spilled out from under a silver helmet, flowing as if under water.

"Mother," he whispered, and her beautiful smile filled him with warmth. "I have failed," he breathed, lowering his head. He felt her arms wrap around him, her horse gone, as she held him in her arms, and for a second he drowned in the love of a mother he had never known. He felt the tears running down his cheek and too soon she released him, holding his shoulders at arm's length and looking him in the eyes.

"Not yet," she smiled. "Your powers are conflicting because they are an extension of you. You have not resolved the two sides of you, troll and Ulfhed, so neither can they. You need to understand what they are and therefore what you are." She wiped his tears with her thumbs, and this brought back a memory of her doing the same thing when he was a little boy.

"A long time ago, before the world was created, a god named

Bor lived next to the vast emptiness called Gingunnagap. He met and fell in love with the beautiful Bestla, the daughter of a giant. Together they had three sons, Odin, Vile and Ve."

"Everybody knows that story," Ash said. "What has that got to do with me?"

"Don't be stupid, Ash. Odin is the result of the union of a god and a giant. His powers are partially from his father, but also from his mother, the giant, and they are resolved in him. The power Odin granted the Ulfhednar is the same power that the trolls and giants have. We are all the same. This is what your father and I understood, and what allowed our union and the creation of you. You have two powers, yes, but they are merely different sides of the same coin."

Ash stared at his mother, realisation dawning on him. The clash between his troll and Ulfhed blood wasn't that the powers were incompatible, they resulted from the conflict within himself. His mind went to Odin and his two wolves. Maybe they were a manifestation of the powers resolved in him? The powers were his to control, not the other way around.

"I need to save my friends!" he gasped at his mother.

She smiled and nodded and pushed him hard in the chest, sending him tumbling away from her, into the darkness.

HE FOUND HIMSELF still in darkness, but now he felt the stone all around him. The powers were still raging against each other within him. Reaching out with his mind, he grasped them and merged them together, like he would with iron and carbon to make steel. The two forces resisted at first, but he was relentless as he forced them together until they merged into one. He could feel them as a tight, uncomfortable ball in his chest and for a second he wondered if he had made a mistake, but then the ball burst and a pleasant tingling spread throughout his body. The pressure of the surrounding stone softened, and he put his mind to task again.

His broken leg was still painful, but he ignored it and soared upwards through the stone, much faster than before, now that he was Shifted and Stonesmithing at the same time. He could sense the shape of the stone around him and followed the wall as it curved into the ceiling of the cavern. He stuck his head out through the ceiling at about the right place and with only a slight adjustment, found himself right above the jotunn. Ash looked down from this height of about two storeys from the cavern floor and saw Torsten's grimace of suffering as the troll pulled his limbs. He heard his friend's cries of pain, distorted by the slowed time.

What he was about to do would probably kill him, but he had no choice, Ash thought as he pushed himself out of the ceiling. He fell like an arrow, body straight, the sword in both hands extended in front of him straight towards the troll. The tip of the sword pierced its left shoulder and with Ash's weight and speed behind it, the weapon sunk into the troll's flesh, all the way to the hilt.

Both heads let out a surprised grunt before there was a loud crack of thunder and a flash of lightning as the jotunn's body was torn apart. Ash was once more sent flying across the room in a shower of stone fragments and gravel. He landed hard and rolled across the cavern floor and something heavy slammed into his side, knocking the wind from his already battered ribcage. When he finally stopped moving, he sat up slowly, his entire body feeling as if it had been crushed. His ears were ringing, having been deafened by the thunderclap, and he rubbed his eyes from the bright flash of the sword releasing its powers deep into the body of the jotunn. When his vision returned, he looked down at what had slammed into him. It was one of the giant's heads, its stone face now frozen in an eternal expression of surprise.

Ash he didn't hear or see the draugr until it stood right above him. Strong arms gripped his shoulders, claws digging into his flesh, as the foul creature opened its mouth, baring sharp teeth in a rotting mouth. Ash was helpless. He was utterly exhausted, and his body was too beaten and broken to resist as the undead pulled him closer, to sink its teeth into his throat.

With a thud, an arrow slammed into its shoulder, knocking it back a step and dropping Ash to the ground. The thing looked up only to have another arrow punch through its eye and come out at the back of its head.

As if in a slumber, Ash turned his head to see Jarl Astrid standing at the entrance of the cavern, readying another arrow on her bow. Her chain mail was torn, black blood streaked her face and mud was splattered over her clothes, but to Ash she looked like a goddess, strong and powerful. On both sides of her, warriors spilled in, spreading out through the cavern and attacking the remaining draugr. Their greater number soon overcame the undead, who were hacked to pieces by the vengeful force.

Ash saw Torsten stagger to his feet, supported by another Berserker as two shieldmaidens kneeled by Yrsa, talking to her and slapping her cheeks as they began bandaging her wounds.

"Oh, good," Ash said, to no one in particular, before letting his head drop back to the ground. He closed his eyes and rested for a moment, when he heard a scraping sound next to him. He opened one eye and looked up at Astrid standing over him, a wide grin splitting her blood and dirt covered face.

"What is it with the youth of today and always lazing about always leaving all the work to be done by their elders?" the Jarl asked him.

Ash, overcome by exhaustion and shock, chuckled at first, but when Astrid joined in, he started laughing and soon tears ran down his cheek and he found it difficult to breathe as the laughter racked his body. Even the pain from his ribcage wasn't enough to stop him.

CHAPTER 36

ROGHALD PEERED DOWN ON THE CAMP AT THE MEADOW
in front of Gurmr and Grundr's cave. Seeing the Jomsvikings
there was all the proof he needed that his master had been defeated. The anger seethed in him. He was lucky that he had spotted the
human sentries in the forest before they had seen him, or he might
have walked straight into their arms. So instead, Roghald had opted to climb the mountain to observe from above the cave instead.
He had perched himself on an outcrop where he had a good view
of the encampment below whilst remaining well hidden by the
rock. Dozens of large tents were erected in the meadow beneath
him, and armed warriors were everywhere.

He had seen Ash carried out of the cave on a stretcher and into
a tent, so that showed that the little scourge must have survived.
As soon as he laid eyes on Ash, he was tempted to launch himself off the rock and tear him to pieces. When the anger rose in
his chest, Roghald lost his concentration and the vertigo returned,
forcing him to lie down whilst the twisting pain in his chest sub-
sided. Roghald felt tears of frustration build up in his eyes as Ash
once again slipped through his fingers. He had fought his way out
of Hornsborg with no problems. After all, that was an effortless

slaughter of people who had never held a weapon before. Below him was a small force of heavily armed and armoured Vikings. He wouldn't stand a chance in his current state. He really needed help, but if the jotunn was gone, where else could he turn?

While all might seem lost, he was determined to seek his revenge. Yes, Gurmr and Grundr was likely dead, but he would still have Ash's head on a stake, with or without the Shaman. He needed to get back into the cave, however. Maybe Gurmr and Grundr had somehow evaded the warriors and he could find some trace of his master in there? But if the jotunn was gone, then the tree was his only connection to Burrugandr, the only one who could help, in that case. It was only a matter of time until the humans destroyed it, if they hadn't already, so he needed to act fast.

He waited all day in his elevated position until the sun set and darkness settled all around him. A fire had been lit in the camp with the approaching darkness, ruining the night vision of anyone there, as he waited for most of the humans to fall asleep. All the sentries would be at the edge of the encampment looking outwards to the forest, so if he was quiet, he should be able to sneak into the cave.

Several hours after dark, he began the slow descent down the mountain towards the cave opening. The moon was up, casting some light around him, but unless anyone was looking straight at him, they would not spot him. In his thursr shape, he climbed with ease, his powerful arms and legs lowering him down quietly and without effort. Before long, he was dangling from the top of the cave opening, holding himself with one arm.

He let go and dropped down, twice his own height, but he bent his legs and helped brace his fall with his arms, landing with almost no sound. He hurried into the dark of the cave where he paused to listen for anyone calling out behind him. When he heard nothing, he continued in.

He could see perfectly well in the dark, so he had no problems navigating the long passageway that took him to the cavern. There were no guards placed in the cave, and he praised his luck. The humans' arrogance would be their downfall one of these days, he thought to himself.

He took in the scene and saw dead draugr scattered about the place, but no sign of the jotunn. Maybe his master had lived after all? When he saw the tree standing in the centre, he breathed a sigh of relief. They hadn't destroyed it yet.

He got to the foot of the mound and had to walk around a round boulder to reach the tree. He didn't remember seeing any boulders here last time, so he inspected it closer.

Bending down, he saw the head of Grundr, now turned to stone, looking back at him with a surprised expression. So, they had killed the troll after all. He straightened up and reached out to the tree. He laid his hand on the black bark and he could feel it writhe slightly under his hand.

At first nothing happened, but soon it became warm under his hand and dark tendrils rose from the bark to climb up his arm. When they reached his shoulder, they swirled around his head and neck before finding their way in through his nose and mouth. He felt a twinge of panic, wondering if he had made a mistake, when he realized that his hand was stuck to the tree. Soon he heard a hissing voice in his head.

"Thursr Roghald. Where be your master?"

"The jotunn is dead. Fallen to the Ulfhednar half-breed," he thought back in reply. "The humans have taken this cave and I do not have much time."

At first there was only silence, though soon he could hear the voice again and there was an edge to it. *"He has come to strength sooner than expected. You will not be able to stand against him now. No doubt the One-eye will send his cub to the source and seek to destroy it. Here in Jotunheim your strength will be doubled. You will seek his death here."*

Jotunheim? Roghald wanted Ash's death more than anything,

but he wasn't sure if he was prepared to travel to another world for it. Couldn't he find a way to kill Ash right here? Yes, he was an Ulfhed now, but Roghald knew him better than anyone, and the long and the short of it was, the boy was an idiot. His hesitation must have been felt through the connection because a burning pain shot through his body, forcing him to his knees and for a second nothing existed but the voice and the overwhelming suffering.

"You will do as you are told, thursr. There will be worse things than this waiting for you, should you stray from the firm hand of Burrugandr."

Roghald submitted in his mind to the voice, and the pain ebbed away. "Y-yes, my lord," he stammered, weak from the exertion.

"Gurmr and Grundr had a portal stone in their possession. Find it and use it to open a portal to Jotunheim. The cave you are in is a shallow point and close to Yggdrasil's branch beneath, which will allow you to use the stone. Do not disappoint me, thursr Roghald."

And with that, the voice was gone and Roghald's hand fell away from the glossy bark. Not wasting any time, he stood up and went to the corner of the cave where he knew the troll slept. He rummaged around a pile of animal skins and soon found a small leather sack. He opened it and shook its contents out on the makeshift bed.

Several bones marked with runes, a rusty knife and a grey stone fell out on the skins. The stone drew his attention, since it had a softly glowing pattern of runes etched into its surface. He picked it up and he could feel a slight vibration in the palm of his hand. He stood up and walked back to the centre of the cavern, close to the tree.

He held the stone out in front of him and hesitating for only a second; Roghald dropped it at his feet. A red light sprang up as the stone hit the ground and a large, red circle spread out around him. A band of glowing runes surrounded the circle, and Roghald felt the very ground beneath his feet vibrate. Then it fell away completely and Roghald tumbled into the hole, leaving the world of Midgard behind.

ASH SAT UP with a jolt. It took him a second to orient himself to the tent he was lying in. A small lantern hung from a hook on the central pole, casting a soft glow around the canvas tent. On bedrolls across from him, he could see the sleeping forms of Yrsa and Torsten. Yrsa, he recognised because she was facing him and Torsten's snoring, rattling the tent, was as familiar to him as the man's voice.

Yrsa looked battered. A nasty bruise covered half her face, and her arm and shoulder were bound in thick bandaging. Yesterday's events came flooding back to him, as did the pain in his leg. He pulled away his blanket and saw that his leg had been set straight and was bound with tight bandages and two splints on either side of it.

Something had woken him, but all was quiet, besides Torsten's snoring, so he couldn't put his finger on what. With some pain and care, he rolled over and got his one good leg beneath him and was able to push himself up to standing. Yrsa's spear was leaning up against a tent pole next to her, and Ash borrowed it. Using it as a support, he hobbled out of the tent, every step of the way causing him pain.

The tent opened up to a clear area dominated by a crackling campfire. Several other tents like the one he was in were arranged in a circle. Two hirdsmen, sitting by the fire, turned to him and nodded when they recognised him. He gave them a half-hearted wave before looking around the campsite. A flapping noise made him turn his head to the right just as a raven landed on one of the tents to the side. Since normal ravens slept during the night, it could only mean one thing. He sighed and started hobbling over towards the tent.

The hirdsmen looked up at him with raised eyebrows, but when he indicated to them that he needed to relieve himself, they quickly turned back to the campfire. Perhaps to avoid a request for assistance due to his injuries. When he made it to the tent, the raven swooped away into the darkness behind the campsite. As Ash passed between the tent and the one next to it, he found himself facing the dark mouth of the cave.

Of course, he thought bitterly. Once his eyes had adjusted from the bright light of the campfire, he could see the moonlit ground before the cave and the raven waiting for him there. He slowly made his way over to it, mostly hopping.

The darkness inside the cave was as solid as a wall, and it didn't take long before he smacked his head on an outcrop.

He paused for a moment, cursing himself for not having brought the lantern from his tent. Then an idea came to him. He gave up trying to see anything in the pitch dark and instead closed his eyes. Clearing his mind, Ash focused on the surrounding stone. Soon the tunnel lit up as he sensed the shape of the stone around him, the minerals glittering in his mind's eye.

He limped in and in a short while he turned the corner into the vast cavern. Sensing that he was not alone, he opened his eyes and saw a figure standing in front of the sickening tree, looking at it, holding a torch. Even in the dim, flickering torchlight he recognised the grey robes and slouch hat with long grey hair spilling out from underneath. Ash limped towards it. When he got closer, he could see that not only did the figure have a raven perched on each shoulder, two large wolves also rested at its feet. The figure didn't turn, even though he made quite a bit of noise hobbling up to it. One of the wolves lifted and turned its head to look lazily at Ash for a moment, before resting its head on its paws again. Drawing level with the god, Ash greeted him.

"Allfather," he said, looking up at Odin.

Odin, still looking at the tree, smiled and replied. "Ash of the Ulfhednar."

He turned towards Ash, and his one blue eye locked on him. Ash felt like the old man could see right through him, deep down into his soul, to his darkest secrets.

"You have had a busy day." Odin commented.

Ash wasn't sure how to answer that, so he just nodded before turning his gaze back to the tree.

"Ugly thing, isn't it?" he said, making the god chuckle.

"To say the least," the old god replied, an edge to his voice. He swung his torch around and held it out to Ash. "Burn it."

Ash looked at the flames as he accepted the torch and saw they had a blue tinge to them. He could not feel any heat radiating from it as the torch passed by his face. Holding his hand close to the flames, he felt only a chill on his skin. Looking at Odin with his eyebrows raised, the god said, "Frost fire of the Aesir, from Bifrost, the burning rainbow bridge that leads to Asgard. Nothing from Jotunheim can withstand it."

Ash nodded and limped forwards a few steps, putting the torch to the base of the tree. As soon as he did, a shiver went through the tree and as the flames spread, licking up the trunk, its branches twisted and shook, bending in on themselves like a dying spider. The fruits burst, with putrid slime dripping to the ground while the fire ate away at them and Ash had to step back to avoid getting splattered. Soon the whole tree was engulfed in the blue flames and the light became so bright that he had to shield his eyes. Within minutes the tree had turned to ashes, and the fire died back to only a few blue embers where the last of the exposed roots were burning away.

"This is not the end of it," the old god sighed. "Its roots still reach to the source and unless it is destroyed, the tree will grow anew in a few years, but somewhere else in Midgard, and this will all happen again." He turned to Ash, who was wide-eyed but meeting his gaze. Ash swallowed; his mouth suddenly dry.

"I have to go to Jotunheim, don't I?" he said, trying to keep his voice steady. "That's where the source is, isn't it? Behind the gates of Burrugandr's mountain?"

Odin smiled at him. "You take after your mother." Then the god's face became serious once again. "Yes, Ash. You have to go to Jotunheim, the home of the trolls. Midgard's fate depends on it."

THE END

The saga continues in the second book 'Thursr'.

ACKNOWLEDGEMENTS

First, I need to acknowledge my editor-in-chief, my partner in crime, beloved and mother of my child; my wife - Hasna Ameti - who not only keeps firm track of every poor life decision I have ever made, but also inexplicably supports every hare-brained scheme I come up with. Such as writing a book, to mention only one. The truth of the matter is that this book would never have existed if it wasn't for her.

Furthermore, I would like to thank Corey Crossin, Dzeneta Ameti, Chris Jansson, Mirry Sinani, Matt Carson, Monica Gunturu, Cham Karunarathne, Inoka Amarasekara, Anders Stromfeldt, Gemma Kelly, Emma Carson, Priya Shenton, Taz Flammea, Doug and Kate Rajkovic and Vicki Lesis for their invaluable input into the creative process. A special thank you to the beautifully creative brain that is Beau Oakley.

I would also like to thank Olavi Mikkonen, Johan Hegg, Ted Lundström, Johan Söderberg and Jocke Wallgren from Amon Amarth for thirty years of daily inspiration. Many chapters of this book were written with their music in the background.

Finally, a big thank you to the people making this book look great: Johnny Greenteeth for the cover art, Scott Colliver for the Yggdrasil illustration and Emily Snyder for the interior design.

ACKNOWLEDGMENTS

Last, but certainly not least, I would like to thank you, the reader, for making it all the way to the end. This is my very first publication, and as an indie-author I am highly dependent on reviews, so please, if you have enjoyed it, leave a review on your favourite reading platform or Goodreads. Or why not both? If it turns out you didn't like the book, just use these pages to line your cat's litter box and never say a word about it to anyone.

If you would like to leave me any personal feedback, drop me a line at afnjansson@gmail.com.

Thank you,
A.F. Jansson